s/21

LETTERS
FROM
THE
DEAD

D0993462

Sam Hurcom was born in Dinas Powys, South Wales in 1991. He studied Philosophy at Cardiff University, attaining undergraduate and master's degrees. He has since had several short stories published and has written and illustrated a number of children's books. Sam currently lives in the village he was raised in, close to the woodlands that have always inspired his writing.

Also by Sam Hurcom
A Shadow on the Lens

LETTERS FROM THE DEAD

SAM HURCOM

ORION

An Orion paperback

First published in Great Britain in 2020
by Orion Fiction,
This paperback edition published in 2021
by Orion Fiction,
an imprint of The Orion Publishing Group Ltd.,
Carmelite House, 50 Victoria Embankment
London EC4Y 0DZ

An Hachette UK Company

1 3 5 7 9 10 8 6 4 2

Copyright © Sam Hurcom 2020

The moral right of Sam Hurcom to be identified as
the author of this work has been asserted in accordance
with the Copyright, Designs and Patents Act of 1988.

All rights reserved. No part of this publication may be
reproduced, stored in a retrieval system, or transmitted
in any form or by any means, electronic, mechanical,
photocopying, recording, or otherwise, without the
prior permission of both the copyright owner and the
above publisher of this book.

All the characters in this book are fictitious, and any resemblance
to actual persons, living or dead, is purely coincidental.

A CIP catalogue record for this book is
available from the British Library.

ISBN (Paperback) 978 1 4091 8992 3

Typeset at The Spartan Press Ltd,
Lymington, Hants

Printed and bound by Clays Ltd,
Elcograf S.p.A.

MIX
Paper from
responsible sources
FSC® C104740

www.orionbooks.co.uk

For my parents, June and Tim.
Thanks for all your love and support.

LONDON BOROUGH OF WANDSWORTH	
9030 00007 4163 3	
Askews & Holts	
AF THR	
	WW20011270

Contents

A Note to Reader
July 19th, 1914

A veil of darkness spreads. I fear its ever-growing reach. For months I have been troubled by a sense of foreboding, greater than any mere anxieties of the superstitious kind. What lingers at the forefront of my thoughts is a swirling, vulgar cloud of ideas that disturb my every waking hour. Horrors on a grand scale, where scenes born of hell and its inferno play out, with bloodied men trudging through pestilent fields, fighting in derelict streets. The world of the near future burns, and to what end I cannot say or begin to understand. Death is coming, on a scale as never before seen.

This growing distress spurred me to write of my time in a small Welsh village; it is now what compels me back to the page.

Many still think 'The Wraith of London' lives. For much of the year nineteen hundred and five, the capital was paralysed in fear, locked in the grip of an unknown foe who seemingly killed without prejudice, taking men and women of every class and creed in the dead of night. There are those who believed then (and still do to this day), that the Wraith was not truly human, rather a phantom of sorts, an ungodly being with the power to move through walls unhindered, to pass through doors locked thrice. Holders of such beliefs congregated at the scenes of the Wraith's crimes, hoping to glimpse this devilish being for themselves. They were lambasted for such actions, moved along by officers of the Metropolitan Constabulary, harangued and heckled in the streets by many who mocked them for their foolishness.

'They are mad,' rang out the raucous fury of the bystanders. 'Surely those people are mad!'

Surely.

My account of that year of dread is written in the following pages; the truth of the Wraith is a story deeply intertwined with my own.

Most of nineteen hundred and five is but a blur to me, a haze of dreary consciousness, where I drank away days, and hid from the world, fearful I may somehow *infect* it.

Seeing the ghosts of murder victims – first in photographs and then the everyday world – knowing such phantoms move about us, having the evidence to hand, does strange, unhealthy things to the mind. And where there was one there came many; in that year alone so many of the dead came to me in my fragile state.

Nevertheless, I shall write this account as best I can. Let me assure those of you who fear the Wraith still lives that the demise of such a wretch was witnessed by my own eyes. Yet, take little comfort from that knowledge, for the miserable villain still moves about this world, though you, and almost all others, will fail to notice.

The clock has struck eleven. As with many nights previous, the Wraith has stepped through the door of my chamber and stands beside me as I write.

On occasion we have spoken, though nothing of any worth is said.

Madness.

Surely madness.

A Suspect

September 4th, 1905

There was no ashtray. They never gave ashtrays to suspects.

I pulled out a cigarette and struck a match, flicked it to the corner of the room. Was I a suspect in some way? Was I guilty of some crime?

My nerves were rattled but I couldn't show it. I had to maintain my composure, had to fight the urge to snatch the hip flask from inside my coat pocket and down the contents in one quick swig.

His eyes – *his contemptible eyes* – watched me from the corner of the room. Ice-blue and vivid, their unflinching gaze worsened my discomfort, made me fidget. How they made me fidget; the damned twitching, tapping, scratching of petty thieves and killers alike, the type of fidgeting I had seen over so many years, the fidgeting of men forced to wait in interrogation rooms for hours on end, with no bloody ashtrays or explanations to speak of.

They suspected me of something, and I had no idea what. That, in truth, was what made me nervous, for so much of the past year was unclear even to me.

As the minutes dragged by, my mind wandered to dark places, memories I longed to forget, nightmares unleashed from blackest nights whence surely they should be banished, were they not so devastatingly real. I tried to push such thoughts aside, though the more I struggled the more I was overwhelmed. My heart fluttered; my pulse quickened…

The tip of the cigarette burnt the skin of my fingers and I stubbed it out on the table, irate.

'Are you going to tell me what this is all about, Jack, or shall I book myself in with the desk sergeant downstairs?'

Detective Inspector Jack Lavernock said nothing. He folded his arms and looked down his slender nose at me. We'd worked together for years and in many ways, he was the closest thing I had to a friend, though it didn't feel like it in that moment.

I grunted, lit another cigarette and took a deep drag. I rubbed at my dry eyes. I'd been asleep when Lavernock had come knocking at my door and had struggled to rouse myself despite it being late morning. I needed a drink, was growing desperate for even a small sip from my hip flask.

Ten minutes later, the urge had only intensified.

'You woke me up, made me dress, marched me down to the Yard and even now won't have the decency to tell me what it's all about.' I growled suddenly, looking from Jack to the closed door of the interrogation room. 'Did the superintendent put you up to this? Wants to know what the hell I've been doing all this time; wants me working a case I imagine?'

Jack clenched his jaw as though he were trying to refrain from speaking.

'I told him I was on a leave of absence,' I continued quickly. 'An *indefinite* leave of absence, and he has no right dragging me into something, regardless of the circumstances.'

Jack finally spoke, with something of a sigh. 'You sleep in till midday often, Tommy?'

Tommy. He'd called me that since the day we'd met, and I hated it now as much I did then.

'It's my life,' I snarled. 'I'll do what I damn please.'

'We've been coming around, knocking on your door the last few days.' His North London accent was thick, unashamed. 'You been sleeping in every day, or just ignoring us?'

I stood to leave.

'I wouldn't try it.'

'Am I under arrest?' I snapped.

'No—'

'Then unless you have something to tell me, I'll be on my way. You have no right, Jack, none whatsoever, to bring me here, and ask me about my business, without telling me what it's all in aid of.'

'Sit down, Tommy. There are important people who want to speak with you.'

'I'm sure,' I huffed. 'Tell the superintendent if he wants to talk, he can do me the courtesy of coming in pers—'

The door swung open; Assistant Commissioner, Peter Critcher, stepped in, followed by the Commissioner of the Metropolitan Police, Robert Henley, and the Superintendent of the CID, Daniel Blair. The men gathered around the table quietly, barely even glancing at me.

I was stunned. I'd never met the commissioner in person, had only spoken briefly with the assistant commissioner when he was chief constable of the CID. The full severity of the situation hit me like a bullet, be it a case I needed to work or some suspicion hanging over my head. Without a word I sat back down, meek and nervous once more.

Henley pulled up the chair opposite me, his chin raised slightly, as though the stiff white collars he wore were holding his head in a fixed position. His thick moustache was perfectly combed; not a strand of slicked grey hair out of place. He sat rigid, his forearms lent against the table, fingers interlocked.

Critcher sat at the head of the table, though his presence was somewhat less imposing. He fiddled with a small pocket watch before pulling a pipe from his long black jacket and lighting it carefully. His features were kinder than Henley's, his eyes softer around the edges. But I had every respect for the man, a great admiration for him in fact. He'd joined the CID in eighteen eighty-nine; had investigated the Whitechapel murders; had his theory on the Ripper. There was something of a mythos around him, rumours that he knew the Ripper by name, even held information on the villain. He and Henley were investigators, real police, through and through.

Blair, a dour-faced man with ruddy cheeks, stood just behind Henley. He leant down, dropping papers from a stack he carried under his arm, and asked if they should get started. A moment later the door opened once more and a figure I didn't recognise entered the small room with no word of greeting or apology. He was at least six foot five and built like a Grecian statue. His face was severe, his jaw thick and chiselled. He was completely bald, though wore a thin moustache speckled with grey hair. His ruby scalp shone dully in the yellow light cast in the room. His brown three-piece suit was smart if poorly fit; his black boots unblemished by any dirt. He too carried paperwork, which he slapped on the desk, before sitting down on my left.

Henley cleared his throat as my hands tremored in my lap.

'Nothing said here leaves this room, Bexley. None of it.' His words were rough as bark, his voice low and quiet. 'You know most of the men here?'

I nodded in silence.

'I believe Superintendent Blair is your direct superior?'

I nodded again. 'Yes, sir. Due to the nature of my role, I work outside the conventional hierarchy. My rank of special invest-igator was given to me by the superintendent's predecessor, Elliot Johnston, who I reported to directly until his retirement.'

'Your *rank*,' Henley muttered dismissively. 'You never trained as an officer, don't even meet the basic requirements.'

'There are plenty of men an inch or two taller than me who couldn't determine the hind end of a mule from its head, let alone enact a decent police enquiry, sir.'

Jack smirked in the corner of the room. Blair's neck and cheeks turned crimson.

Henley smiled thinly. 'I suppose that's true.' He raised a hand to Blair and took the stack of papers from him. 'I've known about you since, well, before I even took this post, Bexley. Your work speaks for itself. Until last year you were a welcome talking point in police circles, and the general public. It seems things have changed quite dramatically since then.'

Last year, the year nineteen hundred and four, the year I had gone to that contemptible village in Wales. The year my life had changed irrevocably, the year I had first lain eyes on a ghost. I began to panic; sweat clung to the base of my neck and shoulders. Moving with no thought, I put another cigarette to my lips (whilst I had smoked for much of my adult life, the habit had greatly increased in the past six months – now I was rarely without one alight) and tried to find a match. As I rummaged through my deep pockets, I heard a snap and Critcher held a light out across the table for me. I thanked him quietly before turning back to Henley.

'I'd greatly appreciate, sir, knowing what this is all about.'

He nodded slowly.

'We've asked you here today, Bexley, to gather some information pertinent to an ongoing enquiry – our top enquiry. I must stress that you are not being formally charged with anything – we merely wish to ask you some questions.'

His words and flat, unwavering tone, were little comfort to me. This felt nothing short of an inquisition.

'I'm sure you're aware,' Henley continued, 'of the recent spate

7

of kidnappings that have been perpetrated across the city by an unknown criminal known colloquially as the Wraith of London?'

I frowned, looked from Henley to Critcher and then to the man sitting on my left. I was completely baffled.

'The ... the what?'

Henley glanced at Critcher from the corner of his eye. 'You haven't been reading the papers lately.' He opened a thin dossier and slid a stack of tattered newspaper clippings towards me. I glanced over the pages; they reported a string of kidnappings, seemingly random, involving men and women from all corners of the capital. North and south of the river, the wealthy West End and the slums of the East. Specific details of the victims were sparse and even less was known of the perpetrator. It seemed the *Daily Mail* had provided the rather distasteful nickname.

I skimmed each clipping, growing ever more confused with every byline and front-page spread I looked at. 'How ... how have I not known about this?'

'You tell us,' Henley replied. 'We have on our hands what many fear is the most dangerous criminal in all the country, an individual who strikes such fear, many think he is the phantom of the Ripper, able to walk through walls and locked doors. Everyone is talking about it, staying late in public houses for fear of going home, sleeping as little as they can, afraid they may never wake. Eleven known kidnappings so far, and we believe every victim to date is dead, though we can't find any of the bodies.'

'Our investigations have been ongoing for months,' Critcher muttered. 'Every paper has been running stories every day, trying to learn more about the victims, making wild accusations about the guilty party.'

Henley leant forwards, his eyes narrowing.

'You must surely be the only man in London who doesn't know about it. You've certainly buried your head deep in the sand since taking up your leave of absence.' He picked out a letter from his stack of papers, glanced at it briefly. 'Your *overdue need for recuperation* was requested December of last year, some nine months ago. Not read any papers in that time?'

I stammered and mumbled, struggling to find words. What was I to say of the endless days shut away, hiding from the world? How could I possibly explain the countless hours I'd spent holding the barrel of a gun to my head, willing myself to pull the trigger?

Henley was unflinching.

'We can return to that. There's a more pressing matter we must address, and our time today is limited. I need to ask you a simple question, Bexley, one which is nevertheless of the utmost importance and one that requires a straight and honest answer.'

He met my gaze, and the blood stopped pumping through my veins. This was it: the moment I was to be found out, the moment the world would learn the truth, and surely come to think me mad.

Do you see the dead, Bexley? Do you see ghosts, as real as any man or woman you may pass in the street? Do they torment your every waking hour? Have you gone completely insane, Thomas?

Henley cleared his throat.

'When was the last time you spoke with Professor Elijah Hawthorn?'

My chest heaved. I looked from Henley, to Blair, to Lavernock, in total confusion. Everything was happening so fast – too fast. I needed a drink, a mere sip to calm my nerve.

'Elijah? Elijah Hawthorn?'

Henley nodded.

'Y-years,' I said quite truthfully. 'Yes, surely, it's been years. We were close once – very close indeed when we worked together in the Forensic Crime Directorate. But when that all ended, when the Directorate was disbanded, we … had a disagreement – he took things badly, thought I'd wronged him. I thought it well known around the Yard; we haven't spoken since then …'

I looked down at the newspaper clippings, plucked one from the table absently.

'Why are you telling me about this, these kidnappings, this Wraith, and then asking about Elijah Hawthorn?'

Even as the words left my mouth, my heart sank with such remorse and regret that I could hold back the urge no longer and took the hip flask from my pocket.

'He's dead, isn't he?' I muttered, struggling with the flask's small silver cap. 'He's one of the victims?'

Henley remained silent.

'Well? You must surely think something of that nature. There's nothing in these reports to say otherwise; you've dragged me here today, want to know when last I spoke to him.' I was rambling without any real thought.

Henley still said nothing. I looked from one man to the next, their blank expressions filling me with dread.

'You think I had something to do with this? You think I've done something to Hawthorn?'

Critcher began to speak but I cut him off, dropping the hip flask to the table with a clatter.

'What reason would I have to kill the man – you think I had some part in all these kidnappings as well?'

Henley raised a hand and hushed me, though it took me a moment to settle down. He tapped a finger on the table twice, thrice, as he mulled over his next words. He nodded, at last, before meeting my gaze once more.

'We don't think Elijah Hawthorn is a victim, Bexley. Far from it. We think he is the man carrying out these kidnappings. We think he is a killer.'

Questions from Superiors

September 4th, 1905

Grey-blue smoke swirled about my face. In the basement several floors below, where the Forensic Crime Directorate had been stationed and where I had worked for some seven years, smoking tobacco had been strictly prohibited.

I opened my flask, smelt the heady scent of cheap rum. Superintendent Blair began to protest but Henley waved a hand at him as I swallowed the contents in one long swig.

'For the purpose of clarity,' Henley said before I had finished, 'it would be best if you explained your relationship with Elijah Hawthorn for the record.'

I gasped, my throat searing. 'You must have evidence to suspect the man.'

Henley nodded. 'In good time. Tell us about your relationship first. I believe Hawthorn hired you to work for the Metropolitan Police owing to your training as a photographer.'

I rubbed my brow, composed myself as best I could.

'Professor Hawthorn hired me in the late autumn of eighteen ninety-one. He was forming a new department, the Forensic Crime Directorate, in the wake of the Whitechapel murders. As you rightly say, they needed a photographer. I was fully trained though had no knowledge or experience of forensic photography.

Nevertheless, I was interested in the proposal and willing to learn.'

'And how did you meet?' Henley was leaning forwards once again, his fingers clasped tightly together.

'I was making a living, where I could. On occasion I would go to the docks, photograph the sailors when they came back from overseas, immigrants fortunate enough to have some money for a family portrait. In the summer I would often spend my days in Hyde Park, where the money was easier to come by. That's where I first met Hawthorn.'

Henley raised an eyebrow. 'By chance?'

'No. He'd been in touch with an old friend of my father's, a Herbert Timberwell, who worked in the trade. Hawthorn had been asking around for men who wouldn't be perturbed by photographing serious crime scenes; it seems this old friend sent him my way. At the time, Mr Timberwell was kindly letting me reside in the storeroom of his photographic boutique for a mere four shillings per week.' I smiled fondly. 'If not for his kindness, I'm not sure how I would have survived back then.'

Henley nodded. 'This Timberwell, is he still alive today?'

I shook my head with some shame. 'I don't know. His boutique was on Leman Street in the East End; I haven't kept up with him.'

'So, you met Hawthorn, and he offered you the role in his new Forensic Crime Directorate?'

I flicked the end of my cigarette. 'Not straight away. We spoke for several weeks before he explained his real purpose. By then I was in desperate need of work so leapt at the chance.'

The alcohol was quickly having an effect on me; I realised then I hadn't eaten properly in several days.

'I know for a fact that when you began in Hawthorn's Forensic Directorate, you were working closely with Detective Inspector

Lavernock, amongst quite a few others. Your role to begin with was strictly photographing crime scenes?'

I nodded. 'Hawthorn wanted experts from outside the force to take on specialist roles. His grand vision was to understand the deviant criminal, learn why the most perverse crimes are committed. He believed the role of policing wasn't simply to maintain order but stop crimes from happening entirely. I always thought the notion was somewhat absurd; there will always be crime and those who wish to commit it. Nevertheless, I admired his conviction.'

Henley continued. 'And as I understand it, you began taking on a greater investigative role some two and a half years later, in the spring of eighteen ninety-four? The documents we have on file suggest Hawthorn wanted you to work as an inspector.'

The unmoving eyes of those watching was becoming insufferable.

'Yes, yes he did. We were a close group in the Directorate, and all worked together well. I'm sure Ja— DI Lavernock would agree. We took on only a select number of serious cases and everyone offered their own views and opinions as the enquiries unfolded. You learnt quickly, working in such proximity to police constables, doctors, ballistics experts and the like. I demonstrated an ability to piece together evidence, formulate my own theories; Hawthorn saw some promise in me and often looked for my opinion.'

'He made two formal requests to the then commissioner to have you join the force and fast-tracked to the rank of inspector. Both requests were denied outright as you did not meet the basic requirements of a constable. That must have been frustrating for you.'

I shrugged. 'Men need to earn their rank; I'd never worked a beat, never worn the uniform, dealt with drunkards in the night or chased down a thief. What right had I to wear the rank of inspector, when men struggle for years to do so?'

'This is true,' Henley said. 'But if the commissioner had bent the rules, let you be a constable, you could have worked your way up.'

'Maybe.' We were opening old wounds that had long since healed. 'It makes no difference when one considers my current role.'

'Indeed. Hawthorn was persistent. He persuaded the commissioner to let you investigate informally, under close supervision. Though you didn't carry the title of "special investigator" back then.'

My head was feeling light, my vision beginning to blur. I rubbed at my eyes, trying to think straight. 'My remit was widened, and I began heading up investigations under Hawthorn's direct supervision.' I slurred the last few words, though Henley didn't seem to notice. 'Now please, sir. What evidence could you possibly have to suspect him of murder?'

Henley hesitated, before gesturing to Critcher. He began talking quickly.

'If you're not aware of the Wraith kidnappings, you likely have no knowledge of the Farrow murders and the convictions of the Stratton brothers?'

I shook my head.

'The Stratton brothers were convicted of murder when they robbed an oil and colour shop in Deptford. They beat the owners to death and all we had to identify them was one fingerprint on a cash box.' He raised a bony finger to emphasise the point. '*One.*'

'A few short years ago, those men would likely have walked free,' Henley said coolly. 'Had it not been for the diligence of officers understanding the latest in investigative forensics, they would never have hung from the gallows. That's thanks in great part to Hawthorn's Directorate; the work pioneered there is now standard investigative practice. The fingerprint bureau holds over eighty thousand men and women's prints on file, and such records are growing every day.'

He pulled a small photograph from one of the files before him and slid it across the table to me. It took a moment to interpret; the image depicted the bottom of an ornate vase. A dirty mark was clear on a smooth area of cream porcelain. The mark was a dark thumbprint, no doubt made in blood.

'That evidence was collected from the house of James Mortimer, aged sixty-eight.' Henley said. 'He's the eleventh known victim we are connecting to the recent spate of kidnappings and presumed murders. That print was taken from his home just under two weeks ago; it's the first solid piece of evidence we've had.'

'Mortimer lived in Marylebone,' Critcher continued. 'Since the Farrow murders, it's standard practice to compare a print of this kind to all those on file, including those of our own officers, to rule out any human error.'

'Hawthorn's prints were on file from his days in the Forensic Crime Directorate.' Henley slid another piece of paper across the table to me, a fingerprint record with both the left- and right-hand digits documented in black ink. 'When we compared his prints to the thumbmark on that vase it was a clear match – even with blood smearing, you can no doubt see the clear distinction of the concentric whorl.'

I could. I was dumbfounded, aghast. 'What – what could possibly be his motive?'

Henley didn't answer. 'This is the first piece of solid evidence in the eleven kidnappings that links us to a suspect. Had it not been for a strange marking left at the scene of each crime, we'd have had nothing to connect any of them.'

He reached across the table with a report marked 'Confidential'.

A symbol was drawn in the middle of the page – a symbol I'd never seen before.

'Do you recognise that?'

'No.'

I studied the image carefully. It appeared to be a rudimentary arrow, drawn diagonally across the page, with the arrowhead facing downwards. Seemingly random curves and lines spun and interwove around the arrow itself, with a wide V drawn beneath it.

'We've had academics study this symbol, though in itself it is not identifiable. Their working theory is that it is a possible derivative of alchemy symbols, denoting purification of some kind. We've therefore concluded that it is a reference to the occult, a means of adorning the homes of those taken, of hon- ouring them.' Henley glanced at Critcher, who nodded solemnly.

'It's been found scratched somewhere in the domiciles of every victim,' Critcher explained. 'Door frames, mantels, headboards. It's the only thing that connects each crime. There are no shared relationships between the victims that we know of, no family connections, no geographical significance to the scene of each kidnapping. Nothing – the rich, the poor, everyone and anyone seems to be a target. That symbol was the only lead for months. We've done our utmost to keep it out of the press. The last thing we need is for someone devious enough to muddy the waters by copying that mark and trying to connect their own misdeeds to this case.'

'Then this thumbprint appears,' Henley sighed. 'A single error on the part of the guilty man. At least the first real error we can positively attribute to him.'

I asked what Henley meant.

'On the thirteenth of August, some nine days prior to the kidnapping of James Mortimer and the discovery of this print, we received a report of a break-in south of the river. A man named Daniel Pinkney claimed he discovered a lone individual, dressed in black with his face concealed. He managed to scare the perpetrator out of his home but lost sight of him in the streets. It may simply have been a burglary.'

'But you suspect otherwise?' I said.

Henley nodded. 'A failed kidnap attempt most likely. This thumbprint appeared at the very next crime scene. It suggests our man is getting weary, lazy even.'

'Making mistakes,' Critcher cut in. 'Mistakes are good for us. Every criminal starts making them eventually.'

'It's fair to presume the individual in question has a broad knowledge of forensics, or at least police practice. Enough to ensure he left no trace of himself that we could uncover for the first ten kidnappings.' Henley paused. 'But the assistant commissioner is right; every criminal eventually makes mistakes. We've had some other partial sightings that are still being chased up, but with this thumbmark, and his expertise in the field, Hawthorn's our top suspect.'

The hulk of a man beside me spoke for the first time. He was loud, and Irish. He made no effort to subdue his words.

'Are you sure Hawthorn hasn't contacted you recently?'

I turned to him, moving my chair away as I did.

'I'm sure he has no interest in ever speaking to me again.' I glanced to Critcher. 'Who is this?'

'Jeremy Flynn,' Critcher replied. 'He's assisting with enquiries.'

I went to take a drink, standing up in frustration when I recalled the flask was empty. 'This is absurd.' I paced a little, from my chair to the door, thoughts unhinged, wild. Henley didn't wait for me to settle.

'You say Hawthorn has no interest in speaking with you. Why?'

I rubbed my brow. 'The way it ended, how the Directorate was shut down. We all know the rumours and stories so what point is there getting into it?'

'Enlighten me of your opinion,' Henley said crisply.

I struggled to grasp the words.

'Hawthorn had friends in high places, we all knew that. He schooled with the Home Secretary and they were still close – it's how he convinced him to set up the Directorate in the first place.' I recalled anecdotes Hawthorn had told me of he and his dear friends' youthful conquests. I moved back to the chair and sat down.

'Despite changing politics, Hawthorn had influence inside the Home Office, and the commissioner, Christopher Bolton, didn't appreciate it. You can see for yourself from the requests Hawthorn made about my role, he could be arrogant and demanding. He had sway over the entire CID and was beginning to talk in ever more radical terms about criminal prosecutions. He didn't view the world in terms of good and evil but more in circumstance, in the physical and mental defections of the deviant and the criminal.'

'Wanted to rehabilitate murderers and rapists,' Critcher scoffed. 'And ban the death penalty.'

I nodded. 'Regardless of one's opinions on such things, it's fair to say they were not widespread views. The hearsay was rather lurid from there but suffice to say Hawthorn eventually got pushed out. I'm not sure about the murkier details, but in time, the Directorate was divided and absorbed into other areas until nothing of it remained.'

'That doesn't quite explain why Hawthorn would hold any animosity towards you, Bexley.' Henley's tone remained even and flat, as it had throughout the entire conversation.

I concurred. 'Before the Directorate was shut down,

Superintendent Johnston, with permission from the commissioner, offered me the position of special investigator. Greater autonomy; working on cases nationwide. I may not have been an inspector, but it was the closest I would ever get. I saw it as a promotion, never as a slight against Hawthorn. I had no idea what was about to happen to the Directorate or Hawthorn himself. He saw my taking the job as a betrayal, no doubt wanted me to leave in protest, with him...' I trailed off at the end, remembering the last, furious conversation I had had with him in the basement.

'Is that all it was?' Henley asked quietly.

I shrugged. 'There had been quite a change in Elijah's character over the years. Maybe it was the nature of our work, the dreadful scenes he saw, the crimes we investigated. He had steadily grown more... erratic – difficult to read. By the time the Directorate was shut down, his state was of great concern to me – in my mind, it was no bad thing for him to be relieved of his duties. It seemed to be destroying the good in him, if you take my meaning.' I fidgeted awkwardly. 'I let my feelings be known to some colleagues; word got back to Hawthorn and he claimed I had conspired against him for my promotion.'

'DI Lavernock says you and Hawthorn were close throughout your years working together. Held each other's confidence.'

'That's a fair assessment.' I glanced to Jack, still standing with his arms folded in the corner of the room. 'If you want the truth, I saw the man as something of a father figure, not merely because of his professional support, but a great deal of other things he did to help me in my life. He had no children, and I think he probably saw me as—' I sighed. 'Saw me as his son.'

I fell silent then, stewing in the memories of that time. I saw Hawthorn's face clearly, his rage, his wrath, his disappointment. His grief.

Henley pulled me back to reality. 'Where have you been since your last case, Bexley? Aside from your request for a leave of absence, no one's seen or heard from you in almost ten months.'

I tried to maintain my composure. My body grew hot; thick needles prickled across my back as my heart rate intensified again.

'I needed some time, sir. My last case was a difficult one.'

He held up a few papers, the writing on which I recognised, even from across the table.

'This was a preliminary report you wrote, with a Sergeant Davis of the Glamorgan Constabulary. I have it on his authority that you were in high spirits when you left the village of Dinas Powys in Wales. A murderer thwarted; a handful of arrests regarding obstruction of the law, fraud and embezzlement.'

I saw Betsan Tilny's burning spectre in my mind, thought of the letter she had written from the dead, now tucked in a lockbox, concealed beneath the floorboards of my attic.

'The case was very much successful, in that regard, sir.'

'And yet you haven't been able to return to work.'

I hesitated, looked at the men around me who all stared back, steely-eyed.

'Things happened, sir. Things I am still trying to move on from.'

Blair sneered, shaking his head in contempt. 'Not so tough when a man's put a gun to your head, Bexley. Real police cope with it like real men.'

I wanted to scramble across the table and ram my fist down his throat. Better judgement kept me sat in silence.

Flynn stood and left the room without a word, though no one seemed moved by this. Critcher tapped his pipe against the table and brushed ash onto the floor with his hand. Henley flicked through documents before sliding a cream sheet of type paper towards me. The document was again marked 'Confidential', though there was very little written on it. What drew my eye was a list of eleven names.

Mathew Fletcher
Yasmin Modiri-Whitmore
Dorothy Clarke
Elanor White
Helena Fenway
Louis Krovac
Judith Norris
Amanda Granger
Norman Scott-Thomas
Heather Warren
James Mortimer

'Recognise any of them?'

I tried to think straight, but by now I was in a poor state, inebriated by the rum and badly shaken by the whole sordid affair. I took my time reading through the list. One of the names, Yasmin Modiri-Whitmore, sparked something, but nothing substantive.

'No, not that I'm aware of.'

Critcher leant across the table.

'We've tried to keep the names out of the papers as much as we can, though quite a few have been circulated. The hysteria has been magnified due to the whereabouts of some of the kidnappings; Marylebone, Mayfair and so forth. It's worse than the Ripper – the public's fear I mean.'

'As someone who lived in the East End through those bloody years, I must say I doubt that, sir.'

Critcher shook his head. 'The Ripper was a sexual deviant whose victims belonged to the lowest dregs of female humanity.'

'Meaning what,' I snarled. 'You think they deserved—'

'For God's sake, man,' Critcher rasped.

'Meaning,' Henley cut in, 'that there was a pattern, a connection between the victims. The Wraith is taking men and women of every class from across the capital. There's no pattern or connection. From beggars to Etonians, people are being snatched away. And the city is very afraid.'

'You said you feared all who've been taken are dead?'

Henley nodded. 'There've been no requests for ransoms. We think this occult symbol – if indeed that is what it is – points to a darker, sadistic motive. In truth, we can't be certain until we start finding bodies.'

'But if you now suspect Hawthorn, you must have some theory about his motive. Other than puzzles and cryptography, I never knew him to have any interest in occult symbols—'

'That may be,' Henley interrupted. 'But it could be a misdirection. Hawthorn's old friends had been pushing for him to regain some role in the force but that was completely out of the question. He met with Assistant Commissioner Critcher who informed him of this and he took it badly. That was in January of this year; nobody has seen or heard from him since. We believe the first kidnapping was in April.'

'We think he's trying to outsmart us,' Critcher said, shaking his head and smiling wryly. 'He wants to prove he's better than us.'

'Then what of the bloodied thumbprint at Mortimer's home?' I replied. 'He's too much of an expert to leave something so obvious.'

'An expert perhaps, but no less fallible than you or I,' Critcher scoffed. 'The man's sixty for God's sake, breaking into homes and subduing men and women alike. He would know to wear gloves, but would he expect Mortimer to fight back? Maybe there was a scuffle, maybe he lost a glove and cut his hand. In his haste to get Mortimer out, he could have easily failed to spot the bloody thumbprint he left.'

'You rightly say the man's sixty yet still you suspect him of all this?'

'Our working assumption,' Critcher hissed, 'is that he is drugging the victims. In the case of Mortimer, something must have gone wrong.'

It was plausible. If Mortimer was the first victim to cause a struggle, to put up a fight, then Hawthorn would no doubt be panicked, perhaps nervous enough not to check every inch of the house before leaving with Mortimer – be he alive or dead.

'You must surely have other suspects though?' In spite of all that I had been shown, I still couldn't believe what I was hearing. 'How could Hawthorn even move the bodies at his age?'

Henley pulled a pocket watch from his waistcoat and checked the time. He began gathering the papers he had spread across the table and neatly organised them.

'Elijah Hawthorn is our top suspect in all this, though we have no real idea if he is being helped by another man. His rather … high regard … among those of better standing, let alone the nature of his career here, make this an incredibly sensitive matter. You'll forgive my rather blunt manner, but I must be certain. Think hard on this now – have you been in contact with Hawthorn at any time in the last twelve months?'

'No. No. I wouldn't even know how to contact him.' I pushed back my chair and looked at Henley with a very real concern. 'You think I have some part in this?'

'Until we have all the facts, we must explore every avenue.' Henley gathered the documents and handed them back to Blair.

'I won't waste time asking about your whereabouts on the date of each kidnapping as I doubt there is anyone to corroborate your statements. But if you would like to prepare an account of your movements, we'll examine it all the same.'

Both he and Critcher stood. Blair moved to the door.

'If Elijah Hawthorn contacts you, you will let us know immediately,' Henley said as he moved out of the room. He turned back to me from the doorway.

'Stay in London where we can contact you if necessary. And try to gather your senses, Bexley. I'd advise you return to the man you once were, and quickly.'

With that, Henley and Critcher left, the superintendent on their heels. The door slammed shut and I was alone with Lavernock, too mortified to say anything.

The Unread Letters
September 4th, 1905

We stepped through the lobby and out the front doors into the fresh air of the afternoon. Beneath the granite archway of the Yard's entrance, a burly sergeant with a poorly trimmed moustache gave directions to a tall constable. The pair acknowledged Lavernock with a courteous nod. When the sergeant eyed me, he fell silent; he turned his head and watched as I moved past him.

Lavernock led me away from the red-brick building, stepping quickly along the embankment towards the Palace of Westminster. Big Ben struck three of the hour, and I rummaged mindlessly, as all smokers do, for a cigarette. I cursed when I couldn't find a match and was surprised when Lavernock barged me into the road.

'What are yo—'

'Don't say anything to him, Tommy. He's a bloody hack.'

The young man was beside me before I knew what was happening.

'Afternoon, DI Lavernock. Lovely one ain't it?'

'Not when you're out of your kennel, Sanders?' Lavernock snapped. 'Piss off.'

'It's a free country,' the young man laughed. He was a little shorter than I and grinned up at me. His teeth and gums were stained with freshly chewed tobacco. 'We've never had the pleasure before, Mr Bexley.'

He held his hand out to me though I was minded not to take it. Lavernock reached out and roughly pushed the man away. For a moment, the fellow stopped in his tracks.

'Oh now,' I heard him sigh as he scampered alongside us once more. 'There's no need for that, DI Lavernock. I was only 'ere to say hello to yourself and the good Mr Bexley.'

'You're sniffing around for something that you won't get. Clear off before I have you—'

The young man stepped in front of us, walking backwards, meeting our pace.

'You'll have me what, Lavernock? Done over? I think the editors at the *Mail* would be quite happy to print a piece on police brutality, get some pictures on the front page. How would that suit the commissioner?' His face twisted and darkened, though his dreadful, stretched smile remained. 'You're already making a mess of the Wraith enquiry. Not much love for coppers 'round at the minute.'

Lavernock lunged clumsily for the man's collar. The reporter sneered and stopped before me, so that I near clattered into him. He stared at me, as a snake may look upon a mouse, his eyes ever widening.

'Things must be desperate. Enlisting the help of the deranged investigator here.' He raised his chin and held his face close to mine. 'Still hearing things bump in the night, Mr Bexley?'

I was stunned, too shocked to react. The man's nostrils flared; his lips twitched as his pupils dilated. He held his ground a moment longer, until Lavernock sent him spinning to the floor. A few passers-by gasped and moved back away from the scene; Lavernock yelled at the man to leave as he clambered to his feet. His dreadful grin seemed only broader, slashed across his face. He said something to me as he walked off, though I wasn't listening or taking much in by then. Only when Lavernock led me away, when I felt the breeze of the day swirl around my neck and face, was I roused enough to say something.

'That man, wha— what did he mean?'

Lavernock shook his head. 'Forget it. He's a worm.'

I grabbed Lavernock's arm. 'What did he mean, *hearing things bump in the night?*'

'There's been rumours, Tommy. Rumours going around the Yard, rumours about your last case. Someone got wind of statements from witnesses, statements from a few of those who went down, they said you were seeing … seeing things.'

He scratched his eyebrow, a tick I recognised from my days of working with him. He was annoyed, growing impatient.

'It's just rumours and hearsay, and some idiots in uniform who speak to scheming hack writers like Eddie Sanders there, probably bigged the whole lot up for an extra few bob.' He stepped closer to me then and jabbed two fingers in my chest. 'For Christ's sake, get yourself cleaned up, Tommy, and fast. Stay in London and stay on the right side of this. I got places to be.'

He turned up his collar and walked away, leaving me in the street with an unlit cigarette hanging limply from my lips. I looked in the direction of the reporter – Eddie Sanders – and wondered if he was still grinning.

I wandered the streets till dark, my mind addled, uncertain of where I had been but soon finding myself at Golden Square and Lower James Street. My home at 7b was a modest townhouse, far grander than anything I had ever dreamt of owning in my youth. I fumbled for the key as I stood in the empty street outside my door. My hands were shaking badly, though the cold air had nothing to do with it. My addiction by then was ravenous and in constant need of succour. I hadn't taken a drink in hours.

I touched upon the brass key and dropped it to the floor as I pulled it from my pocket. I cursed, knelt and collapsed onto the cold stone of the pavement. There I sat, my head held in my hands, a shivering wreck of a figure, a wretch like any vagrant drunkard sleeping rough across the city.

I was overcome by it all. How could Elijah Hawthorn be a kidnapper – a killer? The man had been a father to me, better in so many ways than my own. Though we had parted company on the worst of terms, many a parent and child have separated in similar tone and manner; such discord does not break the bonds of kinship that connect fathers and sons, mothers and daughters. Years had passed since we had spoken, yet still I cared for Hawthorn deeply. The news of his apparent misdeeds, his monstrous brutality, was utterly devastating.

I didn't want to believe any of it. But the image of the bloody thumbprint was burnt in my mind's eye and troubled me deeply. What could it be if not proof – proof that Hawthorn had played some part in the terrible spate of kidnappings?

I needed to drink the image away, to drown myself in liquor and sleep a thousand years. The gas lamps had not been lit, and my hands searched clumsily on my doorstep for the key.

As I touched upon it, an unnatural breeze cut across the back of my neck. Strange laughter drifted down the narrow road. Footsteps quickly scampered across Golden Square, mere yards from me. The sound was unnatural, distorted in a most unpleasant way. I stood, not daring to turn around, all miserable thoughts of Hawthorn and Henley and the Wraith of London gone in an instant.

I jammed the key into the lock and thrust the door open just enough to squeeze inside. I lurched backwards and felt the door slam shut behind me, the noise rattling through the empty house.

I leant my head back and tried to draw in breath. I was weak, and in need of water, of food. But I craved a drink, groaning aloud as I tried to think where a bottle might be.

Something unseen groaned back at me.

My eyes couldn't adjust to the gloom. The pain in my head intensified, spread down the back of my neck and across my shoulders. I clenched my teeth until the pain peaked and partially subsided. Then I held my breath, listening for any sounds.

Nothing stirred. The air was still.

I moved cautiously, stepping lightly across the tiles of the hallway that led to the stairs and the rooms of the downstairs floor. At the foot of the stairs, I gripped hold of the bannister, pulling myself towards it as a mariner would cling to the mast of a sinking ship. Something thudded, the sharp snap of a door being slammed in its frame.

Such things had happened countless times in the last year. I knew these were no mere noises of the night.

Something was with me. Something was moving inside the house.

A squeal, quiet and soft, like a nail slowly being pulled from a rotten piece of timber.

My breathing was uncontrollable – shallow, wavering. It was all I could do to drag my eyes from the darkness of the first-floor landing. With great effort, whimpering like a child, I ran into the lounge and charged towards the mantel. I trod over papers laid about the floor, heard glass shatter beneath my feet as I cracked over a discarded tumbler.

The mantel was almost bare, save for a pair of china jugs sent to me as a gift from my cousin. My fingers set upon matches, and I knelt and struck one against the hearth, watching as the burst of white light illuminated before me. With it came no solace or comfort, for the minute flame only served to deepen the darkness that engulfed me.

A creak, a footstep moving down the stairs.

It was coming for me. The matchlight was dwindling.

Another step, then another. The thing was drawing nearer. Faster.

I struck at matches desperately and gazed about the room for candles. One was propped lazily in an iron candelabra on a bureau beside the fireplace. I grabbed at it clumsily, knocking a stack of correspondence and unopened letters to the floor as I did. I hurried to light it, gripped it tight but to no great relief. It was not enough. In all the desperate months, no light had ever been enough.

Panicked, I took the candelabra and brazenly set it down in the open doorway. The light revealed a hand, a delicate hand, with slender fingers and dreadful, putrid skin, sliding slowly down the bannister, leaving something oily, greasy, in its wake.

I fled to the adjoining dining room, clattered against my erect camera stand, grasped hold an oil lamp with a fractured shade from the top of a wooden sideboard. I flung off the shade, lit the wick, watching as the exposed flame rose. But only for the briefest moment. The lamp began to dim. So too did the light coming from the lounge behind me.

I clutched the lamp to my chest, feeling it shudder in my hands. The flame near died, till nothing but a fine line of simmering orange glowed along the wick. I closed my eyes, tears rolling down my cheeks as I waited, and waited.

The footsteps across the hallway were soft, barely audible. But they seemed to take on a dreadful weight as they stepped into the lounge. The candelabra in the doorway was thrashed to the other side of the room. I whimpered like a child, pleading for mercy under my breath.

Something wheezed; a wretched, gargling noise. Bones cricked and snapped as they moved in ways they never should. A nose sniffed; teeth ground against each other. I felt heat at my back, a noise like the cracking of dried wood.

The dank smell, like aged dirt, overpowered me. The presence of the thing bore down upon me, began to draw my life, feeding off what strength I had. My legs weakened; my hands nearly dropped the lamp.

This night would be the night. This thing would take me to an unknown hell.

An awful blood-soaked cough made me yelp. I heard the ghost dash across the floor to the hearth. I heard it scramble, opened my eyes with a yell and turned to the darkness, catching the faintest glimpse of movement in the shadows as the wretched thing clawed up the chimney. Light burst back into the room. The flame of the oil lamp near scorched my chin.

I crumpled to the floor and gasped and cried.

In spite of how many times I had borne witness to such things, it never grew any easier.

In time I lit the whole of the lower floor. Everything was unclean and cluttered, neglected in the months of my disarray and sorrow. Books were pulled from cases and strewn across chairs and side tables; photo negatives and old crime-scene materials were spread out across the floor, with note pages torn or spotted with liquor. The large dining-room table had been tipped to one side and propped against the wall, my dusty camera and stand now discarded beside it.

The rug was grubby with cigarette ash. Empty glasses and decanters were spread out everywhere along with brown bottles of ale and clear bottles of rum. I gathered the shattered pieces of glass I had trodden on, collecting them onto a plate with some mouldy food.

I found a few loose cigarettes, some stale bread to eat and set about consuming what liquor was close to hand. I dwelt on the day, lingered on Hawthorn's motives and the bloodied thumbprint, the only real evidence against him. Not till the clock struck eleven did my eyes settle on the pile of letters I had scattered from the bureau and a curious thought came to mind.

Has Hawthorn contacted you recently?

That question had been put to me more than once. In truth I didn't really know.

I gathered the letters and tore them open one by one. Many were months old, and I tried to recall when exactly I had stopped opening them. Most likely, it was the same time I had stopped answering the door.

Some were of a mundane nature, concerned with day to day matters of the home and amenities. A number were from my cousin, each growing more and more distressed at my lack of response, and the manner in which I had last spoken with her. Her most recent (dated the fifteenth of August) stated she would soon be travelling to London, though she couldn't be certain when, due to the ill health of her husband. She near begged that I reply, and I felt awash with guilt for causing her such sorrow.

Many of the letters were formal requests for my services from constabularies across the country, and I gave these only the briefest glance before disregarding them entirely. After almost an hour, I set upon a slim, cream envelope, with my name and address scratched in rich, sepia ink. As with all the letters, I had no recollection of when it arrived, and growing tired (and drunk), opened it carelessly.

When I read the name at the foot of the letter, I sat bolt upright, and moved closer to the lamp at my side.

Your friend, Elijah.

I began reading frantically. The letter was dated the twelfth of January.

Dear Thomas

Whilst my writing to you may come as something of a shock, I would stress my deepest regret that I have not been in contact with you sooner. My actions in the past were beyond mere rashness, for I took my anger and resentment out on you, a friend I still hold dearly. Perhaps my current state of affairs has brought a sharper focus and perspective on the whole miserable time surrounding our last meeting ... perhaps some foolish sense of pride held me back from reaching out till now.

In recent weeks I have thought much on our friendship. What work we did, Thomas – what good we did! How I long to return to those days when we watched the guilty led from the dock clapped in irons, when we celebrated our triumphs in the contemptible Fox and Hound pub and sang songs of ill repute until last orders were served.

Such good times, such good memories I cling to.

I cannot dwell on this, for my immediate circumstance is a desperate one.

I fear someone wishes to take my life. I have uncovered a deep corruption that has spread throughout the Metropolitan Police, perhaps even higher, to the upper echelons of government. If I am right, such corruption is of an abhorrent and wicked nature; evil men conspire to hide their evil acts.

I must speak with you in person, for the brief words I send you can do nothing to explain the full gravity of what I have learnt. I have fled London and sought refuge as far afield as I can. Though in truth I do not wish to state where in this letter – for fear it may be waylaid prior to reaching you – I must take the necessary risk of sharing these details:

Travel north to Glasgow, and further still to the tip of Aberdeenshire. Wait for me at Donalbain Station at one o'clock, on the twenty-fifth day of this month.

I pray that you are the man I believe you to be, the man who I know would have no involvement in this terrible conspiracy I have uncovered. You have my deepest trust, Thomas, and for my sake as well as your own, do not trust in anyone else.

Your friend, Elijah.

I spent many hours reading the letter again and again.

A Bitter Morning

September 5th, 1905

I woke suddenly, my head clear for the first time in many weeks. I had slept where I sat on the floor, with my neck resting against the couch. Hawthorn's letter was on my chest, and to be certain that I had not concocted his words in some corner of a deep dream, I re-read the contents twice over.

The signature was his. He spoke of times we had spent together. The letter was no forgery.

Noise murmured from outside. I eased myself up, spread open the curtains and looked out to the bustling street. Men in dark suits were hurriedly moving to and fro, with satchels in hand and papers tucked beneath their arms. A cart trundled by, with a flat-capped driver calling out to clear the road. The day was fair but not overly bright and a chill lingered in the lounge and across my skin.

As I looked out onto the morn, I wondered: *what was I to do? Who was I to believe?*

Henley, Critcher, Lavernock. All of them claimed Hawthorn a madman, a killer. What evidence did they have? A thumbprint, the threads of a motive. The disappearances had begun after Hawthorn had vanished. The man was an expert in forensics, and if anyone could leave no trace at so many crime scenes it was surely him.

The narrative was sound, if not fantastical.

And yet the letter. The cryptic letter cast the smallest doubt in my mind. What dark conspiracy could Hawthorn have spoken of; what could have filled him with such an apparent sense of dread?

Reason would say none, nothing. I was aware his letter may have been part of his strange and bloody criminality. Perhaps he wanted an accomplice. Or even another victim – maybe Hawthorn was simply trying to lure me from safety.

All such ideas overwhelmed me. I grew restless in spite of the crushing questions. I searched for a cigarette and realised I had none to hand. I fidgeted about the house for a short time, trying to decide what best to do. In truth, I wanted no part in the whole miserable affair. I wanted to know nothing of the kidnappings, nothing of Hawthorn's absence or suspected guilt. It was all too much for me to cope with.

Thinking of food – and alcohol as well – I gathered some money and stepped out into the chilly morning air, my coat wrapped around me tightly. Vacantly, moving carelessly through the crowds, I headed for a tobacconist just off Piccadilly Circus. With each step, my thoughts flitted between two opposing plans.

Hand the letter from Hawthorn into the police.

Head north. Go in search of Hawthorn alone.

The latter was a foolish notion; I was in no state to carry out any type of policing. I knew it was right, and sensible, to give Hawthorn's letter over to the Yard and rid myself of any more trouble. Still, the urgency in Hawthorn's words consumed me. I carried the letter with me and regularly felt for it in my pocket. Whenever I built up the resolve to march to the Yard and find Lavernock, some niggling doubt played on my mind, and I was back to deciding a best course of action and letting the whole, dreadful quandary play out again.

By the time I reached the tobacconist, I felt exhausted. A clock on the wall told me it was only nine in the morning, yet I already wished to return home and climb into bed. The matter would be decided when I was better rested, when I had had some time to think on it.

I bought cigarettes and a small bottle of rum, managing to fight the urge to take a slug of the liquor in the street. I busied my hands with lighting a cigarette, realising I had bought no food. As I inhaled the rich tobacco, a young voice rose up above the bustle and clatter of the street. The voice was a boy's, breathless and winded, yelling at the top of his lungs, though at first his words were not clear to me.

As the voice grew louder, I spied the boy, walking up the centre of the road, dodging between the carts and horses that clipped along, gaining the fury of the carters and cab drivers who yelled at him to get out of the way. I shook my head and headed for the butcher's. Only then did I catch some of what the boy was saying.

'…another one! The Wraith has struck again! There's been another one. Get the *Standard* – twelve pages a penny!'

The boy was close to me then, and I dashed towards him and grabbed him roughly. He thrashed at me as I dragged him to the pavement, though there I thrust thru'pence in his hand and snatched a paper from him.

'There's no mention of another disappearance here,' I snarled, after flicking through the first three pages.

'Just 'appened,' the boy said, his face grimed with dirt. 'East by Spitalfields. Well, I dunno when it 'appened but they just found a body. Shoutin' about it helps me sell papers.'

I thrust the paper back to him. 'They found a body? How could it be the Wraith if they found a body?'

The boy shrugged. 'Lots of coppers around, that's wha' I 'eard. You wan' your paper or not, mate?'

I shoved the lad on his way. He spat on the pavement by my feet before walking along, yelling once more.

I stood motionless for a time as people skirted around me. The boy must surely have been mistaken, for if there was a body, there could have been no kidnapping and thus the crime could not have been committed by the Wraith. It didn't fit the profile.

I started off towards the butcher's. The boy's voice still rang out as he made his way from me. My stomach lurched and I hacked on the cigarette I was smoking. I turned and looked after the lad for a drawn-out moment, then flicked the cigarette to the cobbles and headed east quickly. I was dashing along the pavements and through the crowds, making way through central London to streets I knew only too well. The streets I was raised on; the streets of my old home.

I moved slowly along Brushfield Street and, glancing left, spied the bustling market. The vendors cackled and called and yelled out like wild animals. They spat fire and spoke words, seemingly of another language, profanities rarely uttered west of St Paul's. Each, it seemed, had the finest wares in the East End; none could have their prices beaten. They were vying with one another, though the mood was not of ill will. Laughter cut through the cacophony of voices.

The wives jostled for the finest pieces of rancid meat, barely fit for dogs to consume. Their clothes were tatty and frayed, the hems of their pinnies and skirts blotched with mud and dust coughed up from the street. To wealthier eyes, such women seemed unkempt, dishevelled and barbarous. They spoke as vilely as the men and gave no quarter to stretch their measly pennies a little further for the family meal that coming eve. Yet, to take a moment and look a little closer, one could see the care such women took with their appearances. Their hair was wild, yet always tied; their clothes unclean, but visibly mended; their coats thinned and worn through, yet the buttons polished and gleaming. It is most often the women of the impoverished classes who sacrifice their needs and wants for the sake of their families, who forego new clothes or repairing their shoes, to ensure their husband and children take food in their bellies and have soap to clean with. They struggle with what little they have and run the household on less than a pittance, much to their credit.

The smell of filth rose from the very ground and caught on the dirty air, clinging to hats and worn-out coats. Costers with barrows piled high with vegetables, drained of all colour and vitality strolled by slowly, silently, for there seemed no great need to shout about their goods. Even in the cold, flies danced and sprung from the miserable assortment.

Another cart with rotting fruit trudged by me as I came onto Commercial Street. The man peddling the lot was as wasted as the wares he sold. His eyes were bleak, miserable, his clothes dirty and riddled with lice. Probably less than ten years my senior, yet so close to death, doing nothing more than merely trying to survive.

I stepped out into the road as a rider dashed along the street, south towards the river and dockyards. The road was empty of cabs, for no one in all of Whitechapel, or Spitalfields, or Wapping or Bethnal Green or anywhere else much near, could afford to waste money on something so frivolous. Yet still the street was a hive of activity.

Children skipped past me, some barely five or six years old. They were trailed by hounds who barked and yapped, and as I turned to look over my shoulder, I saw the horde gather around the feeble coster, who swung his arms out limply to stave off the gang. A young lad with filthy blond hair gathered as many yellowed apples as his arms could carry before running in my direction, followed by the other children and dogs alike. The coster yelled out, and as the lad came closer to me, I was minded to grab hold of him roughly and clip him for his misdeed. But to what end? The boy, like the children he ran with, was scrawny and pale, his arms thin as bone. Who knew when any of them had last eaten; who knew how many of them would live through the coming winter? Such was (and remains) the cruelty of the East End – the sprawling slum – that children born of poverty rarely escape it until the often-premature day in which they die.

The children sped away from me, except the last, a girl who fell and landed heavily in the road beside me. She moaned and tried to scramble to her feet; not even the dogs stopped for her. She was seven at most, and struggled on the ground, reaching down to her knees that were scraped and bloodied and speckled with black dirt.

The coster was yelling from behind me. The girl sat on the ground by my feet and rubbed at her eyes, stifling tears. I knelt down, looked inside my coat for a handkerchief to wipe away the blood. The girl began to sob loudly as the coster slowly came closer; another voice spoke from a little further down the road.

'What's this? What you yellin' about?'

I looked up and saw a young constable stepping quickly towards us. When I glanced over my shoulder, I saw the coster standing at my back.

'Those thieves took my apples!' I felt sharp fingers prod in my back. 'You saw it – tell 'im.'

I craned my neck and scowled at the wretched fellow. The constable stood right over the girl.

'That true? She stealing from this man?'

'They all did – 'ole lot of 'em just scarpered off,' the coster growled.

'Well?' the young constable said. 'Is that true, mate?'

He shoved his boot into me. For a moment, I seemingly forgot my position and the events of the last year. I stood quickly and eyed the constable an inch from his face, minded to give him what for and remind him of my rank. Yet, in an instant, I faltered, for I was as much a special investigator then as I was a prime minister. The sudden flash of anger quickly left me, though a look of recognition passed over the constable's eyes and he even moved to take a step back from me.

'Aren't you—'

'Yes,' I snapped. 'The girl didn't take anything; it was some boy who has since long gone.' I reached down and rather indelicately took the girl by the arm, lifting her to her feet. Then, for some sympathy had come over me, I reached in my pocket, felt for a sixpence and gave it to the girl, before sending her on her way. She stumbled off as quickly as she could. The coster shoved me roughly in the back.

'What's your game?'

I turned and shoved him back. 'Be gone with you!' I glowered at the man until he stepped away. When I turned back to the constable, he wouldn't meet my gaze, nervous even to speak with me.

'I . . . I didn't realise it was y—'

'I've heard there's been a murder,' I said, keeping my voice low. 'The discovery of a body?'

The constable nodded slowly. 'I didn't know you were back on duty, sir.'

'I'm not,' I replied sharply. 'Where's the crime scene?'

He hesitated, rubbing his jaw, his face cracking into an awkward smile.

'I'm … I'm not sure it's wise—'

'I know the crime was committed around here, man. You'll just save me the trouble of wasting time looking. Was it nearby?'

He nodded. 'Flower and Dean Street, sir.'

I brushed past the constable and stepped a few paces from him, before stopping and turning back.

'Is it the Wraith?' I asked. 'Is this crime connected to the others?'

The constable looked visibly uncomfortable. He shook his head and shrugged. 'I really shouldn't say.'

'Just tell me, damn you.' I stepped back to him and waited for an answer.

The constable nodded.

'The Wraith has made an error then, failed to kidnap their victim.' I thought on the notion for a moment, and began to walk away once more, before the constable called me to stop.

'It's not like that, sir.' He gestured for me to come closer and spoke in little more than a whisper. 'The body isn't of a victim, so to speak.'

He fell silent as two young men stepped quickly by us. When they were out of earshot, I impatiently asked what he meant.

'The body they found was a little 'un, a baby. Neighbours discovered him early this morning. He was dead, had starved to death.' The constable sighed, shaking his head. 'Seems the Wraith had kidnapped the little nipper's mother.'

A Baby's Tears

September 5th, 1905

The sky was as dark as the blackened houses of Flower and Dean Street. The cracked cobbles were thick with scum and festering water; voices echoed from open or broken windows. Men stood in doorways smoking tobacco, their wives or daughters scrubbing at their feet or rubbing clothes against heavy washboards.

As I walked up the centre of the street, I spied the gang of children who had pilfered from the fruit seller, though saw no sign of the young girl with bloodied knees. They laughed and span as their dogs howled and called out; I crunched over a few measly apple cores, stripped of flesh and even the pips.

From somewhere amidst the dense rows of three-storey houses, a baby was crying. A man yelled as a woman wailed for him to be still. Two men with no shoes stepped towards me, and as they passed, I caught a fragment of their conversation.

'…useless bastards, lo' of 'em.'

'They won' catch 'im. No 'ope in 'ell.'

A broad man with a ruffian sack jogged quickly up the road before me, turning back to the Commercial Street end and yelling, 'I think it's true. I think it's 'ere.'

The crowd gathering around the home towards the far end of the street was hard to miss. People were packed together, jostling and straining their necks to look at the door of the property where the crime had been committed. As I came within twenty yards or so, a whistle blared, and two constables led by a sergeant came into view, roughly pushing people away with truncheons.

'There's no circus 'ere. Clear off!' the hefty sergeant yelled, though he only served to cause more intrigue, as a new wave of passers-by gathered on the edge of the crowd and asked what all the commotion was about. Short, sharp whistle blasts rang out for over a minute, as I stood and watched the chaotic scene, until at last, defeated, the sergeant turned and yelled to someone out of sight, 'We'll need more men if this gets any worse.'

I stepped towards him, as he continued in vain to push people away.

'Sergeant,' I said, though he didn't hear me over the clamour. 'Sergeant!' I called out louder. I recognised the man – Greene was his name. He'd been a constable stationed with H Division when I'd worked in the Forensic Crime Directorate. He eyed me up and down quickly before telling me, in no uncertain terms, to move along.

'Greene, isn't it?' That got his attention. 'Bexley. I need to speak with a senior officer here.'

After a moment, the sergeant's demeanour changed, and he nodded his head. 'Didn't recognise you, what with…' He pointed to his face, and I took his meaning. My appearance was far scruffier than was suitable for a police officer. 'DI Lavernock's inside. You wan' me to fetch him?'

I nodded, though the sergeant seemed aggrieved. He rolled his eyes before yelling at the wall of bodies surrounding the front of the house. Slowly, he disappeared into the crowd, and I lit a cigarette as I waited for his return, doubting Jack would have any great desire to come and speak to me.

I was still torn between keeping Hawthorn's letter a secret or handing it over there and then. The latter was the more sensible idea, and if indeed this was another kidnapping linked to the Wraith – Hawthorn being the lead suspect – my keeping the letter would be withholding key evidence pertaining to an ongoing enquiry. I had to do it; I had to speak with Jack and show it to him. With it handed over, I could rid myself of any connection to the whole thing; I could return to my solitude and my demons.

Yet still, my doubts plagued me, for it made so little sense why Hawthorn would have committed such terrible acts. Maybe his letter was sincere, or some conspiracy was at play against him. My personal feelings for the man overcame my better judgement. My heart began to race as I continued to smoke, and suddenly I had a very strong urge to leave Flower and Dean Street and burn Hawthorn's letter in the hearth at home. That would surely be the best thing for it – whilst I doubted I could do anything to help my old friend, I would do him no wrong by incriminating him further.

The crowd was only growing bigger, and seeing no signs of the sergeant or Lavernock, I turned up my collar and began walking back towards Commercial Street. I made it ten yards before a voice called out to me. Lavernock was inching his way through the crowd; a moment later he stood before me.

'It's chaos, Jack,' I said, gesturing to the crowd as I tried to keep my voice steady.

Lavernock nodded, his jaw flexing as he looked behind him. 'Vultures,' he hissed. 'Want something to talk about down the pub.'

'Is it true?' I asked. 'Another kidnapping?'

Lavernock nodded solemnly.

'You found the cult symbol somewhere about the home?'

He hesitated, then nodded again.

'And the baby?'

He eyed me suspiciously. 'How the hell do you know that? How do you even know about any of this?'

'Word's already spread. People know there's a body in there; with all this ruckus it won't be long till they learn there's been another Wraith kidnapping. It was a constable in the street who told me about the baby,' I muttered, noticing the weight of the rum bottle in my inside pocket. How badly I wanted a drink at that moment.

'The family in the room next door said they hadn't heard the child crying for at least two days. Smelt something that wasn't right.' Lavernock rubbed at his eyes, his face waxen and tired. 'They went in, found the baby dead. We reckon the mother was kidnapped perhaps three or four days earlier.' He folded his arms and sneered. 'No trace, no forced entry. A family of five in the bloody room next door and none of 'em heard a thing!'

His voice was getting louder, and he stopped himself from saying any more. I could see how upset he was. Examining a body at a crime scene is never easy, but to look upon a dead child in such a manner is hard for any man to take. I offered Jack a cigarette, which he took with thanks.

'He's still in London,' I thought aloud, mindful of those around us. Jack shrugged.

'Could have left by now. We've got no leads, a body found three, four, maybe five days after the event. Who knows where the hell he is?'

'And other than the strange symbol, there's no link,' I rasped, 'no link between this victim and any of the others?'

Lavernock shook his head once more. 'Not that we know of. We're going door to door; hopefully someone will have seen or heard something.'

'You may get lucky.'

'I doubt it.' Lavernock looked from me to the crowd and then up to the sky. He said nothing till his cigarette was a withered stub. 'What you doing here, Tommy? You're not working this. It doesn't concern you.'

I nodded. 'It's just … it's just hard to believe that Hawthorn could be behind it all.' I felt my fingers curl around the letter in my pocket, the very ink seeming to burn against the skin of my hand. Lavernock must have read something in my face.

'You got something you want to tell me, Tommy?'

My body tensed, as my hand closed and crumpled the paper. I came so close to snatching it from my pocket and thrusting it to him. I fought hard to still the tremor in my fingers.

'No. No, I don't. I just had to see this for myself.'

Lavernock stared at me. After a moment he nodded slowly.

'You think of anything, you come find me, Tommy. You find me straight away, you hear?'

I nodded. A hand clapped against my back, startling me. Lavernock's face grew twisted and angry.

'Out of here, Sanders.'

I turned and saw the reporter, the man who had accosted me and Lavernock in the street the previous day. He reeked of musty garlic, the sweat on his hand seeping through my thick coat and shirt.

'Just doing my job, DI Lavernock, public interest and all.' He stepped around me, smiling wickedly. 'Good to see you here, Mr Bexley. Any comment? No doubt you have some insight about this latest crime?'

Jack walked away, back towards the crowd and the crime scene. Sanders called after him. 'Lucinda Chenko – that was the victim's name, right DI Lavernock?'

Jack said nothing and vanished into the throng of bodies without so much as a cursory glance. I turned and stepped away from the fellow, keen to be rid of his company. He goaded me as best he could.

'I could write an interesting piece on you, Mr Bexley. The strain of modern policing – the toll it takes on officers and the like.'

I heard him laugh but carried on walking. As I headed back towards Commercial Street, three cloaked constables marched quickly towards the victim's house, followed by a handful of curious men and women, looking morbidly toward the crowd.

I stood before the house we had moved to, the home in which, for three blissful years, I lived with my father, my mother and my younger sister. It was indistinct from the other houses around it, identical to many throughout the East End, no less squalid, nor any finer than the one we had left in Spitalfields. The paint on the door was peeling, just as the paint on the neighbour's door peeled. The window frames were rotting, as were all the window frames on this street.

Thomas Street. Quite foolish, really. My five-year-old self had been so proud of being Thomas Bexley of Thomas Street, Whitechapel. I didn't think on why we had moved, nor did it occur to me to ask my mother or father. I was just happy to live on Thomas Street, with my family. Happy for three years, happy until that night.

There were no lasting signs of the fire that killed my mother and sister, though I took little time searching for any. That terrible day was barely a memory, for I recalled little of what had happened, besides the dreadful look of my father screaming, crying aloud as he carried me around the corner to find the flames bursting out into the street, engulfing the exterior brickwork.

That fire had killed him as well, though not on the day it took my mother and sister. Walter Bexley was a good man, but grief can make good men do such terrible things.

Though it was barely eleven in the morning, a line was forming before the door of the workhouse that commanded the opposite side of the road. Men murmured and grumbled in the cold, pulling and scratching at the rags they wore. I knew from experience they would stand and wait in drudgery until the coming eve, when at last they would be allowed inside, allowed a place to rest and given some measly scraps of food, only to have to work like dogs for it all day tomorrow. I remembered the pity I once felt for them as a boy, the filthy men who lined up all day, withered, and worn and tired.

Only after one such beggar dared leave his spot in the line to approach me, asking for a penny, did I realise how long I had been standing, motionless, lost in thought. It had been so many years since I had come to this place. *Why was I here now?*

I gave the old man a penny vacantly, stepping briskly south to Whitechapel Road. With no great concern for who may have seen me, I took the bottle of rum from inside my coat and drank. It did little to settle me, or the growing unease that was building from deep in the back of my mind.

Head north. Look for Hawthorn. A voice was repeating the words over and over; I began to struggle to think of anything else. If Hawthorn was in Scotland, as his letter claimed, he couldn't be the Wraith. Maybe he *was* being framed; maybe he was the victim of some deep and unknown conspiracy.

But maybe he was mad. His letter was eight months old – there was nothing to say that if he had been in Scotland he was still there now.

Head north. Look for Hawthorn. The voice persisted relentlessly.

Soon, I found myself on Leman Street, my subconscious mind carrying me to places of my past. I gazed across the road, looking for the photography boutique of Mr Timberwell, the man who for so many years had treated me well and given me a place to call home. To my dismay, I saw the shop front, tatty and dishevelled, the sign above the door split and broken, 'TO LET' printed in bold white paint across the front window. I grabbed a man by the arm and asked him if he knew what had happened to the shop.

He eyed me darkly, then shrugged.

'Old fella died a little while back. Place closed up.'

I was filled with regret. I had become so closed off from the world in recent months, I had failed to notice the passing of an old friend. For a few minutes I stood, miserable with my contemptible lot, angry that such strange and unnatural things had come to haunt my every day and destroy the world I once lived in. I mourned Mr Timberwell, as well as my former life.

As I stared at the vacant shop, I took the bottle of rum and drank half in one, gasping swig, vomiting the whole dreadful lot on the pavement only a moment later. No one who passed paid any great notice.

When I straightened up, spitting sulphur to the road, my head pounding and sensitive, I had settled on a course of action. The voice from deep in my mind was growing too loud to ignore.

Head north. Look for Hawthorn.

A foolish course of action, but one I am certain I would take again under such circumstances. At that moment, it seemed I could do nothing else.

If I found Hawthorn, I could learn the truth from him first-hand. Either grave forces were at deadly play, acting against him, or his sanity had completely gone. In that instance I wanted to be responsible for bringing him in, for the sake of our old friendship, for the sake of the man I still thought of as family.

And maybe for the sake of my old life as well, a life I wished to have back, but one I knew I would never return to.

The Journey North
September 5th, 1905

I returned home to gather more money, for I wanted to act quickly. I intended to head to Euston Station, to enquire about a train that could take me north. As I stood at my front door though, I was stilled by a troubling notion, annoyed I had not thought of it sooner.

Henley wanted to know if Hawthorn had contacted me. Henley suspected Hawthorn was being assisted with his crimes. My absence was being viewed as suspicious.

The Yard were no doubt watching me.

I couldn't let them know of my intentions, for if they suspected I was leaving the city they would no doubt arrest me. I pulled out Hawthorn's letter once more.

I fear someone wishes to take my life. I have uncovered a deep corruption that has spread throughout the Metropolitan Police, perhaps even higher, to the echelons of government. If I am right, such corruption is of an abhorrent and wicked nature; evil men conspire to hide their evil acts.

Either he was mad or truly desperate. I had to find him – of that I was now certain. I pulled up my collar and stepped outside, glancing at either end of the street as casually as I could. Voices called, heads turned, hands shook. I spotted nothing untoward, no one of great suspicion. Nevertheless, I decided to conceal my steps as best I could.

I headed south, moving toward Piccadilly Circus. I walked steadily, with no great urgency, nor glancing over my shoulder. I stopped at the very same tobacconist I had visited that morning and bought two packets of Woodbine cigarettes along with a small box of matches. I lit one in the street and inhaled deeply before allowing myself to be carried along by the bustle of smart-dressed gentlemen and scruffy labourers alike.

At Piccadilly Circus, a group of women, numbering thirty or so, gathered around the memorial fountain, holding placards aloft demanding the right to vote. They chanted with vigour and a furore was brewing, as men (and a number of older women) began to yell and spit venom their way. Two mounted constables rode into view as I came within twenty yards or so of the group.

I watched and waited. A horse-drawn omnibus was standing idle close to my right. As the constables began barking orders, pushing back some of the men who were attempting to pull at the Women's Social and Political Union placards, the driver cracked his whip and the carriage lurched away. It circled around the fountain, its two horses plodding slowly.

The commotion was now growing. One of the constables was barged and harangued by men and women at either flank, his nag neighing as it was jostled and surrounded. The constable grabbed his whistle and began blowing on it. It only served to draw more crowds into the skirmish, with those defending the WSPU's cause squaring off to those who opposed it. Insults were yelled, punches thrown.

I waited as long as I dared, then walked quickly into the throes of the mob. I pushed roughly through, forcing my way to the steps of the fountain where I was confronted with three women who chanted in my face. I slipped around the fountain to the rear of the departing omnibus where the conductor stood, and barged indelicately onto the carriage, thrusting a shilling in his hand and ducking behind him, out of view.

'We're only going as far as Highbury Barn.'

'That's fine,' I muttered, keeping myself hidden. 'Keep the rest for your wife.'

I travelled as far as New Oxford Street, waited for the carriage to depart after a short stop, then skipped past the conductor into the road. I moved quickly then, for there were only a few milling on the pavements, talking and glancing into shop windows, and I was easily seen. I walked north, but began twisting down narrow streets, turning at every opportunity I could. Just south of Euston Road a beggar played a fiddle in a shaded alcove. I threw him a penny before pulling off my coat, which I handed to him. I gestured for his, a moth-eaten, navy rag that was in a far worse condition than mine.

'I'm obliged, sir,' he said as he pulled mine on, 'very much obliged.'

I moved away from him with my head down and collar turned up, travelling east for a time before arcing back in the direction of Euston. Suffice to say that by then I was somewhat assured that anyone attempting to trace my route would have lost sight of me. Nevertheless, I dallied as little as possible in the station. I was informed at the ticket office of the overnight flyer, heading to Glasgow at eight o'clock that evening.

By now the afternoon was wearing on and I headed home in much the fashion I had left. I gathered my things hurriedly: a fresh coat, clothes and such. For a time, I was resolute that I wouldn't need my camera, but the notion of taking it played on my mind.

Strange as it may seem, I had grown scared of it. It was the camera that had first revealed the spectre of Betsan Tilny to me, the camera that had seemingly unlocked this nightmare world in which ghosts that only I could see now lingered. I feared what may be revealed to me should I find cause to use it. It had a power that I had not as yet truly come to understand or fathom. I blamed it wholeheartedly for changing my life irrevocably, for showing me things that were unnatural, unreasonable, evil in many ways.

For a short time, I argued with myself. Nevertheless, I began gathering the necessities I would need for the camera's use piece by piece, and placed them in the camera's travel case, the handle of which remained broken. Spare glass quarter plates from a stack I kept in a third-storey room; developing and fixing chemicals in small brown jars; a slender thermostat. I checked the stand I had knocked over the previous night and finally examined the camera. The wood was scratched in places, the brass in need of a clean. I wiped the lens before placing the camera in its case and shutting it away carefully. When I found myself fashioning a handle from a leather belt, I realised my mind was made up.

I used a small pair of clipping scissors to trim the unsightly beard that had grown over the previous months and to neaten my hair. Both were done with great difficulty, for my hands shook badly. I realised I had not had a drink since I stood on Leman Street and found another unopened bottle of rum at the bottom of a chest of drawers. I noticed my Enfield pistol discarded on the bedroom floor, and remembered how close I had come to using it several nights previously. More than one dreadful spirit had come to me that night, a great many in fact, in a ceaseless, disturbing parade. I tossed the gun into my case and found what few other things I needed.

For nearly an hour I smoked with Hawthorn's letter in hand. Dusk was settling when I finally donned my coat and a black derby hat. My home had no rear entrance, so cases in hand, I left via the front, heading north and crossing Golden Square, moving towards Regent Street. There, I gently set my cases on the pavement and flagged down a Hansom cab; as I lifted my cases into the carriage, I called up loudly to the driver, asking him to take me to Paddington. As we trundled away, I waited, and only when we dashed past Marble Arch, did I call up to the driver through the trapdoor in the roof, informing him to turn us in the direction of Euston.

It was a vain effort to evade anyone who may have been following, but it was all I could do. We arrived in good time, and after I had paid the fare, I moved into the station quickly and bought a ticket for the flyer as well as a copy of *The Times*. I found a corner where I could sit and read, holding the paper high to obscure my face, all the while sipping on my refilled flask.

At ten minutes to eight, I headed for the platform. Darkness had descended; gas lamps shone as porters dashed with cases and packages in hand. I found the sleeper and a stout conductor examined my ticket before helping me onto the train. He guided me to my narrow cabin. We passed no one as we went.

Soon after, the train shunted slowly out of the station. I watched the city, orange embers dashed across streams of heavy smoke rising from hundreds of chimneys. I turned my attention back to the paper, until the words became blurry and I drifted into a light sleep.

It was short-lived. The train rattled heavily, and I woke to find no more than forty minutes had slipped by. My stomach growled as I lay on the compact bunk, and I decided to get some food in the dining car. I stretched upwards and looked out into the black of night, seeing nothing of the landscape but the soft reflection of my own face and the room around me.

I rummaged through my coat pocket for some money. The

whistle of the locomotive screeched, a long, piercing sound that cut through the steady rumble of the carriage. I glanced at the window.

Eyes looked back at me, set deep in a gaunt and withered face.

I cried out, falling back against the cabin door. The face remained; its mouth opened as the whistle squealed once more. Then the face swept away, and I stared in horror at my own, terrified reflection.

When I gathered the courage, I drew shut the cabin's navy curtains with a sharp thrust and stepped out into the narrow corridor; there I kept my eyes to the floor until I reached the dining car.

It was modest but well kept, with high-backed, rich green leather chairs, deep rouge curtains and small yet gilded light fittings that hung from the ceiling. They jingled with each movement of the train. A few people were eating and conversing. None heeded me when I entered, except an elderly man in a white jacket who approached me with a thin smile.

'Good evening, sir.'

I nodded politely, my body still trembling with fear.

'The dining car is serving light refreshments for the next half hour or so. Would you like to browse—'

'No, thank you,' I said, sitting myself down at a table close to the door. 'I'll have what you recommend, along with a dark rum if you have any.'

The man's smile wavered. 'I'm afraid we don't serve any rum, though we have a number of fine brandies, whiskies—'

'Double scotch then,' I muttered.

The man nodded and left me alone. I let the conversations of those around spill over me, before lighting a cigarette and inhaling deeply. When my drink was brought to the table I consumed it quickly, though fought the urge to ask for another immediately. I ate my food, a plate of cold meat and trimmed vegetables in a thin sauce, before settling into the normality and calm that surrounded me. After a second drink and another cigarette, my sense of disquiet eased. I grew tired but had no desire to return to the small cabin.

A woman to my left, dressed in an exuberant gown, laughed wildly as the handsome man she sat opposite chortled at his own anecdote. Her eyes met mine as she threw back her head, and her demeanour changed in an instant. Whether it was the raggedness of my appearance, or something else that unsettled her, I couldn't be certain. But she raised her elbow onto the table and flashed her companion a forced smile. Their conversation seemed to die down quickly after that, and five minutes later from the corner of my eye, I spotted her subtly gesture for them to leave.

Another couple further down the carriage left shortly after, leaving myself and only two other men in the entire car. One had his back to me, though I could tell by the flecks of white hair sticking from his sideburns, and the weathered hand wrapped around the cane propped lazily by his foot, that he was of some age. The other was far younger, with broad overbearing shoulders that leant over the table. He was reading a newspaper, though I noticed he hadn't turned the page in some time. He had a glass of brandy or cognac next to his heavy hand. It had barely been touched.

I watched him carefully. He glanced up from his paper and our eyes met. His face was rugged, hard-edged and ugly. His eyes were small and close together, though I saw how quickly they darted away from me. He fidgeted awkwardly then, flicking over the paper and playing with the knot of his deep green tie.

I paid my bill in full and left the dining car promptly. I had no great cause for suspicion, merely a troubling instinct. In spite of my best efforts, perhaps I hadn't been cautious enough.

*

I fought the urge to sleep, though the passing hours took a heavy toll on me. A drip of doubt had slowly burst a heavy dam of paranoia and my mind now raced with all such delusions of who the man in the dining car might be.

An inspector from the Yard perhaps, newly promoted into the CID, an unknown to me? Perhaps someone under the command of Flynn, working for another branch?

Sometime in the small hours of the morning, I realised I was holding my Enfield tight, pointing it at the cabin door. I had no recollection of taking it from my case. I set it down carefully on the bed, though left my fingers resting upon the handle. As the train clattered and swayed, my eyes grew ever heavier, and I drifted into a fitful sleep.

I was roused by voices outside my cabin. Two men, their words muffled by the train. I leapt from the bed and moved to the door, straining to listen. The first voice was gruff, abrupt, the second far softer. I was only able to make out the end of the conversation.

'…I'll keep you posted.'

'Thank you.'

Silence after that; I gathered the men had moved away from my door, and nervously I opened it. No one stood outside. I craned my neck into the corridor. To my right, the conductor of the train was moving up the carriage away from me. To my left, the man from the dining car was entering the cabin a few doors down. He didn't notice me watching.

In my tired, inebriated state I was then certain he was police. His conversation with the conductor was surely about me – there were constables and officers already waiting at Glasgow, standing by to take me into custody. My leaving London was cause enough for my arrest; I'd disobeyed both Lavernock and the commissioner, as though I were trying to flee the city, as though I were trying to run from my crimes.

I had to get off the train, had to get away in the cover of darkness. When I peered between the cabin curtains, I realised to my horror the first light of dawn was breaking. I hurriedly opened my case, rummaged through clothes, thought of what I would need, what I would have to leave behind…

Some sense overcame me. I took a breath, thought for a moment about all I had seen, all I had heard. My leaving the train would be a foolish endeavour, making my situation far worse than better. I sat on the bed, tried to calm down, tried to think straight.

I found myself reading through Hawthorn's letter. I still didn't know what to believe, whether the man was sincere or truly mad. I was balanced on a precarious rope, one that was ready to snap at any moment. Whatever I chose to do could be my downfall. If I withheld the letter from the police, they could lose a lead on Hawthorn, the top Wraith suspect. If I handed the letter in, I could fuel a dangerous plot, and risk the life of a dear friend.

If I wanted to track Hawthorn down alone, to learn the truth first-hand, I realised I had to discover who the man from the dining car was. I had to know if I was being followed before I continued my journey north of Glasgow.

I moved from the bed and opened the door of the cabin, stepping back impulsively to take my gun. I had no intention of using it, none at all. But I felt better holding it.

Quietly, I crept along the carriage glancing each way as I went. When I came to the stranger's cabin, I felt my face and lips begin to twitch and my neck and shoulders stiffen. My whole body grew tense, panicked at what I was about to do.

I knocked on the door twice before my nerves got the better of me. I heard a groan and mutter from the other side. A moment later, the door opened a crack; the train rocked heavily as it did, and I was knocked off balance, falling against the door and the bulk of a man who stood behind it.

'What th—'

I pushed hard against him, and he clattered roughly to the floor. I stepped into his cabin, the gun raised, and closed the door behind me.

'Keep quiet.'

The man yelped at the sight of the pistol. His brutish, ugly features softened as his face began to quiver. He raised his hands up to me.

'Jesus. Take what you want!'

He spoke with a heavy Glaswegian accent, though his voice was gentle, ill-fitting to his broad stature and features. I frowned.

'Speak plainly and this won't be used. Did Henley send you? Are you following me by his order, Critcher's even?'

The man shook his head. 'I don't know what you're saying.' He muttered for mercy.

'I know why the Yard sent you. I have no part in any of Hawthorn's misdeeds.'

The man wept, tears dripping onto his navy blue pyjamas. I looked about the small space, at a case in the corner, at a pair of shoes tucked neatly beneath the narrow bed. It shook my resolve, for all appeared so … *normal*. I loosened my grip on the gun and took a small step back towards the door. The fellow edged further away from me, desperately clutching hold of the bed.

He groaned, words that were barely audible. I ordered him to speak once more.

'I don't know what you're talking about. None of it.' He was on his knees, his eyes shut. 'I'm a salesman. Just a salesman.'

'A salesman?' I exclaimed. 'You were watching me in the dining car, you followed me onto the trai—'

'I didn't,' he cried. 'You were looking at me! You stared at me.'

He groped for his suitcase and began undoing the straps, even as I told him to stop. He threw open the case revealing an array of garments, with brochures tucked neatly in pockets.

'We make clothes, specialise in gentlemen's wear. I had a meeting with a department store owner in London. I swear it – I swear!'

I leant back against the door, as the man continued to grovel. I watched him for a moment, enraged by my own idiocy. I looked at the gun, reviled, and tucked it into the waist of my trousers. I squeezed tight the bridge of my nose, thinking what best to say. After a moment, I crouched down slowly, my hands held out.

'There's been a dreadful mistake.'

'Don't hurt me!' he begged, a pitiful wreck.

I spoke as reassuringly as I could. 'I'm police, Metropolitan Police.' I paused. 'We had a tip about an escaped prisoner, I thought you fit his description.' The lie felt forced even as I said it.

The man seemed to calm a little. His bright red face creased as he looked at me quizzically.

'Wh-what?'

'An honest mistake. You have my sincerest apologies, sir.' I stretched a hand out to him and helped him to his feet, though he still looked at me nervously.

'I'm not in any trouble? You're not going to hurt me?'

'Not at all,' I smiled. 'Just a misunderstanding.'

He frowned. 'Bu-but you said I was following yo—'

'It doesn't matter,' I insisted, backing away from him. I needed to get out of his sight; no doubt he would raise the alarm, tell the conductor, or worse still the authorities in Glasgow. 'Try… try to enjoy the rest of your journey.'

I mumbled more apologies as I hurried out the door and

back to my cabin. I had no idea what time it was, or how long remained of the journey. I needed to get off the train, needed to get as far away from the poor fellow as I possibly could.

I cursed myself for my wariness, for my stupidity, for ever thinking that I had been followed. I barged into my room and locked the door shut behind me.

A voice yelped in surprise, and I in turn nearly screamed in terror.

A young woman was sitting on my bed; Hawthorn's letter lay open beside her.

I was too stunned even to grab my gun.

'Who-who the hell are you?'

A Sister Searching

September 6th, 1905

The woman stood.

'This isn't what it looks like.'

'Breaking and entering?' I growled. 'I think that's exactly what this is.' I stepped forwards and snatched the letter furiously from the bed. 'I could have you thrown off the train for this. Arrested, even!'

I was aware of the irony of what I was saying.

The woman seemed unmoved. A little over five feet tall, I guessed she was in her early twenties. Petite and fair-haired, her features were delicate; thin blue eyes above a slender nose and finely sculpted lips. She looked like no woman I had ever seen before, however. Her hair was pulled back, tied and almost entirely hidden by a brown flat cap. She wore men's clothes: an oversized dockers jacket with large round buttons, a slacked pair of brown trousers and shin-high boots.

'You're Thomas Bexley, aren't you?' She spoke confidently, her voice eloquent.

I was taken aback. 'Y-yes—'

'I've read about you in the papers, about your previous cases across the country. They claim you're a brilliant investigator.' I was astonished when she sat back down on the bed. 'I knew it was you,' she said, seemingly to herself. 'I knew it.'

I looked from her to the door, wondering if the man I had accosted had raised the alarm already. 'Would you mind telling me who you are, exactly?'

The young woman nodded. 'I'm looking for my sister.'

'You won't find her in here. Answer my question.'

'Beatrice,' she said, her voice filled with nervous excitement. 'Beatrice Monroe. I'm looking for my sister, Dorothy Clarke.'

I recognised the name from the list of kidnap victims Henley had shown me.

'Your sister?'

She nodded. 'She's been missing for months. The papers ...' Her voice broke somewhat. 'The papers say she is a victim of this monster, this Wraith of London.' Her expression darkened as her lips tremored slightly. 'I need to find out what happened to her, Mr Bexley. I need to know if she's still alive.'

She stared at me with such sorrowful eyes that pity got the better of me. I was speechless, truly, for so much rushed through my haggard mind I couldn't think where to begin. All the while I glanced back toward the cabin door and thought how best I could flee the train.

'Miss Monroe, the enquiry into your sister's disappearance is an ongoing police matter. Your questions or concerns must be raised with the CID at Scotland Yar—'

'I've done that!' she blurted. 'I've spoken to the police, to inspectors. I've spent hours – days – trying to get answers, hanging around that contemptible place. No one will tell me anything.'

'It is an ongoing enquiry,' I said, as evenly as I could. 'There are protocols to follo—'

'No one is doing anything to find her.' Her words took on a furious venom, an anger that startled me. Her eyes seemed to grow. 'They're hunting this criminal, this madman, but not trying to find my sister.'

'I'm sorry for everything you've gone through, Miss Monroe, believe me. But you will need to speak to the police about your concerns.'

'I thought you were the police? A *special investigator*, an expert. That's why I came after you.' She looked away from me and muttered beneath her breath.

'What? Came after—'

'Yes,' she interrupted, her hands balling into fists. 'I saw you outside Scotland Yard, recognised you from the papers. A young constable confirmed who you were for me.' She hesitated a moment. 'I . . . I followed you as you wandered the streets, to your home off Golden Square.'

'How dare you!'

'I came back the following morning,' she continued, unperturbed. 'Thinking you would be working the enquiry, thinking that I may be able to appeal to your better nature, perhaps learn some information. Then I saw you leave your house, a wreck. I followed you to the East End – and back again. Managed to stay with you when you enquired at Euston Station about a train ticket.' She leant forwards, pointing at me quizzically. 'You were trying to evade someone then, but you couldn't have known it was me.'

'How . . .' By now I could barely speak.

'If you are the best the Metropolitan Police has to offer, perhaps I was wrong getting on this train.' She stood, commanding the small space, despite her smaller stature. 'Who did you think was following you all this time? Are you running from someone?'

I didn't answer; she was unrelenting.

'And who is your *dear friend Elijah*?' She gestured to the letter I still held.

I looked from her, to it, and saw how badly my hand was shaking. My heart thundered; this woman knew too much. I began to speak, stuttered, mumbled like a fool. The cabin swayed and I heard voices from outside the door.

'Well,' she demanded. 'What do you have to say?'

I took the letter from her, folded it indelicately and thrust it in my pocket.

'I … I need to get off this train.'

Fortune favoured me that morn, for unbeknown to me, as I so brashly confronted the man from the dining car, there were a mere forty minutes remaining of the journey to Glasgow. In retrospect, it seemed too little time for the terrified salesman to regain his courage. Nevertheless, they were a dismal forty minutes, in which I waited, expectantly, for the train conductor and other staff to come marching to my cabin door to have me detained.

When the steamer finally dropped speed, and we began passing the silhouettes and shaded contours of the city, I moved swiftly, gathering my things. Miss Monroe continued to badger me for answers.

'What's wrong? Why are you so desperate to get off this train?'

'I near attacked an innocent man who I wrongly thought was following me.' I glowered at her. 'Seems my fears were well justified.'

She was quiet for a time after that.

As we came into the station, I put on my hat and pulled the brim down low. I took my cases, and cautiously moving up the carriage, headed towards the lounge car, which was all but deserted. I waited impatiently for the train to halt, looking nervously at the platform, expecting to see a half dozen officers in dark uniforms waiting to arrest me.

Miss Monroe stood at my side. 'If you don't tell me why you have come all this way, or who this man, Elijah is, I'll be forced to speak with the authorities when we alight.'

'I need to get away from this train quickly,' I muttered, glancing over her shoulder. 'After that, we can find somewhere quiet to speak.'

'You'll try to run from me—'

'You have my word,' I said.

The platform was bustling despite the early hour. A postal steamer was being loaded on the opposing line; men with stacked trolleys were moving briskly and calling out to one another. Carts were piled high with packages and luggage; I felt as though eyes watched me as our steamer rattled to a jolting halt.

To my relief there were no police in sight. I opened the carriage door and hopped down to the platform. Steam billowed out around my feet as I looked quickly left and right. Head down, I walked briskly from the train, losing myself in the bodies, though Miss Monroe stayed close on my heels.

In the station's grand concourse, I spied a small tearoom with plush chairs and white tablecloths. Without a word I found a table in a dimly lit corner, and sat silently for a time, watching the door to ensure no one was searching for me. Miss Monroe stared at me all the while.

An elderly waitress came to the table, her back arched so gravely, she stood barely four feet tall. 'What can I get ya', darlin'?' She looked to me from the corners of her eyes.

'Um. Just tea, please.' I glanced to Miss Monroe across the table. 'Unless you'd like anything else?'

She was sitting low in her chair, her heavy cap pulled down over her eyes. She shook her head. 'I'm fine, thank you.'

'Tea for one, please.'

The elderly waitress glanced from me to Miss Monroe, slowly looking her up and down. She frowned, and I realised then that she had likely thought the young woman a man until she spoke.

She muttered as she left the table, and when she returned a few moments later with the tea, she said nothing to either of us.

I was somewhat calmer then, though still kept a close eye on the tearoom's door. As I stirred my dark brew, I pulled the silver flask from my coat and spilt my last few drops of rum into the cup. I sucked back the hot mixture with no grace or decorum before offering Miss Monroe a cigarette, which she declined.

'I didn't think police officers started drinking this early in the day,' she said, pulling the cap up a little to tuck away a few strands of her long hair.

'You'd be surprised what vices police officers succumb to at this hour.' I was being coarse and regretted my tone immediately. I smoked a cigarette, uncertain what to say. 'I'm sorry about your sister,' I mumbled with sincerity. 'I'm afraid I don't know the full circumstances of her disappearance.'

'You're not working the enquiry?'

I shook my head. 'My position is somewhat more … *complicated*.'

The young woman folded her arms as she stared down at the table. 'Well, my sister was taken from her home five months ago. Lived in Chelsea with her husband, though he was overseas at the time – there were no signs of forced entry, no damage done to the property itself. Nothing was even taken. The police won't tell me why they believe this is connected to the Wraith – can you explain that?'

I shook my head silently.

'Then what do you know, Mr Bexley?' she scoffed.

'Enough.' I rubbed my hand against my right temple, which was throbbing mercilessly.

We sat in stubborn silence for a short time, as more and more people began to congregate and gather in the room around us. Miss Monroe fiddled with her hands and bit on her thumbnails.

I could see she wanted to ask me more questions, and was no doubt wracked with panic and misery for the fate of her sister.

I sighed. 'This is surely a difficult time, and I understand your frustrations for they are more than justified. But I swear to you, my being here is in the interests of discovering the truth, nothing more. With the greatest respect I can't sit here wasting time that would be better spent—'

'So you *are* working the enquiry, or following some sort of lead?'

I looked away from her.

'Your sister's disappearance is one of a number, and there are several lines of enquiry, one of which I am pursuing. I admire your spirit, for following me this far. But I'm afraid I can't tell you anything, and it would be best you returned to London—'

'I'm not returning to London or leaving your side until you give me some straight answers.'

'As I've said, the enquiry is ongoing, and I can't discuss it.'

'You're lying to me,' she growled. 'Have you always been this bad at lying?' She spoke with anger, with a simmering intensity, leaning forwards onto the table, her expression darkening. 'You're afraid someone's following you – who?'

'Keep your voice down.' A man close to us looked at me briefly, before staring back down at his breakfast. 'It's of no concern.'

'Is it someone to do with the enquiry – a suspect?'

'I can't tell you …'

'If it were, you'd be hunting them and not vice versa. You're not merely keeping your head down but fearful someone has actually followed you from London.' She frowned, looked me up and down slowly. 'You're a drunkard, a mess.' Her eyes widened then, and she stretched even closer to me. 'They don't know you're here,' she whispered furiously. '*The police*. They have no idea what you're doing?'

My heart leapt; I feigned disbelief as best I could. 'This is absurd.' I took my hat and stood to leave.

'Tell me I'm wrong,' Miss Monroe snarled. 'I read that letter, the one from your friend, Elijah.'

I sat back in my seat quickly and leant closer to her.

'You had no damned right—'

'Tell me who he is.'

'Miss Monroe.'

'For God's sake, call me Beatrice. That man spoke of some corruption in the Metropolitan Police. Is someone covering up mistakes in the Wraith enquiry? Or worse?'

I sighed 'I can't tell you—'

'You have two choices, Mr Bexley. Either speak plainly with me and tell me why you are here or leave me at this table and see how quickly I can get the police to Donalbain in Aberdeenshire.' Her eyes narrowed. 'That's where you're heading, isn't it? I saw it mentioned in the letter.'

'All right!' I pinched the bridge of my nose in frustration, the pain from my temples now spreading across my brow. It seemed the woman had me cornered; I would have to give her something.

'All right. You're correct, I'm not working the enquiry. I've been ... *incapacitated*, for a time, and unable to carry out my duties.'

'So why were you at Scotland Yard the day before last?'

'So that my superiors could judge my state; they're desperate for manpower.' I was lying again, and she saw straight through me.

'That's not it – if things were so desperate, they would have brought you in months ago.'

I nodded, reluctantly. 'There's been a new piece of evidence, something that points to a suspect.'

'What evidence? Who?'

'I can't—'

'The man who wrote you that letter, Elijah. Is it him?'

'No ... I ...' There seemed no sense in pretending otherwise. After a moment I nodded. 'You would have made a great sleuth in another life, Miss Monroe.'

She scowled. 'He is the suspect then? From what he wrote, it seems you once knew each other.'

'We worked together at the Met. I knew him well. Many of us did.'

'Yet he chose to reach out to *you* alone?'

'We were close,' I hissed.

She held her emotions in check, for her face seemed barely to twitch.

'That letter was written eight months ago; you had it in your possession all this time.'

'I only discovered it the day before last – I have neglected many things in recent months.'

'You expect me to believe ...'

'It's the truth,' I croaked. 'The Yard told me Elijah Hawthorn was a suspect, and I went home and discovered a letter where he claims his life is in danger. Either his letter is genuine, or he is truly mad; either way, I wanted to find out for myself.'

'So, you've come looking for him *eight months* after he sent this letter, even when Scotland Yard have evidence against him?'

'I think they are wrong.' I stopped myself from saying anything more.

Miss Monroe was unrelenting. 'And?'

'You have my sympathies,' I continued, 'but in truth I don't know who you are. Please, I implore you, return to London.'

I stood abruptly, grabbing my cases and walking away. Miss Monroe followed close behind.

'I'll tell them you're here,' she spoke quietly. 'Believe me I will. I only care about finding out what happened to my sister. For all I know, you could be lying to me, running from the police because they suspect you!'

My stomach lurched. 'Miss Monroe—'

'You may not know who I am, Mr Bexley, but I don't truly know you either. Maybe it would be best if I *did* tell the police.'

We had left the tearoom then and she stormed away from me quickly. I took her threat seriously and charged across the concourse towards her. She called out to a station assistant, asking him to direct her to the telegraph office. He looked at me in utter bemusement when I explained it wouldn't be necessary. I didn't speak until he had wandered out of earshot.

'This is no foolish matter.'

'I am not acting foolishly.' She stepped away from me and I walked alongside her briskly.

'This man, Elijah Hawthorn – I fear someone intends to frame him.'

'Why?'

'He was an expert in crime-scene forensics. I doubt the evidence the police have discovered would have been left by him.'

'So you think...' She rolled her eyes. 'Oh God. You think the police are conspiring against this man?'

'I didn't say that, I am merely investigating—'

'But you won't tell the police you are here. You're afraid they are following you and want to keep all you are doing secret. Tell me, Mr Bexley, does that not seem a little suspicious? For all I know you are my sister's killer, on the run, now trying to deceive me.'

'That's not it.' I was struggling to keep pace with her. 'I knew this man well; it seems impossible he could have committed these crimes. Listen to me – listen!'

She stopped abruptly. I set down my cases, noticing a few passers-by glancing at us strangely.

'I owe this man, Elijah. If he is the guilty party, I need to find him, to bring him in myself. He was…' I ran a hand across my face. 'He was important to me once. Still is.'

She seemed to think on it for a moment, glancing around the concourse with her hands thrust into her jacket pockets. 'Fine. Then I'll come with you.'

'What?'

'The police aren't telling me anything and it seems you are chasing up the best lead to date. We both want the same thing – to learn the truth – so I'll come with you.'

'That simply—'

'Won't be up for discussion.' She cut in. 'The police haven't learnt what happened to my sister in the last five months and I fear they won't get any closer to knowing in the next five.' I began to protest but she stopped me. 'Either I come or I tell them where you are. I'm willing to bet they'll catch up to you before you find this Elijah Hawthorn.'

'And how do I know you weren't sent by them, impersonating a grieving sister to follow me?'

She seemed genuinely hurt by my assertion, a wild one that even I didn't truly believe.

'It is a risk you will merely have to take,' she muttered coolly.

I saw the determination etched into her face and knew then there would be no dissuading her. All manner of reservations and concerns flitted through my mind as I found myself nodding slowly.

'We'll need to find our connecting train, Miss Monroe. Hopefully there's one leaving shortly.'

'Good. And for God's sake, please call me Beatrice.'

Donalbain and the Hamlet of Pike Ness

September 6th, 1905

Neither of us said a word on the journey from Glasgow to Aberdeen, the point of our next connection. We sat in a compartment that was deserted for most of the way, and whilst we stared out of the large windows, watching as heavy clouds blew in from the east bringing cold rain and hail, each of us fought the urge to sleep. We were both hellbent on watching the other.

From Aberdeen, we headed further north still via a short steamer with three long carriages. With each stop, passengers vacated the train, until few remained. Only when we were close to our destination, having stopped at two empty stations called Turriff and King Edward, did Beatrice say a word.

'This man, Hawthorn, if you are coming all this way to find him without telling anyone ...' She scratched at the back of her hands nervously. 'He must certainly be important to you.'

I could see she was afraid. After the furore and excitement of the morning, her mind had surely settled, realised the rashness of her actions. To be following a man she barely knew, taking his words at face value, believing all he said. No doubt she still feared I may be the main perpetrator in her sister's disappearance.

'He was,' I replied quietly. 'We worked together for many years.' I kicked gently at the camera case down by my foot. 'I am ... *was* ... a photographer by trade – it's how we first met. I worked under Hawthorn in a specialist unit of the police that investigated the forensics of crime scenes.'

'You said he was an expert.' She looked a little embarrassed. 'Though I must admit I don't fully understand the meaning of forensics.'

'We examined scenes of crimes for any scientific clues, tried to learn new ways of determining the guilty parties.'

She nodded but said nothing, turning her attention back to the view from the window, looking out across the flat, windswept fields and the leaden, murmuring sea that grew steadily on the horizon.

At Donalbain, our final destination, we were met by the elements. The wind whipped and sliced around us; rain beat down in sudden, irregular bursts. The station comprised a single platform and shed, perched above a slope of beaten, weathered rock that led straight to the churning waves of the North Sea, a mere hundred yards away. Salt laced the chilling air that pierced my skin and made me shudder; the gales were deafening. Beatrice and I moved quickly away from the train towards the shed; it took a great effort to pull open its chipped green door.

We gathered ourselves in a tight room that was warmed by an iron stove in the far corner. The room was cluttered with chairs and bookshelves, an oversized desk lined with papers. Timetables were nailed into every space on the walls; a terrier sat panting in a small wicker bed.

An old man looked at me, his deep wrinkles creasing as he squinted.

'Didn't know there was anyone left on there.' He laughed, showing what few, yellowed teeth he had. 'You from the head office? Heard you were doing some kind of inspection at each station.'

I went to speak but he carried on.

'I wager you've never even rubbed down an engine like that

one out there before. Boys like you don't get your hands dirty, no matter how much dirty money you get your hands on.' He laughed once more and hit his hand on the desk. 'Not even a wee smile for me then?'

I cleared my throat. 'I'm afraid there's some confusion, we're not from—'

'Speak up, laddie?' he barked, furrowing his brow.

'I'm not from any train company.'

'You're not from Aberdeen?'

'Further afield,' I replied. 'Are you the station master here?'

He seemed offended by my assertion, despite the fact he wore no type of formal uniform, except a dirty black cap.

'Aye. Have been every day 'cept Sunday since eighteen seventy-two. Why you asking?'

I stepped further into the room, knocking clumsily against a chair as I went. I was worn out and in need of a drink.

'We're looking for a man who was here eight months ago.'

The station master wheezed. 'Eight months is a long time.'

'You would remember him. A gentleman from London, about six-foot, sixty years old, slightly portly. Last I saw him he wore a moustache and white beard; has some measles scars around his left cheek.'

The old man smiled wickedly, his eye twitching visibly.

'Aye, so what if I remember him?'

'Was he staying here?' I asked. 'I assume there is a town.'

He nodded. 'Aye, if you can call it that, just down the road a wee ways.'

'And he was staying there?'

He shrugged. 'I'm old, laddie, often need more than just words to remind myself of things.'

I sighed, glancing back at Beatrice who watched quietly by the door. I pulled out a sixpence and hit it down onto the table.

The old man only shook his head. With growing anger, I took out another and slid both towards him.

'I never seen a man the ways you describe, not here or in the town.'

'Never?'

The old man shook his head. 'Never.'

I glanced back to Beatrice, who seemed as perplexed as I. 'You're sure you'd remember?'

'Do you think we get many'a you English boys these ways? I'd remember him as well as I'm sure to remember you.'

I nodded, stepping away from the table and back to Beatrice's side. The old man watched me all the while through his squinted eyes.

'He could be lying,' Beatrice mumbled.

'Perhaps, though I see no reason why he would.'

'Speak up, English,' the station master bellowed, 'cannae hear you when you mumble.'

I felt my blood boil. 'He may not have been staying here,' I continued to Beatrice. 'Maybe there's somewhere close by—'

'What you sayin'?' the old man snapped again, standing from his chair.

Beatrice groaned. 'He's not talking to you. He's talking to me.'

I concurred. 'I'm talking with *her*.'

The old man shook his head. 'There's no lass.'

Beatrice snarled, taking a step towards the old fool. 'I may be dressed like a man, but I am a woman through and through!'

'If he wasn't staying here,' I said sharply, 'he must have been close by. Where's the next town?'

The old man looked from me to Beatrice, chewing on his lips. 'Pike Ness. Just a wee place east about a mile. Not much else for a while from there, until you hit Adanburgh.'

I nodded. It made sense; if Hawthorn had been concerned

others might intercept his letter to me, he would undoubtedly take precautions. If he wasn't staying in the town of Donalbain, he'd surely be somewhere nearby. He'd never specified meeting me in the station; perhaps he'd merely had eyes watching it from afar.

'Is there a road that can take us to Pike Ness?' I asked. The old man gestured roughly out of the station. It seemed all the help we would get from him. 'We shan't take up any more of your time then.'

I turned and opened the door for Beatrice when she wouldn't move. She tore her dark eyes away from the station master. 'Ignorant fool,' she murmured beneath her breath.

Outside, we walked quickly, glancing back towards the station to see the driver and fireman of the steamer watching us with some fascination.

'I don't know what you expect, dressing like a man,' I said over the rain and wind. 'We're hardly maintaining a low profile.'

'And what of it?'

'We need to maintain appearances. I am police, you are not. From now on, just keep quiet.'

Beatrice turned crimson. 'I'll talk when I damn well please.'

'Why in God's name *are* you dressed that way?' I sneered, irate.

'You think it more suitable that I should follow drunken policemen in petticoats and a bonnet?'

'You have some nerve—'

'Indeed, I do. And you are bloody insufferable!'

She glared at me with burning fury, and for the briefest moment, it was as though I could feel the heat from her body.

We were hit by a strong gust that swept us both off balance. The winds bellowed from the sharp edge of the horizon, where the charcoal sea met black, rolling storm clouds. Gulls cried out as they searched for any nook or crack in the rock to hide

LETTERS FROM THE DEAD

away. A thin trail wound down from the station to a dirt road, hemmed in on one side by pebbles and driftwood, pushed up onto the shoreline. Without so much as another word, we moved as quickly as we could along the path, before heading down the road, passing through the single, quiet street of Donalbain without encountering another soul. As thunder drummed far off in the distance, we trudged slowly towards the hamlet of Pike Ness.

'You're police?'

The innkeeper looked from me to the woman beside him. She stood a few inches taller than he; her wide eyes stared unblinking at mine. It was somewhat unsettling.

'Yes,' I replied. 'Working out of London. We need a room. And a drink.' My hand shook as it rested on the bar.

The innkeeper raised his eyebrows, and he scratched at his thick beard with both hands.

'You've come all this way to investigate Douglas and Willie?'

I frowned, as heavy drops of water rolled down my face and fell from my coat. It seemed that between myself and Beatrice, we had brought a gallon of rainwater into the pub; it pooled on the stone floor.

'Um, I'm sorry. There may be some confusion.'

'The two brothers, they went missing a few weeks back. We reported it to a constable, said he'd get in touch with the police at Aberdeen but we've heard nothing.' He looked to the woman beside him cheerily. 'Never thought we'd get men from London, eh, darling?'

The woman only shook her head. She wore a thin wedding band and I assumed she was the innkeeper's wife.

The innkeeper spoke brightly, 'Are there any more of you coming, Inspector...'

'Bexley, Thomas Bexley. I'm a special investigator.' I glanced at Beatrice. 'And no, my colleague here will be assisting me. She's new, an investigator as well.'

The innkeeper's wife seemed shocked. 'They have women in the police in London?'

'Of a sort,' I replied, before Beatrice could say anything.

The innkeeper shook his head, glancing towards the door. 'It's a miserable night to be out *investigating*.'

'We arrived a short while ago at Donalbain; we thought it best to come here.' I paused. 'There does seem to be some confusion, however, for our business concerns a different matter.'

The innkeeper seemed crestfallen. 'What could that be?'

I hesitated to answer; impatience was getting the better of me as I struggled to still my hand.

'We need a room. For a day or two. Do you have any?'

'Well aye, there's some space up above, but what's all this about, if not—'

'All in good time,' I snapped. 'Perhaps I could trouble you for a drink first.'

The innkeeper shook his head and smiled awkwardly.

'Aye. A drink. Could you take one or two of these cases upstairs darlin', whilst I fetch the policeman here a drink.'

I sat myself down on a small stool as the innkeeper's wife gathered up my cases. To my surprise, Beatrice followed after her.

'I think I'll head up, try and rest a little.'

I nodded and watched as she left the bar and followed the innkeeper's wife up a flight of stairs.

'What'll it be?'

'Rum, preferably,' I replied. He placed a glass before me and filled it with dark liquid. I drank it down in one quick swig and asked for another straight away. He filled the glass once more and stared as I finished it just as quickly.

'Do all police drink this much in London?' I didn't reply and pointed to my glass. He filled it once more. 'No wonder there's still so much crime.' I flashed him a look and he smiled politely, stepping to a man at my left who clasped a silver tankard. I stared down at my hand and clenched my fingers. The tremors eased after a moment.

Our walk had not been an easy one. The station master had lied or been mistaken, the mile to Pike Ness in fact being some two and a half. Dusk had settled when, with some relief, we'd reached the peak of a steady climb and spotted a few faint lights nestled in a small cove. Our descent to the hamlet had twisted and bent, made all the more difficult by the miserably cold rain.

Fifteen houses were all that stood in Pike Ness, in a single row that looked out to the sea, that lapped and foamed only a short distance across a narrow beachhead. All were built with the same rough stone and topped with faded clay tiles. A crumbling jetty stretched out from the houses into the roaring waters. The inn had not been difficult to find.

I sat in silence, letting the liquor take its effect on me, and thinking over the day. Those few around me murmured quietly amongst themselves: all men, all aged, all sailors by the manner of their dress. Only when the innkeeper's wife returned did I stir.

'I'm drawing a bath. Seems you and your *colleague* will need one.'

She disappeared once more before the innkeeper could reply. He smiled faintly at me, clearly uncertain as to what to do with himself. I lit a cigarette, before asking him some questions.

'The two men you were speaking of, Douglas and Willie. You say they disappeared?'

The innkeeper nodded. 'Aye, nearly four weeks ago. They're brothers, work the lighthouse just up and over; you probably didn't see it as it hasn't been lit since they've been gone.' He pointed meekly to my cigarette and I offered him one.

'Fine tobacco,' he beamed, inhaling deeply.

'When did you first realise they were missing?'

'We all knew straight away – the boys run shifts on the light-house, but we couldn't find either of them.'

The connection was somewhat troubling, two men having seemingly disappeared with Hawthorn possibly nearby. *Possibly;* there was nothing to say he was still here, his letter being eight months old.

'Do they have any other occupations?' I asked. 'I assume most around here are fishermen?'

'Not Douglas and Willie,' the innkeeper leant his pasty fore-arms onto the bar, 'but they had a boat that no one's seen since.'

'Drowned then,' I muttered. 'Gone overboard in bad weather?'

'Perhaps,' the innkeeper shrugged. 'Can't think why they'd be on the water though.'

'Don't be a fool, Gregory,' the man with the tankard rasped suddenly. 'We all know what those two boys were doing, and we all know they were keeping it quiet.'

'Ah, get away—'

'No. It's the truth.' The old man shuffled from his stool to-wards me. He hit a powerful hand down on the bar, the dark skin of his forearm wrinkled with thick veins. He came close to me, his thin face split as he opened his mouth; I could smell the dank ale on his breath.

'We share the wealth here. Always been the way. Those boys was out for themselves, takin' a cut of their own.'

'How?' I asked.

'The island. North east, 'bout a mile. They were up to some-thing on that isle and I know it…'

'You're talking nonsense, Lachlan,' the innkeeper said.

'I saw them.' The old man hit his hand down on the bar again and pointed a finger close to the innkeeper's face. 'I saw them going out that way in that wee keel they called a boat. You knew the sort of men they were – do you think they were both sitting all night in that lighthouse?' He flicked his fingers dismissively. 'They'd take it in turns going out there. Probably smuggling if you ask me.'

'No one is asking!' the innkeeper snapped.

'Do you have anything substantive to support that claim?' The old man creased his face. 'Can you prove what you say is true?'

He shrugged. 'I suppose not. But what other reason have they for being out on the water? Their father was no sailor; pair wouldn't know a reef knot from a bow line. And why would they be heading for the island? 'Part from the old manor, there's nothing there.'

'The manor?'

The innkeeper nodded as the man – Lachlan – slurped from his tankard. 'There's a manor out there, we call it the Birdhouse. Fayweather Manor is the real name, I think. Been shut up now for about twenty years. The family who owns it hasn't been back in all that time.

'Probably where them two boys were hiding their loot.' The old man belched and smacked his tankard on the bar.

I sipped on the last drops of my rum, wondering if Hawthorn could have known anything about such a place and whether, if he did, he may have seen to use the remote island as a safe haven. If he had, he'd need men to ferry him to and from the mainland, men who would keep quiet about it.

'You say there's been no police here but myself and my colleague. Anyone else who sticks to mind in recent months, anyone English perhaps?'

The innkeeper took my glass and filled it once more. He

shook his head. 'Not that I recall. We deal with the folks from Donalbain and once some years back we had a few rich fools, rambling all the way from Adanburgh, who were lost. But you're the first Englishman round these ways for some time now.' He folded his arms then and puffed out his chest. 'Why are you here for that matter, if not for Douglas and Willie?'

'We're looking for a man we believe is somewhere along the coast up this way.' I turned the glass slowly in my hands. 'However, I must admit, I am quite concerned to hear of these two men disappearing. Have their homes been searched?'

'We had a wee look a day or two after they were las' seen. They share the house at the far end.' The innkeeper gestured with his hand.

'And did you find anything?'

The innkeeper began to speak, his eyes darting to Lachlan, who interrupted him.

'We're not police, English,' the old man croaked.

'That's not what I asked,' I replied sternly.

The two men shared another cursory glance. The innkeeper hesitated, then shook his head and gathered a dark brown jug from the top shelf above the bar. Lachlan tried to stop him, muttering something frantic, before sighing aloud and grumbling beneath his breath.

'There was this, tucked inside Douglas' mattress.' The innkeeper placed an unmarked brown envelope before me. I looked down at it for a moment, before carefully opening it with a handkerchief in hand. Inside were banknotes, all in five-pound denominations. I counted some seventy pounds; curiously they were Bank of England tender.

'I imagine they wouldn't see this sort of money in a year working the lighthouse,' I said quietly.

The innkeeper shrugged. 'It could be savings.'

'That much!' Lachlan growled. 'And English money. Don't be a fool.'

The old man slurped on the dregs of his tankard and moved close to my ear.

'Them boys could never earn money like that with honest work. However, they got their hands on it, I'd bet it had something to do with that island.'

We had one room in the inn, with a single bed and little more. I found Beatrice lying on the bed staring at the ceiling. She leapt up when she saw me in the doorway.

'Did you find out anything?'

I stepped into the room and closed the door quietly.

After a moment's hesitation, for I admit I was still not comfortable sharing all that was discovered of the case with Beatrice, I reached in my pocket and pulled out the brown envelope. 'The innkeeper found this in the home of the two missing brothers, tucked inside a mattress. Seventy pounds in English bank notes.'

She raised her eyebrows. 'You work fast. Do you think it has something to do with the man you're looking for?'

'I can't say. If Hawthorn wanted somewhere to hide, this seems a remote enough place. The men downstairs spoke of an island, abandoned but for a derelict manor. He could have stayed there – could still be there for all I know.' I shrugged before pulling off my sodden coat. 'Perhaps these two brothers have been ferrying him back and forth. Perhaps they have nothing to do with him. Maybe they got deep into some illegal racket and wound up in trouble. Hawthorn may never have even been here. First thing tomorrow, we'll look over the lighthouse the brothers worked in. We may learn something then.'

'There's a tin bath in the innkeeper's room,' Beatrice said. 'It's the one at the end of the hallway. The water is warm.'

I gathered a fresh set of night clothes, and found the inn-keeper's room, with the bath tucked away in the corner, where the ceiling slanted down at an acute angle. The room was well lit; some six sconces held tall beeswax candles around the walls. A small framed photograph of the innkeeper and his wife hung above a bed, just below a crooked, wooden cross.

Steam rose from the bath, and by now I was badly chilled. It was more than inviting, and I stripped quickly before lowering myself in.

It was just large enough for me to stretch out. I let myself settle, my body consumed by the warm, pleasant water. I watched as the candlelight shifted in the fine ripples caused by my steady breathing, felt the heat soften the muscles around my neck and shoulders.

The speed and strangeness of the day's developments struck me then, and my mind flitted between thoughts of Hawthorn and Beatrice, a supposed killer and an indirect victim. There seemed too much to dwell on – the whole affair almost suffocating – as I tried to make sense of things and posit some order to it all. I turned my focus to the burning question of Hawthorn's motive. The man was a scientist, of logical mind and high repute. The fact he was being shut out of the Metropolitan Police for good, never to work in investigative forensics again (if I was to believe what Henley had told me), seemed a poor excuse to succumb to such barbarity and madness. For him to indulge in such wicked-ness would surely have required a far more gruesome, unseemly trauma to have been inflicted upon him.

I remembered a conversation Hawthorn and I had once shared whilst returning from a particularly unpleasant crime scene. He had told me that all that separated man from beast was arrogance, not intelligence or divine right. Mankind was arrogant enough to believe itself better, to have fashioned and shaped years of culture and values around this misplaced belief. Given the right circumstances, any man could fall from his lofty pedestal, to depths of depravity and cruelty no beast would ever descend to. Arrogance made us think ourselves better, when in many ways, we were far, far worse.

My eyes were growing heavy. The peripheries of my vision were blurring, and the golden light of the room seemed to be dwindling away. I should have left to get some rest but allowed myself a few more minutes to linger in solitude. I rubbed my face and listened to the soft patter of drops falling gently into the water from my hair. The winds were still ghastly outside. I closed my eyes. Footsteps creaked outside the door and I realised the innkeeper was likely waiting for me to leave. With a sigh, I stretched my neck upwards and looked about me.

The room had darkened. The lights of the sconces had dwindled to almost nothing.

At the far end of the bath, just between my ankles, a hand stretched upwards from below the surface of the water.

I struggled even to scream.

The hand was misshapen, sore and blistered, skin festering. Fingers curled with slow, deliberate poise – cracked, sharpened nails pointed towards me. The wrist and the forearm rose up before I was able even to move. I scrambled out of the bath and onto the floor.

True darkness engulfed the space as a figure emerged from the water, naked and vile. I clawed backwards as the room began to vibrate and tremor, as strange colours shifted and melded, as walls warped and curved.

The figure – seemingly a woman – turned and looked down upon me, illuminated by a reddish hue that seeped through each fissure and lesion in her dreadful skin. Her eyes flared a ferocious yellow, speckled with dots of crimson blood. My back hit hard against the wall beside the door. I hadn't the strength to reach up and claw at the handle, for all courage was ripped from me as the spectre raised a leg and stepped out of the bath. It seemed her skin was as hot as a raging fire, for the water boiled on her flesh.

I begged for her mercy, curling my arms around my bare body. Her steps were laboured and noiseless, and they were all the more terrifying as a result. I suffered as she moved slowly towards me, as her eyes never left me, as vile, flaming blood gushed from a deep wound in her neck. I buried my head in my arms, crying aloud.

The door beside me burst open; I glanced up to find another of the terrible spectres reaching down towards me. This one too was cast in a pale light, shifting and pulsing with each movement of the arms or twitch of the eyes. It grabbed hold of my shoulders and coldness enveloped me. Screeching, I tried to scramble away from it.

A hand slapped my face, twice, thrice. The sting of each blow brought with it clarity, and when I finally opened my eyes again, everything looked normal. I moaned as the figure shook me roughly by the shoulders.

'Bexley. Bexley!' Beatrice's voice finally brought me back to the world. She stared at me with real concern, her lips parted in shock.

'What the hell is going on in here?' another voice, that of the innkeeper's wife, called sternly. I was confused and shaken for quite a time after and little remains very clear to me. A towel was wrapped around my body, and blood trickled from my nose over it.

'What the hell were you screaming at?' Beatrice asked me sometime later, as we sat together in our room. 'What happened?'

I hadn't the strength to think of a reply.

The Lighthouse
September 7th, 1905

I slept a sleep that no one would envy, for I wished only to wake from it. When at last the light of morning roused me, I felt some sense of relief, though it was short-lived. My waking hours were as bad as any nightmare. Beatrice had seemingly woken before me, for she was not in the room, or anywhere in the bar below.

When the innkeeper brought me a bowl of oats, he asked me timidly about the previous night.

'Seems you were troubled by something very real.'

'Yes.'

I reached inside my coat and pulled out my silver flask, gesturing for the man to fill it, which he did obligingly.

As he handed it back to me, he smiled meekly. 'Is your um … colleague all right?'

I nodded, without paying much attention to the man. 'She's fine; has already left this morning for some air.'

The innkeeper smiled broadly at that. 'Oh, glad to hear.'

I left a short while later and found Beatrice sitting on the stone jetty. Only when we had ascended the winding road that led away from Pike Ness and begun along a narrow footpath that crept above the row of tiled houses, did she speak to me.

'Last night you were screaming as though there was something in the room with you. As though there was something right before your eyes.' I didn't reply; she persisted. 'What was it?'

'Nothing of any concern to you or the matter at hand,' I said bluntly.

'When you finally slept, you kept talking to this man – Elijah.'

'A bad dream and nothing more.' I stopped and looked straight at her. 'It would be better if we focused on the *matters at hand*.'

Beatrice was clearly aggrieved and walked quickly ahead of me.

The day was grey, though the sky was rubbed with a muted shade of pastel blue along the horizon. The sea stretched away to our left, murmuring and thrashing against the cliffs below us. Our path was soft underfoot and more than once we clambered over a dilapidated wall or cut through a heavy brush of nettles and brambles. Grass rose up as high as our thighs in patches, yet the gentle bleating of sheep could be heard on occasion when the northerly breeze settled.

Shortly after, we each gazed out to the ocean, to a low expanse of brown rock that was no doubt the island. It was entirely flat, and from where we stood, I could see trees but no sign of the manor. Then we spotted the lighthouse, its peak rising above the clifftop we walked along. Ten minutes later we stood before it.

I guessed it perhaps ninety feet tall, though its wide base sunk down onto a heavy outcrop of rock that stretched out into the water. Its rough, white paint had been cracked and beaten by the ceaseless winds and sea. The glass of the lantern room was visibly grimy; the black, wrought iron of the widow's watch tilted dangerously on the farthest side from where we stood. It looked close to collapsing off the structure entirely.

Looking down, I watched as the grey waters of the tide churned against the rough rock only ten or twelve feet below the lighthouse's wooden door. A ramshackle set of stairs, cut into the stone and lined with wooden posts linked by rusted lengths of chain, spindled down from the clifftop path we walked along. Beatrice pointed to two sections where the chain had broken and swayed flimsily.

'Who's to say those two brothers didn't just fall? It's quite precarious.'

I concurred. As Beatrice began slowly descending the steps, I stood and stared at the lighthouse a little longer. The strangest sense overcame me – if only fleetingly – the feeling that I had stood on that very patch of cliff before, on the same stretch of coastline, observing the same decrepit lighthouse. As I caught up to Beatrice and edged cautiously down the steps, I recounted my life and the journeys I had taken, merely to be certain that I had indeed never been to this remote corner of the world before.

We stood before the wooden door, visibly rotting from the sea air. There was no knob or handle, only a metal key lock. Beatrice pushed against it; the door was locked tight.

'How do you suppose we get in?' she asked curtly.

After a moment's thought, I rather rashly stepped back and kicked heavily against the hinge side of the door. Two kicks and the whole thing buckled in its frame, the rotten wood snapping under its own weight as it collapsed to the floor.

'That doesn't seem like something a proper policeman would do,' Beatrice muttered.

I ignored her and stepped inside.

Our steps echoed in a chamber some thirty feet high. A wooden stairwell wound around the wall to the floor above us. Bronzed metal vats, marked as kerosene, were stacked beneath a winch, lowered through a trapdoor from the ceiling above. Looking up through the trapdoor, I could see the winch rope continued even higher, likely to the lamp room. Light filtered in through a few slim windows cut into the rear-facing side of the structure. It was enough to examine the space carefully.

Beatrice scampered up the stairs. I looked over the metal vats, large enough for sixty gallons perhaps. A few were full, though most seemed empty. I climbed up to the next floor. Here, a bed was made beside a small stove. A few mugs and plates cluttered a rough set of shelves built into the stonework; a coal bucket sat empty. Some pieces of paper and a pencil were strewn across the bed.

I took one of the pieces of paper and saw a series of dates and times scrawled by a rough hand, some crossed out, others unmarked.

'There's one of those vats up here, and a ladder leading to the lamp room.' Beatrice said, appearing in view as she stepped down from the next floor above. 'It's some kind of gear room. Nothing out of the ordinary.'

I nodded. 'It seems Douglas and Willie have been keeping up with their duties, though they may have been more concerned with other matters.' I waved the piece of paper in my hand. Beatrice came to my side and glanced over it.

'If I were to hazard a guess, I'd say those are tide times?'

I nodded. 'It looks like a timetable, preparations to go out onto the water. These dates go back to mid-August. They've scratched out some, but everything from just over three weeks to the present remains unmarked.' I folded the paper carefully and placed it in my pocket. I glanced at the winch rope, rising through another trapdoor to the gear room. 'There is no way they could have manoeuvred those vats down the steps from the clifftops. There has to be other means to get them in.'

We both returned to the bottom floor. There, I began pushing aside some of the empty containers. After only a few moments, I uncovered a large wooden hatchway, with two metal rings set into the wood. It took effort on both our parts to lift the hatches open. It revealed a deep pit that descended some fifteen feet. Metal rungs had been hammered into the stone.

Cold air surged upwards, laced with a dank smell of spoilt fish and wet seaweed. I crouched down, squinting into the gloom. Anxiety overcame me, and I felt a great sense of shame for my fears. Once I would have delved into such frightful places with little thought or care. Now, I was halted, my mind observing in an instant all manner of terrors that could be lying in wait.

Beatrice was breathing heavily, her eyes looking wide into the darkness.

'We'll need to find lamps,' she said breathlessly. 'For the dark.'

'I saw none upstairs,' I said flatly, trying desperately to mask my fear. 'There may be some down there.' I recalled the words I had once uttered to a young constable, before descending into a dark and terrible place. *Our duty is to carry out these unpleasant tasks.*

I stepped down then without much further thought.

Jumping a short way from the last rung, the temperature dropped significantly. The floor beneath my feet was lined with a fine layer of grit or sand. Two heavy wooden beams, topped with a thick rafter, marked the entrance of a passageway, though the light from above only allowed us to see a few feet ahead.

To my relief, a lantern hung from a nail. Fumbling in my coat, I found my box of matches.

'There is a light,' I said to Beatrice as she clambered down the rungs. With the lantern fully illuminated, the dark passageway was far less imposing. It was some eight feet wide, though the ceiling hung low, particularly where the wooden beams above were thickest. The passage seemed all but straight and I knew it would lead us into the cliff rock, farther from the sea. We moved alongside each other at a steady pace.

A fine breeze gradually grew to a noticeable draught.

'Can you hear that?' Beatrice asked after a few minutes.

I listened with greater care. Something was gently tapping and creaking up ahead.

We walked a little further. A thin beam of daylight appeared, before vanishing with an audible thud. We came to a set of heavy, rattling doors. With a heave we pushed them open and I squinted at the brightness of the day.

I stepped onto a single track that cut through a large rolling field. A mound of earth and grass rose up around the doors of the passageway. Climbing up onto it, I could look out across the sea and spotted the top portion of the lighthouse jutting from the cliff.

'There's a broken lantern down here,' Beatrice called up to me. I returned to the entrance of the passageway and saw splintered glass and a broken oil lamp lying on the floor to one side. It was close to the wall; as my eyes moved further back from it along the floor, I spotted a few strange impressions made in the sand along with a dark, dirty stain. I knelt to examine the marks.

'Someone fell,' I said, pointing to a long scratch. 'They slipped here and dropped the lamp there.'

Beatrice crouched by my side. 'They must have been running.'

I nodded.

'Do you think they were running from something?'

I didn't reply, looking up the wall above the markings, now clearly visible in the light of day. I ran my fingers along the bumps and points of the stone, stopping when I spied something distinct from the deep shades of brown and grey, some three feet from the ground.

'What is that?' Beatrice asked.

'Blood,' I replied. 'You can see the splatter indication.' I pointed to the distinctive shape formed, a large globule with thin streaks splayed out in the direction of the doors. I knew in an instant what the stain represented. 'Whoever this was, they were shot. It must have caused them to go down.'

I examined the blood stains closely, before running my fingers along the wall, moving inch by inch. I knew what I was looking for but had no idea if I would find it. With some fortune my fingers touched upon something cool embedded in the stone. Clasping it gently, I felt it loosen with ease and managed to prise it from the wall. I showed it to Beatrice, who stared in fascination.

'Is that—'

'A bullet,' I said. I stepped across the passage to the opposing wall, judging the position from where the gun had been fired. 'Someone fired from over here. They shot once and missed, fired again and struck.'

'Do you think they were chasing all the way from the light-house?' Beatrice asked, pointing down the passageway. 'It seems strange that they fired so close.'

I had stepped backwards and nudged up alongside one of the heavy wooden beams lining the edge of the walls. It moved under my weight, and when I turned, I realised that there were in fact two standing alongside one another. No rafter was set in the ceiling above the beams; when I ran my hands along the crack made between the stone wall and the wood, I felt the lightest breath of wind.

'There are false beams here,' I said. 'Help me move them.'

We grappled clumsily with the wooden beams, letting them crash to the floor of the passageway with a deafening crack. Where they had stood, a cut-through or entrance to a branching tunnel was revealed. It was four feet wide and meticulously carved into the stone wall. Steps descended out of sight into the gloom.

'I guess this is where they were coming from,' I muttered, climbing over the fallen beams and stepping into the tunnel. I awkwardly made my way down a few uneven steps. The carved walls were tight around me.

The faintest light rose up through the tunnel. Beatrice and I descended further down and the narrow space around us grew and widened. Soon, the wall to our left disappeared entirely, and a wide cavern emerged and spread away from us. Fifty feet below, we spied sand and large pools of still seawater; two natural archways let daylight flood the space. The sounds of crashing waves echoed softly. Our stone steps were replaced by wood, as a huge stairwell, constructed of scaffold and thick timbers, wound down to the cavern floor.

Stepping outside, we looked up to our left, at the huge outcrop of rock, dashed in mustard yellow moss and topped with the lighthouse. The cliffs rose up to our right as well, penning in the tiny cove. Smooth pebbles gave way to white sand as we moved closer to the tide. It washed up around our feet and ankles before I spied a misshapen bundle, covered in deep seaweed and propped against a few sharp rocks that projected up from beneath the sand.

We cleared the seaweed carefully, uncovering the front quarter of a dashed and broken rowboat.

'Do you think this is Douglas and Willie's?' Beatrice muttered gravely. I couldn't help but nod.

'I fear they may have no use for it anymore.'

Making Way to the Island

September 7th, 1905

'Did you find anything?' The innkeeper, Gregory, asked sombrely.

I looked down at my drink. 'It's now a police matter; I'm afraid I can't tell you anything. We'll need to take a look at the island and the manor, as part of our enquiries.'

Gregory frowned. 'Why? Do you think they were smuggling?'

I shook my head. 'We can't be certain. Will anyone be willing to ferry us over to the island?'

Gregory sighed. 'Lachlan, the old fool in here last night, will do anything for money. Only fishes when he damn pleases. Shall I fetch him?'

I nodded and the innkeeper obliged. Beatrice and I were left alone in the bar, for it was still only early afternoon. She whispered to me sharply.

'Why didn't you tell him about the gunshots? You know as well as I that those men are dead.'

I shook my head. 'That's not how police enquiries work. We don't know anything yet and we have no cause to rouse fears or swell grave suspicions. Besides, there may be more to all this than you and I realise.'

'You think others here may be involved somehow?'

I pulled out the small, flat bullet I had prised out of the wall.

'In a place this remote and insular, we have to entertain that possibility.'

I set the bullet down onto the bar and took my Enfield revolver from my coat. I unlatched the barrel, the cylinder of the gun pulling forward smoothly as I did. A spent cartridge bounced onto the bar; I quickly stuffed it in my pocket. I fiddled to pull out a live cartridge, turned the gun over in my hand and opened the loading gate.

Beatrice drummed her fingers lightly. 'You seem to be struggling with that.'

'You point and shoot,' I snarled as I finally freed a cartridge. 'The army hated these bloody guns the moment they were given them – Hawthorn managed to get hold of some when they were surplus to require—' I stopped myself and took hold of the live cartridge and the flattened bullet.

'They seem a similar size,' Beatrice muttered, leaning closer to me.

'Similar, though I can't determine a calibre by just comparing the two. An expert may be able to identify that upon closer examination, though I imagine it would be near impossible to identify the specific gun this bullet was fired from.'

She huffed. 'So that doesn't tell us much either.'

I reloaded my gun and pocketed the lot. Beatrice rubbed at her forehead and temples; her face wrinkled with discomfort.

'Are you all right?'

She shrugged. 'A little unwell. My head is aching, that's all.' She feigned a weak smile. 'I think I'll take some rest – come wake me if you need me.' She stood, her arm brushing against mine as she pulled it from the bar. Her hands and wrists were deathly cold. She moved slowly to the stairwell that led upstairs and I watched as she went, a grave and miserable notion forming slowly at the back of my mind. *I grew sick as I first began to see the dead. I was being poisoned by a madman, but perhaps there was more to it than that. What if seeing the dead had made me ill, as though an infection were spreading through my body? What if I were somehow infecting Beatrice now, by merely being beside her? What if Beatrice were to start seeing the dead as I did?*

The innkeeper returned with the old man, Lachlan, who stormed into the bar, near jubilant.

'Here he is – the policeman. Mr Bexley, am a' right?' He wheezed through haggard breaths. 'What did I tell ya?'

He sat down beside me with the same stretched grin he had had the previous night, one that revealed his bloodied gums and contorted the skin around his eyes until they were non-existent. He hit a hand against my shoulder.

'Gregory tells me you want to head to that island. Told ya, did I not? Those boys were up to something out there.' He cackled as though he was pleased with himself. His left hand pulled on the thick silver sideburns that grew down to his jawline and he began regaling us with all the mischief and trouble the two brothers had caused when they were children. 'Just knew they'd end up this way – always had a feeling.'

'We need to get out there as soon as possible,' I interrupted as he took a heavy breath. 'Are you able to do it?'

'Of course, I'm the best damn sailor—'

'How much?' I asked coolly.

The old man's demeanour changed; he rolled his eyes and scratched his chin. 'It's a hard place to get to. High tide floods the only quay that you can dock on; we'd have to go this eve, as the waters recede.' He hammed his part, twisting his face in mock concern. 'Even then it's not easy; every chance you can wind up clinging to flotsam and praying to your mother you don't get struck into the cliff.'

'Just name your price, Lachlan,' the innkeeper sighed.

'Ten shillings there, ten shillings back.' He cackled once again. 'I assume you plan on coming back?'

'Fifteen shillings when we return,' I countered. 'I'm sure others would take us up on that offer.'

He raised his hands. 'Fine. Fine. I assume that's for the uh ... *both* of yous.' His devilish little smile took on a more wicked appearance for a moment. I looked from him to the innkeeper.

'Yes, the both of us. Would you have something to say on the matter?'

Lachlan shook his head wildly.

'Where is your colleague?' Gregory asked.

'Upstairs. She is feeling a little unwell.'

'Well, I'm sure she will be well soon.' Lachlan chortled. 'Are you planning on staying on the island long?'

I was somewhat perturbed by the man, for it felt in that moment as if he were having some jest at my expense. I had not the faintest idea what was wrong with him, though looking at the innkeeper, I could see he was somewhat embarrassed on Lachlan's behalf. I let the matter drop. 'One night and day should suffice. I gather there's no means of communicating with the mainland, so we'll be reliant on you to collect us?'

'All the more reason to ensure a fair price—'

'You'll have your money when we're safely back on dry land.'

The old man smacked my shoulder once more and got up to leave. 'You drive a hard bargain, policeman; maybe you wee English boys aren't as soft as you all seem. I'll meet you on the jetty at seven o'clock this eve.' He sauntered away, whistling a dreary tune off key. At the door of the inn he stopped and turned back to me.

'The winds never die around Pike Ness y'know. Be ready for a choppy journey.'

*

That afternoon I took my camera case and walked along the cliffs alone. I headed back in the direction of Donalbain a short way, to a point where the coastline slunk further away from the encroaching sea. The day by then was fine and clear, and I could see the tip of the tall white lighthouse standing firm against the battering waves, as well as the slender brushstroke of the island.

I set up my stand, and with great care, began fixing my camera. My intentions were fairly whimsical, for my purposes then were not wholly concerned with the investigation. It had been some months since I had even toyed with the notion of taking a single photograph, fearing what I might see in any image I subsequently developed. I wanted merely to overcome this fear in a setting I thought would be best or safest. In spite of unpleasant circumstances, the scene itself was breathtakingly beautiful.

I captured one image alone, for any more would be a waste of my limited glass quarter plates. I then sat upon a ridge of grass and stared out across the sea, thinking of everything and nothing at once. Morbidly, I wondered how long it would take me to fall from the cliff edge to the rocks below.

'If it weren't for last night, I would say you were almost at peace.'

I was startled by Beatrice, standing with her arms folded some ten yards down the path from me.

'There is no peace,' I sighed, loud enough for her to hear. She ignored me and sat by my side, pulling her legs up to her chest.

'I once came somewhere like this when I was a child,' she said softly. 'Down south mind, along the Cornish coast. Wasn't as cold as here.'

'We never went on holidays when I was a boy,' I muttered. 'Got to the city limits along Mile End Road once.'

I reached in my jacket and pulled out my cigarettes, offering her one, which she declined. I smoked in silence for a time. The strange sense of having visited this place returned to me as I stared out at the island and the lighthouse. I had no great recollection of any of my cases involving a hamlet positioned so precariously at the edge of the sea. Yet, still, the feeling of walking amongst the homes of Pike Ness, of clambering along the cliffs to the lighthouse, of even glimpsing the distant island, lingered and deepened. I tried to recall a book I had perhaps once read, with a similar landscape, or even a lighthouse and remote hamlet. Such things were not uncommon, I wagered, and it was the most reasonable conclusion I could draw as to why I felt I had been here before.

'We've spoken little of your sister,' I said at last. 'I know as much about her as I do you.'

I'd questioned enough people in my career to know the visible signs of discomfort. Beatrice stayed silent a long moment, ran her hand up her arm before shrugging. 'She's a good woman, I suppose.'

'You *suppose?*' I muttered, surprised by her choice of words.

'Well yes,' she said quickly. 'I suppose she's generous, thoughtful. She married a man for the wrong reasons as women often do, for money, comfort, security.' She shook her head as she looked down towards her feet. 'He's honest and kind, but I know …' She trailed off, sighing as she pursed her lips together. 'I know she does not love him. It's quite miserable in many ways.'

'You disapprove of their marriage then?'

She nodded slowly, as though the notion were a great revelation. 'I guess she thought marrying him was the right thing to do.'

'But it's not the life you seek to lead?'

She turned to me, smiling sadly. 'No. No, not me. Ever since I was a girl, I've always dreamed of travelling the world, heading off somewhere with no real idea where I'm going, seeing things most only read about in books. Wandering across endless deserts, delving into thickest jungles to uncover all manner of rare and exotic beasts.' She brushed her open palm aimlessly along the grass by her feet.

'What's stopped you?' I asked bluntly.

'Circumstance. Not everyone can live their dreams, Mr Bexley, no matter how much they'd like to.' She looked out to the ocean, her face taking on a grave expression. 'Some day, in good time, I'll have my adventure,' she said defiantly. 'Once I know what's happened to Dorothy, I'll see the world, all the beauty it has to offer.'

I spoke with little thought, for in truth I have never been a man capable of offering much comfort to those who have suffered a terrible loss. Not for lack of empathy, for I am not completely heartless. More a necessary detachment, a feeling that one must maintain some emotional distance from those around them.

'I'm afraid you must be prepared for the worst.'

Beatrice scowled at me. 'I know she's dead. I'm no fool. My parents still hope she's alive; Dorothy's husband still thinks she may walk through the door, that she may return to him. But I know…' Her voice wavered, as she wiped a tear from her eye. 'I'll be damned if I don't find out the truth, if I don't get some sort of justice for her.'

I nodded, regretting my words. 'Do… do your parents know what you're doing; do they have any idea where you are right now?'

Beatrice shook her head. 'In all honesty, they haven't really noticed me since Dorothy died.' She changed the subject quickly. 'Do you have any siblings?'

'I had a younger sister,' I said. 'She died a long time ago.'

Beatrice apologised. 'It's none of my business.' Strands of her long hair swirled and blew around her face.

I sighed, feeling as though I owed Beatrice some solace. 'I know what it's like to lose people. I know the anger and resentment you feel, the questions that torment you day and night.' I flicked away my cigarette, stopped myself from saying much more. 'It will pass, in time.'

Beatrice looked at me closely. 'Are you sure about that?'

I didn't answer.

Gulls glided across the sky before us, laughing to one another. They swooped and fell with no apparent direction, silhouettes against a hazy blue backdrop. One landed close to our left, its beady eyes observing us carefully as it skulked in our direction. It snapped its beak and ruffled its wings, before letting itself be carried away by a gust that pushed it further inland.

'What happened to you last night?' Beatrice asked. 'You were terrified, as if some great terror stood right before you.'

'I shan't let it happen again—'

'That's not what concerns me.' She spoke with authority. 'If we are to uncover what happened to Dorothy, I need to know that you are what you say you are, not some madman deceiving me.'

I struggled to think of a reply – what was I to tell her? The truth, that I was haunted by spirits, by ghosts? She would run from my side, run all the way to the nearest police station and have me clapped in irons.

'It was merely a dream,' I said at last. 'A most visceral dream that took hold of me quite suddenly. In this line of work, it is not unheard of.'

She nodded after a moment, though appeared unconvinced.

'Fine. We should head back, get everything ready. That old man won't be pleased if we're late meeting him on the jetty.' She stood and began walking away. I called after her.

'I should take some brief statements from the residents before we leave; ensure they corroborate Lachlan's claim that the brothers were travelling to and from the island.' I shrugged. 'It may be relevant.'

Beatrice nodded, before marching back towards Pike Ness without so much as a glance at me.

Lachlan had not lied. Freezing water lashed over my legs as we rolled dangerously in his meagre rowboat, barely large enough for the three of us, my camera case and the small provisions Beatrice and I had gathered. He laughed heartily with each sudden rise and dip, calling out and singing like a fool. He regularly barked at me, for I sat near the stern and laboured with two heavy oars as he did behind me. My arms were weak and exhausted, for we had been out on the water for almost an hour.

With each glance over my shoulder, the island loomed closer. Its rocks and sheer cliffs grew in the twilight. The rain had held off, though the wind swept from the Arctic and chilled me to the bone, despite my exertion. My hands were curled rigid around the oars, completely lifeless and numb.

'You alrigh' there, policeman?' Lachlan cried out from the bow. 'Almost there. Just a wee ways. We have to skirt around to the western side – that's where the quay is.' He started singing about a woman from the tropics, and it was all I could do to block him out and focus on my rowing. I had grown quite sick of the man and his strange remarks.

Thirty minutes or so later, with the island passing on my right side, I felt a heavy whack on my shoulder. I craned my neck, feeling a shock of pain from the jarring of my stiff muscles. Lachlan had lit a lantern, and pointed to a narrow bay, blanketed in a thin sheen of white mist. It was barely visible in the growing darkness.

'There's the quay. It's best I bring her in on my own to keep us from the rocks. Keep your wee eyes on the water in case I get too close.'

I did as I was told, and kept a careful watch as Lachlan eased the boat towards the quay. It looked ancient, carved out of the stone and covered entirely by dark green moss and urchins. Metal cleats had been driven into a low-lying dock; the water lapped and splashed around them. Steps, haphazardly laid and badly broken, rose up a sheer bank of mud; a few lowly growths of shrubs twisted alongside them.

We moved in slowly, Lachlan easing his oars gently through the water, looking behind him as he went. He didn't sing or yell but muttered under his breath with each small flex of his hands and wrists. He growled at me once when we came within a few inches of a black crop of rock that I barely noticed through the mist. Shortly after, he pulled up his oars and let us drift towards the dock.

When he stood suddenly, the boat rocked enough for me to throw out my hands instinctively. My right forearm was submerged in the water, and when I pulled it back, I saw that my hand was covered in grime and filth. Lachlan waited a moment, then stepped onto the dock with one large stride.

'Throw us the rope there,' he called to me. I slung the thick length at my feet the short distance to him, and he moored the boat down quickly. Beatrice clambered off. I hauled my camera case from the boat before taking another lantern.

'I'll wait here until you make it up top, then I'll head back,' Lachlan said, gazing up the dreadful climb of stairs. 'I cannae recall where that manor is, but if you get to the eastern side of the island you've gone too far.' He laughed wickedly.

I looked out onto the water, seeing the darkness of night and feeling the wind grow stronger with every breath. I struck a match to light the lantern. 'Would you not stay here – it seems safer—'

'I'd much rather take my chances with the water than be creeping round an ol' manor,' he smirked. 'Away with you.' As we stepped across the slimy dock and gingerly made our way up the first few steps, he called after us. 'And be sure to come back at four o'clock tomorrow, so I can get paid.'

Neither of us replied. Beatrice hurried ahead, leaving me with the lantern and my cases. The stone steps were surprisingly sturdy, though more than once I cursed myself for looking over my shoulder towards the scene below. I tried to focus on my footing, as my thighs began to burn and sweat began to roll down my brow. Finally, and with a great sense of relief, I heard Beatrice thank God as she reached the last step and the very top of the cliff. We each collapsed on a thick bed of grass and looking downwards, waved our hands at the quay. It didn't surprise me to see Lachlan, already in his boat, rowing back towards the mainland.

'Bloody fool,' Beatrice murmured.

We sat for ten minutes and gathered ourselves, before rising slowly to go in search of the manor. Neither of us had paid any heed to the landscape beyond the cliff edge. As with the quay below, mist spread and swirled about us, growing denser towards the edge of a forest of black trees. The conifers – Scots pine it seemed – rustled and scratched as limbs swayed in the wind.

We walked steadily, moving along the forest edge until we found what appeared to be a path trodden in the dirt. We stepped beneath the forest canopy, gingerly and with a keen eye, twisting and turning through the rough undergrowth, our soft circle of light illuminating the irregular knuckles and scars of each tree limb.

My foot snapped upon a fallen branch and the noise made us both judder with fright. A strange hue enveloped the forest, a sickly yellow that was born of dirty moonlight. I noticed then how nothing was stirring about us.

'Do you hear anything?' I whispered harshly. 'There's nothing. No owl calls, no sounds of life.'

Beatrice stood still and held her breath. She shook her head slowly after a moment.

Dread scourged me, for my imagination filled the silence with all manner of beastly things lying in wait, peering at us with gruesome eyes. Beatrice continued, and I stepped close behind her.

We walked perhaps fifteen or twenty minutes before the forest trees began to thin all around.

'There,' Beatrice whispered. 'There's something over there.'

She stepped ahead of me. A structure began to form out of the gloom, small and compact. It was shrouded in growths of creeping ivy, the material of its walls and roof completely hidden. It was some kind of wooden shed, too small to be a work room for gardening or carpentry.

Beatrice shook her head. 'I think it's a children's playhouse.'

I cast my eyes about, spotting something else in the darkness. Another structure, much larger but still by no means a home. This one was peculiar, made in cast black iron and finished with a domed roof. At first I thought it a glass house, though upon closer inspection I saw it was encased in wire mesh, broken in places and badly rusted by the elements. Weeds grew over a few exotic tree stumps that had been carved into smoothed perches.

'There's an aviary here,' I called back to Beatrice, who stepped over and examined it with me. 'The manor can't be far.'

It wasn't; only a short distance further we spotted it, spread out across a clearing in the forest. It loomed tall, a huge building with some three grand floors. Its grounds were distinguished only by a dead lawn, blanketed in moss. Whether we were at the rear or the front seemed hardly to matter; we stopped beside a crumbling fountain brimming with stagnant water. Before us were the remnants of a stone path, lined by barren hedgerows, heading to a set of stairs that stretched the length of the manor. These led to a veranda of sorts; fine French doors spread the entirety of the wall, though many were visibly boarded up. Much of the brick, deepest black in the darkness, was grotty and damaged. Ledges were crumbling; a second-storey window was shattered, allowing the torn remnants of a set of curtains to billow outward into the night.

We moved silently up to the veranda. Eagles, ravens and other birds carved in stone watched us with distrusting eyes from the edge of the roof. One, particularly grotesque, its features eroded by the elements, seemed to lean down, clinging to the walls of the estate. My eyes were drawn to it. In the dim moonlight, it appeared most un-birdlike.

Beatrice moved to a French door, its boarding broken, glass shattered. Tentatively she stepped inside, and as her feet clipped upon tiles, I heard her gasp.

She muttered something, and I moved to follow her inside. Glancing back up at the stone monstrosity on the roof, I saw that it was gone. I jolted and caught my breath. I looked further along the roof's edge but spied only the empty place it had been but moments before.

Beatrice muttered something to me again and staring out into the eerie forest, I backed through the French doors and into the manor.

'They said the family liked watching birds,' Beatrice whispered. 'That was surely an understatement.'

Still in shock at the disappearing golem, I turned and looked about. We stood in a hall, grand and vast, rising up two storeys, and stretching the length of the property. The floor was chequered in white and dark tiles, entirely empty apart from a commanding fireplace, resplendent with stone carvings that rose high above the mantel.

And the birds – hundreds, maybe thousands, of stuffed birds. They lined the entirety of the wall we now looked upon. Their lifeless, frozen eyes glared down at us.

Creeping Through the Manor
September 7th, 1905

The birds were not pleasant, or intriguing or curious, to look upon. They were grotesque. They had wasted and rotted in the years since the manor had been abandoned, each appearing most unnatural and squalid. Wings were all but stripped of feathers, plumage discoloured and crawling with lice. Their glass eyes were ignited by the dim light of our lantern, and it seemed at any moment the terrible assembly would begin to move, to take on life once more and lurch and swoop down from the great wall towards Beatrice and I. She looked at them morosely, though my revulsion was mingled with something of perhaps far graver concern.

A feeling – a most dark and dreadful weight burdening my shoulders. Beatrice said something, though I barely noticed; an intense pressure built suddenly from the back of my neck and clawed upwards through the inside of my skull until I was wholly detached from the real world and lost in a strange, disjointed chasm of memories and dreams.

I heard voices whisper from the shadows, saw scenes of such depravity even when I closed my eyes. Figures clawed upwards through the tiles of the floor; the very world seemed to split and tear asunder ...

The sensation departed with such suddenness I felt limp. Like venom being drained from a vicious wound, I was brought back to life, but in a most incoherent fashion. I stumbled towards Beatrice, who looked at me with some alarm.

'What's wrong?'

I shook my head, doubling over. 'Nothing.'

'Tell me the truth, Thomas. What happened?'

I pulled myself upright, nodding weakly. 'I ... I was overcome by something ... I'm not sure what.'

I stumbled further into the hall, rubbing my eyes. My temples began to throb lightly as Beatrice came to my side.

'What? You have to tell me.'

I was in no mood to keep secrets. 'I had a sudden feeling that I had been here before. It felt as if some memory was revealed to me.'

'A memory?' She looked baffled. 'You had a memory of standing in this room?'

'I don't know,' I groaned. 'It may have been a memory; it may have been ...' I shrugged, for in truth I had no idea. I took a drink from my flask and after staring at the floor for a few moments, felt the throbbing in my head ease. All that had been tangible mere moments before faded, till nothing of the sensation, of the feeling, of the memories, remained. I shrugged it all off, even as Beatrice asked me more questions, her voice filled with concern. I assured her all was well, and together we stepped fully into the hall, creeping towards the fireplace. A huge log was damp and riddled with fungi, caused by a persistent leak that dripped down the chimney. I noticed then how cold the space was, for it felt even chillier than outside.

Beatrice was clearly unhappy, but I moved to a heavy set of double doors standing beside the fireplace and framed by a gilded surround. I grasped an overly large, brass doorknob with a hand I was struggling to steady. I didn't want Beatrice seeing the effect the strange 'vision' (for lack of a better word) had had on me. We had barely begun looking about the place, and I was already terrified of what lay in wait.

The door opened, the hinges creaking quietly. I looked into a dark corridor that was starved of any light or exposure. The smell of dank carpets and mildew swept out into the grand hall. I stepped into the corridor with Beatrice still some feet away from me. I wanted her to be at my side but had to show some resolve and courage. I carried the lantern and my case, though wished I could grip my revolver.

The corridor was wide, though cluttered. The lantern revealed a few paintings along the walls; some of pleasant landscapes, others of mythical gods and loathsome tragedies. The carpet beneath my feet was weathered and worn, a deep shade of green to match the faded, floral wallpaper. In some places it was damp and soft, where water dripped from the low ceiling. The light was suffocated by the thick, swirling dust that choked the air, as heavy as winter's fog and yet far more invasive. It clung to my skin and stifled my breath; I was compelled to cover my mouth.

Beatrice stepped alongside me and gestured to a door ahead. It opened ajar, though thudded against something on the other side. Together, we heaved against it and finally managed to open it enough to squeeze ourselves into the room. Book-lined shelves rose high to the ceiling. We were in a library.

A fixture built around the door had collapsed, jamming it shut. I pulled it free to open the door fully, then cast my eyes about. The room was not large, though had a small fire built into the left side wall and a few high back chairs placed around it.

I saw the darkened husks of a few charred logs in the hearth. A stack of dry wood was piled beside the fireplace.

'It's true,' I said, trying to quell the excitement in my voice. 'Someone has been here recently.'

My beating heart told me it was Hawthorn, and it was all I could do not to rush from the room and call out to him, in some vain hope that he may reveal himself and make sense of the whole affair. The wood, however, was cold to the touch, and I realised it had likely sat in the hearth for some time. Even if Hawthorn had been here, he could have left months ago.

'I'll leave my case here,' I said quietly. 'Are you all right?'

Beatrice nodded, though her expression said otherwise. I noticed how laboured her breathing was, and the deep shadows that had formed beneath her eyes. She looked gaunt, tired, as though she had aged in merely a few minutes.

'This man,' she muttered, looking about the room and towards the door. 'How certain are you of his innocence?'

I shook my head. 'Not certain at all. He may be telling the truth,' I paused, dread churning in my gut, 'or he may be mad. For the sake of our friendship, though, I need to find out for myself.'

Beatrice fidgeted nervously. 'Have you considered he may have lured you here for some ill purpose?'

'Yes, but it still seemed right to come.'

She nodded feverishly. We agreed to search the lower floor first, before moving upwards. Candles fixed in silver holders stood at either end of the mantel, and these I took, though I chose to pocket them, and continued carrying the lantern. Free of my camera case, I felt a little more at ease knowing I could reach for my gun should I need it. Together we stepped out into the corridor and continued our cautious shuffling along the carpet.

We came to another door, a room adjacent to the library. Looking inside, we saw a billiards table, a few large couches and an upstanding clock, adorned with a carved eagle. A drinks cabinet contained a dozen half-empty bottles of port and brandy; tall portraits of steely-eyed men in suits or military attire covered the walls. There was no fireplace in the room, but we lit a few candles in sconces upon the walls, though the light only served to sharpen the callous, indignant features of the men in the paintings. We searched a little but found nothing of intrigue.

We left the door wide open as we moved further along the passage. Another, far narrower, branched off from the main corridor, though this only led to a single door. I peeked through, a tremendous effort of nerve, for behind each door I fathomed could be a hundred, *a thousand*, terrible ghouls and phantoms. The light of the lantern barely penetrated the room. Beatrice whispered to me, and I turned to see her looking at the opposing wall of the passage.

'Notice anything?' she mumbled.

At first, I shook my head. Holding the lantern close to the wallpaper, I finally spied what she saw. The faint, floral pattern that had continued throughout the corridor, stopped abruptly. Identical colour paint was used instead, only for half an inch or so, before the wallpaper continued. Beatrice knelt and pointed to a brass peg, similar to the pedal of a piano. The thing was almost entirely concealed by the thick skirting that ran around the base of the walls. I knelt beside her, and with the slightest hesitation, pushed a hand against the peg. A portion of the wall, a few feet wide, swung back a little. Beatrice looked at me aghast, as I pushed the concealed door open entirely and we stepped through.

'It's a kitchen,' she muttered. 'Why have it concealed in such a way?'

My light bounced off an array of copper skillets and pots. A huge wooden table, cluttered with plates and glassware, filled much of the centre of the room.

'I don't know,' I replied quietly. 'To allow the staff to move unseen, I imagine. No doubt there are more doors like it.' A dreadful smell emanated from the far corner of the room, and walking around the table, I spotted a shrouded stairwell leading down below. The smell rose from there; it was pungent and cloying, sticking in the back of the throat.

'A larder maybe?' Beatrice said, her words muffled by a hand that covered her mouth and nose.

I nodded. 'We'll return once we've searched this floor and those abo—'

Something flinched, jerked in our light. A scratch and a scurry; a flicker, thin and long.

'Rats,' Beatrice hissed.

I felt my stomach fall from me. 'The last time I followed the sounds of rats ...'

Beatrice asked what I meant but I didn't answer, turning and leaving the kitchen via the hidden door we had uncovered. I stepped back across the passage and together we entered the opposite room. We found a large space, both a sitting room and gallery, where everything was covered in white sheets. We searched carefully for a time, though I was soon pulling off each sheet roughly, uncovering chairs, ornaments, even a baroque harpsichord. In my haste, I knocked an ornate vase perched on a table, and it tumbled and smashed on the floor before I could catch it. The sound was dreadful, bouncing off the silence through each room as though I had fired a stick of dynamite.

We each held our breath, until the echo died away. With some annoyance, I gently kicked the broken pieces of the vase beneath the table.

'I'm sorry,' I muttered sheepishly.

'It's all righ—'

From somewhere deep inside the manor, something fragile and heavy shattered, just like the vase I had knocked. I reached inside my coat and pulled out my revolver, petrified.

One minute became two, two became three.

'Maybe … maybe it was just an echo, a delayed sound?' Beatrice whispered at last, though it was clear she didn't believe herself. Perhaps someone lurked in the manor with us; perhaps another vase or similar object had broken by coincidence. I felt hot quite suddenly and removed my coat, leaving it on a chair. Though I said nothing of it then, I was grateful – beyond grateful – that Beatrice stood by my side. *How*, I wondered, *could I have done this on my own?*

I forced my legs and body to move. 'That way,' I said, pointing to a door to the right of where we had come. 'Let's head that way.'

We found a dining room, and in the dim light that seeped in through large glass windows, I noticed the sickly glow of Beatrice's skin. My concern for her – that she may be ill, that her involvement in all this may reveal the dead to her as they had been revealed to me – was growing. I asked how she felt, and she shook her head slowly.

'I'm … I'm fine. Let's just keep going.'

We didn't linger and headed left out of the room, through a small door that was hardly noticeable. It needed a shove to open, and when we finally stepped through, we gazed morbidly at what we found: cages, hundreds of them of all sizes and shapes. All were empty. They creaked from wires bolted to the ceiling, stood on tables and littered the floors. Some were brass and some were rusted; some had perches, and some were laced with decayed straw. More of the miserable stuffed birds decked the walls, and the smell was unconscionable, foul and heavy.

'There's nothing here but stuffed birds and moulding furniture,' Beatrice murmured, wiping at her brow, after we had searched for a time. I nodded, taking the flask from my pocket and offering her a drink, which she declined. I guzzled from the flask before heading out the room.

In a large foyer, occupied almost solely by a stairwell that curved upwards to a second-floor landing, we gathered our bearings. This was surely the front of the manor, for a heavy set of wooden doors were shut and barred. We elected to head along another thin passage that branched away from the foyer. I kept my gaze upwards, to the landing. Anyone could have been watching, standing right over us, and I found it hard not to call out and ask who was there.

Midway down the passage, my foot hit upon a loose floorboard, which thudded as though it had not been properly fixed in place. I thought nothing of it until we reached the end of the corridor and came to a door that was locked and bolted. Only then did I point back the way we had come.

'There're no other doors along here,' I said quietly. I was mindful of the concealed entrance to the kitchen we had found. I focused on the spot where my foot had struck upon the floorboard, crouched down and held the lantern towards the skirting board, looking for a small brass peg. There was none.

I looked at the walls. Here, they were covered in a brash, busy wallpaper. In the dim light it was hard to notice any break or crack in the masonry. Beatrice began looking with me.

Without meaning to, I stood on the very spot – the seemingly loose floorboard – as I pressed my hands hard against the wall. Another concealed door swung back a few inches and with some astonishment, I stepped through.

It struck us immediately that the proportions of the room were completely wrong. It stretched nothing of the length of the corridor we had come down, nor spread to the depth of the manor's exterior wall. It was a study, with a table embossed with green leather, pushed up against the left-hand wall. Shelves contained paperwork and documents, which we began to thumb through carefully. Some were over fifty years old, business transactions and ledgers, accounts regarding staff salaries and wages. There seemed nothing extraordinary in the papers, nothing illegal by any means. A large painting of the manor, dark and foreboding, hung upon a wall. A bookshelf in the corner of the room was half full, the titles bland, mostly concerned with economics.

'This room doesn't seem right,' Beatrice muttered. Only the right wall was fully exposed, and Beatrice stepped to it. After only a moment she crouched down, pushing against something toward the floor. Another hidden door opened then, revealing a tight set of stairs that wound down into chilling black. The smell we had noticed in the kitchen hit us once again.

'They must be able to lock the door from this side somehow,' I said as Beatrice dared to move down the first step. She stood in silence, her body completely still. Then she came back into the study and quickly closed the door behind her.

'Did you hear something, see something?' I asked her feverishly.

'No,' she replied, her skin drained of any colour. 'But sometimes the imagination runs wild.' She quickly changed the subject. 'A lock, some means of locking this door from the inside.'

She began running her hand along the seam of the door. Something still troubled me about the room, and I began looking along the wall with the bookshelf. There was no sign of any door, no matter how hard I looked. After I had been crouching and running my hand along the skirting for some minutes, I noticed a few scuff marks on the floorboards beside the bookshelf. They were faint, as though something had been rubbed or grazed against the wood.

I stood before the bookshelf. Tentatively, I tried to slide it to the left. To my surprise, it moved with ease, as though it were set on casters. It squeaked a little as it moved, but revealed a cut-through to another portion of the room, a space a little larger than the study. There were no windows, or a fireplace, but I noticed a stove, tucked in the far-right corner, with a steel flue rising up to the ceiling. There were a few travel cases and chests in the room, and a makeshift bed, low to the floor. I spotted clothes, scattered about the bed and hanging from empty bookshelves, as well as dried biscuits and a few jars of preserves.

We began looking through the cases; Beatrice opened a chest.

'There's a camera in here,' she said with some surprise. 'Looks a little like yours.'

I stepped over to her. Indeed, the camera was of the same manufacturer as mine, a Lancaster and Son, though this was a Le Merveilleux model. I recognised the very camera itself, for immediately my eyes settled upon a set of small initials, neatly scratched in the front standard above the lens. I recalled the day I had helped the owner purchase it.

'This camera—'

'There're pictures on the wall here.' Beatrice had stepped away, and when I turned, I saw her pull a framed photograph from the wall. She held it close to the light, squinting to make out those who were in it. As I looked at the photograph, I recognised it in an instant.

'Is that—'

'Me,' I cut in, my voice near breaking. 'That's me and Hawthorn and the others from the Forensic Crime Directorate.' My hands were shaking terribly, but I was able to point out

Elijah Hawthorn and Jack Lavernock to Beatrice. 'This picture was taken the first day we all met. The start of something new…'

I trailed off, staring at the photograph. There were some twenty of us in all, each man standing with his arms folded across his chest, some wearing new suits and smart ties, others in black waistcoats, with their white shirt sleeves rolled up. Lavernock stood in his constable's uniform, his helmet pulled low over his forehead. Hawthorn sat on a chair in the middle, his face beaming with happiness and pride.

I looked so young, so incorruptible. So hopeful.

I turned to Beatrice, and then gazed at the chests and clothes in the room.

'He was here. Hawthorn was here. We have to find hi—'

I was stopped by a noise that made us both leap in fright. Somewhere from deep in the house, another heavy crash was met with an electric scream, a painful, high-pitched shriek.

'Oh God,' Beatrice whispered. 'Someone's with us.'

The Horrors in the Rooms Above

September 7th, 1905

My palm was coated in such heavy sweat I could barely grip the handle of my Enfield.

'It came from above,' Beatrice quivered, looking down the passage towards the foyer and the stairwell leading upwards. 'I'm sure of it.'

On cue, the petrified voice shrieked out once more. The noise was painful; blood-curdling.

We each stood still, willing the other to step that way. Finally, Beatrice did, snatching the lantern from my hand. Her skin was as cold as ice. As we crept towards the stairs, I felt every fibre of my being tingle. My mind yelled, telling me to run and leave this place as fast as I could. Yet I knew I had to find the bearer of that terrible scream, or else it would morph and worsen in my mind's eye and I would never dare sleep or walk in darkness again.

As we ascended the stairs, my hand gripped the bannister so tight I felt certain I would snap the wood to splinters. The landing above slowly emerged to us, a wide space with three separate corridors leading from it. They were narrower than the ones below and seemed to drain the very life of Beatrice's lantern.

'Which way?' she whispered. I listened carefully but heard nothing, for not even the wind whimpered now. I pointed to our left and we began inching along the deep red carpet.

The corridor was not long, but it took an age to reach the first room. I glanced behind us often; I couldn't draw my eyes away from what lay at our backs. If I did, I knew things would move, would suddenly thunder and charge for us. The most gruesome sensation overcame me, as though my skin were being peeled away, as though watching eyes stripped me of my very flesh. How I shuddered then, and oh, how the finger resting upon the trigger of my gun did quiver.

I yelped a little when I bumped into Beatrice stopped before a door. She looked horrified, not just for our peril but at the sight of me. Her wide eyes flitted from mine to the darkness over my shoulder. I wished in that moment I could be of more comfort to her, but courage was seeping from me like a wound and I was fast losing the strength to hold my ground.

I spun quickly, feeling as though something had brushed against my ear. My eyes darted around the ceiling as Beatrice opened the door.

Our feet trod across a thin film of water, which covered the tiles of a large bathroom, once opulent and splendid, with a huge bath set in the centre atop a raised step. I lurched at our own reflection, heightened and stretched by a grand mirror fixed against the far wall. It was set between two windows, their heavy drapes closed. Gold-leaf cupboards stood empty and bare; a wooden divider lay clumsily on its side.

The lantern light, reflected as orange fire in the water, danced across the ceiling where a delicate collection of images – cherubs upon clouds, angels with arms outstretched – looked down upon us. Hell glowed up to the heavens. Our feet splashed lightly.

I moved towards the bath, looking to my left and right, at the dresser table draped in thickest cobweb, at the gown that had been carelessly left on the back of a chair, putrid and tattered. I imagined that if I held it between my fingers it would disintegrate.

'Did we ever know why they left,' Beatrice mumbled quickly, her words reverberating strangely. 'The owners – why they never came back?' She was stepping around the edge of the room, beside the cupboards which she glanced in quickly.

I had no answer for her, for so little had been said of this place. My eyes were darting from the ceiling to my own shadow growing beyond the bath on the vast, empty wall beside the mirror. My hand holding the revolver, wobbled and twisted, the shaking in my arm exaggerated by the soft sway of the water and the flicker of the lantern flame. The dark image grew towards the finely sculpted castings of the ceiling as I reached the platform on which the bath stood. I looked at the shape of my neck and shoulders, at the place where my eyes should have been.

My legs hit the bath edge. Cold lapped against my thigh. I looked down – the bath was brimming with dirty water. A body lay motionless, sunken at the bottom.

I screamed in fright, lurched backwards and slipped on the wet tiles. My back hit the floor hard, and I scrambled to try and get purchase. Beatrice rushed to my side, asking what was wrong, shouting after a moment when I only continued to scream and crawl backwards. She stood, panicked, charging towards the bath as I yelled for her to stop. She stared down into the water.

She stood motionless for a few seconds, then hurried back to my side, her expression grim and focused.

She knelt beside me.

'There's nothing in there.'

'The body. The bod—'

'There's nothing,' she repeated slowly. Then: 'What did you see?' Her eyes were wide, staring into mine as if searching.

I shook my head and stammered. 'There's a body in there. A

body, the throat was cut…' I couldn't finish, as I recalled the gruesome spectre that had appeared from the bath in the inn at Pike Ness.

'There's nothing in there, Bexley. Nothing.' She gasped a little as the light of the lantern flickered and dimmed. I hauled myself upwards and timidly moved back to the bath. There, still struggling to breathe, I looked down.

I saw the water, the dirt and grime swirling and congealing at the surface. And nothing more. There was nothing of the body I had seen.

'It – it was there. I saw it there.'

Beatrice didn't seem to hear me. She was staring at her hand, holding it against the wet floor.

'Dark and wet. The place was dark and wet…'

'What?'

The light of the lantern dimmed once more. She grabbed at it suddenly.

'There's oil in here,' she said desperately. 'Why is the light dying?' The flame grew smaller and smaller, until nothing remained.

In pitch darkness, we listened to each other's ragged breathing. I clumsily took out my matchbox. With my hands shaking so badly, I dropped some half dozen of the tiny matches into the bathwater, leaving only a few that I could grasp. I cursed terribly, scratching the match against the rough box paper, snapping my first match after only a couple of strikes. The second match lit, and I held it out to Beatrice.

She was gone, nowhere to be seen.

I spun about, the little flame dying as I did. I tried once more to light another match but wholly in vain, for my hands couldn't be steadied and I dropped the matchbox entirely. Grasping my revolver, I fumbled from the bath side, crying out for Beatrice, wailing out her name.

By some miracle I found the door of the bathroom and stepped out into the corridor, spinning all around, looking into the darkness. I was lost then, not knowing whether to return to the stairwell or continue deeper into the manor. I whispered Beatrice's name, croaking louder when I dared. Hot tears rolled down my face, for in my heart of hearts I truly thought the curse that blighted me – the phantoms that haunted me – had snatched her from my side.

I moved blindly and hit the handle of a door, though when I tried to open it, I found it was locked. I carried on. Something rapped against the wall beside me, and I turned and thrust my gun and free arm outwards, though I felt nothing there. I continued until I reached a turn in the corridor, realising then I was moving away from the stairs. I thought to go back, but something hacked from the direction I had come. I lunged around the corner, trying to be as quiet as I could. It seemed I was being stalked.

The faintest glow of light kissed against my right arm, and looking down the new passage I stood in, I saw a set of large arched windows at the very end. A pallid full moon shone through them

I moved down the passage hurriedly, looking over my shoulder with every other step. When I came to the windows, I realised they marked a corner of the manor. I found a few chairs that I knelt and hid behind. A set of stairs on my left led upwards and out of sight to another floor.

I tried to gather my thoughts, though I broke down in an instant. I muttered Beatrice's name under my breath and dwelt on what had taken her. The gun in my hand seemed to grow heavier with every passing moment, and I stared at it despondently.

It would bring an end to the horror. It would give me some peace.

Something metallic clattered on the floor above. Voices, unintelligible and distant, mingled with my heavy gasps. Their volume grew as they began to cry out. Soon, what sounded like a hundred souls screamed over one another. I clasped my hands around my ears.

Heavy footsteps thudded, drawing near from both the passage I had come down and the stairs descending from above. I twisted my neck, looking from one direction to the next. The voices continued to scream at me. I began to distinguish them: men, women, old, young.

Something coughed from the passage once more. A white light burst forward and near blinded me – I shielded my eyes and cried out in pain. The footsteps grew faster as the terrible voices screeched in agony.

The gun in my hand became too much to hold. I asked for forgiveness, though to whom I spoke I do not know. A shadow appeared from the stairs to my left and charged towards me, thin arms outstretched. The light grew closer from the passage. The screaming reached a painful intensity.

In total fear I fired a shot blindly down the passageway. The blast of the gun silenced the voices instantly. The shadow on my left disappeared, though the white light grew closer, its bearer unstoppable. With a sigh I turned the gun on myself and thumbed back the hammer. I closed my eyes as the light enveloped me, and pulled back the trigger.

The hammer snapped. No bullet fired. A hand wrestled against mine and I screamed and thrashed out. The gun was pulled away from me. My face was struck, once and then twice. The voices returned, though now they were different. There was only one in fact, and it said my name. The voice was beside me, a woman's voice I began to recognise.

'Bexley! Stop it for God's sake, stop it! Bexley.'

I opened my eyes and saw Beatrice crouching over me. The unlit lantern was dropped on the floor by her side, along with my revolver, the barrel of which was still smoking. I struggled for another few moments, for I was badly confused and in shock. She grabbed my jaw, her hands viciously cold, and held my face so that we stared into each other's eyes. I saw total fear distorting the blue of her irises.

'Look at me. Look at me!'

I began to still, my arms growing weak and limp. I slunk away from her, looked towards the stairs and then down at my hands. She collapsed onto the floor before me, panting heavily, hair sticking to her forehead and temples.

'Wha-what…'

'Jesus,' she muttered. 'You shot at me.'

'I didn't know,' I mumbled. 'I thought. I thought—'

'You thought what?'

She sunk her face into her trembling hands and groaned. I shook my head.

'You vanished, from my side. You were there and then you weren't.'

'The lantern died!' she snapped. 'I told you to follow me back downstairs, to gather some candles.' She glared at me. 'You almost shot me. For God's sake, can't you see that?'

The Grim Search

September 7th, 1905

We had returned to the hidden study, our lantern and candles now lit. Neither of us had spoken in nearly an hour. Beatrice sat on the low makeshift bed and asked if I needed any food or water. I chewed absently on some dry biscuits; I was hungry but didn't feel like eating. I drank the contents of my flask and brooded in the corner, staring at the photograph of myself and the others of the Forensic Crime Directorate.

'Tell me what happened!' Beatrice finally blurted as if she were no longer able to contain the question. 'You almost shot me.'

'I'm sorry for tha—'

'To hell with your apologies.' Her face was flushed, filled with wrath. 'I don't care for them. Nor your excuses. I want the truth. All of it.'

She came close to where I sat and knelt beside me, resting her hands upon my arm. They were still dreadfully cold, despite the stuffiness of the little room; I recoiled from her touch.

'You saw something upstairs; in the inn at Pike Ness as well. They can't just be mere visions, or some *dreams* you haven't fully roused from, I won't believe it. Just tell me, please.'

I tried to hold my tongue, but my mouth and lips quivered uncontrollably. The shaking spread throughout my body, and the more I tried to take hold of my shudders, the worse they became. The immense weight of all I had seen and lived through began to snap and crack the recesses of my skull, as though a dark scourge were trying to break free and burst from my insides. I could hold my secrets back no longer.

'Do you believe the dead linger, in some afterlife we cannot see, we cannot fully touch upon?'

'Uh … wha—'

'Last year, I was contacted by someone … *dead*, seeking justice. I know it to be true and not my own insanity or delusion, for I have proof of it, a letter I received from a young girl whose murder had already been committed. She drew me to her, brought me to a village, the place of her death, to uncover the truth. She even played some part in my discovery of her killer, and since then I have been haunted, for there is no other word for it, by spirits … most terrible spirits.'

I looked down at my lap as a swell of emotion overcame me.

'At first, I saw her in photographs – the scene where her body was found, where her corpse was kept. Then she came to me, walked and moved as you do before me. When I returned to London, I thought it would all be done with, thought I could go back to my normal life. But more spirits came to me; day and night I see them. They torment me, for now I see so many people, so many of the dead wherever I go. I can't work, can't live anything like a normal life. How can I? And never does it get easier; never do they cease. Each time I see them is like the first, for I am powerless to stop them, to do anything to appease them.'

I hurriedly grabbed my flask but feeling it empty, flung it across the room in a frenzy as tears rolled down my face. I waited for her consternation, for her sudden unease, for her to leap from the ground and run, yelling, pleading for help on an island where no one could save her.

'You see–'

'My camera,' I groaned. 'My camera revealed things to me about the case. In photographs I saw things that were never there in reality. Then the girl, I started seeing her in pictures as well. Finally, she came to me – her ghost – just as real as I see you before me. Now ... now I see so many. All the time. She was unique, different. A young woman at times, a malignant demon at others. But all those I see now are like monsters, beasts hellbent on punishing me for some wrong I have done them.'

She glanced about my person and for a moment I couldn't make sense of the way her eyes shifted so suddenly. Then I realised – she was looking for my pistol, trying to fathom where it was. Surely, she did think me mad.

'Were we in London, I could show you the letter,' I insisted, pleaded. 'It may act as some small proof ...'

'Your camera has some strange power then?' she asked quizzically.

'W-what? I don't know, truly I don't know, I don't understand any of this.'

'And the girl's killer,' she continued coolly. 'In this village you were brought to. You found out their guilt because of the camera, had them arrested?'

I paused, but there seemed no sense in lying. 'He ... he's dead. I killed him.'

She only nodded, slowly. Her face was steely and unmoved. She looked down at her hands and said nothing for a short while. I assumed she was thinking how best to flee me, how best to escape the island before Lachlan's return. With a rashness I was becoming ever more prone to, I pulled the gun from my pocket and handed it to her. She looked at it with total bemusement.

'Just take it. I'll make no trouble for you when you figure out how best to leave.' I wiped tears from my face roughly. 'There's likely no way to get off this rock without that fool Lachlan, so you'd be wise to wait for his return. I'll make no trouble.'

She held the gun loosely, with no great care, before tossing it back to my lap.

'The girl – the dead girl who wrote to you. You brought her killer to justice.'

I nodded slowly, though with some confusion, for it seemed Beatrice wasn't really speaking to me but more to herself.

'Perhaps it is why you see so many now.' She nodded her head as she spoke. 'Perhaps they have all been wronged. Perhaps they seek justice as she did.'

'I-I have no idea. Truly I don't.'

She remained silent a little longer, before she stood slowly and gestured to the door.

'We need to keep searching,' she said, her voice grave but resolute.

I nodded, rubbing at my face. I was somewhat gobsmacked by her demeanour. 'You ... believe me then?'

She shrugged. 'I don't know. You seem a good man to me; I trust my instincts on such things. Yet what you say is madness, and perhaps you are mad, and I am wrong about all this.' She wouldn't meet my gaze. 'Perhaps you have brought me here to kill me. There are easier ways to go about such things ...' She was scared, it was obvious, but she was trying not to show it. 'People pray; people talk to gravestones and photographs. What do I know of the afterlife, of the dead?'

'Maybe I am mad,' I muttered. She didn't seem to notice.

I returned the Enfield to my pocket; merely holding it took such a great effort. I had come so close to shooting Beatrice, maybe even killing her. Shame and guilt washed over me, a deep sense of remorse. How far I had fallen; how lost I had become from the man I once was.

'I'm sorry,' I mumbled. 'I'm sorry for ...' I trailed off.

Beatrice didn't answer – I could tell she wasn't listening to me. She moved back to the bed, pulled off the blankets with a sudden thrust.

'The innkeeper said he found the money of those two brothers tucked safely in a bed.' She ran her hands across the surface of the mattress. 'Help me with this.'

At first, I didn't understand. Even when she beckoned me to her, I was slow to rise and move to her side, roughly wiping the last of my tears away.

'What do you hope to find?'

'Lift the mattress.'

'Can't you—'

'Just do it,' she snapped, and I did, somewhat begrudgingly. To my surprise, at the head of the bed, I spotted a tatty book with a hardback cover. We looked from it to each other.

'How did you—'

'The brothers, the money,' she smiled. 'Seems a sensible place to keep important things.'

I took the book and looked through the first few pages. It was wholly nonsensical – the letters were all misplaced. I smiled rather thinly.

'Do you know what it means?' Beatrice asked.

'It's Hawthorn,' I muttered dryly. 'A notebook written in cypher. A code to conceal his messages.' I took the book and thumbed through it. It was perhaps half full, with pages scripted in fine writing. 'Hawthorn has a passion for cryptography, often showed me his more complex cyphers. This first page seems simplistic, which puzzles me.'

'Why?'

'If Hawthorn had meant to conceal anything from the world, he would no doubt have used something far more sophisticated.'

Beatrice shrugged. 'Perhaps he didn't want it concealed from everyone, just enough who may get their hands on it by mistake.'

I didn't answer, tucking the book in my pocket. 'We'll look at it later. There are more pressing matters at hand.'

Beatrice nodded, though I saw her resolve was already fading. Fear was creeping back across her face. 'Do you think we'll find them, the person who screamed?'

I stood and shook my head. 'In truth, I think we are the only ones here.'

Beatrice scowled as though I had wronged her. 'But I heard them. I heard that scream. I heard it as well as I hear your voice now.'

'I know,' I muttered. 'Perhaps you are right. Or maybe you are descending to madness as well.'

We returned to the second floor, though moved with greater purpose, lighting what candles we found in a few sparse sconces, only ever straying a few feet at most.

From the bathroom, we came to the door I had found locked. Here, I used brute force to kick at it until it snapped open. Slowly we stepped inside, to a wide and luxurious bedroom. Like the other rooms, it had been abandoned, emptied of any real contents except furniture and a few scattered items.

No sooner had we entered the room than we hastened to step out of it. A rhapsody of fluttering wings sped towards us and our light – a thousand brown and mottled moths, a swarm far greater than any I had ever seen. They swooped and swirled from every corner, nattering quietly as they moved. Some were small, others wildly overgrown.

In the corridor, it took us a great effort to disperse the

wretched lot, for they landed on our hands and coats and faces and wriggled and writhed amidst our clothes. We yelled as we batted away at them, which was no great shame, for the sound of our voices seemed to disperse them. After a few moments, much of the swarm had leapt to a few lit candles further down the corridor.

When we stepped back into the bedroom, hundreds of the moths remained, yet we searched as best we could. It wasn't long before I spotted the stains on the four-poster bed. A thin sheet had been left draped over a rotting mattress; dark marks stood against the grime and dead insects.

'Blood,' Beatrice said. I nodded. 'The person who screamed. The person we heard—'

'It's old,' I cut in. 'Dried quite some time ago.'

She pulled at the sheet, disturbing a few moths. 'Can you do anything with it, find out something about it?'

'Not here. There are tests to distinguish human blood from that of animals, even means of categorising different types of human blood. I can gather a sample before we leave, but with no suspect or known victim . . .' I trailed off, before muttering uneasily. 'I'll need to photograph this room at first light, and as many other rooms as I can.'

'You think you will find something? The camera will reveal something to you?'

I nodded. 'Perhaps.'

From there we moved to the place I had fired my gun and up the stairwell that led to the third floor. We came into an observatory, fitted with huge windows and spyglasses draped in sheets. There were servants' quarters on the top floor as well, through a small, unremarkable door that led away from the observatory. These were meagre, compact rooms barely able to fit a bed and table, built abreast of each other along a narrow walkway that came to a dead end. A sickly pool of rainwater and mould had formed at the end of the walkway, seeping down from the ceiling and congealing at the floor. Another hidden doorway, like those we had already found, was revealed by the decay of the wall. We stepped through into a dark antechamber, frightfully cold and covered in cobwebs. Stairs led down and above us the roof beams of the manor groaned.

'Shall we go back the way we came?' Beatrice asked, running her fingers along the dank brickwork. The cobwebs around us moved, caught in a light draught that rose from below.

'No,' I whispered, though in truth I wished to do nothing else. I took one tentative step down into the darkness, then hurriedly began to move, with Beatrice at my back.

I moved so fast that I nearly tumbled down the narrow stone stairs. They seemed unending. With blessed relief, I finally came to an unlocked door, and barged through into the familiar surroundings of the kitchen.

As I took a breath, Beatrice slammed shut the door. 'There's so much more up there,' she said. 'More passages, more hidden chambers.'

I had to agree with her; it seemed our venture had left so much undiscovered.

'Shall we go back up, start from the main stairwell?'

I shook my head. I was staring at the corner of the room, from where the terrible smell was rising.

'We should go down,' I said. 'There could be a basement below.' I began to walk before Beatrice or my nerve could persuade me otherwise, clipping across the kitchen and down the steps quickly, dispelling any thoughts of rats or worse.

The smell worsened with each tentative step. When I came to the bottom, I looked upon a vast space, shrouded in total darkness. I waited for Beatrice to appear at my side, then gingerly moved forwards.

After only a few feet she moved to her left, and through an archway made by thick pillars of stone, came to a wide alcove, with empty wooden shelves and hooks hanging from the ceiling. 'The larder,' she whispered. 'That smell—'

'Isn't from here.' Claws scampered near my feet and I swung around to look for the vermin. I saw none, though I heard their terrible natter close by. It filled me with the most primitive fear.

We stole into the heart of the cellar, moving past more of the heavy pillars that were spread at equal intervals of about fifteen feet. We found sconces and candles, though the wicks wouldn't light, dampened perhaps over many years. A long wine rack covered the left wall beyond the larder, though there was not a bottle in sight. A wooden dinghy was propped on its side with a single broken oar lying beside it, along with other clutter, like rusted shears and lawn furniture.

Beatrice screamed suddenly and with such ferocity I was unable to move or even aid her. *Aid her;* it was I in need of help. A dark mass fell and clung to my shoulder, all fur and teeth. I saw the oversized eyes of the rat stare into mine, only for an instant. Then I spun where I stood, and with no grace, swung out and batted the creature from my shoulder, trying in vain to stamp on it before it scurried into the shadows. Above us, tails hung from a wooden beam that stretched between two of the stone pillars. Dozens of round eyes glimmered. We hurried away, though casting our gaze upwards, saw even more of the horrid creatures scurrying and climbing over one another. It was no use trying to evade them, and we started back in the direction of the stairs and the kitchen, for our courage was spent.

The smell was unbearable by now, acrid and invasive. The pillars had grown rougher, the stonework less defined. Rubble and bricks were spread about the floor, mingled with red clay dirt. As I moved to flee, Beatrice stopped me. She was staring wide eyed into the corner. I followed her gaze, and in the gloom, was able to make out a single wooden chair. A length of rope lay looped around it on the floor.

For a moment, I forgot about the horde of rats that nattered and scratched above us. Together we stepped to the chair. It was simply made and seemed solid, though I was minded not to touch it, and advised Beatrice to do the same. When she asked why, I pointed to a few dark marks that had stained the wood. We knelt and looked closer at them.

'That's more blood,' Beatrice exclaimed, loud enough to disturb the rats. Some were now on the floor, scurrying around the edges of our dim light. She pointed to the sides of the chair, to the tops of the legs as well. 'What are these?'

I couldn't be certain. 'Scratch marks, perhaps. Though whether they were made by someone or the vermin is hard to tell.' From a cursory glance, it was impossible to judge, but they were most troubling all the same. With the length of rope around the chair, it seemed a reasonable assumption that someone had likely been bound there, possibly even tortured.

I thought of my time in a basement with a maniac, thought of how he had tied me to a chair. Something more than good fortune had saved me that day. Something far more powerful . . .

Beatrice pointed to the floor. 'The blood trails off. God, there's lots of it.'

There truly was. Behind the chair, perhaps three feet or so, a pool had dried on the floor. We stood over it, and saw a gruesome mess that led away to the wall of the cellar. We followed it, our bodies crouched as we moved. As we came closer to the wall, the light of the lantern revealed the mouth of a passage, barely five feet high. The blood trail disappeared into the gloom.

I took out my handkerchief and held it to my nose. 'Stay here,' I said as calmly as I could. 'Wait for me to return.'

With my back arched, I crept down the passage alone, much to the protestations of Beatrice, who whispered sharply after me. The passage was propped up by wood and nothing more. Earth fell upon my face as I moved; tangled roots hung from above. At one point I had to crawl along on my hands and knees, where a joist had split, seemingly close to breaking entirely. Had I had the space to turn, I surely would have, for the prospect of being trapped beneath tons of earth and soil seemed very real to me then. I was greatly relieved when I came to the end of the passage and crawled into a chamber that was neither wide nor long, but stretched upwards a considerable height. It appeared as though I was standing at the base of a dried up well. The walls and floor were lined with stone similar to the cellar. I spied at least ten rats nesting and snarled at them when they scurried towards me. Thrusting my lamp out, they fled away up the passage; I heard Beatrice cry aloud a moment later.

'Stay there,' I called to her.

'Well, hurry!' she cried back.

I looked about the tight chamber, placed my hands upon the cold stone, holding my breath to listen carefully. I heard nothing, for there was nothing in the space to hear. And yet the smell, a smell I recognised now to be the heady smell of death, hung thick and putrid in the air. Something was in the chamber. Something was hidden close by.

I held the lamp close to the walls, running my fingers slowly along them. They were set with a rigid mortar, wholly solid. I took my time, despite Beatrice's repeated pleas for me to hurry. I knelt down at the right-hand wall, and some three feet from the ground, noticed a change in the mortar's colour. It felt different, crumbled when I rubbed and picked at it.

'I'm coming in,' Beatrice called out.

I tried to stop her, but she came nonetheless. 'Be careful. The passage is not secure.'

Thirty seconds later she was at my side, grimacing at the awful smell. I showed her the crumbling mortar.

'Have you a knife?'

She shook her head. I cursed and scratched at the mortar with my fingers. Had it been rendered hardier and thicker, the task would have been impossible, though it seemed someone had been hurried. Soon I had loosened a stone the size of a fist, which I began to grapple and pull on. It came away from the wall, whereupon Beatrice recoiled and dry-heaved, for the smell became truly palpable. I admit my eyes watered, and I had to breathe steadily through my mouth to maintain my composure. Fat beetles and brown centipedes crawled from the hole I had made.

'Wh-what in God's name is in there?' Beatrice had moved back towards the passage and was taking shallow breaths.

I didn't want to answer, for I feared then I knew. I wanted desperately to be wrong. I wanted desperately to find something else. *Someone* else.

I slowly placed my hands on the cavity, trying to flick away the insects as they latched onto my skin. I pulled on the stone, shifting my weight as pieces fell away. With one heaving effort, a large portion of stone crumbled around my feet, revealing a small hollow, dug out of the dirt. Jostling my position, I was able to crawl a little way forward and cast my lamp into the newly uncovered space.

I touched upon wet, dank mud, then something solid, cool and smooth.

I noticed the exposed area of the ribcage first, for the slithering worms that weaved between the visible bones made it seem for an instant as though the chest was still full of life, expanding with steady breath. My hand rested upon a shin bone, lined with sickly tissue, moist to the touch yet dreadfully thin. I felt every bump and knock that shin bone had ever taken through what remained of the muscle and skin. The pelvis was buckled below the ribs and torso, for the space was not overly large and the body had been left in a most dreadful and undignified manner, forced into the cavity with what was surely great force. It sat horribly upright, bending forwards towards me.

As I cast my gaze upwards, I was met with a rotten, decaying face, with a gaping smile, the jaw broken and unnaturally slack. For the sake of decency, I shall not describe the deterioration of the body in full, but shall merely say that between mutilation, decay and the feeding of rats upon the corpse, the individual's face was wholly unrecognisable. The body, however, was that of a man; there were no clothes or personal effects that I could see.

My revulsion nearly overcame me – it was all I could do not to vomit on the miserable fellow.

Beatrice had been speaking though I'd paid her no heed. She prodded me in the back and rasped with some frustration. 'Are you deaf?'

'What?' I replied, gagging.

'The rats are coming back. What's in there?'

'A body,' I said flatly.

She didn't answer for a moment. 'Is it—'

'A man,' I replied. 'I can't be certain who.'

I was lying, for in my heart I knew. From deeper in the small cavity, I noticed some movement. A dark shape bobbed upwards, revealed in the light of my lamp, before disappearing into shadow. A moment later, it appeared again, though this time the meagre silhouette seemed closer. I leaned forwards, pressing myself against the corpse, my face mere inches from the body. I held my breath, listened intently. A rat slowly emerged, creeping over the left shoulder blade, which protruded, exposed from the flesh entirely. It bared its teeth at me, and I struck it away, only to see another crawling across the corpse's stomach, and another scrambling over the buckled knees.

'The rats,' Beatrice yelled. 'They're coming through the tunnel!'

'They're in here as well,' I croaked, reeling. 'They've found some way to get to the body.'

I crawled backwards clumsily, only then noticing the hands resting at the body's side. The fingers and thumbs had all been removed; bloodied stumps were all that remained.

'The rats!' Beatrice snarled once more, her voice shrill and filled with panic. I could feel one on my leg, crawling quickly along my calf. It lunged at a heavy beetle by my side, gnawing through the shell, before moving on to another, midway up the body's torso. It climbed up the exposed ribs as though they were a flight of stairs, and I tried to push it away, though the task was a vain and hopeless one. Already, more were scrambling from every shadow.

I backed quickly out of the tight space. As I did, my lamp light touched upon a glint in the dirt, something small and solid that was all but concealed a little distance from the mutilated right hand. I grabbed at it blindly, for by then the rats around me were numbering some five or six, and were growing vicious, biting at anything that moved, including each other.

When I returned to Beatrice's side, I understood the extent of her fear. The rats were coming from the cellar in droves, moving down the passage two or three abreast of each other. She glanced at me, petrified, and asked with some real desperation how we were going to get out. I told her to follow me closely and started down the passage without another word. We hurriedly moved past the terrible vermin, who seemed uninterested in us. Only when we had returned to the cellar and walked quickly back to the stairwell that led to the kitchen, did we stop and gather ourselves.

Beatrice shuddered and groaned. I opened my hand slowly, for in my palm I still held the little trinket I had found beside the body. I wiped away some of the dirt, revealing a gold signet ring. My heart sank, my body erupting in panic and fire, when I looked upon the initials.

'E I H,' I said slowly.

Beatrice looked down at the ring. 'What's that?'

'A ring I found beside the body. E I H; Elijah Isaac Hawthorn.' I held back tears, but was instantly overcome with grief and remorse.

'He's dead. He's … he's actually dead.'

Retrieving the Body

September 8th, 1905

When I awoke, my first instinct (as it was for each of the days so far written and the months that preceded them) was to have a drink, and numb the aches and pains that coursed from my head down my body. My flask, however, was empty.

Addiction is not something one merely sets aside when it becomes an inconvenience. I fidgeted, tried distracting myself by thinking of the case at hand. But that only made things worse, for thinking of Hawthorn's corpse lying in such an abhorrent state, broken, bloodied, decaying and covered with rats, filled me with such misery that my clear and sober mind couldn't cope with the reality of it all.

I'd wanted to recover the body immediately, to drag it from that wretched place. But my grief was so overpowering it had become difficult to think straight. Reluctantly, I had let Beatrice lead me back to the study, where, after very little time, I had fallen into a restless sleep.

She remained curled on the bed, breathing lightly, her back to me.

When my thirst for liquor grew stronger than my fears, I stood and hurriedly took a candle in hand. I slipped into the corridor carefully, and spurred by the courage of an addict, hurried in the direction of the billiards room, where I recalled a drinks cabinet with a few half-empty bottles.

The heavy weight of night's darkness had lifted somewhat; whether it was the promise of dawn or unblemished moonlight I couldn't say. I hurried to the room and began rifling, like a starved animal, through the decanters and bottles in the cabinet.

I sipped on a few dregs of brandy, coughed on bitter whisky that burnt blissfully against my throat. Bottle after bottle, I sniffed, sipped, spat, drank, until I came upon some measly dregs of port which tasted so vicious and foul, I felt terribly sick the moment it passed my lips. In disgust I hurled the bottle at the wall. The sound of it smashing made me flinch, and then I cried out, yelling at the steely-eyed men in the portraits around me, enraged at the fear I felt. I had grown so weary of being afraid. Under the gaze of the eagle, which stood atop the large clock, I slunk onto a couch, weeping for the man I once was.

To say I felt overwhelmed would be a gross understatement. Hawthorn was dead. I had no idea who conspired against him, but a conspiracy was surely at play. His missing fingers and thumbs – his bloodied thumbprint at the scene of a crime. Someone was acting to ensure he was framed for the disappearances and murders. I tried to understand motive, thought of his letter to me where he spoke of terrible secrets held in the upper echelons of the Metropolitan Police, as well as the government. Fiction surely, and yet now his body lay in the cellar beneath me. Why? Because he had learnt of such things? Such questions seemed unanswerable with what little I knew. I found myself holding the diary, written in cypher. I turned my attention to it; if nothing more, it was something of a distraction.

Glancing quickly at the first page, it seemed (as I had suspected) that the cypher was far from a complex one. I rummaged through a sideboard and found a stubby pencil to begin decoding. The liquor made my work slow and laborious.

Hawthorn initially employed a substitution cypher, a replacement of plaintext by letters shifted in the alphabet. The cypher text was simple to decrypt, provided one knew how many steps the alphabet had been shifted. Hawthorn had not made the task difficult, going so far as to draw a grid at the bottom of the page, with the plaintext alphabet written out above empty squares where one could fill in the substitution letters. He'd even filled in two of these, so that the decryption was mere child's play.

Words and sentences formed quickly, even where whole paragraphs of the text were written in blocks with no spaces between words. Still, they were not of the calibre I expected. Nothing was addressed to myself, or a generic reader, nor was anything written with any order or formality. In truth, very little made sense. I was confident of my decryption, yet it appeared as though Hawthorn had merely been transcribing random sentences, lines of fragmented poetry. On occasion, whole sentences would read true, yet they offered nothing to me, despite a niggling sense that I may once have read them in their original context.

I turned to the second and third pages, though here things became drastically difficult. Hawthorn had altered his cypher, deepening its complexity far beyond the simplistic substitution he had first employed. I struggled to discern patterns, or commonly used words such as THE or IT. I grew frustrated quickly and flicked through to the final page Hawthorn had written, finding a series of carefully drawn symbols – angled and well-shaped hieroglyphs – that were far more foreign than any ancient language. I slammed shut the book.

'What the hell were you trying to say!'

I cradled my head and sat in silence, until a timid voice roused me.

Beatrice held out her hands. 'I'm sorry. I didn't know where you had gone and wanted to find you.'

I settled back on the couch. 'I couldn't sleep.'

She nodded, though looked over the shattered glass about the floor and the empty bottles lying haphazardly on the liquor cabinet.

'It's nearly dawn,' she said, wrapping her arms around herself. 'Do you want to go back below, gather the … um, remains?'

'Yes,' I replied bitterly. 'We'll need to examine the body somewhere and photograph what we can of the cellar and the rooms above.' I sighed and rubbed my brow. 'There is much to be done.'

Beatrice sat beside me. 'I am sorry.'

'For what?'

'That you had to find him like that. That someone left him in such a way.' Her face fell, her eyes filling with tears. 'The world can be such a cruel place.'

I saw her sorrow then. Finding Hawthorn was a loss for her as much as I, for now she was even further from learning the truth of her sister's disappearance. I imagined that her mourning was not truly able to begin. Each day, each hour, she was no doubt bombarded with all manner of terrible thoughts pertaining to Dorothy's death – did she suffer, where now did her body lie? And yet her resolve had been unwavering since the moment our paths had crossed. In that moment it offered me a flicker of strength. She wasn't crumbling, letting her grief destroy her, or succumbing to any vice that would null her pain or distort her mind. She was resilient, determined. I longed to be like her.

'We'll uncover the truth of all this,' I said with only the smallest doubt creeping into my voice. 'We – I – will do everything possible.'

She smiled, though it faded quickly. With a deep breath she gestured to the notebook resting on my lap.

'Did you learn anything?'

I held up the book. 'Not yet. It's rather peculiar. The first page is easily read, yet the words are nonsensical. Beyond that there is much I cannot fathom, no doubt a message Hawthorn was nervous to leave. I guess he was right to be wary.'

'If you want to talk about him—'

I merely shook my head. Beatrice said nothing for a little while.

'The letter Hawthorn wrote to you – he feared someone wished to take his life. He spoke of a conspiracy in the Metropolitan Police.' She shifted nervously, her left eye twitching as she looked at me. 'Do you think…'

She trailed off, and I said nothing, for I didn't know what to say.

We waited for dawn's full light, then moved about the manor and threw open every curtain and window we could find. The day was overcast but dry; the air felt muggy and dense. The winds from the previous night had stilled and all was quiet; even the trees surrounding the manor stood motionless.

I didn't know how to retrieve the body, nor did I truly want to look upon it again. I decided it best we take a pragmatic approach and deal with each scene in the order they were discovered. I therefore took my camera to the second floor, to the bathroom, where I thought I had glimpsed a body lying in the water. Beatrice was somewhat sceptical but said nothing as I set the angle of my camera and exposed my first plate. After I had removed it from the camera, and held the closed plate holder in hand, I noticed Beatrice staring at it with some confusion.

'Now what? Will um … an image reveal itself when you pull the glass plate out?'

I shook my head. 'I need to develop it, as I would any normal photograph.'

'Oh, I see.' She seemed a little embarrassed.

I chose to take only one image of the bath, then moved to the bedroom filled with moths. With the curtains pulled back and the windows wide open, many of the insects had escaped into the day. Many more remained though, and they were an infuriating presence. They landed on my camera, fluttered before the lens as I tried to set my image of the bed and the stains upon the sheets. Beatrice did what she could to brush them away, but to no great avail. Finally, with some defeat, I captured my image, and moved hurriedly to leave the room, but not before I took a sample of dried blood from the bed, which I gathered in a small, empty vial from my case. When we stood in the corridor, Beatrice asked where next to go.

'The cellar, the chair.' It seemed there was no point prolonging the unenviable task any longer. 'Then the body.'

Beatrice looked miserable. 'You'll need more light down there.'

I nodded. 'We'll be quick taking a photograph. Then we'll gather the body quicker still.'

The rats had grown in number, crowding the passage leading to the body. It made the task of photographing the chair and rope somewhat easier; the space was well illuminated with candles set about the floor. But the truly gruesome task at hand was still to be done, and neither of us wished to dwell much upon it.

'We'll hurry,' I said to Beatrice, attempting to sound reassuring.

Only then did I see the true horror in her eyes. She nodded, feebly.

'I can do it alone,' I said then, wholly uncertain if I could.

'No, no I can…' Her eyes were wet, her hands trembling.

She didn't say another word and I made no quarrel, for even I, someone who had dealt with the dead for many years, had no desire to do what was necessary.

'Stay here.' I tried to smile, though it only seemed to make Beatrice more upset.

I took aim and fired a shot with my gun into the sprawling mass of rats. They began to flee up the tunnel into the cellar, running in droves, yellow teeth and riddled fur, scurrying about our feet and ankles. The gunshot still rang in my ears when I finally stepped forward, camera in one hand, lantern in the other, the stand tucked under my arm. I dashed and crawled along the passage as quick as I could. It was awkward, and I clung to my camera tight, lest I trip and tumble. When I came to the stone antechamber, the rats were still gathered in great number. I kicked at them, set my camera stand upon the floor and thrust the lantern into the little opening beside the remains. More of the body had been eaten and chewed away, much to my horror. I quickly set about my work and captured an image – a gruesome, deplorable image – before fleeing back towards the cellar. Breathless, I placed the camera and stand beside the wooden chair. I admit I was somewhat surprised and disappointed; Beatrice was nowhere in sight.

I looked about the cellar. The rats shrieked from everywhere. We had brought a linen sheet from the rooms above, something in which to wrap the body. This I now took in hand, hurrying back down the passage, the pistol bouncing in my pocket. In the chamber, I wrapped the sheet around the ankles. With a revolting tug, I pulled the body towards me. It was stiff, for rigor mortis had long set in; skin peeled below the sheet. Nevertheless, I pulled again, harder, shifting the body out of the tiny space into which it had been crammed. When I had done enough to reveal the pelvis, I was forced to stop – a terrible throb of pain overcame me, spreading down my head and neck.

The sensation, the most dreadful and surreal sense of the world around me being clawed apart, paralysed me where I stood. I became limp, somewhat lifeless, just as I had when we had first entered the manor, when I had looked up at the birds upon the wall of the great hall. I cradled my head, lost now from the rats and the smell and the darkness and the spiders. I stood, wavering, 'seeing' things that were both tangible and visceral, yet unreal and dreamlike.

I think I called out to Beatrice, as I lost all sight of the chamber and was overcome with dizziness. I fell against the wall, barely able to hold myself upright. The strange spell lasted seconds, minutes … I couldn't tell. When it began to recede, pain – a most terrible migraine – took its place.

In a haze I leant down, disorientated, my heart beating irregularly. I grabbed at the ankles once more and struggled to free the body. The sheet was rancid when the task was finally done; I wrapped it around the corpse as best I could. Manipulating the arms, I was able to clasp my hands around the chest and exposed ribs. With painful effort, I was able to heave the body backwards out of the passage. It was an indelicate and odious task. It was all I could do.

The rats latched onto the body as it moved, despite my best efforts to ward them off.

Beatrice had not returned to the cellar when at last, I fell beside the chair, the putrid corpse resting against me. Weakly, I called out to her, though heard no reply. My words echoed through the vacant cellar, and the rats seemed to respond, chattering in unison. A few were still circling close to me, and with trembling hand, I took hold of my gun and fired off a round, striking one, to my surprise. It seemed to dispel the remainder to the shadows, much to my relief.

Despite my tiredness, I didn't linger. Rising, I grabbed hold of the body and pulled it across the cellar floor. At the stairs leading to the kitchen, I rasped out Beatrice's name, but heard no reply. My sympathy for her was now gone, and I admit I felt great anger at that moment. The dreadful errand had been made all the more difficult by her absence. Weakly, I began hauling the body up the stairs.

Breathless, I made it to the kitchen where I stopped, crying out, my arms and legs burning from the physical toil. I stank, my shirt bloodied and stained. Grimly I laid the corpse out as best I could, though any dignity for the dead had long gone. Suddenly, Beatrice's voice startled me; I had not noticed her sitting beside the large table.

'I'm sorry.'

I thought to yell but held my tongue.

'Say something,' she groaned.

'There is nothing to say,' I snapped. 'I have to get my camera, before the contemptible rats eat it!'

I near crawled back down the stairs.

'Thomas,' Beatrice called out. 'Thomas, wait.'

I turned and glared at her.

'Your nose,' she said gravely. 'Your nose is bleeding.'

I touched my fingers to the top of my lip, looked down at them and saw a thick layer of red blood spread across my fingertips.

'Why are you bleeding?'

I thought of the strange sensation, the terrible, pulsing pain that had spread through my temples.

'I don't know,' I growled angrily. 'How the hell would I know!'

Questions With No Answers
September 8th, 1905

Beatrice dozed quietly as I worked. When she woke, I was examining the remains and making notes. The body was still on the floor, though it was now laid across the sheet with another draped across the midriff. It had taken me a great deal of time and effort to move and shape the limbs – the figure was still awfully contorted and twisted around the pelvis.

Beatrice stood and stepped over to my side; she gazed down at the body with tired, bloodshot eyes.

'The fingers and thumbs have all been removed,' I began before she said anything. 'I can't be certain whether it was done prior to or after he – the victim – was killed. It was done with a heavy blade though, and with no great skill.'

'Torture?' Beatrice croaked.

'Possibly, though I fear it was a fouler purpose.' I explained to her then the bloodied thumbprint found at one of the victim's homes, how I had believed it strange from the outset, how I doubted a man as knowledgeable about forensics as Hawthorn would be so clumsy.

'Perhaps he learnt of this deep corruption in the Metropolitan Police, what he wrote of in his letter. If he thought his life was at risk, he likely came all this way to hide. Regardless, someone tracked him down and silenced him. Maybe, as an added protection, whoever took his life sought to discredit him entirely, frame him for the Wraith kidnappings.' It struck me then. 'Maybe the kidnappings are at the very heart of the conspiracy, somehow.'

'That's a ludicrous assertion,' Beatrice scoffed.

'Yes. Perhaps.' I ran a hand through my greasy hair. 'But if we assume Hawthorn's thumbprint was planted to frame him, then someone, or some few, in the Metropolitan Police would be best placed to plant evidence.'

'It's still preposterous.'

I concurred. 'Yet I fear the possibility. The thumbprint was only discovered at a recent crime scene and – well – there's something else troubling about this body.'

I stood and pointed to areas that were most unpleasant, the stomach and gut in particular, where internal gasses had bloated much of the abdomen.

'The victim was not killed long ago. It's difficult to ascertain a time when the crime was committed.'

Beatrice frowned. 'How so?'

'The rats,' I groaned. 'They have fed on much of the flesh and soft tissue. The chest, the face, areas of the limbs. The presence of flesh that does remain tells us that the body has not been left for a great deal of time. Anywhere from four to six weeks I'd say.'

'And the thumbprint at the Wraith kidnapping was discovered—'

'Just over three weeks ago. Meaning the killer had ample time to dismember the digits of each hand, return from here to London and plant the thumbprint at the crime scene.'

'It fits in with the brothers,' Beatrice nodded. 'They were reported missing roughly four weeks ago.'

The thought hadn't even occurred to me. 'Indeed. The old fool Lachlan suggested the brothers were smuggling, taking goods from here to the mainland. What if they weren't? What if Hawthorn had convinced them to bring him here in secret, and to ferry regular supplies of food and provisions?'

'It would explain those English bank notes found at their home.'

'And the tide times in the lighthouse.' I paused. 'Suppose the perpetrator convinced Douglas and Willie to bring them here somehow, on false pretences. Maybe even bribed them.'

'And then killed them both, to cover their tracks when they had returned to the mainland.'

'They would've had to be silenced,' I said gravely. 'It's only a working theory but it fits.'

Beatrice folded her arms, bit nervously on the nail of her thumb. 'It's far from proof that the police – or anyone in the police – had any involvement. There's too much left uncertain.' I beckoned her to speak on. 'If someone went to all the effort of tracking Hawthorn down, why leave his body so easily found? Someone tried to conceal his body behind the walls of that well, yes, but left so much evidence to lead us there. The blood around the chair; the rope used to tie him. All remained on show.'

It was a valid point. 'Maybe the perpetrator had little time. Maybe they were interrupted in the act, or one of the brothers returned to collect them.'

'Maybe,' Beatrice shrugged. 'But how do you even know this is Hawthorn? The face is so—'

'Damaged,' I snapped. In the full light of day, the extent of degradation done to the facial features was truly revealed. The nose was almost gone, as were large portions of the ears. The skin around the eyes and temples had been removed, cut away or gnawed at by the vermin. The jaw was very much broken, as was the left cheekbone. Thin wisps of white hair remained on the head, though no sunspots or identifiable marks were visible.

'This is the body of a man in his early sixties, as Hawthorn was. He had scarring caused by measles on his left cheek – the skin on this body has been removed or damaged so there's no means of positively identifying him via such scars. I would estimate the body to be just shy of six feet tall, as Hawthorn was, and the general frame and proportions of the man seem accurate.'

'It's still not proof,' Beatrice insisted.

'You're right; a wholly positive identification is nigh on impossible due to the body's condition. But still.' I pulled the gold ring from my pocket, rolled it between my fingers. 'This ring was his.'

'A convenient discovery,' Beatrice muttered.

'A discovery nonetheless.'

'Is there no other way of identifying him?'

I thought on it for a moment. 'Teeth, perhaps, though Hawthorn had dentures even when I knew him. There are no teeth or dentures in the victim's skull. Whether someone removed them; whether they were knocked, or *pulled* out...' I sat myself down at the table and looked through the notes I had written with great unease. 'This is policing,' I said as Beatrice stood staring at the body. 'It is not straightforward – it is not easy.'

'This body gets us no closer to the truth.'

I hit my hand down against the table, overcome suddenly with anger. 'It proves something fouler is at play here than both you and I understand right now.'

She tried speaking but could only utter a few words inaudibly. I tried to empathise with her, for I too was struggling to come to terms with the whole miserable affair.

'It is unbelievable, truly I know. But Hawthorn feared someone wished to take his life as far back as January this year. With this body, found in such a way and with another two men missing, suspected dead, this man *has* to be Hawthorn. There seems no other explanation as to who else it may be. Had he not written to me, who's to say anyone would have found him – if they had, they would surely have struggled to identify him.'

'The ring—'

'A mistake,' I insisted. 'Someone hurried, someone clumsy; most killers often are.'

Beatrice mumbled under her breath, and I could feel her fear permeating through the room for it mingled with mine.

'What ... what killed him?' Beatrice asked, pointing to the body.

I sighed. 'It is not pleasant ...'

'Just tell me.'

I nodded. 'The gash across the neck there. It's not easy to define due to the later damage caused by the rats, but I believe that it was the final, fatal injury. Whatever they used to take off his hand they used to cut his throat as well.'

Her skin visibly paled before my eyes. She left the kitchen quickly and I was alone to continue my examination. I noted down other injuries: bruising and bleeding below the skin, likely caused by blunt force trauma. Some smaller stab wounds, around the legs in particular. I photographed the remains, took close-ups of the hands and the wounds to the neck. Then I went in search of Beatrice. She was sitting outside on the veranda, in the close air and overcast light. I offered her a cigarette though she barely seemed to notice.

'There seems little else I can do with the body. I – we – can't take it back to the mainland with us.'

Beatrice remained completely still. 'Why?'

'Until I know the truth of who is behind this, I can't risk going to the police.'

'This is madness,' she groaned, her head dropping towards her knees.

'There is some chance, unfathomable as it seems, that individuals in the Metropolitan Police could be behind this. I have to rule out that possibility before we approach them.'

She nodded, her eyes unblinking, distant.

'You really believe some corruption, some conspiracy involving the police, could have caused all this?' she said quietly. 'Based on what? A letter from a man you once were close to, a letter from a man you haven't seen in years? What's to say it wasn't forged?'

'It wasn't. The letter was from him and in all honesty I–I...' I didn't answer for I didn't truly know what I believed. After a few moments, I flicked my cigarette to the floor.

'I have to bury him. I'll find something to dig with.'

The afternoon was wearing on. The dense clouds were parting, and brief streaks of light were shining through the rich green pines. No buzzards or insects swarmed about me, despite the heavy sweat running from my brow. I had rolled up my sleeves, my hands now dirtied by heavy soil and grimy stones. The shallow grave I had dug would suffice. Beatrice and I stood on either side of it; the body, wrapped in sheets, lay between us.

'I'm not really religious,' Beatrice said quite bashfully. 'It never played into my view of things.'

I was trying to think of some words to say, something of brevity that would define the moment in my mind, that would pay respect to Hawthorn in a manner he truly deserved, but I couldn't think of anything insightful or compassionate. I couldn't define his time in any words that would do justice to the good work he had carried out, to the guilty men he had thwarted, to the lives he had no doubt saved. I couldn't define his character, his wisdom, his dark humour. I couldn't speak of his friendship, of his sense of duty and loyalty. All I could dwell on was the deep injustice done to him and the barbarity of his end – the circumstances were so terrible I could think of nothing else. With great effort I was holding myself together, pushing down my grief.

I didn't want to leave him in such a way, but with nothing to mind I began covering his body with dirt and soil. I dug my shovel into the mound of earth I had formed, before Beatrice began to sing.

Amidst the misery of it all, her voice was angelic, soothing and delicate. She sang a song I had never heard before or since, words of which I can't recall but were all that needed saying in that moment. She sang with her hands clasped and her head bowed. Her voice carried on the faintest breeze and gifted the woodlands around us new life, revived vigour. Her words eased my heart and made me want to fall to my knees beside her. She sang all that needed to be said, and far more.

When she was finished, she nodded to herself. She looked to me and I thanked her. Her smile was filled with such melancholy, and I knew her song had not just been for a man she had never known, but for her sister as well.

The Truth in Rhyme and Cypher

September 8th, 1905

The time of Lachlan's return was approaching, and I sat with Hawthorn's cypher book in hand. I was still attempting to work on it, piecing together a few of the cypher text letters from the second page. But what I found was as nonsensical as that I had already decrypted. Poetry. Lines of it. Jumbled, confused, broken. Scraps I recognised, most I didn't. I scratched my brow and wondered what Hawthorn had meant by it all, if anything. I was tired then and struggling to focus.

I was sitting on the veranda, cooled by a billowing breeze that cut through the forest and whipped around the manor.

'What do you think it all means?' Beatrice asked as she came and sat beside me.

I shrugged. 'Nothing to me yet. Truly it is quite puzzling.' I flicked to the last page, where the cypher changed from letters to symbols. 'This I hope may have the answers, though I can't even begin to understand it.'

'Does any of it make sense?'

I nodded, turning back to the first two pages. 'Keats. Chaucer. Tennyson, Elizabeth Barrett Browning. There are several lines of hers I recognise.'

'My sister loved her work.'

'She shared something in common with Hawthorn then. He was something of an admirer of both her and her husband.'

I flicked from the first page to the second. Beatrice stopped me. 'She appears on this page too. Quite frequently in fact.' I began circling lines in pencil that Beatrice pointed out to me.

'I guess Hawthorn had her words in mind when he wrote these pages,' I muttered uneasily, returning my attentions to the bizarre latter entries.

'They may have some of her books in the library. I could look before we leave?'

'There's some time,' I said rather dismissively. 'I'll gather our things and make rea—'

I stopped short and looked at Beatrice. Her eyes were cast down on the pages. I stood and headed inside the house hurriedly. She called after me and I heard her follow quickly.

'What is it?' she asked as I stepped into the library. The room was dreadfully dark, and I began looking with my eyes squinted, struggling to read the titles embossed onto each leather spine. Some were unmarked, and I pulled them out quickly and turned to the inside pages. As I moved from book to book, I carelessly slung them to the floor.

'What is it?' she asked once more, as I skirted around the hearth and looked upon the shelves across the other side of the room.

'Poetry,' I said breathlessly. 'Look for Keats, Chaucer, and Barrett Browning in particular.' She didn't ask why but began looking through the lower shelves. A few minutes later she called me to her, and I knelt down at her side.

'Barret Browning, two volumes of poems,' she said. 'And Keats, Chaucer…'

I pulled out a volume of Barrett Browning, and cast my eyes carefully over each page.

'What are you looking for?' Beatrice asked.

'I don't know. Writing perhaps, a message of sorts. Maybe the cypher text was just a sign to look here.'

I continued to flick through. A single piece of thick paper, used as a bookmark no doubt, fell to my knees from between two pages. I read on, gazing at page after page, my eyes running from top to bottom. When I reached the outside cover, I grabbed at the next volume, though this revealed as little as the first. I was baffled. I tore at the paper that lined the covers inside, though nothing was there. This I did on the front cover as well but to no avail.

'There's nothing?' Beatrice said after a few minutes.

'Maybe the others.' We looked through Chaucer, Keats, any poetry we could find.

'There may be more,' Beatrice said, grabbing my wrist. 'We should look—'

'Don't bother,' I said, wrenching my hand free, rubbing at my wrist reflexively. 'Whatever Hawthorn was doing did not concern these books.'

I felt a sudden regret for those I had tossed to the floor and damaged. I collected them up clumsily, for strangely it seemed wrong to leave the fine library in such a sorry state. I gathered up the thick piece of paper that had fallen from the collected works of Barrett Browning. On the back, I noticed something written ever so faintly in the corner. It was small, and difficult to make out.

'A-G-B-R,' I muttered. Beatrice looked at me quizzically.

'What does it mean?'

'Perhaps more cypher, though it could be anything. To me it represents the chemical formula—' I stopped abruptly and she implored me to speak on. 'It's the chemical formula for silver bromide. It's a principle compound in the making of photographic plates.'

I sped from the library. Beatrice followed close behind, her voice rising as she asked what the paper meant.

'How long till Lachlan returns?' I called to her as I made my way to the hidden study and opened Hawthorn's camera case.

'An hour or so.'

I lifted out his camera, the camera I had helped him buy. Tucked neatly beneath it, I found a single glass quarter plate in a closed plate holder. My heart pounded as I held it in my hand.

I gathered a few things quickly from my own camera case, including the plates I had exposed from the rooms above. 'I'll be as quick as I can. Head to the quay and wait for him. When he arrives, come and find me.'

Beatrice tried to protest, but I didn't listen, rushing from the study as fast as I could.

I wasted no time. After maybe forty minutes, I had concocted enough developing and fixing fluid, gathered what I needed and headed to the empty larder in the basement – it was dark enough. In searching for pans and pots to mix my chemicals, I had some luck in the kitchen, for nestled in several large drawers were tablecloths of various colours and sizes. One was burgundy, in truth a dusky rag, but more than sufficient for my needs. I had wrapped it around a lantern before descending to the larder – now the red hue of light gave the rough walls and broken arches a gruesome appearance. All around me bled, just as Hawthorn surely had. I pushed aside the thought, and the intrusive chatter of the rats close by.

I submerged Hawthorn's glass plate, uncertain then if I was being foolish, if the letters written on the slip of paper were trivial, meaningless. Beside it, I submerged one of my own plates, that which I had exposed in the bathroom above. Bile boiled in the pit of my stomach.

I waited impatiently beside the submerged plates, my hands quivering with unbridled excitement. As I saw the first dark shadows appear, I noticed the scratch of vermin about my feet, and felt one dreadful creature sneak across my shoe. I didn't move, however, my eyes fixed on the glass and the images appearing. It was my own from the bathroom that came clear first.

I saw the bath, filled to the brim with dirty water. Black negative light streaked in through the two large windows out of shot. And there, barely concealed between each discernible beam, I saw the face of a woman, grim, bloodied. Crying.

She held something in her hand, something glowing, burning through the very image. A knife – no doubt the blade that killed her.

I reached to take hold of the negative, but stopped myself, too afraid even to touch it. A moment later my eyes were drawn from the gruesome spectre, as words began to emerge on Hawthorn's plate. An image of a note appeared, scrawled in large capital letters. I read the words as they remained submerged.

TOP FLOOR LAST ROOM BENEATH BED

It would have been wise to fix the images then, to ensure that what I saw in that moment was indeed all that the photographs had to offer. But I didn't: for the rats, for the blood-red walls and for my own miserable fear. I left all as it was, sped from the cellar, up through the manor to the top floor, where large windows revealed the pallid light of day. I hurried along the narrow corridor with the servants' quarters and came to the last compact room. I stamped over woodlice and fell to my knees beside the low bed. In truth I could see nothing beneath it and moved then to pull the bed away from where it stood. Nothing was revealed at first, and manically then I ran my hands along the rough floorboards.

In the corner, I felt a loose board rock ever so slightly. I flung the board to one side and thrust my hand into the space revealed. I touched upon something wrapped in linen and pulled it free. It was a book. As I opened to the first page, I read the first line scrawled in sepia ink. I felt a flash of jubilance, sullied quickly by crippling fear.

Dear Thomas,

I write this to you, for you alone are the intended recipient. If you read these words, I am surely dead.

This book contains all that I know, all that I have uncovered of the conspiracy and plot that now festers at the heart of the police force and government we so dearly care for. My death should emphasise to you the severity of the situation, for if they have found me, they have done so with eyes and ears all across this land, far from the halls of Scotland Yard and Whitehall.

It is imperative, for your own safety, that you heed my words, so I shall write as plainly as I can and summarise what I know in these first few pages. In the last twenty years, a revival of the occult – that which concerns the unscientific, the superstitious and the overtly wicked – has spread through much of Europe. I believe this fascination goes beyond mere intrigue, for there are those – weak-minded enough! – who believe such mischief and dark spiritualism can unlock power, true power to dominate others and seize control of the state. As unfathomable as it may be, I fear such a revolution, a coup of sorts, is close at hand within our empire, for a cabal of great influence has formed in secret and now lies in wait.

This cabal – this cult, for that is truly what it is – was founded late in the last century. How it originated I cannot say, but it began within the Palace of Westminster, with those who swear to govern the state and protect His Majesty's subjects. Its primary goal is to overthrow all that they have sworn to protect – to destroy our monarchy and its bloodline; to disband our government and seize power absolutely; to tear down each fine institution our great nation is built upon and thereby lead the empire into a new dawn. An age of dark spirituality – _an age of blood_ – that which fuels their perverse rituals, initiations and gnostic ceremonies. The blood of the innocent, of the pure at heart.

The cult needs it. Already they have taken to seizing it where they can. Unexplained disappearances, mysterious deaths and bodies found, brutalised and savaged. For years they have instigated kidnappings and low-profile murders, though now, as they draw closer to enacting their vile schemes, they intend to wipe out those few that stand before them, those who knowingly or otherwise scupper their well-laid plans. By the time you read this, some furore may have been made, some high-profile individuals taken from their homes in the midst of a seemingly random crime spree. That is the work of the cult! Do not be led to believe that it is the misdeeds of a lone man, another Ripper, for it is simply all lies and misdirection.

I have learnt of this madness, this cult, from the mouth of our own commissioner, Robert Henley, who plays a key role within the group. He, foolishly, believed I would be willing to join this dreadful band, to stand and support their foulness, their depravity. For a time, I played the game, I played the uncertain man, dubious, afraid, but willing to join, willing to hold my tongue and move in secret circles. Only then did I learn the true breadth of this rot, for it delves far deeper than our commissioner, for also involved are the assistant commissioner of Crime; the former Home Secretary whose friendship I once cherished; senior members within the Commons and Lords; along with almost every department head within the Metropolitan Police, including that of the CID. Other heads of police forces no doubt play a role, so that a web of darkness stretches from one corner of our fair isle to another. They will soon be ready, Thomas. They are close to setting their ultimate plan into action and seizing control of the state. They have the means to maintain order, and will use it, if necessary, in brutal fashion.

I simply do not know how I can guide you. Part of me wishes only to tell you to run, to flee the country as fast as you can and never return or look back. I know in my heart the character of man you are and that your first and only thought will be to charge into the tiger's gaping mouth. What always shone in you was your need for justice, to stand by those whose voices were taken – in this I know you will surely wish to see terrible wrongs righted, even if all the odds are stacked against you.

Therefore, with heavy heart I tell you (for I fear desperately that this may lead to your end) that the cult meets primarily outside of the city of London. It is a measure to ensure secrecy and security; for years they have gathered within the walls of the Lord Cavendish-Huntley's estate at Burton Lodge, which stands outside the village of Burton Haxteth in Cambridgeshire.

If you wish to stop this wicked group, you must uncover all the evidence you can find at Cavendish-Huntley's estate. It is worthless trying to apprehend Cavendish-Huntley or anyone else you may find, for that would serve no other purpose than merely revealing yourself. Look for those who will listen; look for those who will take what evidence you are sure to discover and will use it to bring down this terrible plot. And beware this symbol – _this brand_ – for it is the mark of the terrible cult . . .

At the bottom of the page, Hawthorn had drawn a symbol that chilled me to the core. It was the strange mark that had been found at each of the Wraith kidnappings, the symbol Henley claimed had been used to 'honour' each of the victims.

I intended to read on but heard from the floors below Beatrice calling out my name. I rushed down, holding the book in hand ready to show her. But she was clearly shaken and spoke before I did.

'The time has come and gone. Lachlan – there's no sign of him anywhere. I don't think he's coming for us.'

Fleeing from the Coast
September 8th, 1905

'Could something have happened to him?'

I looked from Beatrice to the book in my hand, my heart thundering.

'I don't know. We can't stay here another night.'

Beatrice looked confused. 'But wh—'

'We need to leave! Something terrible is at play.'

She nodded silently. 'How do you propose we go?'

I thought for a moment. 'There was a dinghy in the cellar. If it is seaworthy, it may well be our only choice.' I looked rather grimly out of the French doors, past the veranda to the encroaching dusk. 'I have no great skill at seamanship.'

'Neither do I,' Beatrice replied. 'Would it be best to stay, to wait. Perhaps he is merely late – perhaps he will come in the morn.'

I shook my head. 'No, he wanted his pay. Something, or someone, has stopped him returning. I fear we may need to take our chances.' The manor seemed to creak under the buffeting of the wind. 'I have no desire to be here any longer.'

Beatrice gestured to the book I clung to. 'Did you learn anything?'

'There's much to tell,' I said, looking down at the book with a swelling sense of dismay. 'But for now, we have to get off this island.' I turned to head to the cellar.

'I can't go back down there,' she muttered to me. I barely noticed, charging into the red light and bleak shadows. I found the little dinghy and, along with the single broken oar, dragged it across the cellar and manoeuvred it up to the kitchen. In the dwindling light we inspected it. Its blue paint was badly chipped; I pulled away a rusted cleat with my bare hand. Yet, to our untrained eyes it seemed solid enough.

'We'll gather what we need and take this with us to the quay.' Beatrice was pallid. 'I can't—'

'You can't what?' I barked, my impatience growing.

'Thomas, I have to tell you something.'

I looked at her for the briefest moment, saw the deep anxiety in her wide eyes. This was all too much for her – she was no police investigator, no officer or trained expert. She was an innocent bystander, a sister who had come in search of the truth for all the right reasons, who now found herself at the heart of a deeply disturbing case, one that was unravelling, growing more surreal, more complex. I felt pity for her, but couldn't let myself dwell on it.

'What do you have to tell me – we have no time for this!'

She went to speak, stopped herself. She held a hand out and touched my shoulder, the sickly cold of her fingers seeping through my shirt.

'I-I …'

I pulled away from her, brashly.

'If you are too afraid to stay here any longer, I understand. Perhaps you should just wait at the quay. Maybe we are wrong, and that old fool will be there.'

I turned away from her, pretending to examine the dinghy some more. She said nothing and left the kitchen quickly. I felt guilty, for my tone, my callousness. In truth I was still in shock. When I was certain she was gone, I fell to a knee and vomited on the floor. It took such an effort to get a hold of myself.

*

In less than half an hour I had gathered my things and dragged them in the dinghy to the edge of the cliffs above the quay. Beatrice was nowhere in sight. The daunting uneven steps were my only way to the water's edge below. Already I could see the rising tides lapping over the moss-strewn platform. I cursed aloud, looking back towards the trees, hoping to see Beatrice behind me. I thought to go back and search but knew I first had to get the boat down to the water.

I took my camera case and the lantern from the dinghy and left both on the cliff edge. Slowly, I stepped downwards, my back to the water. I slipped on the second step and my spine jarred painfully as I managed to retain my footing. Gripping the front of the dinghy, I gingerly pulled it towards me. As it tipped over the edge of the cliff, its weight pressed against me. My tired body struggled to maintain balance, as step by step I descended towards the quay. It was awful, a lengthy struggle compounded by my exhaustion and fragile state. Had I fallen, it would surely have been to the rocks below, and to my certain death.

In time I was forced to move more quickly, for my tired arms struggled to hold the weight of the little boat any longer. With blessed relief I came to the bottom, my feet splashing in the icy water as I stepped onto the platform. With a thud, the wooden boat smacked against the stone.

I left it there and hurried back up the steps to fetch my camera. At the top of the steps, I began to cry out to Beatrice. Once, twice, thrice, I heard nothing of her. Then, to my surprise, she yelled up to me from the cracked and crumbling recesses of the quay below. I was startled and infuriated to see her there.

I made way back down, my anger fuelling my confidence. Not once did I slip.

'What the hell were you doing watching me from down here!'

I didn't yell, for I hadn't the strength. 'Did you not think to help me or were you curious to watch me fall to my death?'

'I can't—' Beatrice mumbled meekly.

I ignored her, shunting the dinghy off the platform, dropping my camera case in it roughly and stepping across the short gap of black water. Beatrice stood motionless on the quay.

'Come on, we have to go.'

She stepped carefully into the boat. It barely seemed to rock under her weight. She sat at the bow and I placed the lantern between us. Looking about the hull, I saw no signs of water leaking in. She turned and set her gaze out, leaning forwards to the water.

'I'll guide us,' she said quietly. I didn't reply as I struggled to push off.

As we headed out, the back of my neck began to burn, as though a hot blade were searing into my flesh. I twisted and looked over the flooded quay, let my gaze rise up the steps to the clifftop above. A figure stood there, unmoving. Their hands were held at their sides, their face concealed by wet, unkempt hair. I stared with a sick fascination, as all manner of devilish voices whispered in my mind.

Their words were filled with malice and blood. I couldn't look away, had no desire to do so. The figure raised its arm and pointed towards me.

The voices in my head grew louder as they tried to drown out another screeching sound. They failed.

'Bexley!'

I gasped back to life and turned to Beatrice.

'We have to go.'

We had been drifting, the oar held limply at my side. Beatrice began pointing out our course, and I obeyed her as best I could. I glanced back over my shoulder more than once, though the figure on the cliff had vanished.

We knocked and bumped and scraped our way from the

island, skirted back around its western edge in the direction we knew roughly to be Pike Ness. Mist smothered us, even as we ventured to the open sea. Blessedly, the breeze was steady, the waters calm. Switching the oar from one side to the other, I tried to keep us on what I believed to be a straight course, though in truth we had no idea how far we were drifting.

In time I became troubled, as did Beatrice.

'The mist,' she whispered. 'It seems only to thicken.'

I didn't reply. An hour passed in silence. Another half hour after that. My arms were so weak by then I could barely raise the oar from the water after each stroke. Beatrice was growing ever more concerned.

'We should be able to see something now. Why won't this mist clear, why can't we see anything!'

It was most unnatural. Another ten minutes passed. The cold air was sucking the heat from my exertion, and I shuddered as I laboured with the oar. Arctic waters lapped into the boat when we began to rise and fall over rougher waves. The cold soaked into my trousers and burrowed deep into my skin.

Beatrice was growing frantic. 'The mist. I can't see anything! I can't—'

I tried to calm her, but the wind began to whip and whisk around us. A shape swooped close overhead and Beatrice cried out in surprise. Another creature dashed down beside the boat. Another fluttered close to my side. Then a laughing call rose out and both Beatrice and I looked at each other and then out beyond the dinghy's bow.

'Gulls,' I muttered. 'We have to be close to the coast.'

I stopped rowing, stretching my body precariously from the boat's bow. Over the gentle lapping of the water, I heard the churn and wash of the tide against the rocks.

'We're close to land.' And how we were, for looking up then I distinguished depths of darkness breaking through the fog and realised the cliffs of the coast were less than fifty yards from us. I grabbed up the oar and thrust it into the waters on my right, curling the boat starboard. By now, however, we were being sucked in by the tide and all I could do was struggle to stop us lashing against the rocks. I pushed with all my strength as we were rolled by the waves, though by then I had lost all control. As we came up against the cliffs, I thrust the oar out and tried desperately to push us away from them. It did little good, and we struck a scarp hard, both of us nearly knocked out of the dinghy entirely. We were pinned against the rock.

'Now what?' Beatrice asked desperately. I cried out, for the impact had caused a sharp pain to surge up through my arm and erupt in my shoulder. I tried pushing off from the cliff, and we bobbed a little way, drifting some five yards along the coastline, before being thumped back into the rock. Again and again this happened, and the dinghy snapped and moaned each time we smacked against the cliffs. We were taking on a dangerous amount of water, the icy chill now up to our ankles.

'If we can't move off, we'll have to swim.' The idea pained me. I lost my footing and nearly went overboard, fortunately falling back into the boat. I stretched the oar out to Beatrice.

'Take it – push us on.'

'I can't,' she near wailed.

'Why the hell not!'

'I can't,' she said again, her voice almost pleading. All seemed quite hopeless as we thundered against sharp rock once more, and I looked at my camera case, now half submerged, knowing that if we were to abandon our boat, I would need to leave it as well. I considered the very real prospect that Beatrice and I would both drown.

'We swim for it, along the coastline. Stay together—'

'Look,' Beatrice cried over the crash of the waves. 'Along the cliffs.'

I squinted, looked into the mist. A silhouette rose up, shaped by the skyline. It rose above the cliffs, a few hundred yards from where we were. After a moment, I recognised it as the peak of the abandoned lighthouse.

Invigorated, I began pushing us along once more. I moved with purpose rather than care, so that beyond the deep crags we began to grind against the rock, the waves lashing us like vicious nine tails. The peak of the lighthouse disappeared as we came closer to the little cove, the dinghy now half sunk. I pushed us as close as I could to the shoreline, before Beatrice leapt out, waded through waters that rose midway up her thighs. I grabbed my camera case before nearly falling from the dinghy and following her to the narrow beach. On dry land, we each collapsed, lying on our backs, shuddering and exhausted.

'I need to tell you— I need to tell you something,' Beatrice wheezed between laboured breaths and chattering teeth. I reached for a cigarette, finding only an empty sodden box.

'Right now, I couldn't give a damn,' I groaned bitterly.

Darkness descended, and despite our lack of light we fumbled along the path from the lighthouse back to Pike Ness. As we stood on the road looking down into the tiny hamlet, we shared an uneasy glance with one another. Not a single light shone. Nothing moved.

We walked along the cobbled path that passed each small house and dwelling. Thin curtains, and even a window or two, were left open, despite the frightful chill of the breeze. We made our way straight for the inn, walking with such quiet steps, for even then, the churning of the sea – so close to where we stood – seemed distant and strangely noiseless.

Hesitantly, I tried the door of the inn. It opened with a soft creak, and we stepped inside to the little bar area. Beatrice shut the door behind us before we each timidly called out to the innkeeper and his wife. There came no response. We called out again, this time louder, moving a little into the bar, knocking against chairs set around tables. I struck upon a candle with a matchbox at its side and struck one alight. The bursting flame hissed, as Beatrice began to scream.

The innkeeper was slumped at a table beside the bar. His eyes were open, his left hand clutched to his collar. His skin was grey and lined with deep purple veins. His wife lay collapsed on the floor, staring at us, her arm stretched back towards her husband.

I rushed to them, felt the coolness of their skin, the rigidity of their bodies. They had been dead some time, twelve hours or more. I looked into the glossy pupils of the innkeeper, saw threads of blood around the irises and whites of the eyes. His right hand still clutched a mug, now tipped to one side, its contents spilt across the table. I prised the mug from his grasp, held it to my nose and smelt the faint odour of tea leaves and milk. Beneath that was something subtler, barely distinguishable. Almonds, or at least the smell of them.

Beatrice was struggling to breathe. She had collapsed into a chair, was resting her head against her hand and talking quickly with each haggard intake of breath.

'They're—they're …'

I knelt beside her. 'It's all right, Beatrice. Look at me, it's all right.'

She shook her head and swung her arm at me. 'No, it isn't! There's so much death, so many dead.' She sunk her face into her hands, her body trembling as she wept. I looked from her to the eyes of the innkeeper, panic and dread setting in.

'Beatrice. Beatrice. We can't stay here. We can't stay.'

She ignored my words and the desperation in my voice. 'How did they die? Do you know how they died?'

'Poisoning. I think they were poisoned with cyanide. We have to go.'

Still she wouldn't move. She cradled her head in her hands and continued to weep. I stood and stepped out of the inn, looking both ways up the cobbled path before turning left and going to the house next door. I stepped into a dark sitting room and kitchen but saw no one. Upstairs I looked through each small room; in the last I saw a woman's body, face down on the floor. Back in the kitchen, I found her breakfast, cold upon the table, a mug half empty, smelling as bitterly of almonds as the innkeeper's had.

In the next house I found an elderly couple, both dead. In the house after, parents and a young child. All dead. All staring with the same mixture of confusion and fright. The look on the child's face made me splutter and gasp and rush back to Beatrice's side. There was no need to look through the other houses for I knew that I would find the same terrible scene in every one.

'The water. Someone's poisoned the water of every home. We have to leave,' I said sharply.

'Why?' was all she could answer. 'Why would someone do this?'

'I don't know yet.' We hurried from the inn and climbed up and out of Pike Ness.

'Are we going to Donalbain?' Beatrice asked meekly.

'No, we can't go back that way. We'll walk the coast till we find a town, a station.'

'Then what?'

'Then we head south,' was all I said, for then and there we began to walk briskly, and I spent every ounce of my strength listening to the sounds of the night and searching in the darkness.

A killer was somewhere near.

The Eyes that Follow

September 9th, 1905

I shan't detail here how we spent the night running from Pike Ness, hiding in what refuge we could find, like fugitives with bloodhounds on their trail. Exhausted, broken and afraid, we tried to rest as best we could, though sleep was near impossible. Every call of the owl, every rustle beneath the hedgerows, the bitter bite of the midnight air, kept us awake and petrified. I would cling to my gun, look for a man – or men! – draped in black clothes, walking reapers. I saw faces move in the darkness more than once, and in one drowsy moment before falling into a nightmare, screamed aloud when I felt an infested hand fall upon my shoulder.

No one was behind me. No one was around us. Yet still I stood and spun, goading the unseen ghouls to appear. I lied to them, telling them I was not afraid, that I was no coward. In stinking clothes and with shaking hand, I ordered they stand before me, yelled that I was police, real police, police who stood for the good and righteous.

Beatrice finally silenced me, soothed me as I collapsed to the ground, whereupon I regained some sense after a time.

'Talk to me of better things,' she whispered softly. We both shivered, yet neither of us dared to try lighting a fire. I thought on it for a moment, until memories, distant and almost forgotten, crept to the forefront of my mind.

'My mother was born in Poland, came to London in eighteen sixty-six. She was Jewish and her family wanted to go to America – only got as far as Spitalfields. When I used to say I was cold as a child, she'd tell me, "It was nothing like east of Warsaw." As a four-year-old lad I never really understood what she meant.' I smirked, recalling the dreadful pair of short trousers she had made me wear come rain, sleet or snow.

'I didn't know you were Jewish,' Beatrice whispered.

I shook my head. 'Mother renounced much of her faith when she met my father. The day she arrived in London, he was down at the docks, trying to get those coming off the boats to have their photograph taken. A foolish errand – none had a penny to their name. Yet he always said it was worth it. He found my mother down there, was smitten ...'

I stopped, for all the fine memories began to tarnish and sully. So much joy had been taken from my father, so much life and exuberance. The man he became before he died was just a shell, as much a ghost as those that haunted me. I hated him for so many years, hated all that had happened to him, all that he'd had to endure.

'You didn't speak much about your family before,' Beatrice said, looking down at her feet.

'Josephine, my younger sister, meant the world to me. At three years old, she was already the queen of the East End,' I smirked. 'Used to order the other children around, would stand up to the boys her age.'

I saw the flames, lashing from the broken windows and up the brickwork of our home. The smile faded slowly.

'She and Mother died in a fire when I was only a boy. A house fire – no one knew how it started. It was just me and Father after that. He was a good man, but the grief ate away at him like a cancer till there was little left, till he finally got hold of a rope and put an end to his misery.'

'Oh.' Beatrice fidgeted with her hands then. She slunk down a little where she sat.

I felt somewhat embarrassed. 'Hawthorn was something of a father to me after we met. He took a great interest in my life, in all my world. Taught me a great deal; set me on a new path when I was perhaps at my lowest.'

I noticed Beatrice's eyes were shut. She slept quietly as the first grey haze of dawn began to lift all around us.

I couldn't settle. I turned to Hawthorn's diary and re-read the first pages in the dim light. His assertions, his *absurd* claims, were dreadfully terrifying in the light of what we had discovered at Pike Ness. Understand that even in my state of unrest, suffering the pains of addiction and clawing to the shreds of my sanity, I found the notion of a cult, a secret, murderous society, ludicrous. And yet the bodies – Hawthorn on the island; the men and women poisoned where they sat and ate. The growing list of the dead proved that something foul was at play, something wicked and scheming. As much as I wished not to believe the words written in Hawthorn's hand, I soon began to hear the voice of my former friend speak directly in my ear. And in a short time I grew most assured, that what he spoke of was, indeed, the dreadful truth.

Hawthorn detailed meetings he'd attended, listed those he'd met with, who'd offered their support to the terrible plot. He spoke of the one occasion he had travelled to Burton Lodge, the manor of Lord Cavendish-Huntley. There he described a cere-monial room, the former grand hall. He had watched a macabre scene, the desecration of a young man's body and a sordid ritual performed with his bloodied remains. He claimed Henley, a prominent leader within the group, had been in attendance. When he wrote of dark blood being wiped across the man's brow, I could take no more, and slammed the book shut with force.

Almost an hour had passed, and the calling of birds drifted on the fresh morning air. I roused Beatrice and we walked on, checking over our backs as we went.

'We have to move unnoticed,' I said, looking down at the large, sprawling town below us. Clattering metal hammers, voices, the clopping of nags' hooves, drifted on the air. We stood on the edge of high clifftops, the ocean now shimmering in a golden light. I turned back to look along the coastline, and in the distance, thought I spied the island, a tiny pebble standing in the water. It was merely a delusion of my own making, for I knew in truth we had walked too far to be in sight of that dreadful place.

A busy dock bustled with ships heading out to the open water. At the centre of the town we saw a plume of steam rise and mingle with the clouds above, before hearing the unmistakable ring of an engine's whistle. A few moments later the locomotive emerged into view and hurtled off into the countryside.

'What do you plan on doing?'

'Heading south,' was all I replied, gazing at the last wisps of the locomotive's steam as I started down the road that led to the town. In my heart I knew my intentions, to head to the manor of Lord Cavendish-Huntley, the man so prevalent in Hawthorn's accusations. I wished to look upon his estate myself, as if it alone may shed some light on the truth.

We walked through the streets, our heads bowed. Beatrice wore her cap low over her eyes, and moved with her hands thrust in her deep pockets. Her carriage was bent, either on purpose or as a symptom of her exhaustion. People walked by us, though few paid us any attention. My heart seized when, upon rounding a corner, I spotted a constable in dark uniform and buttoned overcoat. He was standing across the cobbled road, watching drearily as the world moved around him. His helmet stood high above his head and raised his stature significantly. I noticed the bullseye lamp hanging on his left side, saw the soot smeared across his left cheek. He had been on night watch, was likely tired and waiting to be relieved. I dared not take any chances though and in a moment of panic, as he turned and looked our way, slipped into a grimy coffee house.

We sat in a corner, far from the few who ate and spoke. Before I had chance to breathe, a young man came to my side and I ordered both Beatrice and I tea with bread and eggs. Only when the waiter, hacking and wheezing, left and returned to the kitchen, did she lean over and whisper to me.

'Do you truly believe every police constable in Scotland is out to get us?' I opened Hawthorn's diary on the table, and she read through the first few pages quickly. 'This is insanity.' Her voice was raised, and I quickly seized upon the diary and concealed it in my coat. 'You can't truly believe that?'

'Why not,' I snarled. 'You saw the state of the manor. And Pike Ness!'

She grimaced at the name, shook her head and clasped her hands together. 'It can't be true. None of it can be true. You really think a lord, a respected peer, would be involved with something so—'

The waiter returned with two portions of food on a single plate and one mug of tea.

'Two teas, man,' I said with more than a little irritation. 'Two.'

'I don't want one,' Beatrice said.

The waiter recoiled. 'Uh—'

'Just get her one, please,' I said sternly.

'Really, Thomas, I don't want one!' Beatrice snapped, her face turning red.

I raised my hands to her. 'Fine, leave it.' The waiter stepped back from me slowly. He nodded even more slowly, before disappearing behind the counter and back into the kitchen.

'Dim-witted fool!' I turned and scowled at Beatrice. 'You need to eat and drink something to keep up your strength.'

She shook her head, her lips trembling. 'I said I was fine. You're hardly keeping a low profile causing a ruckus like that.'

I ignored her, tearing ravenously into my food.

An old man a few tables away glanced more than once at the state of our dress and condition. The young waiter, wiping something brown and red onto his grubby apron, returned timidly once, asking if we wanted more tea. I handed him some change and we both stood to leave.

'Where's you from if you don't mind my asking?' His voice wavered as he spoke.

'I do mind,' I said bluntly. I noticed then the silence of the place, and how everyone was glancing up at me from their measly meals or stale mugs of coffee. With a sense of sudden urgency, I beckoned Beatrice to hurry and we left with our eyes to the floor.

We were in Adanburgh, though this only dawned on us when we entered the train station and asked for tickets heading south.

'Where you going?' a grizzly station assistant asked from behind the wrought-iron bars of a kiosk.

I thought of Beatrice, for I had said nothing of my plan. I needed to be honest with her and give her a chance to get away if she so wished. Mindful not to tell the station assistant of my true destination of Burton Haxteth, where the manor resided, I thought quickly.

'Cambridge,' I said flatly. From there, either I or us both could get a connection onwards.

He raised an eyebrow. 'Long ways to go. You'll need to go to Edinburgh via Aberdeen, then head down the East Coast line and change for Cambridge.'

'That's fine, thank you.'

He handed me a third-class ticket. I glared at it, then back to him.

'I need two tickets. And *first class*.' I pushed the ticket back to him. He eyed me suspiciously.

'First class?' he sneered. I handed over the fare and he shrugged. 'No mean to be rude. But the way you look...'

I took my tickets and stormed away from him. Beatrice was standing further along the platform. We had only a short wait till the train arrived.

'I have tickets to Cambridge. We can decide what best to do en route.'

She only nodded.

'I need cigarettes, and a—' I stopped myself from saying drink though that was what I desired.

'I'll wait here.'

I hurried away from the station, only realising as I found a tobacconist that I was still carrying my camera case. I rushed inside, and asked for two packs of cigarettes, a box of matches. 'And rum, if you have any.'

'Aye,' the shopkeeper said quietly. 'I have a few bottles.' He turned and gathered what I had asked for. 'Anything else y'need?' he asked over his shoulder.

'No, that's fine, thank you.'

I heard heavy boots behind me. When the shopkeeper turned around, he smiled to the figure at my back.

'Morning, constable. Fine one.'

'Aye.' The voice was gruff and low. I glanced behind me, spying the height of the man. He was at least six foot three and built like an ox. He held a packet of tobacco in his meaty hands.

'Morning, sir,' he said dryly.

I nodded and tried to smile.

He stepped around me and dropped his tobacco on the counter. 'English, are you, sir?' I nodded again. 'Up this way for any reason?'

'Photographing the coastline,' I said politely, meeting his gaze and kicking at my camera case lightly.

He nodded. 'Are you alone, sir?'

The shopkeeper laid my wares on the counter and I began rummaging in my pockets. 'Yes, soon heading back south. Keep the change.'

I thrust everything into my pockets and stepped over to the door. The constable raised an arm at me. 'Not by chance had breakfast little ways from here, at a coffee house, sir?'

I smirked and shook my head. 'I'm afraid not, officer.' With a nod I left the shop and walked as calmly as I could across the street. I heard the door open behind me, and the constable call out to me. I ignored him. I heard him step quickly after me, and picked up my pace, rounding a corner. The constable hurried after, yelling as he went.

I acted before I really thought. I dropped my camera case and pulled my revolver from my pocket. The constable lurched into view and I swung out and struck him hard against the jaw with the butt of the gun. He didn't fall but groaned and cried out in alarm. Stumbling away from me, I grabbed and struck him harder. I felt the force of the impact as I hit his cheek; he collapsed awkwardly onto his back. I checked he was still breathing, felt a surge of guilt and torrid excitement as I realised what I had just done. I took up my case and walked away quickly. It was a miracle no one had seen me.

I wound my way back to the station, hoping then that our train wouldn't be delayed. To my relief I saw a steamer and carriages alighted at the platform. Beatrice was standing beside the train, looking nervously for my arrival. When she saw me, she smiled thinly, though it faded when I came alongside her.

'Get on the train, sit somewhere away from me.'

'What's happened?'

'Just do it. Get off at Aberdeen, we'll need to switch trains.' I hurried her on, then walked to the farthest carriage and got on myself. I sat in a dingy seat, watched with bated breath for a pack of constables and sergeants to charge into the station and order everyone off. Each minute we waited was agony, and I grabbed at a cigarette to try to calm my nerves.

Finally, the engine's whistle chimed; the station master gave the signal and the train lurched forwards. White swirls of steam billowed across the platform. I eased myself back into my chair, though we were far from safe. I opened my meagre bottle of rum and guzzled almost a third, thinking on the rashness of what I had done and the state of my paranoia.

If the conspiracy is as deep rooted as Hawthorn claims ... If that constable had arrested me ...

I felt I had lost all sense of what was real.

I stared out the window. A man stood at the end of the platform. His body was almost entirely consumed by steam. His posture was grand; he leant on a cane or stick, though that I couldn't fully see. He wore a white beard, or at least a moustache for that was what I noticed. The tone of his skin was ugly, particularly the deep red around his left cheek. As he passed my line of sight, I craned my neck and even managed to open the carriage window, whereupon I pushed my head and shoulders through and looked back towards the station. The man had seemingly vanished.

I sat back down, my eyes wide, my mouth dry. I near dropped the bottle of rum as I raised it to my lips, horror consuming the world around me so that I sat alone amidst black and shifting shadows with little else but my fears to comfort me.

Though he appeared somewhat different from when last I had seen him, I knew in my heart that I had just gazed upon Elijah Hawthorn. Or at least the ghost of him.

Memories Forgotten
September 9th, 1905

We got off the train at Aberdeen. There was no police presence on the platform, nothing untoward or suspicious that I could see. I gestured to Beatrice from some twenty yards away, and we both got back on the train as it pulled away. I found her in an empty compartment and sat opposite her, glancing nervously at the closed door.

'I saw him,' I muttered. 'On the platform, as clear as I see you now.' My words were frantic, agitated.

'Who?' Beatrice asked.

'Hawthorn.' I had leant close to her and hissed out his name. 'His spirit, his image. Did you not see him?'

'No,' she muttered. 'How could I—'

'What does it mean?' I muttered feverishly, my fingers rubbing my brow and cheek. 'Why would he come to me in such a way – why not seek to help me or speak with me?'

I lashed out suddenly, thundering my boot into my camera case.

'What the hell does it all mean! What the—'

I silenced myself, eased back in the chair, though twitched and mumbled under my breath.

Beatrice looked at me with a real air of concern. 'Is this why you were so nervous when we left?'

I shook my head as I struggled to light a cigarette.

'No. I saw him after we departed.'

'Then why did you want to switch trains at Aberdeen?'

I flicked the ash to the floor. 'In – um – in Adanburgh, a constable was asking about us. Seems the man in the coffee house must have said we were causing some fuss – no doubt your cross-dressing offended him.'

'You were the one who—' She stopped herself. 'What did you do?'

'I dealt with it,' I replied. 'When he comes to, he'll be no worse than before, bar a sore head and jaw.'

She looked at me aghast, leant back and stared up at the carriage ceiling. 'You struck him?'

'What choice did I have!'

'And now you claim to have seen a ghost in the station.'

'You don't believe me?'

She folded her arms and stared out of the window. I asked her once more but still she held her tongue. For the first time in some days I felt a sudden sense of loneliness. The disquiet between us hung as thick as the grey plumes of tobacco haze. As the train rattled on, it became almost unbearable.

'What do you plan on doing?' Beatrice asked at last.

'I have to learn the truth. I have to see things for myself. I need to go to the manor, the manor of Lord Cavendish-Huntley. Hawthorn claims it is where the cult—'

'The *cult*? You believe in it now?'

'I don't know what to believe! Whether you wish to come with me or not is your decision, but I am going.'

'All of this is such madness,' Beatrice muttered, shaking her head.

'You wished to learn the truth of your sister's death,' I said petulantly. It seemed to ignite something in her. She glowered at me as her pupils dilated, to such a degree, they seemed to consume the whites of her eyes. The soft features of her face grew sharp and callous in an instant.

'What were you doing before all this?' she asked bluntly. 'After *that* enquiry, the one in the village? You said you couldn't work; have you been working since then?'

I sighed. 'I was dealing with things.'

'Drinking yourself half to death, I imagine.' She thrust a finger at me. 'Where were you? When the disappearances began, whilst all this was going on, what were you doing?'

I was taken aback by the venom in her voice. 'Is this an interrogation?'

'It's an exercise in trust,' she snapped. 'Now answer the question.'

'I was in London, wishing myself dead most days, toying with the wrong end of a gun on others.' I resented my own words, my own insufferable self-pity. 'You think I had some hand in this, or at least want to ask the question.'

'I want to know that all you say is true, that this lunacy – this cult – is not some concoction of your own making.' She seemed furious then; my anger erupted at her incredulity.

'I had no part in this!' I growled. 'You think I am responsible for the graveyard that is Pike Ness?' I was shouting then, for the rum had dulled my sensibilities. My fists were clenched so much, the knuckles shone white.

'That's not what I meant,' Beatrice said, her voice more subdued. She tried to hush me. 'I meant—'

'You think me a killer, a deranged man?'

'That's not true—'

'To hell with you!' I grabbed up my camera case, left the compartment and walked back down the carriage. I waited by the door for the next station. I'd get away from Beatrice and uncover the truth of the whole affair on my own. I'd leave her behind and learn who had slain Hawthorn, who had done such wrong by him. I didn't need her – I needed no one.

My sudden resolve was short-lived.

I stood, a man alone, a man afraid.

Maybe I *was* insane.

How many days in the past year could I fully recall, could I truly distinguish? How many had been spent blind drunk, where hours vanished in the blink of an eye and weeks flit by, barely acknowledged? How much could I truly remember, could I truly discern as reality or dream? How many nightmares had I forgotten, or worse still, relived?

I stopped myself. Such thoughts were absurd. No matter my state in recent months, I had no part in any of this. I knew it in my heart.

Five or ten minutes later, Beatrice appeared down the carriage and approached me slowly.

'I'm sorry,' she mumbled, 'it's not what I meant.'

'It is,' I said. 'Maybe from here it would be best we parted company. I don't know in good conscience if any of this story, this cult, is real, or if Hawthorn was badly deceived, or if something even more bizarre and unknown is at play.' I pulled out Hawthorn's signet ring. 'But I saw his body, saw those at Pike Ness and have no other lead than this Cavendish-Huntley and his estate. Maybe it will come to nothing – maybe not – but all I know is that I hope for the best, yet fear the worst to be true. I don't want you to have any further part in this if it is the latter.'

She nodded slowly. 'I've come so far, all this way, to learn the truth of my sister. I shan't stop now.' I tried to discourage her for a moment but she would have none of it. 'We'll learn the truth of all this in time. I know that.'

She turned and looked out of the window. It was hard to read her, to know what was going through her mind.

'You remind me of my sister,' I said quite abruptly, surprising even myself. She turned and looked at me, not knowing what to say but smiling, nonetheless. I felt embarrassed and looked down towards the floor.

I must have closed my eyes at some point, for in an instant, Beatrice, the compartment, the very train itself, were all gone. I was outside, sitting at a fine garden table, looking out across the ocean. Hawthorn was next to me, the man I remembered, the man I recognised as my friend.

'I always wanted to come here,' he said, face serene and calm, his voice gentle over the soft breeze.

'Where … where is here?' I asked, looking towards the horizon, tasting something ashen and bitter in my mouth.

'Not London,' he chuckled. 'It's always good to get out of London. That place eats you like a nest of vipers.' He sipped on a cup of tea, and I realised I held one as well. I couldn't look behind me, but didn't feel the need to. After a moment I felt very peaceful.

'Do you remember when we first met?' Hawthorn beamed. 'In Hyde Park, that fine summer. You were touting for business with the wealthy mothers and nannies, taking pictures of them with their children at play.' I smiled as I thought of that day. 'Sometimes,' Hawthorn continued, 'I fear I took you from a better life.'

'A poorer one,' I laughed.

'A simpler one,' he smiled. 'A life that didn't involve …' He waved his hand absently. 'We are such a miserable species, doing such terrible things to one another. You may have been poorer before, but you were free of all the depravity, of all the bloodshed the world of policing revealed to you.' He glanced over to me. 'You wouldn't be in the position you are now.' He said it as though I had a grave illness.

I looked at him. He sighed deeply.

'Yet some are born to do things in this world. I think you were born to be an investigator. Born to seek justice, to do your duty towards others.' He raised his mug to me, and we toasted that notion. The warmth of day seeped through my clothes and I settled back in my chair and stretched my legs out. I watched as a few yachts, with crisp white sails and vibrant flags like a peacock's plumage, drifted across the horizon, following each other one by one.

'I still can't believe this is all happening,' I said, speaking of my life that now seemed very far away. 'This madness, this cult. How you came to know of it.'

'I wish I hadn't,' Hawthorn spat. 'Henley and his sadist lot should have known I'd have no part in it.'

I frowned. 'I can't believe you. I just ... I just can't believe any of it.' I looked at him and he nodded solemnly. 'It's just so fantastical, so absurd.'

'You shouldn't believe it,' he said firmly, setting down his mug and pointing a thick finger at me. 'The first thing I, and others, taught you was to accept nothing as fact until you have sufficient evidence, until you have the proof you need.'

I reached inside my coat pocket, pulled out Hawthorn's gold signet ring with his initials embossed on it. 'Is this evidence? Is this proof you are dead?'

He took the ring from me and placed it back on his finger. 'That, and my being here.'

I looked at him quizzically and then pointed out to the sea. 'Where is here?' I asked again, though in my heart I knew.

'Where we go. When one world spits us out, another takes us.'

I scowled. 'Don't joke about such things.'

He shook his head. 'It's no joke. In spite of what we have thought for hundreds of years, this place is not separated into the good and the bad; there's no judgement at a set of gates.' He gestured to the space around him. 'We all just come here. Together.'

'Together?' I said as my skin began to ripple with an unpleasant chill.

'Together,' he repeated. 'Those the world has deemed to be good, and those the world has deemed to be evil.' He clasped his hands on his lap and closed his eyes. Everything started turning cold. The sun began to lose its lustre and all around became tinged in a stark and unpleasant white light. I reached for Hawthorn across the table, but my arms wouldn't move. I tried to call his name, but my words were as quiet as a whisper. The yachts on the horizon slipped slowly below the grey water; it in turn began to freeze and still entirely.

I yelled out Hawthorn's name, pleaded with him to listen. But he was frozen like the water, his eyes frosted, his smile unflinching. It was such a horrid scene that I turned away and tried to run. My legs carried me, and I scampered over hard grass and compacted earth. Then nothing, for all light vanished as if a thousand candles had been snuffed out at once.

In the darkness, I spoke to Hawthorn as if he were still beside me. 'I'll find the truth. I'll find those who took your life and then I'll take mine. I'll come here and find you. I'll come here.'

I was weeping on my knees. My words had no volume, no echo. They fell on no one's ears but my own. I waited. And I waited. For what felt like an eternity in darkness, I stayed where I was and waited.

And only when I thought my wait would never end, did a thousand hands with daggers for nails, reach from the darkness, slit my throat and tear me limb from limb.

I woke suddenly, completely disorientated. I was confused for far too long, lost in the memories of my dream. I had no idea what was happening, yelled with timid voice for Hawthorn to come back. Beatrice stayed beyond my reach, though tried to settle me, her hands raised, her voice calm.

'What's all this?' The conductor of the train opened the compartment and stepped in. I moved away from him, pushed myself into the corner of the tight space. My first real moment of clarity was observing the gold buttons of his jacket, how finely they were polished. Then I looked from his stony face to Beatrice.

'A bad dream,' Beatrice said quickly to the conductor. 'He gets them from time to time.'

'Answer me!' the conductor said to me, dismissing Beatrice entirely. He stepped over to me with one large stride, pulled on my coat roughly and sniffed around my collar. 'If you're drunk, I'll have you off—'

'He's not! Please.' Beatrice tried to squeeze between us, but couldn't.

'Bloody bum.' The conductor stepped back a little. 'I'll have you off at the next station; not having drunks causing a fuss—'

'Wait,' I groaned, reaching for my ticket. The conductor stepped back to me. I flashed it to him, whilst clumsily handing him a shilling. 'For the trouble. It won't happen again.'

He glared from me to the coin in his hand. His face turned crimson; his flat nose twitched.

'Where are you getting off?'

'Cambridge.'

He huffed. 'I hear another peep, and you'll be off the train, no matter where we are.' He left the compartment then and stormed down the carriage.

Beatrice turned to me and knelt at my side. I rubbed my temples, for they seared with pain; my mouth was coarse and dry. I shook so badly that when I tried to reach inside my coat, I struggled to grab what was in my pocket.

'You were yelling. You were yelling whilst you slept.'

I nodded.

'What were you dreaming of?'

'Hawthorn,' I croaked.

She pulled at my shirt collar, rubbed a finger – as cold as ice – along my skin. Her eyes were filled with concern.

'You're bleeding. How are you bleeding?'

I rubbed my neck, saw then the blood on my hands and thought of all those that had come for me.

Beatrice stared in horror. 'How are you bleeding?'

The Village of the Cult
September 10th, 1905

Our journey was long, and delayed so much, that when we finally reconnected at Cambridge and travelled the remaining distance to Haxteth Hill (the nearest station to the village of Burton Haxteth), the hour had long passed midnight.

No one else disembarked from the ramshackle train. A decrepit wooden sign pointed down a black road; the village was a mile away.

We trudged into the darkness, feet blistered and aching, arms sore, eyes heavy. We spotted a barn nestled just off the road and skipped a fence to rest inside. There seemed little else to do; the hour was late, and my exhaustion had only fuelled my paranoia. Even if more comfortable accommodation had been available, I doubt I would have elected to stay anywhere that would garner unwanted attention. I wanted as few eyes upon us as possible.

The barn was completely empty, with not even straw to rest on. Despite my best efforts, I could not sleep, and when the first light of morning broke, it brought with it heavy rain that pattered through cracks in the shabby barn roof. The water splashed around my feet, dripped against my face and hands. It woke Beatrice with something of a start.

'Your neck,' she mumbled, rubbing her eyes and face. 'It's still bleeding.'

I ran a finger across my collar, felt the slender scratch that had not healed, and rubbed tacky blood between my fingers.

'No one scratches themselves like that in sleep,' she said. 'I've never heard of such a thing.'

'Well, how else do you explain it,' I coughed. I lurched up and left the barn, my back throbbing mercilessly.

The day was frightfully cold. We carried along the road until we saw a row of neatly kept cottages with well-tended gardens and thatched rooves. An old woman was sweeping in her door-way. She had the features of a crow: a small head with sharp nose, thin hair pulled back like sleek down. She wore a fine black gown and light blue shawl. We tried to move quickly past her, but she spotted us from the corner of her eye and called out to us harshly. We both stopped and turned; I smiled as best I could, as the rain pelted down on me.

She asked who we were.

'Newspaper reporters,' I beamed. 'Here from London, doing a piece on Lord Cavendish-Huntley and Burton Lodge.'

She stopped sweeping, set down her twisted broom and peered through eyes overcast by heavy wrinkles.

'You don't look like a reporter. Vagrant if you ask me.'

'I assure you, myself and the young lad here are doing work for a paper.' Beatrice scowled at me when I glanced to her. I held up my case and patted it. 'My camera, you see.'

The old woman shook her head, squinting towards Beatrice. 'Young lad?' She gazed back at me, poked her neck. 'You're bleeding.'

I hesitated, ran a finger on the thin wound and acted surprised. 'Oh yes, must have been a cut from a shave.' I said this even as I rubbed the heavy stubble around my cheeks and chin. 'The lodge is up beyond the village, I gather.'

The old woman crossed her arms. Her lower jaw moved from

left to right as she mulled us over. Eventually she threw her arm in the direction we were heading. 'The village is just up here. Go left at the square and follow the track for about half a mile. You'll see the lodge, the castle.'

I thanked her cordially and we walked quickly away.

'She's still watching us,' Beatrice whispered, glancing over her shoulder. Indeed she was. The old crow stood like a statue, her legs bowed under what little weight she carried.

'Just keep walking,' I muttered. Soon the road bent, and we were out of sight, though I felt as though the woman was still surely standing in the deluge, thinking on our brief encounter.

This sense of being watched, of being marked and observed with suspicion, was not new to me. As we came into the village proper, crossing a wide stone bridge that spanned a fast-moving river, I noticed a tailor's and a small general store were both closed. Church bells rang out; the few little streets that led off the main road were steadily filling with men, women and children. They greeted each other heartily with warm smiles and firm handshakes, despite the frightful rain worsening with every passing minute. They began to congregate in the street around us, moving four or five abreast up the road. I cursed under my breath.

We stopped by the general store. 'Too many people have seen us,' I murmured, staring down at the floor. 'They're all looking at us.'

They were. Men in particular stared, their smiles and laughter quickly turning callous and dark when they spotted our dirtied clothes and unwashed faces.

'Just try to stay calm,' Beatrice whispered.

I didn't answer. A young couple, perhaps in their early twenties, stepped over to us. The man, slight and pale, smiled and tipped his cap. His wife, for I saw the simple band she wore on her finger, looked quite pained to be next to us.

'Morning,' the man said, his voice laced with dwindling confidence. 'Morning to you.'

I smiled thinly. 'Morning.'

'Are you, um … are you passing through?' He clung tightly to his wife's arm.

'No, we're from a London newspaper, here to look at Burton Lodge and its owner.'

The young woman beamed. 'You're here to speak with Lord Cavendish-Huntley?' I nodded. 'Well that's marvellous, he's a wonderful man.'

'You've met him?' I asked with some surprise.

'Oh yes,' the young man nodded, his voice gaining volume and enthusiasm. 'He's ever such a kind man, has done so much for the village over the years.'

'His father renovated the castle – the lodge – you know,' the young woman cut in, 'restored it to all its former glory.'

'We have a great deal to be thankful to him for. To the whole family. They're truly marvellous people.'

They continued in this vein until the young man stopped abruptly. 'Strange, for I thought the Lord was away on other business for several weeks. He said he would return for the harvest moon festival.'

I felt my face flush. 'He is expecting us presently; our arrangements were made some months ago.'

The young man hesitated. 'I'm sure. And there are more of you—' He broke off as his wife gestured at him. 'I'm sorry, the sermon will soon be starting in the square. Perhaps you would attend – get some flavour of the village for your article.'

'In the square?' I asked, looking out onto the pouring rain.

'It's tradition,' the young man smiled. 'In the weeks leading up to the harvest, we have our Sunday prayers in the morning air, in all of God's glory. It's to bring good fortune.'

Neither Beatrice nor I said anything. The young woman tugged on her husband's arm. 'Well,' he said cordially, 'it was good meeting you.' He was pulled away then, though looked back towards us more than once.

'I've heard of such superstitious practices,' I whispered to Beatrice. 'Those who wish to indulge in pagan rituals and the like.' I watched as those walking along the street dwindled to all but a few stragglers who dashed through the rain in the direction of the town square. The old crow we had passed sweeping in her doorway didn't seem to notice us.

Beatrice shrugged. 'What of it? It's all harmless.'

'Perhaps. In any other circumstance.'

She scoffed. 'You think it's part of this cult, don't you?'

I began towards the square. Beatrice followed close behind me.

'We should leave it. Let's just get to the lodge, or castle, or whatever it is if that's what we're here to do,' she urged.

I ignored her, and soon caught up to the elderly and infirm who made their way with careful step. We rounded a gentle corner and the gathering crowd came into view. They packed together tightly, for the square was not large. Three roads, including that by which we had come, led into it. Homes and a few more businesses enclosed the space – a church spire rose high above the rooves, though the church itself was barely larger than any other cottage. An overflowing fountain spouted in the middle of the square, its highest tier visible to me. Above the crowd I saw a priest in white robes, his bald head glossed with rain, his features appearing like melting wax. His smile shone out nonetheless, and he waved to those who murmured and laughed in the crowd. He wore a bronze crucifix around his neck, the chain tangled and knotted. It inverted the crucifix, though he seemed not to notice.

We held back, standing in the doorway of a cobbler.

'We should go,' Beatrice insisted once more, though just then the priest raised his hands to hush the crowd. The murmuring stilled instantly, and all laughter died away. With his face now solemn, the priest gently lowered his hands. To my astonishment, the entire crowd – men and women, young and old – dropped to their knees in the rain and the dirt of the stone. Some were quicker than others, though the priest stayed silent till the last old beggar got down to the floor. I pulled Beatrice closer into the doorway, for then we were easily seen. The priest brought his hands together, then looked up to the heavens, as water kissed his face.

'Glory be unto God, for that which comes from the dirt, from the earth, from below, is glorious.' The crowd repeated these words, their voices united.

'Praise be to He whom we worship, whom we offer our thanks to, whom we show our devotion to at this most sacred time.'

The crowd repeated, the eerie chant drifting over the patter of rain.

'Let us give thanks, let us ask for His blessings, and let us sacrifice for others.'

The crowd replied, before joining in a silent prayer. The inverted crucifix drew my attention, for it seemed to shake and glimmer in the dull light of day. The words of the priest filled me with such disquiet and unease that I felt myself shift away from him. I glanced at Beatrice, who looked at me with real concern. She gestured for us to go, to leave via the street we had come from, though in the silence of the crowd's prayer, I dared not move, lest they hear and turn upon me.

The inverted crucifix held my gaze and began to glow, to throb with a blinding light that pained me. My skin tingled, itched, began to burn; my heart raced with such terrible speed I thought it would burst from my chest. The silence of the crowd was terrifying, the light of the crucifix all consuming …

'Praise be to our Lord and Saviour!'

I was startled by the sudden outburst, the roar of cheers that followed as people threw their arms to the air. The priest gestured for all to stand, which they did with laughter and good heart.

'Let us give thanks now to the Lord whom we worship, whom we serve with unwavering loyalty, and whom – if so satisfied – shall gift us a bountiful harvest.'

In unison, the crowd gently drifted into song. I exhaled deeply and grasped my chest with stiff fingers. Beatrice leant close to me.

'For God's sake, we must go. You're in no condition – don't do that—'

I drank the last of my rum. Beatrice cursed and looked around. The crowd's hymn was of the fields and the green pastures, though I hadn't heard it before.

'This has to end,' she said then, her palm pressed against her forehead. 'I can't do this.'

I nodded. 'You do what you feel is best.' I stood straight, gathered myself and made to head to the road bearing left out of the square, that which led to Burton Lodge.

'If you do this, it will not end well. It will not end well for you. I just know it.' I glanced at Beatrice and was taken aback, for tears spilled from her eyes. 'Just run away, just get away from this place and keep running. Don't look back – I'm sure in time you will overcome your demons.'

I shook my head. 'Such demons as mine will never leave m—'

I pressed myself hard against the door.

'What are y—'

I hushed her, then pointed out across the square. She struggled to see what I had spotted, though when they came into view she gasped aloud. The two figures, in their dark tunics and black cloaks, stepped closer towards the priest.

'Why the hell are there Metropolitan Police sergeants here,' I whispered sharply. The polished badges on their helmets were easily recognisable. With slow steps, they disappeared behind the crowd.

Beatrice muttered something, though I wasn't truly listening. 'It's real,' I murmured in total disbelief. 'They must have known we were coming somehow.'

The two sergeants were still out of sight, and hurriedly we scampered away from the square. I looked over my back, waiting for the inevitable cry to halt, the sudden charge of heavy boots. None came, though we didn't stop running until we crossed the wide stone bridge and were back along the country lane. Beatrice brought us to a standstill.

'It's real,' I gasped, my tired mind struggling to find the words, my greatest fears seemingly justified. 'How else could they know we were here?'

Beatrice threw off her cap. 'The constable in Scotland. The man you assaulted—'

'They had no idea we were coming *here*; I bought us tickets to Cambridge. Unless they had men waiting at the station who learnt where we were going, but that seems highly unlikely.'

'Enough,' she said.

'If the Scottish police had wanted to stop us, they could have at Aberdeen, or Edinburgh even. Why would they send for Metropolitan Police – how could they know we would be coming here!'

'Enough,' she said louder.

I rubbed at my face and paced nervously. 'They didn't know

anything about us coming. That must be the truth. The police are here watching this place – they probably have orders directly from Henley, are likely posted here day and night.'

I felt myself growing hot. Thoughts swirled in my mind and I was addled, overwhelmed. Beatrice tried to calm me, but I wouldn't be stilled.

'Cavendish-Huntley's lodge holds the truth of all this.' I pointed at her, standing over her, searing with anger, with dismay. 'We'll find the truth of it all within those walls.'

'Thomas.' She grabbed my hand then, her skin so painfully cold I pulled away from her. 'Thomas, please, get a hold of yourself.'

'We'll find a way around the village. There have to be more ways to get to the lodge.' I began walking along the road, only stopping to turn back to Beatrice.

'Do you want to learn the truth of your sister? After all this time?'

I thought she was afraid, for she stood looking so meek as the rain poured over her, so small and fragile.

She wiped her eyes. With a renewed look of conviction, she nodded and trudged after me.

Revelations

September 10th, 1905

In the cover of tall grass, we lay and looked at the lodge. It was indeed a castle, a Norman age keep. Flags of red and gold flickered in the wind from a single turret; no one entered or left through the tall front doors.

Beatrice had said nothing since leaving the village. I spoke more to myself than to her.

'There has to be some other means in; servants' doors or the like.'

She didn't answer. Her face was wasted of colour, of life. I was dragging her into something far beyond anything she could have imagined when first she found me. I thought to place my hand on hers, to offer her some reassurance. But I kept still.

'You can stay here. Or leave. There's no reason you need come with me.'

She nodded her head. 'I know. I know.'

Her lip quivered as she spoke. I reached inside my coat and took out my Enfield revolver.

'For God's sake, don't.' Beatrice stared wide-eyed at the gun. 'Think of what you did in the manor. Think of what you almost did to *me*. Who knows who may be in there, who may have no idea about any of *this*.' She said the last word quietly.

I frowned, looking down at the gun in my hand. Reluctantly I tucked it back into my coat pocket.

'We'll skirt around the side, see if there's any way in. If Cavendish-Huntley isn't here, the place may only have a skeleton staff minding it.'

'We can still run,' Beatrice insisted. 'We can just leave. *You* can just leave!'

'I can't,' I replied sharply. 'I have to know the truth.'

With nothing else said, I moved from my vantage point. I dashed around in a wide arc, hiding in the cover of a few trees as best I could. Between us and the castle was a shallow decline of open grass. Beatrice scampered behind me.

After a short distance, I stopped.

'We just need to move across the grass,' I whispered. 'Don't run. It will only fuel suspicion if anyone sees us. Just walk quickly.'

After a moment's composure, and leaving my camera case behind, we did, for there seemed nothing else for it. We walked briskly, side by side, quickening our pace as we came to a gravel road that surrounded the castle. We pressed ourselves against its walls, hugging them as we crept around the exterior. We found a wooden trapdoor and I pulled on it gently. It opened freely, with no creak of the hinges. Steps led downwards. Dim light shone from below. Beatrice grabbed hold of my arm.

'You don't have to.' She was pleading then, shaking her head.

Even through my coat I felt the cold of her touch, and almost asked why, since the day we had met, she had always been so badly chilled. But I didn't; I roughly pulled my arm away from her and stepped through the trapdoor. I was terrified yet determined, driven by a gruesome fascination. I would not let myself waver.

The steps led into a kitchen and pantry, the warmest place I had been for some time, for a raging fire crackled and spat in a wide hearth. As my feet touched upon a polished, pristine floor,

I heard a voice humming from somewhere close by. It was a woman's voice, pleasant and at ease. I couldn't see the woman herself, for alcoves and arches concealed much of the space from my view. I spied a stairwell leading upwards to my right and dallied as little as possible. Crouching low, I moved to the stairs and climbed them lightly. Beatrice followed, though hesitated a painfully long time in the kitchen itself. Her reluctance, was slowing her down.

We came to a heavy wooden door at the top of the stairs. I leant my ear against it, and hearing nothing from the other side, opened it as slowly as I could. Still crouched on our haunches, we moved into a dining room, neither grand nor particularly large, but well lit. Gas lamps glowed along every panelled wall. A table was laid, with golden candelabras and shimmering silverware. Our wet clothes dripped onto plush Persian rugs.

I knew what I was looking for: the grand hall that Hawthorn had written of, where the dreadful ceremonies were performed. I imagined a cold and loathsome place, the walls covered with mounted stag and doe heads. I envisaged a chandelier, made with twisted bones and sticks, and saw quite clearly, highchairs, like thrones for aged grandees, arranged in a circle around a bronze or golden font. There would be no blood on the floor, for this would have been regularly cleaned, scrubbed away after each terrible meeting, no doubt by the demented woman who now hummed pleasantly in the kitchen below. All this came so clearly to mind that I had no doubt I would find anything different. It would be enough – enough to prove my worst fears.

I was shaking. The slit on my neck began to throb. I wiped at it and crept through the dining room, coming to a set of double doors that I peeked through carefully. These led to the castle's foyer, a narrow space that was dimly lit. The dark wood panels here were decorated with fine gold leaf that stretched the length of the foyer and upwards across the ceiling. It was a splendid space, yet all seemed a farce to me – a cover, a show – for the real purpose of this formidable dwelling.

Beatrice turned suddenly and I heard the voice of the woman in the kitchen drawing nearer. We dove through the double doors into the foyer and there moved quickly towards the back of the castle. We passed two doors as we went; the first was locked, but the second was open. We ducked into a small sitting room and closed the door behind us. I pressed my body against it and listened intently. I heard the rattling of metal, the woman mutter to herself before she began to hum once more. She drew nearer to the door, and my heart lurched for a terrible instant, when I was certain she would try to come into the room.

But she didn't; she passed by along the corridor, and a moment later I heard nothing of her. I sighed with relief, my body quivering. Beatrice couldn't look at me. Quietly we left the room and moved back along the corridor. It turned right a little further along, and we soon came to a flight of stairs leading to the floor above. Another set of doors was set into the wall opposite the stairs, and I knew in an instant that these would lead to the grand hall of the estate. The door frame was splendidly carved, with animals of all shapes and size twisting and turning up bark and vines that stretched to the low ceiling. The creatures seemed gentle, almost joyous, as they scurried and larked with one another. The sight only made me shudder, for it was surely another dreadful front in this place. I tried the brass door handles, feeling them move; the doors were not locked.

Sweat dribbled down my brow; my stomach twisted with nausea. I pictured the room beyond the doors, seeing terrible men, men of trust, men of high position, laughing, frolicking in the death of others, in the blood of the innocent. I imagined Henley's delight at knowing Hawthorn was dead; I pictured him sitting amongst the mob, telling them of the good news. I pictured a thousand dreadful things in a single beat of my racing heart and could barely contain my emotions. Beatrice took hold of my arm, looking so desperate as she stared down at the door handles, petrified for her life, no doubt thinking of her sister. Her skin was charged – there was no other word I could think of to describe it. Her icy hands gave off a magnetism that made the hairs along my arm stand on end, a power that drew me closer to her. For an instant, I saw inside her thoughts, felt her fear, her anguish. And something else – another emotion behind the wide eyes that looked up at me. In that moment I couldn't place it. In that moment though, I knew nothing of her true self.

I tried to tell her it would be all right, but words failed me, and with no more hesitation, I opened the door to step into the hall.

'Don't,' Beatrice whispered.

I paid her no heed, reaching inside my pocket for my gun, expecting to find a cabal of men standing in ghastly robes, torturing some poor soul.

What I found was far different.

The hall was airy and light. A grand piano stood in the corner, a vase of beautiful autumnal flowers atop it. The walls were lined with spotless white paper; the ceiling castings were gold and shaped like branches from a tree. Thin, tall windows let in natural light. I noticed a child's rocking horse beside the piano, its saddle embroidered with blue stars.

My feet echoed on solid wood flooring. I looked to a fireplace on my left, saw candles lit along the mantel. There were framed photographs too, and I stepped to them – smiling faces, nothing of the formal family portraits I was used to. A man, Cavendish-Huntley I presumed, was in many of the pictures, as was a fair woman and a young boy, no more than four or five. I stared at the photographs with some confusion, for they were far from what I had expected to find. Evermore I looked at the man in the images, the man whom I had grown certain was some dreadful leader, some bloodthirsty tyrant. I recognised something in his face.

I looked back to Beatrice. She was clutching her arm with one hand, looking nervously around the room.

'Something's wrong,' I whispered. It struck me then how easily we had come into the building, how in all the time we had sat and observed the castle we had seen no police presence, not a single officer, despite the pair we had spotted patrolling Burton Haxteth. 'Something's terrib—'

I was cut short. Above the doorway we had come through, a landing from the second floor looked out across the grand hall. In the shadows, for no lamps were lit up there, I glimpsed a flash of movement, an arm with banded stripes across it. A gruff voice called out and I staggered backwards, raising my Enfield.

Beatrice yelled at me to stop. The door behind her burst open and five uniformed constables charged in, bearing their truncheons. I pointed my gun towards them, saw Beatrice move between me and them, her arms raised, her eyes squeezed shut. I held my fire, hesitated, screamed for her to move. In the blink of an eye she was gone. It knocked the wind out of me.

'Beatrice,' I muttered, stunned.

Before I knew it, a heavy hand had knocked the gun from mine. Arms wrapped around me. I tried to struggle, to free myself, screaming Beatrice's name. A voice from above cried out over mine. The constables unhanded me, though one grabbed hold of my revolver. I looked up towards the landing, saw rifle barrels poking out from the darkness, their muzzles aimed straight for my chest.

All became still then. The constables surrounded me, holding their truncheons above their heads. I spun around, searching for Beatrice and looking up towards the landing, waiting for the unseen figure in command to show himself. The rifles twitched ever so slightly.

'You have his gun, lads?' The man who spoke was Irish, his voice brash. I recognised it then but couldn't understand.

'Yes, sir,' one of the constables replied. Silence then, nothing but the clicking of the twitching guns and the heavy breathing of the constables. They glared at me, looked at me with such scorn.

'What have you done with her?' I wailed. 'What have you done with Beatrice? Answer me!'

None of them flinched, though a young man with dark hair shook his head, disgusted. After a few moments, the doors to the hall swung open. Jeremy Flynn, the man Henley had introduced in my meeting at the Yard, stepped in quickly, his three-piece suit badly stretched over his massive frame. Lavernock walked in behind him.

Flynn stood beside the constables; he towered some inches even over them. When Lavernock came close, I growled at him like a wild animal.

'You're involved in all this, Jack – are you running things for Henley and his little band of followers?'

Lavernock seemed genuinely crestfallen. He shook his head, looked me up and down with pity.

'Tommy,' he muttered.

'Mr Bexley,' Flynn said, folding his meaty arms together. 'You're under arrest for multiple charges of kidnap, murder, perverting the course of justice and tampering with evidence relating to a crime. My men here will be taking you into custody and escorting you back to London.'

'*Your* men!' I snapped, looking from the constables to the rifle barrels still aimed at me.

'Special Branch, Mr Bexley, under the authority of Commissioner Henley. We thought, if Hawthorn was the guilty man, he would need an accomplice, someone to help him with his scheming. Never thought for a moment it was all a sham, that you were setting Hawthorn up.'

He gestured to one of the constables who took out a pair of shackles and stepped behind me. I was so confused I barely resisted as he took hold of my wrists.

'Setting Hawthorn up—'

'You'll have our evidence put before you, there's plenty of time for that. With recent revelations that have come to light, no court in the land is going to find you innocent.'

'Beatrice! What have you done with Beatrice?'

Flynn turned to Lavernock, who in turn only shrugged.

'Who's Beatrice, Mr Bexley?'

'Don't play the fool,' I spat, rattling my shackles. 'She was with me just now; she's been with me ...'

'Our men clocked you in the town square,' Flynn snarled. 'We've been watching you since you left and made your way here. You've been alone, alone this whole time.' He gestured impatiently to the constables. 'Take him away, for God's sake, he's soft in the head.'

'Beatrice! Beatrice, what's happening, what's happening?' I tried to crane my neck and struggled with the constable holding my shackled wrists. He struck me hard in the spine with his truncheon, and I bent over double in agony. Flynn stood over me.

'You don't understand what's happening, Mr Bexley, because you're a madman. And you're going to pay for your crimes, rest assured.' He gestured to the constable who began hauling me away. I tried to turn, tried to look for Beatrice but wasn't able to. I yelled for her, screamed out her name, but to no avail. I was dragged from the hall, and the castle, with rifles pressed against my back.

Cold Draughts in Prison Cells

September 11th, 1905

My wrists had been rubbed raw by the shackles, for they were kept on me from Burton Haxteth all the way to North London. My back was so sore that I could barely lie flat on the wooden bed in the cell. There was no mattress, nor a pillow. I rested my head on a wooden block, with my coat wrapped and stuffed around it.

I lay on my side, drifting at times into sleep, for the light shining through the small cell bars set into the heavy door was barely enough to see my hand before my face. Some foul-smelling straw was strewn about the floor, and twice I woke and saw something rustle through it. The night air and the elements rushed and spattered in through bars set just above the head of the bed. I felt the cold, and the wet, for the rain had not abated.

We were in a quiet station – Walthamstow – and had stopped, no doubt, due to the unseemly hour at which we had arrived. I'd lost track of how long I had been crammed in the back of the dreadful carriage, flanked on all sides by plainclothes members of Special Branch. No one had said anything to me along the road, nor when I was dragged into the station. The rifle muzzles I was growing accustomed to were aimed straight at my back and chest as I was marched into one of two cells. I heard no voices of rowdy drunkards, no yells of innocence or angry exchanges from the cell beside mine. The place was eerily quiet, in fact, which did little to distract me. I thought mostly of Beatrice; Beatrice, who I longed to see, whose whereabouts I knew nothing of. I was convinced that she had hidden in the instant the police had barged into the hall; she had flung herself into hiding and had not been seen. It was the only explanation.

I was roused by the sound of heavy keys clinking as they turned in the cell door. It was pushed open slowly; a young constable stood nervously with the keys in his hand. One of Flynn's plainclothes officers pointed a rifle at me.

'Get up,' he snarled.

I didn't move at first. 'Where are we going?'

'Get up,' he repeated, his words more forceful. I sighed – there seemed no point in aggravating the situation. It would only end with me being winded by the rifle butt, or having my lip split open by a heavy punch. I was too weary, too depressed, to struggle or fight back. I slid from the bed, sat for a moment, for the world around me spun a little. The man growled once more, and I stood and faced him.

'Walk slowly from the cell,' he said, before backing away from me. I did as I was told. The young constable seemed mortified to be standing next to me. He took a pair of shackles from the floor and looked from the man with the rifle to me, the whites of his eyes glowing hot in the candlelight around us. I held out my wrists and clumsily he handcuffed me.

'All right,' the gruff fellow said, lowering his gun. 'We're taking him to the interrogation room. Lead on.'

The constable grabbed hold of my cuffs and began leading me from the cells. We walked down a tiled corridor to an unmarked door with a severe-looking sergeant outside. A thick red scar was cut across his cheek. He nodded to both men as they approached, his face twisting with revulsion as he looked upon me. He opened the door, and I was made to sit at a table and wait. I asked for a cigarette, but no one answered. The door was left open, and the men murmured as they watched my back. I heard Lavernock's voice before he walked around the table and sat opposite me.

'That's fine, sergeant, just wait outside.' The door was closed behind me.

Lavernock set his hat on the table, took out a notebook and pencil before reaching for a pack of cigarettes. Without a word he pulled out two, placed both in his mouth and lit them with a match. He offered me one, which I took with a nod. The ashen tobacco taste was heavenly.

'We got a lot to talk about, Tommy.'

'What time is it?' I croaked.

'About one in the morning. They asked me to come and formally charge you.' He spoke gravely, leaning back in his chair. I didn't reply, the links of chain from my cuffs rubbing against each other as I brought the cigarette up to my mouth.

'You can stay quiet all the way to the hangman if you want – it won't make a blind bit of difference to them.'

Still I didn't talk.

He sighed after a few minutes. 'Word from these Special Branch boys is that you snapped, mate, completely lost it some time ago. They found a diary on you, lots of stuff about a cult, some conspiracy that Henley and his government friends were a part of.' He shook his head. 'It's signed off by Elijah Hawthorn. Do you really think he wrote it? D'you really think there's some cult taking over the country; that they're behind the Wraith kidnappings?'

I stayed quiet, though hearing the cult mentioned so lightly filled me with burning fury. I stubbed out my cigarette on the table and looked at the floor.

'They reckon you're seeing things, too. I think I can attest to that, knowing what you were like when we arrested you.' He flicked away his cigarette. 'Flynn had his suspicions, but none of us thought you capable of something like this.'

I kept my gaze down. Lavernock leant forward.

'When that lot from Special Branch said you'd done a runner, snuck out of London somehow, it all kicked off. They were following you the moment you left the Yard, were watching your house even before I brought you in.' He smirked. 'You did well to lose them. They expected you to run but waited at the wrong station. Me and the lads from CID had your door in that night, tore your whole place apart.' He tapped his finger hard down on the table. 'After what we found, Henley had every constabulary in the country wired. You were top priority to find. Of course, we now know where you were, up in that little fishing hamlet. There's men there, combing the place – that island – as we speak.'

I didn't answer.

'Some old bloke raised the alarm.' He flicked through his notebook. 'Fella named Lachlan Montgomery. Claims you were half crazed, delusional. Wanted to be taken out to the island, kept talking about some *assistant* you were with, though you were alone. You'd arranged for him to collect you, but it seems you had other plans.' He looked me straight in the eye. 'He claims you jumped him on the mainland, tried to kill him, beat him near senseless. From what I hear, it's a miracle he's alive. When he woke, he found the whole village poisoned, managed to struggle to a place called Donalbain where he wired the local police from a train station.'

I thought about Lachlan, realised then why he hadn't returned to the island. I didn't understand – how could he think I had tried to kill him? And what was he talking about – he had seen Beatrice with me!

'They think they've found Hawthorn's body, though there's not much to identify him. It hardly matters; the evidence on your person and found at your home is enough—'

'What evidence?' I snarled then, for I couldn't contain myself. It was his turn not to answer.

'This is madness, Jack. You may not be a part of it, but Henley and his band are setting me up—'

'Tommy—'

'If not this cult, how do you explain how I was tracked down? How do you explain Flynn and his men waiting for me at Cavendish-Huntley's estate—'

'Enough, Tommy!' He smacked his hand hard down against the table, threw back the chair he was sitting on. He stood and leant right over me, his eyes desperate despite his anger. 'With the evidence we found at your home, you left us a bloody trail. We knew where to wait for you. There is no conspiracy here, no one is setting you up, no one is trying to deceive you. It's all a fantasy of your own making, a story you're telling yourself.'

I shook my head and tried to dismiss him, though a growing, toxic dread brewed in the pit of my stomach. He grabbed my shoulder and squeezed tightly.

'How many days in the last year can you actually remember, Tommy? How many times does your mind go blank, or do you just recall waking up, having no real memory of where you've been or what you've done?'

'Jack. I know I have no part in this.'

'Do you?' He couldn't hold my gaze and rubbed at his eyes. 'They've got enough evidence to pin all the Wraith kidnappings on you, all of them.'

'What possible eviden—'

'And they want to know where the bodies are, that's their priority now. With those thirty people dead in that hamlet as well, there's no hope for you. They've got no doubt about your guilt; just spare everyone any more misery and tell the truth.'

He spat out the last few words before pacing a little around the floor.

'Ever since that damned enquiry in South Wales, ever since you came back, you were different. Something broke inside of you, didn't it?' He nodded even when I didn't reply. 'We all feel it, getting close to that dangerous edge, the point where you think *one more body, one more murdered wretch laid to waste in the dirt and I'll scream and forget what it means to be a decent man*. We all feel that, Tommy, some of us just stay on the right side of the edge.'

'You really believe I did this?' I was struggling to keep my voice steady. 'You think I kidnapped and murdered men and women? You think what; that I butchered Hawthorn and framed him with a bloodied thumbprint at one of the crime scenes – that I helped myself go to sleep at night by creating a fairy tale—'

'I don't believe it, I know it,' he snapped. For a moment he seemed as though he was going to erupt, to scream and yell at me. But when he spoke once more, his tone was softened by regret. 'I know it. The evidence doesn't lie.' He stepped away from me and gathered his notebook and pencil from the table. 'Your head's gone – your mind's hiding things from you.'

'Jack, I had no part in this. Where's Beatrice?'

'Who?'

'Beatrice, the woman I've been with this whole time. The sister of Dorothy Clarke. She'll attest to my innocence.'

He stepped over to the door. I began to panic and tried to reach out to him. He pushed me back with some force and hammered on the door until it swung open.

'Henley's on his way. He wants to talk to you first-hand, go through all the evidence properly, give you a fair hearing, would you believe.' He sighed. 'I can't do this.' He left without another word.

'Jack. Jack! I had no part in this. Jack!'

He didn't return, no matter how loud I yelled.

The Rough Side of the Law

September 11th, 1905

Sometime in the hours before dawn, I was woken roughly by uniformed constables who grabbed me from the wooden bed I slept on and dragged me from my cell. The young constable who had guarded me earlier was gone, as was the plainclothes Special Branch officer with the gun. The sergeant with the scar across his face stood with an apple in hand. He took a large bite, smiling deviously.

'Give him a good hiding, lads.'

They saw to it that I got a beating. Weak and tired, I was barely able to cover my face, as heavy boots clumped into me, as truncheons smacked against my arms and legs. I was winded and bloodied within an instant, though it lasted for some time, blow after blow, strike after strike. When I felt consciousness start slipping from me, the sergeant called out, his words warbled and unclear. I was dragged back to the cell, left sprawled on the straw that covered the floor. I have no recollection of the door closing, or of any time passing.

Water, colder than that off the shores of Pike Ness, was dashed across me. I screamed out, tasted the blood that lined my mouth and gums before the pain that barraged my skull and seared through my body came into focus. Instinctively I covered my face, lurching painfully, for I feared another beating would ensue.

A figure stood over me, though my vision was blurred and hazy.

'Jesus, Hendricks, you kicked him half to bloody death.'

Another voice, that of the sergeant, spoke up. 'He was causing trouble, sir. Making a few remarks at the men.'

'Like hell he was.' The man knelt down and grabbed me up by the scruff. He patted my face roughly and I focused enough to realise it was Flynn from Special Branch. 'How long did ya' work him over, ya' fool? There's roughing a fella up and then there's this.'

The sergeant stepped into the doorway. 'After what he's done, all those people he killed—'

'You're not a judge and jury here, Hendricks. And the commissioner down the hall won't take kindly to eediots beating men to a bloody pulp before they've been properly questioned.'

He let me fall back to the floor and I groaned aloud.

'Get him up,' Flynn spat, and two men took me by either arm and got me to my feet. I nearly fell straight back down, my legs buckling under my weight.

'Shall I cuff him?' one of the men on my arm asked feebly.

'Do you think he's going to cause any bother?' Flynn rasped. 'Get him down to the commissioner.' He cursed in words I'd never heard before as I was dragged back down the tiled hall to the interrogation room. I was surprised to find Henley already waiting inside. He sat with straight back and hands clasped, papers and documents spread out before him. He barely twitched as I was forced into the chair opposite him; Flynn walked around the room and stood in the corner.

The door behind me remained open. Henley gestured with the smallest flick of his head and the door was pulled shut. No doubt keen ears remained on the other side listening.

Henley cleared his throat.

'What happened?' he asked Flynn without turning to look at him.

'The sergeant here let things get carried away.'

I spat blood on the floor at that. Flynn scowled and folded his arms.

'See to it that it doesn't happen again. This is a serious case, and will no doubt be in the public gaze soon. We must be seen to be acting to the letter of the law at all times, understood?'

Flynn nodded. 'It won't happen again, sir.'

Henley kept his eyes on me. He brushed at his moustache, took a deep breath as though he were contemplating where to begin.

'Would you care for a cigarette?'

That threw me off guard; I shook my head and croaked. 'A drink.'

'We'll fetch you some water.'

I shook my head again. 'A *drink*. I need it.'

Henley sighed. Flynn stepped forwards and for a moment I was certain he was going to lunge at me, despite the words of the commissioner. Instead he reached inside his tight jacket, rummaged for a moment before pulling out a flask similar to the one I carried. He set it on the table, and I took it with no word of thanks. I drank the whisky in three large gulps.

'What happened to you, Bexley?' Henley said as I slid the flask back across the table. I didn't answer, wiping dried blood from my nose as Flynn snatched it up and returned it to his pocket. He stayed at the commissioner's side, glaring down at me menacingly. After a moment, Henley shuffled a few papers.

'There's a lot to go through, so we'll do it chronologically, piece by piece. Before I begin though, I'd like to ask you a plain and simple question, one I hope you will give me a straight and honest answer to, for the sake of – well – yourself, I suppose.' He leant forwards a little, gestured his clasped hands to me.

'I've seen the diary you were carrying with you upon your arrest. It seems to suggest that some conspiracy is at play, some underhanded cult behind the Wraith kidnappings, run in part by the Metropolitan Police, the organisation that you, for many years, worked for.' He pursed his lips together. 'Do you truly believe such a conspiracy is taking place? Can you be certain that the evidence you have seen leads you to such a conclusion?'

He waited for me to reply. I struggled to focus on his face, my left eye swollen and difficult to keep open. I didn't want to give the man any satisfaction, any sick pleasure for having pulled the wool over my eyes. I shrugged. 'Just get on with your bloody interrogation.'

Henley's face remained unchanged. He nodded slowly, leaned back and looked down at his papers.

'All right, Mr Bexley. We'll begin...'

The Evidence Laid Bare
September 11th, 1905

'A statement was made at East Ham Station in K Division on the nineteenth of August of this year, a week after the kidnapping of Heather Warren, the tenth known Wraith kidnap victim, who lived in the area. Miss Warren resided with her fourteen-year-old daughter who was out during the night of the kidnapping, likely making money to support her mother. The statement in question was made anonymously by an individual unknown to the station desk sergeant. The individual claimed to have sighted a man – Caucasian, regular build, under six-feet-tall – loitering in the area of Miss Warren's home in the days prior to her kidnapping on the twelfth of August. Furthermore, the anonymous source was able to give a potential identification for the man in question.'

Henley took a piece of typed paper, held it up and read from it slowly.

'*I recognised the man, seen his picture in the papers plenty of times. He was the police fellow, the investigator type who grew up around Spitalfields way. My mate used to live by him – I think he goes by the name Bedley, or Bexley.*'

Henley set the piece of paper down carefully. I tried not to react or flinch.

'Now that statement on its own is, frankly, no evidence at all. Since the Wraith kidnappings began, we've had hundreds,

223

perhaps thousands, of statements of a similar ilk. Men pointing the finger at enemies; women claiming the Wraith is the husband who abandoned her with three children. We've followed up on the more plausible lines of enquiry, but in general, most are simply recorded and set aside. It wasn't till the thumbprint of Elijah Hawthorn was found, on the twenty-second of August following the kidnapping of James Mortimer, that this particular statement became relevant.'

He slid over the image of the bloodied thumbprint, black against the bright white or cream of the vase it was found on. I stared down at the image, remembering the rank smell of Hawthorn's corpse, rotting in the cellar of the manor.

'You recognise this photograph?'

'Yes,' I muttered.

'You have seen it before, when we spoke at Scotland Yard on the fourth of September?'

'Yes, you were baiting me. Learning what I knew, feeding me information, a mouse for a trap!'

'Quiet!' Flynn roared, his right hand clenching. Henley hushed us both.

'We brought you in for good reason, Bexley. I told you then that we had gone through eighty thousand fingerprint records on file, that we had matched the bloody print we discovered with Hawthorn's. You understand how surprised we were, how shocked to see his name even associated with this. As a precautionary measure I had every written witness statement pertaining to the Wraith brought to the Yard and analysed by the CID. That's when we uncovered the statement I have just read to you.' He brushed at his moustache in thought for a moment. 'Hawthorn's print was a surprise; your name being associated with a suspicious sighting could have been no coincidence.'

I smirked bitterly, shifting uncomfortably in the seat. The

bruising and swelling from my beating were beginning to burn uncomfortably – my breathing was somewhat laboured.

'If you fake something, it's not a coincidence.'

Henley nodded. 'You want that recorded then, that you consider this statement, this *evidence*, to have been forged by the police?'

I said nothing in reply. Henley tapped his fingers on the table, a glimmer of frustration.

'You're not helping yourself; you understand that? Your previous relationship with Hawthorn, the closeness of your friendship, makes this statement more than merely intriguing. It is in fact, quite damning.'

'You hadn't been seen for months,' Flynn snarled, leaning across the table to me. 'Neither had Hawthorn. His thumbprint, and the sighting of you around East Ham connected two men who were both colleagues and good friends to a spate of murders with no other credible suspects.'

'I was nowhere near East Ham—'

'How can you be sure?' Henley interjected. 'Tell me what you were doing in the days leading up to the twelfth of August?'

I shook my head. 'I won't play this game.'

'Tell me.'

'How would I even know?'

'It was less than a month ago; you must surely have some idea.'

I thought, delved into my memories, tried to piece together where I had been, what I had been doing. It was impossible – my addled mind and body could barely recall the last few days. Even if I had not been tired and beaten, what was there to recall? I had been drunk much of the past twelve months, barely conscious of anything.

'I know I wasn't skulking around East Ham.'

'And you're certain of that? You can tell me plainly where

else you were then?' Henley was keen to press the point home. I grimaced at him, felt a surge of contempt lift me a little from my seat. Flynn barked at me to sit down.

'No. No, I can't tell you where I was.'

'What about the thirteenth, the day after Heather Warren was kidnapped? Were you anywhere south of the river, near the property of Daniel Pinkney? Did you try to break into his home that night – did something go wrong?'

'Of course not!'

'Pinkney claimed the man in his home couldn't have been in his sixties – moved too quickly. Did you wake him before you had ample time to subdue him—'

'This is all your miserable scheme, your bloody plot…'

Flynn erupted, stepping around the table in one big stride and hurling his fist into my left cheek. I collapsed from the chair, heard Henley yell at a volume I didn't know him capable of.

'Get him up! One more outburst, Flynn, and you'll be spending the next two days in the cell next to his!'

Flynn grabbed me up, his hands curling around the scruff of my collar, digging his fingers into my skin. He threw me onto the chair so violently I nearly collapsed off it once more. He didn't return to Henley's side but stood at my shoulder, inches from me.

Henley took a moment to compose himself.

'It won't happen again, Bexley. But please, answer my questions plainly.'

'I'll take that cigarette now,' I coughed, the side of my face searing with pain. Henley's eyes flashed up to Flynn; the bull of a man hesitated. I looked up at him, saw the utter contempt he had for me. He reached inside his pocket, took out a cigarette and match and threw both onto the table before me. I managed to light the cigarette feebly, though my lungs stung terribly with each deep intake of breath.

'We brought you in within a day of the CID getting hold of the witness statement linking you to the disappearance in East Ham. Jack Lavernock volunteered to come to your house and collect you; to be frank he didn't believe you could have any involvement in all this. I think he still has his doubts.'

'Haven't indoctrinated him then?' I shook my head, expecting another clout. None came. Henley slowly took hold a paper file and opened it carefully.

'You claimed to have not recognised the victim's names when I presented them to you at our last meeting. Would you care to see the list again?'

I shook my head. 'I didn't know any of them, Henley. How could I?'

He nodded and then began placing photographs on the table one by one. The photographs were of various people, men and women. Henley laid out five photographs in total.

'Recognise any of them?' he asked.

'No,' I replied, though in truth I gave the images only a cursory glance.

'You're sure? You don't want to look a little harder?'

The way he spoke and tapped his fingers against the table made my heart flutter. Coolly, I leant forward, looking from one photograph to the next. Three were portraits of a traditional appearance in front of a plain backdrop. Two were photographs in a field or green space, one I recognised vaguely. These photographs were familiar. I leant closer, my head resting against the hand that clutched my cigarette.

'I've never seen these before,' I lied, for in truth I knew I had, though couldn't recall where. My hand shuddered as I brought the cigarette to my bloodied lips. 'You'll be found out, you realise?

You know that, don't you?' I was speaking quite foolishly, though my head was dazed and I wanted to see Henley squirm. 'You left her out there – she was with me the whole time.' I laughed quite manically.

Henley nodded, his brow furrowed, his expression one of deep contemplation. 'Who is *she*, Bexley?'

'The one who's going to reveal you for what you are.' I looked up at Flynn. 'For what you all are. She's brave, smart; she'll find a way.'

'Who, Bexley?' Henley asked once more. 'Beatrice, is it?'

I recalled screaming her name out whilst being arrested. It didn't seem to matter. 'She escaped you at Cavendish-Huntley's estate. She's probably figuring out a way of bringing you all down. The truth – the bloody truth will come out then.'

'How long have you been seeing Beatrice?' Henley asked quietly, taking up a pen and making some notes.

'I'm not going to help you find her – you can go to hell!'

Henley only nodded. 'You feel close to Beatrice? Some sense of loyalty to her?'

I didn't answer. I consumed the last of my cigarette and flicked the ember down to Flynn's foot.

'The anonymous statement naming you was no solid evidence, of course,' Henley carried on. 'But it was enough to intrigue Flynn and his men at Special Branch. They followed you after you left the Yard, were meant to keep a watch on you, track your movements.' Henley coughed rather deliberately. 'You did well to evade them. How many men was it, Flynn?'

'Just two, sir. I take responsibility for it.' Flynn was clearly embarrassed – I smiled with grim satisfaction.

'We didn't know it at the time, but now know that you headed to Scotland. What drew you there?'

I folded my arms, held my tongue. Henley pulled out a tatty

piece of paper that I recognised immediately. It was Hawthorn's letter, crinkled and torn from all the hours and miles it had spent at the bottom of my coat pocket.

'That's mine,' I growled.

'It's evidence,' Henley remarked. 'We know why you went to Scotland, Bexley. We have the proof here; I've read it. This letter, one you believe to be written by Elijah Hawthorn, asked for you to come to Scotland, asked for your help, begged for it in fact. Were you aware of this letter when we spoke on the fourth of September?'

'I found it that night,' I snapped. 'Hawthorn was trying to warn me of you.' I spat as I spoke, and specks of blood dashed across the table. Henley stared down at them, his face unmoving.

'So, you found this letter – after we had spoken in Scotland Yard – and then travelled north, in search of Hawthorn. This letter is dated January of this year. Are you really claiming that it sat in your home for some eight months, without you being aware of it? That you happened upon it mere hours after we discussed Elijah Hawthorn as a suspect in the Wraith kidnappings?'

I held my silence.

'We took all the correspondence from your property, Bexley, read through them all. We believe this envelope corresponds to the letter in question.' He pulled a cream envelope from beneath a stack of papers, the very envelope that I had indeed torn open to discover Hawthorn's letter. 'Would you confirm that?'

'So what if it does?' I shrugged petulantly as Henley slid the envelope across the table.

'Notice anything about it?'

At first, I didn't pick it up. I stared at it, shrugged once more. I had no idea what path Henley was leading me down.

'Until recently you were one of the finest investigators this force had in its employ,' he uttered, before reaching across the table and tapping on the envelope thrice. 'Look at that envelope and tell me if anything odd strikes you about it.'

I snatched it up, causing a fresh wave of pain to sear through my arm. I looked at both sides of the envelope. My address scrawled in sepia ink; the handwriting I believed to be Hawthorn's. An ordinary Royal Mail stamp – national, first class. The envelope had been sealed neatly at the back. I was truly perplexed at what Henley could be talking about.

I tossed the envelope back on the table. 'There's nothing. Nothing distinct that I can see. What the hell is so special about a bloody—'

'Postal marks,' Henley said, taking the envelope and tucking it back beneath his papers. 'Ink stamps used at sorting offices when letters pass through them. This letter supposedly came from Scotland, all the way from Hawthorn himself – from north Aberdeenshire. There's not a single postal mark on it. Not one.'

I frowned, as Henley looked through his documents. 'Meaning what? The letter could have been sent by a courier—'

'With a Royal Mail stamp on top?' Henley sighed. 'It seems more likely this letter was not delivered, merely given the appearance of being delivered.'

'You claim it's a fake.' I laughed dryly. 'This is your grand scheme, to cry foul the bare evidence put against you.'

Henley ignored me. He took a few moments to read through documents, to make some further notes. His calmness, his empirical approach to this whole sham interview was starting to infuriate me. It seemed Flynn sensed my ever-darkening mood. He inched closer, so that the toe of his boot pushed against the leg of my chair.

'Upon leaving London, how did you travel to Pike Ness?'

Henley asked suddenly. 'We'll ascertain the route you took all in good time, or you can just tell us now, and save us the trouble.'

I held my silence.

'When did you start seeing this woman, Beatrice?'

I shook my head. 'Seeing her—'

'Yes,' Henley replied. 'Seeing her. When do you first recall seeing her?'

'The overnight train to Glasgow.' I regretted saying it immediately.

'And she was with you from then on?'

I said nothing.

'Was she with you when you arrived at Pike Ness?'

Still I held my tongue.

'Do you recognise the name Lachlan Montgomery?'

I saw the old fool's decrepit face; heard the words he had sung as we had rowed to the island. 'He's another man you've brought into this.'

'Really?' Henley nodded. 'All right, how so?'

It was my time to lean across the table, to hammer down my finger accusingly. 'You kept him alive for a reason. It's clever. If you'd killed *everyone* in Pike Ness there'd be no one to testify against me. How much does it cost to change the testimony of a wretched man like him?'

Henley took a deep breath. 'Lachlan Montgomery barely survived a grizzly assault; he was beaten so badly that he sustained several broken ribs and a fracture to the skull. It's quite astounding he even regained consciousness, a miracle he was able to struggle the distance to nearby Donalbain, where he raised the alarm. He has little to no memory of the attack, or his attacker—'

I threw up my arms theatrically.

'—yet claims you arrived at Pike Ness on the eve of September sixth, whereupon, the following day, you asked for passage to the island. Mr Montgomery claims to have never seen you before, nor to have had any prior knowledge regarding your standing within the Metropolitan Police. However, he knew you by name, for it seems you used your real name whilst in Pike Ness, and has since positively identified you via a photograph he was shown by officers questioning him. More than anything, Montgomery simply claims you were acting out of the ordinary. Speaking about your *assistant*, a woman he claims you spoke of as if she were beside you.' Henley's voice turned grave then. 'Is that Beatrice? Was she with you when you were at Pike Ness?'

I laughed bitterly. 'He claims she wasn't? He must have taken a terrible beating.'

'By you,' Henley replied. 'Do you recall the assault? Any of it?'

'No, because it didn't happen.'

'You're denying it?'

'No, I'm saying it wasn't me – how could it have been? I was on that damned island. We were searching—' I stopped myself before I said any more.

Henley raised his eyebrows. 'So Beatrice was with you then?'

I shook my head, angry with myself. How long would they keep me in here – how much of the truth would they get out of me to twist and bend in their favour? They were nailing my coffin, finding every minor detail to ensure I would take the fall for everything.

'Montgomery claims you went to the lighthouse near Pike Ness prior to travelling over to the island. He's told us that two brothers who ran the lighthouse had been missing for almost four weeks, that you were intrigued by this and wanted to investigate. Tell me what you found?'

I folded my arms and shook my head. Henley reached for a small paper envelope, marked and numbered at the top. It was open, and he carefully took out something small, which he set down on the table between us. I recognised it as the bullet I had pulled from the wall beneath the lighthouse.

'This was one of a number of items found in your coat pocket. You didn't speak to Montgomery – or anyone else as I gather – about anything you found in the lighthouse. Is this it? Is this what you discovered?'

I stared at the small, flattened piece of metal.

'We had an expert examine this bullet. We can't be certain, but he has narrowed down the possible firearms from which it was shot. Would you care to see his findings?'

I shook my head. Henley told me nonetheless.

'This bullet is likely that of a Webley revolver cartridge, the mark one, or an Enfield cartridge, the .476 mark two. Both are used in a fairly specific sidearm, the obsolete Enfield revolver you carry.'

I burst up from my chair, though Flynn's heavy hands pushed me down swiftly. 'You're lying. This is all lies and subterfuge!'

Henley reached inside the envelope once more, took out an unspent bullet and placed it beside the small fragment of lead. 'This is a bullet from your gun. Our ballistics expert is confident—'

'So you think I killed them, those two brothers?'

Henley shrugged. 'Did you?'

I scoffed and shook off Flynn's hands from my shoulders.

'I won't answer any more questions. You've set every piece of this up. All of it lies.'

Henley shrugged. 'It's your right, Bexley. You don't have to answer any more questions – you may sit there in silence.'

'I want to go back to my cell.'

Henley ignored me then. He began laying more photographs out on the table, turning them to face me.

'Do you recognise any of these people?'

I looked down at the faces: more men, more women, some in formal portraits ...

I grabbed a photograph of a man, a man in rough clothes, a man with dark eyes and a stern, severe expression. What struck me was what was behind him, surroundings I recognised all too well.

'That's the dock, the East India Docks. Tha– that man.' Though I didn't recognise him, I could tell he was an immigrant, someone who had bought passage to England in the vain hope of starting a new life. I could see it plainly: in his proud stance, in his filthy clothes and matted hair.

'This picture ...' I rummaged through the rest, grabbing some Henley had set down earlier, those that showed families before an open green space. 'That's Hyde Park, I see it now.' I began looking through the pictures one by one, my heart rate growing ever faster. 'I took these pictures,' for then I was sure of it. 'This backdrop was set up in Mr Timberwell's photography boutique, I was there for many years—'

I stopped cold, feeling my chest tighten with sudden severity.

'Who are these people?' I said, my words barely audible.

Henley still held photographs in his hand, he looked from me to them morbidly.

'Who do you think they are?'

I slammed my fist down, my arm trembling terribly. 'No more games! Who are these people?'

Henley shook his hand at Flynn behind me. He stared straight at me, spoke with the same even tone he had maintained through much of the interrogation.

'That's Louis Krovac, the day he arrived from the Baltics. A young man then. He was a labourer, earned a reputation as a good worker. When he didn't show up for work on the twenty-first of June this year, a few of the men he worked with went to his home. He was gone, though it seemed none of his possessions had been taken. We found the mark of the Wraith,' he set down a piece of paper with the pseudo cult symbol etched in pencil, 'on the inside of his front door.'

Henley pointed to another photograph: a portrait of a woman sitting on a chair, clearly pregnant.

'That's Heather Warren, of East Ham. This is quite an old photograph, some fifteen years old to be exact. She lived with her daughter, a daughter who was out trying to scrape together some keep for her mother on the night of the twelfth of August, the time a witness claims you were seen in the area. When the daughter came home, she found her mother gone, vanished with no trace. The mark of the Wraith was scratched into the arm of a rocking chair she owned.'

Henley pointed to another, and another. 'That's Yasmin Modiri-Whitmore. That's Mathew Fletcher. That's Amanda Granger. Victims. Every one of these people is a victim.' He dropped the last few photographs onto the table. I was grabbing at them, panic-stricken, confused, mortified. Then my hand set upon a family portrait, a father, mother and daughter, perhaps as young as six or seven.

'That's Dorothy Clarke,' Henley said, reaching beneath his papers once more. 'The young girl, I mean. That photograph was taken some time in eighteen ninety. Do you recall taking that photograph?'

'What the hell is this?' I could only mutter in reply.

'That girl was twenty-two when she was kidnapped; a young woman, intelligent, from a good family, married to a fine young man. Here is a more recent photograph of her.'

He stretched across the table and set the photograph before me. I recognised the face in an instant: the gentle smile; kind, considerate eyes. I took the photograph, held it close to me. It shook so badly I could barely focus on it; blood surged suddenly through my temples, and I felt close to fainting, simply from the sick, terrible shock of it all.

'A young woman in her prime,' Henley said with regret.

'This isn't Dorothy Clarke,' I stammered, my words barely forming. 'This isn't Dorothy, you're wrong.'

'It's a recent photograph, given to us by her husband.'

'It's not her!' I yelled ferociously, unable to control my wavering voice.

Henley seemed unmoved. 'Who is she then, Bexley?'

'That's ... that's ...' tears dribbled down my cheeks when I finally said her name. 'That's Beatrice. That's Dorothy's sister.'

'Dorothy Clarke never had a sister; she was an only child.'

I wept and moaned. 'What-what have you done to her?'

'It's not about what we have done to her, Bexley. This is about what *you* have done.' As I stared at the photograph through bleary eyes, Henley grabbed up more brown envelopes, marked 'Evidence'.

'We found these photographs at your house, along with others, and an extensive list of approximately forty names, including those of the victims. Records from your final eighteen months working out of Timberwell's shop. Manic notes on how you had tracked individuals and families down, people whose photographs you had taken.'

He began setting down trinkets, mostly jewellery: rings, brooches, a timepiece. Finally, a necklace – a delicate set of pearls on a silver chain.

'We found these as well; we're working on the assumption they are keepsakes, worn by the victims when you kidnapped them.' He stood up, walked around the table with a sudden urgency, leaned over me and snatched the photograph of Beatrice from my hand.

'She's wearing that necklace in the photograph her husband gave us. Look at it.'

Like a child, I screwed my eyes shut – I didn't want to see. Henley stepped back around the table.

'You took every single victim's portrait at some time or other approximately fifteen years ago, before you'd met Hawthorn, before you'd begun working for the Forensic Crime Directorate. That's a significant connection, the first real connection we have established between the victims. Can you explain that?'

'What have you done to her?' I was cradling my head, crying into my hands.

'Would you care to guess who the next name – the next target – on your list was? Bartholomew Cavendish-Huntley. *Lord* Cavendish-Huntley as he is known now. You asked Jack Lavernock how we tracked you down after you fled Pike Ness, how Flynn and his men were able to follow you to Burton Lodge. No one was following you, man; we merely waited for you at Cavendish-Huntley's estate. I had officers escort the lord and his family to safety the minute this evidence came to light; had men scouring the city of London, looking for anyone else named on your dreadful list.'

He rattled the paper on the table, grabbed another unsealed envelope and dropped a tatty notebook before me. He leaned across and opened the first few pages. Each was filled with gruesome drawings, sketches of the strange occult symbol and incomprehensible writing.

'This was with everything else we found at your home. You detailed how you killed each victim in this, where you disposed of some of the bodies.'

'Where's Beatrice?'

'Dorothy,' Henley snapped. 'Dorothy Clarke. She's dead.' He

flicked through pages of the notebook. 'Of all your victims, you mention her the least.'

I tried to stand, tried to break free of Flynn's grip when he roughly took hold of me. I yelled at the top of my lungs. 'This is all your doing! You've set me up!'

'We found all of this hidden beneath the floorboards of your bedroom. We're still tearing your home apart; no doubt more secrets will be uncovered.' Henley continued, his voice loud but steady and controlled. 'You broke. Whatever happened to you in that village on your last assignment broke you. You've gone *insane*, man. I don't fully understand your motive, but I have my theory.'

Flynn had near grappled me back to my seat, though I continued to struggle against him.

Henley set down the last of his evidence, placed it carefully before me on the table.

'Do you know what these are?'

'This is all lies—'

'Train tickets. Train tickets from Euston Station to Glasgow, with connections going to Adanburgh, north Aberdeenshire. Approximately six miles down the coast from Pike Ness.' He tapped on the tickets. 'Look at the dates.'

I groaned and struggled. Henley was unmoved.

'You set off from London on the fourteenth of August, the day after the failed kidnap attempt of Daniel Pinkney, and returned on the eighteenth. That's approximately four weeks ago; the time in which Lachlan Montgomery claims the brothers working the lighthouse off Pike Ness went missing, and the time in which we believe Elijah Hawthorn was murdered on the island. You returned to London four days before Hawthorn's thumbprint was found at the scene of James Mortimer's home, the eleventh known Wraith victim. I don't know what motive you had to travel to Scotland and kill Elijah Hawthorn, or why he was hiding out on that island, but again, I have my theory.'

He held his hand to his mouth, looked at me with such pitiful curiosity.

'When men snap, they usually seek to take the lives of others, to regain some sense of power, of control. I think after that enquiry in South Wales, you wanted to kill. I think you wanted to kill as many as you could but were too afraid at the start. I think you reached out to Hawthorn, made contact with him.'

Henley spoke on even as I continued to mutter and thrash out in vain.

'Whether you met in London or otherwise, I think you told Hawthorn about your illicit scheme, told him you could both get away with it, owing to your forensic expertise.' He grimaced. 'Did Hawthorn tell you to get help? Did he not turn you over then and there out of some sense of loyalty? You claim you saw the man as a father, and he saw you as a son. Is that why he didn't contact us, warn us about your plans?'

I cursed in Henley's face. Flynn clouted me hard over the head, so hard I saw black dots burst before my eyes as I slouched down onto the table.

'I'm sorry, sir, but he's causing trouble.'

'It's all lies,' I mumbled, reaching for Beatrice's necklace, taking it in my hand.

'Hawthorn didn't have the heart to turn you in, but he was afraid of you. Maybe you got angry with him when he refused to help. Either way he tried to run from you, wanted to hide somewhere he felt safe. No doubt you tracked him down though; we don't know how but you're a bloody good investigator.'

'I didn't,' I said sincerely, though then I didn't know what to believe.

'You'd already started the kidnappings then, taken victims,

had your way with them. But Hawthorn – you must have been quite furious with Hawthorn. You finally tracked him down four weeks ago, travelled to Scotland, convinced the brothers to take you to the island, where you tortured and mutilated him.'

'No, no, I couldn—'

'You killed Hawthorn, then got back to the mainland, where you killed the two brothers to cover your tracks. After that you returned to London, where you used Hawthorn's mutilated thumb to plant the bloodied print at the crime scene of James Mortimer. Was that because you feared someone may have sighted you, that we may be closing in? Or was it merely some further way of spiting the man who had refused to help in your devilish acts?'

'Please, this is all wrong, this is all wrong!'

'How much of the last few months do you really remember, Bexley? How much are you really certain of?'

I saw the black nights, the terrible dreams, the demons who haunted me, the early hours, rising, the haze of liquor.

'I-I…'

'You don't know,' Henley said coldly.

Flynn knelt at my side and growled close to my face. 'You don't know, fella, because you've lost it. All of it. Your brain is keeping secrets from ye, hiding the truth as best it can.'

Henley spoke gravely. 'Madness. Caused by trauma, and events of some magnitude. In soldiers it's usually a battle. With you it appears to have been the man who captured you in your last case, who beat and tried to kill you.' He tapped on his papers, on the photographs, looked down across them all. 'It's the nub of this really, the underlying cause. Psychoanalysts – men who study the mind – seem to be understanding it now, the fragility of the psyche. The complexity of the brain and how it can keep secrets from our own consciousness, if I understand the terms correctly.'

'You've been going out at night, snatching people from their beds, and then living a fantasy to keep yourself from cracking entirely.' Flynn smiled wickedly. 'The lengths you've gone to are quite extraordinary – for a madman, it's brilliant.'

'You think it a coincidence that you find a letter from Hawthorn, dated from January of this year, the day *after* we bring you in for questioning?'

'I told you—'

'You hadn't seen it. A letter with no postal marks, a letter that was therefore surely not delivered from Scotland as you believe.'

'It's Hawthorn writing in the letter.' I reached across to it and held it to Flynn's face. 'He speaks of times we had together – his signature is at the bottom—'

'Forgery,' Flynn snarled. 'It's easy to write in another man's hand when you've lost your mind. Easy to think the world is conspiring against you. You worked with Hawthorn for years, would have known his signature. And as for the times you had together…'

'*You* could have written about them,' Henley said plainly. 'You *did* write about them. This letter; the diary speaking of cults and conspiracies. None of it was written by Hawthorn, it was all written by you, just a part of the fantasy you've been concocting.'

Flynn snatched the letter from me, slid it back across the table towards Henley. '*The cult*,' he sneered, shaking his head. 'A conspiracy at the heart of the police, committing a series of kidnappings, murdering your old friend.'

'It is very elaborate, extremely so.' Henley tucked the letter away. 'No doubt there is still some glimmer of your former self, idling in the recesses of your mind. You feel guilt for your crimes. That's why you've created this story, you at its centre, the hero, trying to uncover the truth.'

I was a wreck, sobbing, shuddering, my breathing ragged and

laboured. When I went to stand, Flynn didn't move to stop me. I paced close to the door, moving back and forth along the wall like a caged tiger.

'How long have you been seeing her, Thomas?' Henley had his hand raised to try to calm me down. 'More importantly, when did you last see her?'

'The lodge, Burton Lodge,' I panted, 'but the oth- the othe—'

I doubled over, bile and venom rupturing through my stomach. I hacked and reeled where I stood.

'Is it just her, Thomas? Are there others you see as well?'

His words burnt through my skin. I held my head, as an immense pain began to swell and build.

'The testimony from your last case, from a constable arrested, a disgraced councillor. They both claimed you were seeing things in the village – strange, ungodly things.'

Flynn came over to me, took me by the shoulders and set me back in my chair.

'We know you are behind the disappearances,' Henley said slowly. 'You are the Wraith, Bexley; the evidence is stacked against you. Along with your connection to the victims and the *trophies* you took from them, you kept a sordid record of how you killed each victim after they were kidnapped, and where you disposed of some of the bodies. How you mutilated them, even drowned one. Our men have already uncovered at least two. The things you are seeing – they are manifestations of your guilt. You couldn't even bring yourself to use Dorothy Clarke's real name in the miserable lies you told yourself. You're dangerous, beyond your own capabilities. How you even killed all those people in Pike Ness – to poison the water for them all…'

When I looked at him, I realised Henley's eyes were starting to grow. The whites were starting to glow. They darkened the space around him, sucked light into them.

'It's not true.'

'It is, Bexley. You're sick; very, very sick.' He nodded sombrely. 'There's still some good you can do though; that side of your character still exists in some slim way. Tell us where the remaining bodies are – the records you kept are incomplete. Tell us how you broke into each home, how you stole the victims away.'

I moaned as Henley's eyes grew brighter, as they took on a miserable yellow hue. The walls of the room collapsed, crumbled to the floor revealing nothingness, empty dark. I leapt up from my chair, screaming as I did. Flynn grabbed me, though I fought him off with a savage mania, lashed out again and again.

'This isn't happening. None of this is the truth!' It felt horribly plausible to me then, though.

I saw all the terrible faces, the wretched dead who had haunted me in my home, in the streets of London. I saw each face as a victim, tried to remember what I had done in the long lapses of time that were blank to me. The days, the weeks I couldn't remember. Had I scrubbed all memory from my mind – had I erased the truth so deeply that even now I failed to recall my wickedness?

I'd felt so certain I had been to the manor before, so certain I had seen Hawthorn's body, dismembered as it was.

Beatrice was Dorothy; not a sister searching, but a fragmented delusion of my mind.

Flynn lunged on me. I pushed him back with what strength I had. Henley's eyes flickered, as from the darkness that surrounded us, figures emerged, one by one.

Women – bruised, beaten, strangled, dead.

Men – cut, stabbed, bloodied, dead.

They walked towards me, glared at me, despised me, screamed silent screams. If Henley's words were to be believed, then I was their killer; we shared a grizzly and miserable bond.

I tried to flee from the room, hammered my hands against the heavy door, begging for it to be opened. Flynn grabbed me, swung me down. Still I clawed for the door, the smell of the rotten dead filling my nostrils. The pain in my head became unbearable – I heard ringing, a terrible siren call that deafened me entirely. Cold, stinking hands latched upon my clothes, as the edges of my vision blurred, then vanished entirely. I lost sight of Flynn, and the room around me.

'Jesus, what's happening to him?' The voice was far away, but I recognised it as Flynn's.

'He's bleeding from his nose.' Whether Henley was standing over me I cannot say, but his words were surely the last I heard. 'He's convulsing. Fetch a doctor!'

Do Mad Men Know They Are Mad?

September 11th, 1905

Light spilled through the bars above the cell bed. For a blissful minute, I had no knowledge of where I was or what was happening. I heard voices talking calmly, craned my neck to see the heavy cell door opened wide and a few men gathered in a small huddle. I recognised Henley and Flynn, as well as the rough station sergeant. Their faces brought my circumstance back to mind, and a wave of despair and contemptible misery overcame me. Another man was standing with his back to me – he wore a black waistcoat and white shirt.

I tried to call out to them, but my throat was too dry and bitter. Blood lined the inside of my mouth, and I felt it caked around my lips and nose. I thought of the beating I had taken, wondered if it was merely a result of it. The words of the men began to make sense to me, and I listened as best I could.

'How were we supposed to know that it might happen?'

'I would have thought, sergeant—'

'You listen here, I'm no bloody sergeant!'

'Flynn, please.'

'Whatever your rank, you should be wise enough to know that kicking a man near senseless is going to cause some damage!'

'It came on suddenly.' I recognised Henley's voice.

'I imagine.' The man in the waistcoat turned and glanced at

me. 'It's possible the beating had little to do with it. You said he's been hallucinating?'

'He's deranged,' Flynn growled.

'To you perhaps, but his attack could have been some sort of seizure. Epilepsy, perhaps even a more severe neurological disorder.'

'You're saying he's ill?'

'Maybe, but from what I understand, he doesn't have much longer to live anyway. Illness or not, we can't let deranged men roam the streets murdering people.'

The man stepped away from the door. Henley and Flynn glanced at one another.

'Is he staying here?' the man I now gathered to be a physician said from out of sight.

'No,' Henley replied, folding his arms. 'We need to get him to Scotland Yard. He's a special case; we need him under close watch as soon as possible.'

'Well, I'd hold off from taking him until tomorrow morning. He's in a bad way; imposing any more stress upon him may trigger another attack.'

'You think he deserves kindness?' Flynn seemed baffled by the idea.

'Hardly,' the doctor replied. 'He deserves to stand before a judge and be tried for his crimes. Would you rather he died before that can happen?'

Flynn conceded. 'Can we take him any sooner?'

'Whether you or I like it, that man needs rest. Give him until the morning. If he has another attack, send for me immediately.' The doctor reappeared, shook hands with both Henley and Flynn. 'He's the one who's been causing all this terror throughout the city then?'

Henley nodded. 'We believe so. Let's hope London is safer for it.'

The men walked away still talking. The door of the cell creaked shut. I felt myself grow light-headed. Then I closed my eyes and drifted from one nightmare to the next, where the faces of the dead appeared to me, and where I wrapped my hands around their throats.

I was left alone for hours that day; left to wallow in blood and pain. At times I grabbed at the small bars of the cell, yelled and screamed incessantly for Henley to return, for him to talk to me. On such occasions a heavy whack from the constable's truncheon sent me reeling away from the door. I pleaded, I snarled and threatened. When my voice was hoarse and my body limp, I collapsed to the bed and sat staring at the wall. All the while I longed for a drink, for my body needed it. My addiction ran rampant and caused me to say such foul things to the constable guarding me. What falsities I would have pleaded guilty to for even a mouthful of brandy in those hours; what crimes I would have sworn were carried out by my own hand.

I dwelt on the previous months. I lingered on dates, trying to recall day by day accounts of my movements, my actions. Such a thing is impossible even for the healthy and clear of mind. So much was unclear to me that fear consumed every passing moment of my time alone. Fear of the truth; the less I could recall, the more Henley's theory that I was the guilty man began to feel like the truth.

I thought of Hawthorn, of our supposed meeting as far back as January. With painful effort I tried to conjure some memory of it, anything that might prove it took place.

I saw Hawthorn at the door of my home, saw him come inside, remembered my words of greeting, and the awkwardness in which we broached the bad terms of our parting. Then we were laughing, drinking. Sometime later, for I could see the dusky light through my front window, I spoke to him of something severe, and his demeanour changed quite suddenly. He yelled at me – an argument ensued. He stormed out of my home, despite my calling after him.

Writing the letter from Hawthorn; scribing my address across the envelope and carefully placing on the stamp.

Hiding the photographs, the trinkets from the victims, the records I had kept, beneath the floorboards of my bedroom, tucking them away safely before taking to the bottle.

Memories. Were all such thoughts memories or fiction? It seemed so real, just as my memories of Pike Ness, of the manor, of Hawthorn's body lying at my feet, were surely real.

I tried clinging to the idea of the cult, of a great conspiracy acting against me, blaming me for its evil crimes. But such a notion now seemed childish, farcical even. I felt a fool for ever believing in such an idea, for no evidence had been presented of its existence, no grounds on which I should have believed Hawthorn's claims. *Hawthorn's claims* – if all that Henley had told me was true, then this was all some narrative I had created, some fiction to reassure my broken mind.

I saw myself standing over Hawthorn, as blood dribbled from his throat and he struggled to take his final breath.

Just a thought – just an idea? Or a memory, something real?

My hand scrawling out the cypher, sitting in the library of the manor, laughing as I wrote. Was I drunk; was I lucid? Did I strike my hand against the shelves above the door as I left – did I rip them down in a fit of manic hysteria? A memory, or just an idea?

The blast from my pistol. A young man – Douglas perhaps – crumpled in a heap on the dusty floor in the tunnel from the lighthouse. How did I kill his brother? Did I drown him in the quay on the island, did I row back alone, chase down Douglas and shoot him before he could get away from me, before he could escape and run into the open fields? A vivid memory, clear as any, gone before I could fully grasp it. Or maybe just a fantasy, a treacherous one.

The grip of the cleaver, its handle wooden. Wooden; I felt certain it was wooden. A single thrust at the throat, swing upon swing to remove the fingers. What did I use to carry them in? And where did I dispose of them after I had printed Hawthorn's bloody thumb at the scene of James Mortimer's kidnapping? Had the man whose home I broke into watch me do it? Had he stared at me in petrified bemusement, as I marked a bloody thumb down against a polished vase? Had I dragged him away into the dark night, then? Had he struggled much before I killed him? Had any of them struggled?

I saw faces of strangers, saw how I killed them, how I broke into their homes and stole them from their beds. I couldn't recall then and there where I had disposed of the bodies; my memories were vague on that. But I'd written the details down, which likely made it easier for my conscious mind to forget.

In the slow passing hours, I cried furious tears, scorned myself, thought of how I could end it all. At times I laughed for the absurdity, for the way in which my life had changed in such a relatively short amount of time. Once the papers wrote about me for the crimes I had solved, for the criminals I had thwarted. Now they would forever burn my name against the men and women I had killed. A twentieth-century Ripper.

I cried for Beatrice – Dorothy. I cried for what I had done to her. How real she had seemed to me, yet all those days I had been speaking to nothing, merely some deranged fragment of my broken mind. How I cried in those hours for the terrible wrong I had done her.

I was brought some food, though I couldn't bear to eat it. As evening turned to night and the small block of light streaming into my cell died away, I took the measly blanket offered to me and wrapped it around my shoulders. I sat in the corner of the cell, my back propped straight against the wall. I was pained and uncomfortable, yet as tired as I was, I struggled to sleep.

I waited for something to appear to me. Some corner of my thoughts desired to look upon a ghost, wished to see the spirits and try to speak with them, to learn the truth from their mouths. I had never attempted such a thing before, for fear was the primary emotion when seeing such terrors. But I would muster the strength to compose myself, would hold steady in the corner of the room where I couldn't move and demand that they tell me the simple fact. *Was I the man who had killed them?* I needed to know.

I sat, and I waited, and with each flicker of candlelight that glowed through the cell bars I flinched and twitched. I whispered to the shadows, tried to conjure the dead before me. I asked they do me this small mercy, that my penance was my own self-torture, grappling for the truth, struggling to know if I was a monster, a raving killer. I begged for forgiveness as tears welled in my eyes. With each breath of night air, I looked about the little space for them, thought they would appear sitting upon the bed or crawling out from beneath it.

Nothing came. No sign of the damned and the walking horrors I had spent so many nights reeling from. *They're not real*, I thought, with such self-loathing. *They're just another part of your delusion, of your guilt-ridden mind. You've gone mad, Thomas. You truly have gone mad.* I called out at one point, a sombre, weary cry, met only by the anger of the constable who clashed his truncheon against the cell door.

'You say another word and you'll have *this*, all right?'

I shook my head and muttered back to him. 'I think…I think I've gone insane.'

'Too right, mate. You're as mad as they come.' The constable laughed cruelly.

'Please,' I pleaded with him. 'Please help me.'

'Help is it – help is what you want.' I heard the key in the cell door turn. It swung open slowly; the constable stepped into the confined space, his truncheon in hand. His face was filled with wrath. 'I'll give you all the help you need.'

As I looked beyond him, I saw a figure, just out of view, a pair of eyes glimmering and nothing more. I saw the sadness in those eyes and recognised them immediately.

'Beatrice,' I mumbled.

The figure remained unmoved.

'This is for what you did to all those poor bastards,' the constable said, raising the truncheon above his head.

'Beatrice!' I yelled, scrambling quickly towards the door. The constable was quicker though. He brought the truncheon down hard upon my shoulder, and I reeled to the grimy floor. I looked through the open door, looked for Beatrice. I couldn't see her.

'Simmer down,' the constable said, a ringmaster to a wretched beast. He struck me hard between the shoulders.

I cried in pain, shouted to Beatrice with all the strength I had. He struck me again and again until I could take no more. I lay in silence, the wind knocked out of me, my back arched in a dreadful fashion.

'Next word from you, it'll be a cracked skull, y'hear me?'

The constable stepped over me, slammed shut the cell door and locked it. I whimpered where I lay, muttering Beatrice's name with every other breath.

Old Friends Reminiscing

September 12th, 1905

Before dawn, the murmur and noise outside my cell began to build. The constable guarding me was joined by another, then another and two more shortly after that. The old sergeant began rearing his ugly head, I heard him speak ill words of Flynn, of all Irish men, for he detested them all in equal measure.

'*Special Branch*,' he spat to mutters and laughs. 'Not very much special about them if you ask me. It took 'em long enough to catch our man there.' I heard something hard hit against my cell door. 'You ask me, they're all a bunch of puffed up fools – led by that bastard from Belfast.'

Someone hushed the sergeant quickly as voices approached from down the corridor. I heard Flynn's thick drawl from where I sat.

'Which one of you mongrels spoke to the press, eh? Eh!' The sergeant and his constables remained quiet. 'Was it you? Or you?'

'Look, sir—'

'You can address me as Superintendent Flynn. Now, either one of your men owns up, or I'm going to hold you personally responsible, sergeant.'

'Owns up to what?'

'Speaking to the press, telling them that Bexley is here, that he's the chief suspect in all this. We're not even in Central London, yet there's a mob outside baying for his blood.'

'Look, superintendent, none of my men told any newspapers about this. We were under strict orders from the commissioner himself – he didn't want any of this getting out.'

'Of course he didn't!' Flynn's voice reached fever pitch. 'We have in our custody the most wanted man in the country, a public menace, this city's worst bloody enemy. They'll tear him to shreds before we take one step outside the door of this station – we've already brought in more men from Chingford and Edmonton to hold back the crowd.' He tried to compose himself. 'Now which one of yous spoke to the press? They offered you a bit of extra money, eh? Fat lot of good it'll do you when I flog you to death.'

The sergeant swore at Flynn; a scuffle broke out, though I didn't move to look. After a few minutes the pair were separated as I heard more men crowd into the small space outside of my cell. Tempers flared all around.

'There's families of the victims out there, of those he butchered…'

'You telling me how to do my job…'

'Just feed the bastard to them…'

'Enough!' someone roared over the crowd. His voice carried such a command, a weighty authority, that the room fell silent in an instant. 'Stand to attention.' I recognised the voice as Henley's. Feet shuffled on stone.

He stepped into the room. Not a man was heard breathing.

'The issue of who spoke to the papers will be dealt with at a later time. We have more pressing matters at hand. We almost have a riot on our hands and the day has not even begun. They'll be through the doors of this station if things escalate any further so we need to move our man to the Yard as quickly and as discreetly as we can.'

'We have four carriages prepared, sir,' Flynn said sternly. 'A ten-man group of uniformed officers will accompany the prisoner, along with several of my men. They'll escort the carriages armed with rifles and—'

'It's too obvious,' Henley interrupted. 'If the public see a convoy of carriages with uniformed officers and armed men, they're bound to suspect Bexley is inside. We've had bloodshed transporting prisoners in this city before and I won't have it repeated.'

'With respect, sir, I don't think anyone will try to stop us.'

Henley scoffed. 'You're sure of that? You're willing to bet on the lives of the public, of your own officers? It takes one man to lose his nerve and let off a shot from his rifle. One shot and all hell breaks loose, we'll have a massacre on our hands.'

'Sir, my men are trained—'

'We'll use a single carriage – a cab, something inconspicuous.'

'He'll be seen.'

'Cram him in the footwell. Have a plainclothes driver and two men from Special Branch to accompany him. They'll leave from the rear stables and head west, until they are far from any crowds.'

Flynn tried in vain to raise his concerns. 'Sir, please, with respect—'

'Flynn, I won't have bloodshed on the streets over this. People are angry, and they have a right to be, but we need to ensure their safety above all else.'

The room was silent then, for Flynn had nothing to say. Henley cleared his throat. 'We'll finalise the details. We're moving him within the hour. Flynn come with me and bring your best men.'

I heard Henley and Flynn leave the room. The sergeant piped up once more.

'Damndest idea I've ever heard. We should go out there and show that mob who the law is.'

'And how would you do that, sergeant?' I recognised Lavernock's voice. He spoke down to the sergeant, who hesitated and failed to reply. 'If your idea of law and order is still beating unarmed men and women half to death, I fear you may wish to consider retirement.'

The sergeant said nothing, though I raised my head a little, feeling the rising tension in the room.

'Clear the room,' Lavernock snapped. 'This is no social club, it's a police station. You men have work to do, don't you?'

The sergeant barked an order and feet trudged out and down the corridor. Lavernock said something quietly and I heard the metallic rattle of heavy keys. The door to my cell was unlocked and swung open. Lavernock stepped in; at the sight of me he shook his head with regret, maybe even sympathy. I couldn't tell which. I clambered up and sat gingerly on the bed. I rubbed my aching ribs, tried to breathe as deeply as I could though it pained me badly. I wiped lazily at the blood still dried around my nose.

Lavernock carried a small plate of food. He sat next to me and sighed heavily. 'You've seen better days, Tommy.'

'That's an understatement.'

He handed me the plate and I began eating slowly, my jaw aching painfully as I chewed. When I had finished what little I could, I gestured to the door. 'Is it as bad as they say it is outside?'

Lavernock nodded. 'It's bad.' He reached inside his coat, pulled out a cigarette case and offered me one. With fingers I could barely move, I took one gratefully and held it to my lips as he struck a match. We smoked, even as the constable guarding my cell looked in and eyed Lavernock with disdain.

'There's a lot of anger for you, Tommy. Word is they think

you've got some illness.' I shrugged. Lavernock continued. 'You're seeing things?' I nodded. 'What sort of things?'

'Unpleasant things,' was all I replied.

'Do you remember any of what you did? Any of the crimes you committed, of the lives you took?'

I shrugged again. 'I don't know what's real anymore, Jack. For so long now, I've been living in a world I don't really recognise as my own. I see things – can't tell if they're of my own making or ...' I trailed off.

'I'm sorry you had a rough time in here,' Jack said. 'It shouldn't have happened.'

I rubbed at a lump on the back of my head. 'If I'm guilty of all I am charged then it is no more than I deserve.'

Lavernock fidgeted with his coat. 'You don't remember anything about Hawthorn's death? You don't remember kill—' He took a long drag. 'You don't remember what you did to him?'

'I have flashes, though whether they are real memories ...' I laughed bitterly. 'If we stood in each other's shoes I'm afraid I'd have to believe you guilty. The evidence, the——' I struggled to think of the word. 'Psychosis. Strange really, to think oneself mad.'

'You could plead insanity.' Lavernock glanced to the door. 'You talk to me now as I have always known you. Whatever has happened may be caused by this illness they now speak of.'

I stared down at my dwindling cigarette. 'They'd have me drugged and strapped in a straitjacket for the remainder of my life. I'd rather be dead.'

Lavernock nodded. He looked around the cell, kicked his feet at a fat tail that slithered suddenly out of sight beneath the bed.

'I'll have to testify against you,' he said frankly. 'I was there when we searched your home. It was ... it was me who found all those things: the photographs, the trinkets.' He seemed genuinely pained to say the words, almost apologetic. I had no desire to make him feel worse.

'You do your job, Jack. You were always good at it, always understood your duty.'

He finished his cigarette, sat a while longer before offering me his hand, which I shook feebly. He stood to leave.

'Do you remember when we met, Jack?' I asked him as he went to the door.

He thought for a moment. 'The Forensic Directorate. The first day Hawthorn brought us all together, I guess.'

I shook my head. 'We met just before that, a few days before in fact. You probably don't recall. You were outside the Yard, right outside the door, and when I moved to pass you, you tried to turn me away, thought I was some vagrant causing trouble.' I smiled, though Lavernock looked mortified. 'It's all right, I was all but penniless then, wearing tatty shoes and a moth-eaten rag suit. The only thing I owned, would you believe.' I nodded warmly at the memory. 'I must have been quite the state. Funny, that day Hawthorn showed me the basement, showed me where we would all be working. He loaned me money, told me to buy a suit and see a barber. That first day proper, the day we all came together, I'm not sure you even recognised me.'

'I didn't.' Lavernock looked down at the floor. 'You were always his favourite. No matter who came and went over the years, you always had his ear.'

I felt the sting of tears at the back of my eyes, fought against them as best I could. A terrible pressure drilled behind my forehead and temples. I tried not to focus on the overwhelming sadness.

'Hendricks retired,' Lavernock muttered. 'Finished off his time out of Y Division somewhere. Highgate, I think, maybe Potters Bar.'

'He was a good man,' I said, rubbing my face. 'Duggan, Morgan, the rest Hawthorn found. They were all good men. We made quite a group.'

Lavernock nodded. 'We did a lot of good work. You as well, Tommy.'

'I'd give anything to go back, back to that day when we all met. Back to when it all started.'

'Me too, back when I was a far younger man.' Lavernock smiled. He reached inside his jacket, pulled out a wide but slender wallet and retrieved a folded piece of paper from the inside.

'Would you believe I've kept this for all these years? Just something to remember that day, I guess.'

He unfolded the piece of paper, looked at it with a thin smile, then turned it around to me. It was a picture I recognised, of Lavernock and Hawthorn and me, and all the others of the Forensic Crime Directorate, a picture I recognised all too well, for I had looked upon it so recently.

In the manor. That photograph had been in the manor.

Lavernock was talking to me sombrely from the cell door.

'I saw that photograph,' I muttered, confused, straining to recall which room of the manor it had been in. 'In Scotland, on the island, in the manor...'

Lavernock didn't seem to understand at first – shook his head, still smiling a little. Then he must have seen the look on my face. 'Tommy—'

'I saw that photograph, Jack, with Hawthorn's things, with everything else I found.' I rose slowly from the wooden bed. 'Is this a joke or something? Are you mocking me?' Another, more absurd, idea came to me. 'Were you up there?'

I felt dizzy, my vision blurring badly from the terrible effort it took for me to hold my balance. Lavernock thrust the photograph in his pocket.

'I came to make peace with you, Tommy. Before it all ends for you, before they hang you. Don't let it end like this.'

'Were you a part of all this? Did you do this to me?' My teeth ground together; heat and nausea enveloped me.

'God have mercy on you, Tommy.' Lavernock stepped out of the cell and yelled at the constable. With a snap, the door was bolted. I lurched and stumbled across the cell, shouting his name as I came to the little bars set into the door.

'Jack. Jack! What have you done? What have you done to me!'

He hesitated.

'Nothing,' he muttered, bitterly. 'Nothing you ...' He trailed off, glanced at me briefly, then stormed away. I screamed at him, even when he was out of sight.

After a moment, the constable thundered into my cell. I don't know when or how I blacked out.

A Dangerous Transfer

September 12th, 1905

The hysteria was rising, both inside and outside the station. The physician, who had returned, was examining me as quickly as he could.

'What happened to me,' I mumbled, trying to regain my senses. Our eyes met for a moment, though the malice and contempt he had for me was clear. He hurriedly put away his equipment. I noticed Flynn standing at my cell door.

'Can we move him?' he asked the physician gruffly.

'Seems you have no choice. Whatever brought on this most recent seizure...' He shrugged and left the cell, as I limply fell to my side on the wooden bed. It took a few minutes for me to recall my conversation with Jack. *The photograph*. He'd had the photograph I saw in the manor. I sighed and rubbed my eyes. So what? His having the photograph (one likely given to all of us in the Forensic Crime Directorate at some time or another) was no evidence he had been to the manor. I felt a stab of guilt for accusing the man of having some part in my downfall, based on something so insignificant, so foolish. I shut my eyes but couldn't sleep – the racket from outside my cell was too great.

Nervous voices chattered.

'There are hundreds outside, more coming every minute.'

'They're pushing up to the doors—'

'They'll be coming straight through 'em if we don't get him out of here.'

The sergeant's voice cut above the rest suddenly, and I gathered he had been struck by the mob outside the station.

'Hurled stones when I came out. They want *him*.'

Sometime later I heard Flynn cry out and silence the other officers. 'Right! Everything's prepared, let's get moving.'

My cell door swung open. Three plainclothes men grabbed me up roughly and hauled me out. Shackles were strapped around my wrists; a rifle barrel thrust into my back.

'I'll cause no trouble,' I murmured, exhausted, resigned to my fate.

'Shut him up,' one man snapped.

The sergeant struck me hard in the ribs.

Two of the burly plainclothes officers took me by either arm. Flynn led us away. I felt the hatred of all those in the room who watched me.

'Once these boys are safely clear,' Flynn called over his shoulder, 'we'll look to disperse the crowd.'

'Make it quick!' someone called back.

We wound through tight corridors bustling with activity. Men in uniform moved past us hurriedly. I soon heard the rumblings of voices, bitter cheers, vicious calls, cries for blood. We were approaching the front of the station and the size of the crowd outside was becoming dreadfully plain to me. The voices grew louder, and for a terrible moment I thought Flynn had lied, and in truth was leading me to the door to throw me to the wolves. I glanced in terror at the men beside me, their faces emotionless.

We turned and began moving away from the noise. We came to a door and Flynn threw a hessian sack over my head. I tried not to scream or yell, but the sudden blindness was terrible in my circumstances. I heard the door open and felt fresh air rush against me. I was pulled outside, dragged down steps then lifted onto a carriage footplate.

'Get in.' The man to my right barged me. 'Lie on the floor and don't say a bloody word.' I lay down as best I could, though the space was tiny, and I had to pull my knees up to my chest.

'You know the route, boys?' Flynn asked quietly. The men affirmed. 'John's dressed up like any other driver so try to act as normally as you can. Keep Bexley down at all times and conceal the guns – the mob won't suspect we're transporting him in a Hansom. Once you've headed west a short way you should be safe, as long as they don't see him in the carriage.'

The two men climbed aboard, stepping on me carelessly, their boots pressing into my prone body, crushing me. My back jarred as the Hansom's doors were snapped shut; I barely had room to breathe. My neck twisted at an extreme angle, and through the sack I saw a square of light above me and knew it to be the little trapdoor in the carriage's roof. A shadow moved, and I gathered it was the driver ready to leave. One of the men poked the muzzle of a rifle into my shoulder.

'Keep your head down or you'll lose it.'

He need not have threatened. His foot rested on my neck.

'Get going,' Flynn said. A whip cracked, a horse whinnied, and the carriage lurched forwards. The men above me said nothing. I tried my best to glance upwards.

We veered right. I heard the voices of the crowd close by. One of the men muttered and the other silenced him. The driver cracked his whip once more though didn't cry or yell out to the nag pulling us. A rifle butt pressed against my leg, heavy and cold. I smelt dried dirt on polished boots and felt every bump and stone in the road as I lay in agony upon the carriage floor.

I was startled by a banging. Hands smacked against the cab;

a young voice jeered. One of my guards shifted, his heel digging into my ribs as he moved his weight.

'Get out of it!' he shouted as we continued to drive on. 'Children,' he muttered. Still I heard the crowd. The carriage began to slow.

'What's going on, John?' the guard called up to the driver nervously.

'They're following us up the road, a gang of 'em.'

The rifle butt was lifted from my leg.

'Steady now.'

'If they think he's in here . . .'

'Just stay calm.'

The carriage was moving at a crawl. The guards stayed totally still. I shifted uncomfortably, my right arm numb and tingling. One of the men pushed down hard with his heavy boot.

'Easy now.'

People were talking nearby. Some cried out to the carriage. A man's voice spoke above the rest as he called out to the driver. The driver didn't halt. The man called out again and this time the driver laughed and said something back to him. I strained to listen, held my breath in anticipation for the moment they would realise I was in the carriage. The doors would swing open; a few shots would be fired before they seized upon me and dragged me into the dirt of the road. Then . . . then it didn't bear much thinking about.

'Keep us moving slowly, John.'

'We need to get out of here,' the other guard whispered, his voice harsh and desperate.

'Everyone stay calm.'

A terrible wait ensued, where the soft plodding of the horse's hooves was all I could focus on. I had no idea how close anyone came to looking in the carriage, or if anyone spotted the guards' rifles, or the nerves etched on their faces.

The carriage veered left. With a few gentle yips from the driver we started moving faster. Voices on the street died away as a soft breeze swept into the cab. The two guards relaxed, for they lowered their rifles from their laps and rested them on my body.

'Well done,' one sighed. They sat in silence as we continued.

For some twenty minutes nothing was said. My position was unbearable; my shoulders and back ached mercilessly, my right arm was completely numb. The breeze drifting through the cab grew colder; I began to shiver, a little at first, and then uncontrollably. It seemed the guards noticed the chill as well.

'Winter's coming,' one muttered.

Another twenty minutes passed in this fashion, until the driver whistled and called down into the cab.

'We're clear.'

The two men sighed aloud. 'Thank God we're heading to the Yard,' one of the guards huffed. 'Mercy to be rid of *this*.' He nudged me with his foot and I groaned in pain.

'Be glad for the double pay, too,' the other mumbled.

'You're on double pay for this?' I heard no reply. 'Son of a whore, that bastard's got it in for me.'

'He's never liked men from Londonderry.'

'Why the hell hire me then?'

There came no answer. A foot was kicked into my thighs as the man vented his frustrations. We were picking up pace, swerving and turning up streets this way and that. I wondered how long we had left to travel.

'When else has he paid you doubl—'

'Look, take it up with Flynn, it ain't my doing.'

'*Take it up with him*. He'll have my damn fist down his throat.'

'Yeah, you tell yourself that, Riley.'

'You think I wouldn't?'

'He probably doesn't want to pay you Irish boys any extra in case it's seen as him having favourites.'

'So he pays you English lot more.'

'Look, take it up with hi—'

'Quiet,' the voice of the driver seemed nervous. Our pace dropped quite suddenly.

'What's wrong?' The guards snatched up their guns.

'I don't know,' the driver said, keeping his voice low. 'There's fog in the road.'

'Fog?' The horse continued to slow. 'Jesus, it's getting cold.'

'Pick up the pace,' one of the guards called out.

I heard the driver's pained voice a moment later. 'The horse won't move any faster.' He called to the nag, jeering, begging, his whip cracking over and over. Still, the Hansom slowed.

Finally, we came to a stop. The guards moved nervously in their seats.

'Something's wrong.'

'I can't see anything.'

'Get out an' take a look.'

'You do it.'

One of the guards got out slowly, the Hansom rocking as he clambered over my body. I craned my neck, trying to gauge anything through the hessian sack. But it was in vain; all was merely light and shadow to me. I held my breath to listen.

The driver was still; the guard outside the cab shuffled a single step. The nag neighed, stamping onto the stone or cobbles of the road.

'Get this bloody beast moving,' the guard outside hissed, his voice a panicked whisper.

'It won't!' the driver replied. 'What the bloody hell is happening – this street…'

I didn't catch the driver's last words.

'What's wrong?' the guard sitting above me croaked.

'There's no one out here,' the other replied. 'The street's empty, fog thicker than any I've ever seen.'

'Someone's coming,' the driver called down harshly. He thrashed the whip, but still the horse wouldn't move. The cold worsened with the doors of the cab open. It seeped into the very pores of my skin, as though my blood were soon to freeze. The strange fog seared down my throat, and I coughed and spluttered, my entire body now shuddering uncontrollably. The guards paid me no notice.

'Can you see anything?'

'Just shapes moving.' A moment later the driver yelled out, 'Who's there?'

'Christ, be quiet!'

'There are more coming, get out here.'

The guard on top of me clambered from the carriage, and the man from Derry called out into the street.

'We're armed. Stay back and this won't get ugly!'

'Riley, get over here, there're people moving. It's a bloody ambush.'

'Get that carriage moving!'

Commotion ensued; the guards yelled profanities, threatened to fire. The driver cracked his whip, leapt from the carriage and from what I could gather, tried to pull the horse into life. All the while I lay on the cab floor, choking on the freezing air. I began to panic, for such was the difficulty I had to breathe, I felt certain I would surely suffocate. When hands pressed upon my wrists, I thought it merely the guards moving me. Someone spoke in my ear, their words distorted by my ragged breathing and dreadful confusion.

'What? I can't breathe!'

The hands lingered a moment longer; something pulled lightly on the chain of my shackles and I thought that the guards were likely trying to drag me away. But the hands let go, and with them went the cold, for with a shocking suddenness, I gasped a breath as though it were my first. Instinctively I raised my hands to my throat, realising the bonds that held my wrists together were gone entirely.

My hands were free. I grabbed hold the hessian sack over my head, pulled it up and stared, dumbfounded, at the heavy shackles that had been locked tightly around my wrists. They lay on the carriage floor, just at my side, the manacles broken, split and cracked.

I squinted into the bright light of day, a wall of fog where the guards were almost entirely hidden. They were standing beside each other on the right side of the carriage. When I craned my neck and looked to my left, I saw the deserted street and a thin lane leading away. A route of escape was made clear to me.

Heart lurching, I sat up awkwardly, reeled as a thunderous shot rang out from one of the guard's rifles. Their voices came back into focus.

'Jesus, we have to get him. We have to move!'

'Where the hell are they? I can't see them.'

I stared at the lane that would surely be my salvation and made ready to run. I stopped myself, before my foot even left the carriage.

Understand that in that moment, I had no idea of my guilt or innocence. Some clarity of thought – some reason – dictated that the evidence put to me by Henley was clear and undeniable. I was surely mad, ill by all accounts. I had no true memories of my crimes, no real knowledge of them, but it seemed to matter little. The evidence was found in my home; I had been at Pike Ness when the entire hamlet had been murdered. It would seem

I was guilty, even if in my heart I thought myself incapable of doing such vicious, wicked things. It was surely irrefutable – I was the Wraith of London. I was a killer of the innocent.

Some good still lingered in me – those had been Henley's words. I pulled myself back into the carriage, sat upon the floor and closed my eyes. I would not run; I would not flee. I needed to be brought to justice. I needed to serve penance for what I had done.

Another rifle shot blasted out.

'Riley, they're coming round the front!'

I looked towards the commotion through the haze and fog. I saw nothing of the guards or the driver. I held my hands together, bowed my head. I had no idea what was happening. But I needed to pay for my crimes.

Run.

The voice was quiet, both from afar and inside my mind.

'No,' I replied. 'No.'

The carriage lurched – the horses pulled.

Run. The voice was louder, clearer, the voice of Beatrice – of Dorothy Clarke – the voice of my fantasy.

'You're not real,' I moaned. 'Get out of my head.'

I stared at the broken shackles on the floor, at the fog that had stopped us, heard the voices of the panicked guards. All of it seemed very real.

'The nag's moving,' the driver cried. 'Let's go!'

Run! Please.

'I won't,' I whimpered, rocking back and forth, rubbing at my wrists. The horse lurched forwards again. Another shot rang out.

Unseen hands pushed against my back so hard I fell forwards towards the Hansom's open doors. When I looked, Dorothy was there, in the carriage, her face filled with wrath.

'Run! Run now!'

She pushed me again, so hard I tumbled onto the street.

'He's free!' the driver cried, though I didn't turn to see him. I stumbled in terror, my tired limbs wavering as I made way to the lane.

'He's running – the bastard's running!'

I was, for then I heard another gunshot fire and knew this time it had been aimed at me. I sprinted down the lane, more animal than man, and darted left when I came to another street. I saw no one as I ran up the road and cut down a black and sordid alley, not a soul as I skirted across another street and weaved this way and that to evade my captors. Each time I glanced over my shoulder, it seemed as though the wretched fog were chasing me, concealing me. It was everywhere, bleeding from the walls, from the road and pavements.

Finally, I collapsed into a passage beside a row of lowly tenements. I listened for the guards, waited for them to shout and cry and find where I was hiding. I held my head in my hands, tried to regain my senses.

'You had to run.'

Dorothy was sitting beside me. I screamed and crawled quickly from her.

'You're not real! You're just – you're not real.'

She held her hands up to me, tried to calm me. 'Please, Thomas, listen to me, just listen.'

'No!' I wrapped my hands around my ears like a child terrified of thunder. 'You are just my madness. Get out of my head!'

'I'm sorry I lied to you. I'm sorry I didn't tell you who I really was – I didn't want to frighten you. I couldn't tell you I was Dorothy Clarke.'

'You're not real. You're just some fantasy of my making.'

I closed my eyes, but then felt her dreadfully cold hands upon me. All the times she had touched me, all the times I had felt that frightful chill. The cold touch of something that isn't real, the touch of one's own imagination.

'I'm not some delusion of yours, Thomas, please, please believe me—'

'Get away from me!' I lashed out at her, at *it* – the thing that wasn't there.

'Please, Thomas. I went to sleep one night and never woke up. I have no idea who did this to me, I have no idea why. You have to find the killer, you have to—'

'It was me, all of it was me,' I wailed. 'The evidence is there. I killed you, I killed you!'

'You're being framed. Thomas, please. It may not be the police, but someone is conspiring against you.'

'Stop it.' I struck the sides of my head. 'Stop it, just stop it!'

'You're not a killer. You're a good man – I know you are!'

I could take no more. The words of the fantasy, the voice in my head, became too much. I lunged, seeing red and nothing more. I slammed my fist against the woman, felt cold for an instant and then pain, for my hand struck the brick of the passage wall.

I cradled it, for the pain jarred my wrist terribly. But the terrible figure of Dorothy Clarke was gone. I slumped to my knees, tried to catch my breath, to think straight. With her, it seemed the fog had gone as well, for the street to my right now appeared in full view. After a few moments, a man hobbled lazily past, though he didn't notice me.

I stood gingerly, tried to think what best to do. I knew I needed to return to the police, to either find my captors or hand myself in to the nearest station. But I admit I was terrified, so badly shaken by all that had happened, so stunned to find myself free – a convict on the run! I took a step towards the street and heard voices talking. Whistles then began screeching out, the unmistakable sound of police constables raising the alarm.

I knew I needed to return to custody. I knew I needed to face up to my crimes, to face justice.

But it shames me to say – for even now I look upon this act as a moment of the greatest dishonour, to myself and my moral standing – that I didn't. I thought of all that would happen to me. Facing the families of those I had killed. Facing a judge and jury who would stare with callous eyes and take no pity on me. Left to wait in a dark cell for days, beaten when so desired by my jailers. Left to starve in my own miserable filth. All of this, to finally be dragged out one morning and hauled to the gallows. My end would be a short fall and a tight rope.

In a heartbeat, as I thought of all this, cowardice overcame me. I chose to run. I stumbled down the passage, moved with crouched body, hurried to find the streets I knew too well, and the darkest corners of the city where I would feel safest.

The Loathsome in Loathsome Places

September 12th, 1905

Opium dens were not as common as the wealthy classes were led to believe, though they existed where people knew to find them. I cannot truly say what brought me to such a place, to the door of a ramshackle building that seemed in such a state of disrepair, the wind could surely topple the bricks and timbers. But such a place – so unseen and detached from the rest of the city – seemed to me as safe a place as any to hide.

The night had set in; it was dangerous for me. The constables on patrol gave no quarter to those who lurked in doorways or beneath railway arches – they searched them out down every street and alley. I'd thought to enter a dosshouse under a false name but realised it would be a dangerous risk. No doubt each and every dosshouse of the East End would be raided before dawn as the police hunted for me. The only meagre disguise I wore was the stolen cap of a chimney sweep, and black soot, spread across my face, arms and clothes.

This place – this miserable place – was my best chance for some rest and reprieve. I pushed open the door and stepped through an unseen wall of heat.

A young woman looked me up and down, a wasted, withered creature. Her eyes were wide, empty and bulbous. I could have been her father, her brother, her dearest husband. She wouldn't recognise me, nor know my name for all its worth. She was gone, lost in the euphoria, the blissful confusion of opium. It was a miracle she was standing, for in such a state even remaining upright is a considerable task. We were clearly on different worlds.

I could hear voices, low and distorted, coming through a thin curtain. Heady smoke drifted and wisped around me and the woman. She groaned, a noise barely human. I stepped towards the curtain, though stopped myself from going through. I turned back, and standing close to her ear, asked if she had any money. She didn't flinch or move. I looked about her person but saw nowhere in her rancid dress that could hide even a few pennies. Her left hand was closed, however, clutching onto something tightly. I reached tentatively for the hand, and prised open the fingers. From her palm, I took a single tu'penny piece. She moaned feebly as I moved away from her whilst looking down at the little coin in my hand, curious of the newly discovered depths of my shamefulness.

I tumbled through the curtain, tripped on a man whose legs were laid out just behind it. He garbled something to me in a language I didn't recognise. A fierce serpent wound around the right side of his face, the ink tattoo as unpleasant as the expression he held. He said some more to me, before leaning his head back against a wall and closing his eyes. I saw the serpent's teeth had been drawn upon the right eyelid.

There was hardly any light in the room – such places are all the better for it. The men and women who lay upon makeshift cots, hammered together with rusted nails and discarded timbers from the dockyards, were illuminated by a few faint candles. These were dotted about the room, in the corners and up on low hanging rafters. Thin sheets had been draped down, separating the room in a most irregular way, so that the true depth and scale of the place was hard to discern. All manner of fine and rotten things were used for furniture – felted chairs that were surely stolen; crates stacked and lashed together; barrels where glasses and disused pipes were laid to rest. The thickness of the smoke was truly remarkable, for it swirled and rose as a single, never-ending cloud that hid the ceiling entirely. The floors above were no doubt as poorly ventilated as this one; within a few moments I was drenched in a thick sheen of sweat.

The lost souls about me offered no greeting. Though not dead, none were truly living, for it was all they could do to raise their lit pipes to their lips and inhale as deeply as their lungs would allow. They moved in slow and clumsy fashion. Most were no doubt strangers, yet it was hard to be sure, for the small beds and rotten mattresses were cramped with bodies, the waking and the sleeping. They huddled close together, wrapped themselves around each other, drool dribbling onto their grubby shirts. All were unkempt and dirty, for this was no glamorous place, gilded with oriental canvasses and wisemen from China as fictions may falsely narrate. Only the saddest souls, with nothing more than despair and the need for escape, came to places as dismal and torrid as this. Nothing exotic or exciting dwelt within the walls.

I moved about the bodies. Sailors were easy to spot – their skin deeply tanned, their arms marked with the distant names of ports they had visited or women they had loved. Mariners such as these were likely stranded, either by choice or through no great fault of their own. The others, those ragged and bloated, whose faces were lined with sores, whose mouths had few teeth and whose hands were incapable of turning to work of any use, did all surely share similar tales of woe and misfortune. What had brought them to such a pit of foul smells and incivility was no doubt the stuff of great tragedy.

A man stretched his arm out as I inched past him; his hand

grabbed loosely at my ankle. When he rolled on his back, I saw many weeks' worth of dirt and grime dried upon his torn shirt; bones and skin all that lurked beneath. The fellow twisted in such an unnatural fashion, as though possessed by something that crawled and moved through his limbs. His eyelids opened for the briefest moment and I admit I pulled away from him in fright. The bloodshot whites of the eyes were all that could be seen.

"Ere!' cackled the voice of a woman, who leapt across the room, clinging to her purple petticoats. Her hair was wild, her face wilder still. She wore boots that cracked across the wooden floorboards and raised her height to my stature. Her age was hard to define, for the dim light of the flickering candles hid as many wrinkles as it revealed.

'Causing trouble, eh?' she whispered to me when she was close. She smelt faintly of sweet perfume and a heady musty odour, as though she hadn't stepped into the fresh air or even daylight for some time. She hit a hand against my shoulder and truly I saw dust sprinkle from the arm of her dress.

'Speak up or ye out.' Some of those about the floor were rousing as the woman spoke. Those awake sucked on their pipes and watched in vacant fascination.

'I-I need a drink.' I held out the tu'pence I had stolen. The woman looked from me to it and scowled.

'Find a pub.' She barged me back though I held my ground weakly.

'Please, I need something.'

The man on the floor beside us croaked and laughed drearily. The woman kicked her leg out at him.

'Quie'.' She snatched the coin from my hand and walked away. I followed after her, mumbled for my money back, for I was pained to think she had stolen it. She led me through to a back room, one of equal size but far more crowded than the first.

Here, beds were stacked atop each other in bunks, so that men and women alike were piled up towards the low ceiling. The heavy weight of the opium smoke was so compounded that the filthy shirt I wore clung to my back and shoulders. The air burnt inside my nostrils, laced with the stench of sweat.

The woman weaved about the room to a makeshift bar in the back corner. On the wall behind the bar were racks of pipes, all of various sizes but of the same rustic, simple design. The woman had stashed my tu'penny; she reached below the bar and pulled up a small cognac glass and a bottle with no label. She poured what I assumed was brandy into the glass and handed it indelicately to me.

'This is all ye get, scroungin' roun' 'ere with tu'pence.' She pointed to the pipes behind her. 'Charge leas' half shillin' for mixter and pipe. You come 'ere with tu'pence.'

I mumbled my thanks as I sipped upon the vicious drink – it was far from any brandy I had tasted.

'Can I … can I stay for a time?'

''Ere's no kip or peg!' She tapped on the bar. 'Salvation Army's down Blackfriars Road. See 'em for charity.'

'Can I stay till I finish this,' I said quietly, raising the small glass of poison. 'Till I'm done with this …'

The woman looked beyond me. A voice wailed out from behind, a woman screeching, gasping for air.

''E's not breathin'! My William's not breathin'!'

The witch who ran the den cursed and stepped around the bar, completely ignoring me.

'Get off 'im and keep your voice dow'. Is always trouble with ye – always.' She seemed not the least bit concerned by the state of the man on the floor. Even through the haze of smoke and poor light, I could see his complexion was pallid and waxy; his arms twitched ever so slightly.

I used the distraction to my benefit, moved from the bar to a dark and shady place, where the drapes were thicker and the candles far fewer. Through a host of bodies, I shifted carefully, clinging to the little glass – my only means of staying in this devilish place. I squeezed myself between a full bunk and a man whose eyes were barely open. He rested his head against my shoulder and muttered some nonsense, chuckling and scratching at his brow. A pipe still simmered loosely in his hand.

The misery – the sheer misery of it all! What depths I had fallen to. I cried quite suddenly, and felt no great need to stifle my tears, for those around me paid no heed nor offered their sympathies. I drank the vicious liquid and felt it burn down my throat; my stomach churned painfully. I rested my head back and cursed as the little tu'penny drink took no effect on me. My craving for real liquor lingered. All manner of depraved and lurid thoughts bombarded me relentlessly, and soon my mind turned to suicide and the need to rid myself of guilt and suffering and fear. It was surely the best thing I could do, surely more than I deserved.

Through bleary eyes I saw the curtain pull back and a woman step through. I assumed it was the treacherous witch, coming to sling me out. But as I rubbed my eyes clear and regained my focus, I realised with greater horror who the figure was.

Dorothy looked at me with abject pity.

'Thomas, please . . .'

I shook my head. 'I know you are not here – not real. Yet if only I could right the wrongs I have done you.'

'You have done no wrong.'

I hit the side of my head hard. 'You're just my imagination. You're not real.'

She crouched before me, rubbed at the corner of her eyes. 'Thomas, I need you. I need you to help find who did this to me.'

'I did.' I rapped my knuckles against my temple. 'I did, I did, why will this delusion not end?'

The man next to me stirred, the little pipe he held falling to my lap. I took hold of it, looking at it with a morose fascination.

'Thomas, it may not have been the police, but someone has framed you.' Dorothy reached her hand towards me. 'You didn't kill those people in Pike Ness – you were on the island with me when Lachlan was beaten.'

As her hand touched upon my knee, I felt her dreadful chill, and it was surely the last thing I needed.

'Thomas, listen to me.'

'Get out of my head,' I muttered weakly.

I grabbed up the pipe, still barely lit, and sucked on the mouth-piece. The embers glowed softly as smoke filled my throat and lungs. The effect was instantaneous, terrible and extraordinary, as though some silent explosion blocked out every conscious thought I had. My senses charged and fired for an instant, and I tasted such strange things, smelt odours most unnatural. I saw the room in its grotesque entirety, before every harsh edge and corner merged and softened. Then the room was merely a blur. My mind eased to a place where all the horror of my circumstance was forgotten, where I slipped into blissful darkness, and rested, for a time, in peace.

Nowhere to Run

September 13th, 1905

I heard a voice, an ugly, angry voice. In darkness, I started to feel pain. It slowly burnt through my body, through lungs that stung with each meagre breath, through limbs that were bruised and beaten. As the darkness lifted, to deepest shades of crimson, the pain grew unbearable. I groaned feebly, as I felt something kick at my legs. The angry voice grew louder. I mumbled words that were barely audible, wishing only to return to darkness and peace.

The voice became coherent. My legs were thrashed at repeatedly. When I opened my eyes, my head erupted and I knew that it was not the result of alcohol, for no such agony could be caused by drink. I rolled to my side and vomited – the voice became clear as I writhed.

'I tol' you 'ere's no kip! I tol' you!'

I looked up to the woman who ran the den. Though I couldn't recall why in that moment, I knew I had wronged her somehow.

'Wha-what's happening?'

'Sling it! Ou' before it gets ugly!'

She grabbed me up roughly and I was too weak to stop her. I regained some memory of the dreadful place as the woman led me out, back through the first room, where now it seemed, far fewer bodies lay about the floor.

'All night. All nigh' on tu'pence and thievin'. You takin' me for a fool?'

She pulled back the curtain to the small entrance room. I saw the space where the young woman had been standing and recalled stealing her money. It was the first of many miserable recollections I was to have.

The door was flung open; I was shoved into cold light. I had to shield my eyes for it was unbearable to keep them open. The woman pushed me once more, screeching in my ear.

'All nigh' ye was 'ere, an' if ye e'vr come back, I'll 'ave ye. You'll be in the river!' With that she stepped back inside her dingy den and slammed the door. I was left reeling, trying to gather my bearings.

I heard the river, the yelling of men and the bustle of work. When I finally looked about properly, I saw the ships anchored at the East India Docks. The events of the previous days lunged back into focus and I was crippled for a moment by fear and guilt in equal measure.

Dockers barged past me. Some turned and glared at me with suspicious eyes. I began walking, though my steps were badly laboured. I ached so dreadfully, and my stomach was pained as if I had been stabbed in my sleep. I had no idea where to go, no idea what to do, for thinking straight in that moment was impossible. I walked, for it was all I could do to keep moving.

It was early morning from what I could gather. The air was bitter, the sky a fine and gentle blue. I moved along the river, towards London Docks. On occasion I was forced to stop, when the pain in my stomach intensified and I doubled over in sheer agony. No one approached me, quite the opposite in fact. Soon the men who set about to work were giving me a wide berth, and I couldn't blame them. I was in a filthy state, groaning and moving in the most deplorable fashion, muttering foulness whenever the pains of my body became too much to bear.

How badly I wished to sit. But I couldn't, for if I did, I wouldn't be able to stand again until I was discovered and dragged to my feet by a constable. That savage, instinctive urge to flee was all that kept me moving.

It wasn't long till the figure of Dorothy Clarke appeared before me again. She came to me as I stood clutching at my chest, as the rupturing pain from my stomach burnt up towards my lungs. I groaned with misery at the sight of her.

'Will this madness ever cease!'

'You look ill.'

'I am.' I lumbered past her and carried on walking. She followed at my side.

'You'll die if you carry on like this.'

'I deserve it. Were it not my cowardice, I would throw myself in the river with a heavy sack bound to each leg.'

She didn't say anything to that, though she continued to walk at my side. I hadn't the strength to tell her to leave.

'I can't atone for what I've done to you,' I muttered, mindful of those who passed me by. 'The *real* you, not merely this … this … manifestation.'

'I am real, Thomas.'

'You're not – you're just my guilt, my guilt and madness.' I turned to her. 'I've seen you move things, touch things. How can you do that if you are a ghost?'

I carried on walking before she could answer, rambling on with my eyes down to the floor.

'If the other things I see are ghosts, why are they so different from you? Why do you come to me as a woman and they as monstrous beasts? I see such horrible things for they are surely my own consciousness; my own guilt-ridden mind punishing me.

Admittedly you seem different, special somehow.' I interrupted her before she could answer. 'If you're a ghost and no one can see you, why not walk into Scotland Yard? Why not discover who the Wraith is for yourself?'

'I did,' Dorothy nodded. 'Well, I walked into Scotland Yard, I mean. For some months after I...' she hesitated. 'After I was killed, I wanted answers. I spent many days in and around Scotland Yard trying to find them. The police weren't lying to you, Thomas; they had no leads on this until that thumbprint appeared.'

I laughed rather bitterly. 'This delusion is worsening.'

'And I wasn't lying to you, either,' Dorothy continued. 'When I said I saw you outside the Yard. By then, I couldn't face going inside anymore; it seemed the police would never learn the truth. I would spend hours standing around, outside on the embankment, hoping – praying – something good might happen, that someone might uncover some evidence, might apprehend the culprit.' Her voice faltered. 'And then I saw you, a man I vaguely recognised from the papers, a man renowned as an investigator. And I felt such hope, as though I knew we had to help each other...'

'If you were really a spirit, you would know your killer,' I said cruelly. 'You would be able to identify the guilty man.'

She grew angry then. 'I told you I was taken in my sleep. I have the vaguest memory of being somewhere dark, somewhere cold, of a silhouette running from me and leaving me alone in the black.' Her lips trembled. 'When I awoke properly, I was in my home. I thought it merely a bad dream, until I realised the worst was still to come. No one could see me. No one could hear me!' A tear trickled down her face. 'There were police searching through my things, questioning my housekeeper, trying to contact my husband. It was hours before I realised what was

going on – that it was no sick trick – that I was in fact … dead.'
She rubbed her eyes with shaking hands. 'We haven't the time
for this.'

'I have nowhere to run,' I muttered, ignoring her completely.
'Nowhere at all.'

'Thomas, please …'

'You're a voice in my head. Just give me some peace.'

'Enough of this,' she growled, grabbing hold of my left arm
suddenly. I tried to pull away from her but she wouldn't let go. 'I
am Dorothy Clarke. I am real, not merely some fantasy of yours.'

'You are—'

'A ghost, Thomas. A ghost bound to you, though God knows
why!' She pulled on my arm, and the most bizarre sensation
tingled to my shoulder. 'There's no time for this self-loathing,
this self-pity.'

'Get off me,' I growled, trying to pull away. No matter how
hard I tried, I couldn't break free. My arm began to sting, and
how strange I must have appeared to those walking by. Dorothy
pulled me closer to her, and though I still believed her a visage
of my own making, she felt very real to me then.

'You need to listen to me. *You are not the guilty man* – I know
it to be true, you can't be.'

'Get away!'

'We were on that island together,' she said angrily, the hollows
around her eyes seeming to deepen, the lines of her face growing
more pronounced. 'We were on that island until we returned in
the boat. You didn't poison the water before you left, you didn't
return and assault Lachlan.'

To my alarm, her cold touch began to grow hot. As I looked at
her hand on my arm, I saw her skin blister and crack. The strange
stinging sensation became a burning pain that swept across the
left side of my body and paralysed me.

'You're hurting me,' I moaned. She didn't let go.

'It may not be some great conspiracy, or some miserable cult, but someone has acted against you and staged this, and I need you to grasp some sanity and *be an investigator.*' The darkness around her eyes gave her face a terrifying appearance. Her voice was furious, and that fury was changing her. I pulled away with all my strength.

'Forget the motive, the reason why. *You* need to think who could have framed you, how they did it.' Her voice was becoming distorted, loud and inhuman. I felt myself nodding, heard myself pleading, as I tried to free myself from her scorching grip.

'Please…'

'If you don't, the real killer will be free to do as he pleases, to kill whoever he chooses, to take them in the night as he took me. Don't you realise how angry I am about this? At him – at you?'

The world around her was lost to me, for she consumed the light, seemed to grow before my very eyes.

'I won't let it happen. I won't let him win! I have to know what happened, and I need *you* to regain some sense and help me!'

Her grip eased enough for me to wriggle free. I fell back against the floor with a thud. In the blink of an eye she was gone. A man walked by, calling me a drunkard.

I stood and turned around to find her. For a moment, I thought she was gone completely. Then I heard her voice at my back.

'So think, who could have staged this against you? Who could have planted the evidence at your home?'

She was calm, her face unblemished by unnatural and dark shadows. I rubbed at my arm where she had grabbed me; it still tingled uncomfortably.

'You could be wrong,' I muttered. 'You surely are.'

'Just think on the question – who had the means to stage this against you?'

I thought on it, indulged in the idea for a time. After a few minutes I spoke feebly.

'The letter from Hawthorn, the one they say I forged, was never sent from Scotland. I have no recollection of it ever coming through my door.'

'Fine, good. So someone had to plant it in your home before you went to the police. Who has been in your home recently?'

I shrugged. 'I am an addict, a wreck. I barely remember the days – anyone could have been there.'

She stepped closer to me, imploring me. 'Who do you remember?'

'Jack,' I replied. 'Just Jack Lavernock. He came to collect me to take me to the Yard; sat in my lounge whilst I got ready.'

I thought of the last time we had spoken; of the picture he had shown me in the prison cell. I set aside my remorse, thought about the day he had come to my home, the time I had spent upstairs when he had been alone.

'He could have planted the letter amongst all the others; I had a stack of correspondence unattended. He had plenty of time to do it.'

'And what of the other evidence,' Dorothy said. 'The photographs, the trinkets – my necklace.'

I shook my head. 'No, no, I would have noticed him, he remained downstairs—' I cut myself short. 'He told me he was there when the CID searched my home. He was in the house when they found the evidence.'

'Did he find it?' Dorothy asked quickly. I shook my head.

'I can't be sure, but …'

I was quiet, suddenly consumed by thought. Dorothy didn't speak. My tiredness, my aching head and body, made any logical reasoning difficult. After a moment, however, I looked up at her, frowning.

'Lavernock has, or had, the same gun as me.' I nodded to myself as I spoke. 'We all did in the Forensic Crime Directorate; Hawthorn got surplus guns from the military – Enfield revolvers.'

'He could have killed those brothers,' Dorothy said excitedly. 'He left the bullet in the wall, knowing full well it was a match for your gun.'

'He knew where I used to work,' I continued. 'Mr Timberwell's. I spoke to him of it many times.'

I saw the 'TO LET' sign on the front window of Timberwell's boutique, remembered what the old man in the street had said, that Mr Timberwell had died 'a little while back'. A terrible thought occurred to me.

'The photographs, the records, the details about the victims would surely have been there. Timberwell died not long ago.'

'You think Lavernock had a part in that?'

I shook my head. 'I don't know. I don't know, all this is circumstantial, it's not hard proof.'

'But it's something,' Dorothy replied. 'Isn't it enough to make you want to find Lavernock and try and get some answers?'

A moment's excitement came and faded in an instant, and I looked at Dorothy, feeling the same resigned fate I had since the evidence was put to me. She noticed it, for her face became crestfallen.

'You have to try. Please. You have to believe that you didn't do these things.'

'Because a voice only I can hear tells me so,' I said bitterly.

'Because it's the truth.'

I bowed my head, realising that all this time I had been standing in plain sight, appearing surely to be talking to myself. Someone may already have flagged down a constable and waved him in my direction. I began hurriedly moving from the docks, though Dorothy remained with me. She was quiet for some time, which I found a blessing.

I headed north and soon came to Cannon Street Road; from there I moved to the early bustle on Commercial Road East. Mindful of officers on the beat, I kept a keen eye, though it occurred to me that Flynn and his plainclothes troop from Special Branch might also be searching for me. I was still grubby, though my chimney sweeper façade was unlikely to get me out of the city. I needed to eat, for then I was dreadfully weary, taking such great effort to move one leg before the other.

'You can't go on like this,' Dorothy said, her words spoken fast. 'Even if you find a way to get out of the city, what will you do?'

'I don't know,' I grumbled.

'When the police catch you, they won't listen to any of your theories then. They won't care if Lavernock has the same gun as you, or had the means to plant the letter, maybe the evidence. You have to find out the truth of these matters for *yourself*, before it's too late.'

'And how should I do that?' I said, quite mockingly.

'Go to Lavernock's home, there may be evidence that can prove—'

'Break in and search his home,' I laughed bitterly. 'Another charge to add to my sheet, for what difference it will make. The evidence points to *me*, your being with me now rather confirms the reality of all this, that I am mad.'

'Don't you want to uncover the truth? Surely, with all that you stand to lose—'

'Lost!' I held my hand up to her then. 'Enough. The evidence was put before me, I am the guilty man and I need no more of this hysteria to ease my shame. You, the voice in my head can just… leave me.'

I stepped away, spied a stall across the street with fruit and vegetables laid out. I considered how best to steal some, and how, if needed, I could run to get away.

'Thomas.'

Dorothy's voice was coming from just behind me. I ignored it, hoping it would fade away.

'Thomas.' She grabbed my arm with her terrible touch, and I turned upon her quickly.

'Just get out of my head!'

'Look.' She pointed to a group of men and women gathered on a street corner. Some were reading papers, others talking amongst themselves. They chattered quietly, nervously. I spotted the newspaper vendor, his stack of papers beside his feet. He was talking to another man, their expressions both dire and concerned.

'Likely news of my escape,' I muttered.

Dorothy stepped into the road without answering. I was pleased to see her go. I looked back to the stall of food and began walking towards it, my hands in my pockets, my eyes focused down on the ground. I moved maybe ten, fifteen yards, before Dorothy startled me terribly. She stood in front of me and pointed to the huddle of people.

'You have to see what the papers say.'

'I have to eat.'

'Look at the papers, then I will leave you if you ask. I swear it.'

I was bargaining with my own consciousness. It was ludicrous. Still I agreed. Together we stepped across the road, and cautiously – for it occurred to me then that the papers may contain a picture of myself! – came to the edge of the group. With my eyes still down to the ground, I asked a man who was nearly as filthy as I, what all the fuss was.

'Been another kidnapping.'

My heart surged to life, began to beat with a manic intensity. I asked him to repeat himself.

'Another one's been snatched by the Wraith. Las' night they reckon. Coppers had him and 'e escaped yesterday. No idea how the 'ell 'e gave 'em the slip.'

I lingered a moment longer, before walking away, wholly dazed.

'You were in that damned den last night,' Dorothy hissed. 'You were there the entire night.'

She was right. The wretched woman who ran the place had turned me out because of it, told me to my face.

'If there was another kidnapping last night, it couldn't have been committed by you, as surely none of these kidnappings have been.'

I stumbled across the road, rubbing my head, my thoughts confused and disjointed. I was shocked to learn of another murder, to realise that what I had come to believe may not be true, that someone with ill intent may indeed be behind all this, framing me maliciously. I forgot about my hunger, about the pains in my stomach and throughout my body. I looked to Dorothy, seeing her anew.

'You, you are … you are a ghost then?'

She nodded. 'I am. You have to believe it.'

I looked back towards the crowd reading their papers.

'I don't know. I don't know what to believe.'

When I turned back to Dorothy, she looked pained, distraught even.

'But we need to find Jack Lavernock,' I said then, my voice stronger than it had been for some days. 'Or at least go to his home.'

Dorothy nodded her head. 'There may be answers there.'

He Who Holds His Silence

September 13th, 1905

Lavernock's terraced home was in Pimlico, a quiet area of the city occupied mostly by managers and businessmen. I'd been there once, shortly after he had bought it, only months before the Forensic Crime Directorate had been disbanded. As he'd shown me the empty rooms with pride, he had talked about his hopes for a family, about a wife and children. It was a rare moment to see the man separated from his work, to witness his deeper aspirations. Perhaps things would have been different had he settled down, had he pursued these personal ambitions more than the criminals and murderers that plagued London's streets. Jack still lived alone in the house, with no wife or children for company.

Rain beat heavily upon me as I sat watching Lavernock's front door, on a park bench in a deserted green space. Dorothy seemed baffled.

'What are you doing?'

'Waiting.'

She looked from me to the house. 'Waiting for what?'

'Lavernock. He should be on duty, searching for me with the rest of the force.' I saw the look of disappointment, of *revulsion*, on his face when he had left my cell at Walthamstow police station. I'd presumed it was the wildness of my accusation that had

sent him away, though maybe it had been something else. *Fear*.
Maybe I'd struck upon some truth and Jack had been fearful of
me then. 'I need to be certain he isn't here before we go in.'

Dorothy nodded reluctantly.

'I don't understand it,' I muttered, looking away from her. 'If
you are truly a spirit and not some manifestation of my own
making, then so are all the others I have seen.' I thought of the
dreadful creatures who, for nearly a year, had crept through my
house in the dead of night, those of most monstrous intent,
who had haunted me mercilessly. I saw the spider-like legs of
the ghoul who had scurried up my chimney, of the woman-like
creature appearing from the bath in Pike Ness. 'Why are you so
different? Why are you so … human?'

Dorothy paused in thought. 'We are all caught between two
worlds. I, and all those you have seen. We are trapped because
of the injustices done to us.' She smiled thinly. 'Death, it seems,
isn't quite unjust enough. The anger, the total fury, the crushing
sorrow you feel when you realise the truth, when you learn that
your death was not of natural causes, that someone sought to
steal your life for their own miserable purpose.' She sighed. 'It's
overwhelming, worse than any grief one could possibly feel in
life, compounded when you watch the world move around you
and know you will never again be a part of it. Every menial,
foolish thing you'll never be able to do comes to mind in an
instant, along with all the important things. Knowing you won't
be able to hold your loved ones, at least in any way that would
be of comfort; knowing you won't be able to tell them all the
things you wish you could.'

She looked down towards the floor, took another deep breath
to steady herself.

'In death, that rage and grief can consume you. It can change
you – can physically change you, if you allow it.'

I noticed how she clenched her fists, how they shook ever so slightly as she spoke.

'I feel it all the time inside of me; this ... wrath, this vengeful presence that wants to control me. The others – those that you see, those who are frightful to you – they've let that wrath consume them. They're lost in their anger, corrupted by it, shaped by it.' She looked into my eyes. 'What else can they be but monsters when they have suffered so greatly?'

She must have seen something in my face, some disbelief.

'They mean you no harm,' she said with conviction. 'I don't understand why they are drawn to you as they are, and I doubt they do either. But they are simply in pain. For us, Thomas, this whole world is pain. Emotionally and physically.'

'You're not like them,' I muttered. 'You still haven't explained why you are so different.'

She sighed, shrugging her shoulders. 'I won't let the anger I feel change me. I *can't*. I *have* to find out the truth of what happened to me and the others this madman has kidnapped. I have to ensure he is stopped.'

I thought on her words for a time and all the things I wished to ask her. But as we sat upon that bench in the rain, I simply could not find the words

'You must be very strong,' was all I said, rather clumsily. 'To ... to not let yourself be changed.'

She didn't reply.

'Perhaps one day your family can see you the way I do. Perhaps you can talk to them as you talk to me now.'

She shook her head. 'I'm afraid I am beyond such optimism. In truth, Thomas, I fear you may be unique in all that you see.'

We watched Jack's home for another ten minutes or so. Nothing stirred. No lights were lit, no curtains rustled. No one came or went; no smoke rose from the chimneys despite the cold.

Finally, with a grunt of annoyance, Dorothy stood and started towards his front door.

'What the hell are you doing?'

She didn't answer. I stood and even tried to stop her, but her strength, and the feel of her terrible touch, was too much. I followed her, angry, my hand tingling with pain. We climbed the few short steps that led to the white pillars and dark front door of Jack's home.

'What do you plan on doing?' I rasped. 'Knocking the front door, ringing the bell?'

She shook her head, grabbed hold of the handle and tried turning it slowly.

'How can you touch things,' I said, staring down at her hand. 'How can you grab that handle?'

'It takes a great effort,' she muttered through gritted teeth. 'Even the simplest things can be draining. It's locked.'

'That's not an answer. You moved things in the manor, carried things, grabbed hold of me. The shackles I wore on my wrists when Flynn's men were transporting me – you broke them!'

'The door is locked,' she said again.

I glanced up the front of the house, at the windows. 'We can find another means to get in.'

'I can move through the door,' she said coolly.

I shook my head. 'How can you grip a door handle yet be able to move through a door?'

'This world is pain to me, Thomas,' she said slowly. 'Just being here hurts, as though I am trapped somewhere I shouldn't be. I can take hold of things – even you. But it causes such agony, such effort. At times I can't bear do the simplest tasks.' She took a breath, as though composing herself. 'Imagine every bone of your hand, the bones in your fingers, shattering to a thousand pieces in an instant.'

Without another word she stepped through the door. I was stunned, for a moment later, I heard a bolt slide and the door creaked open slowly. I stared at Dorothy, her appearance grave. Her skin was deathly pale, her eyes and lips bled of colour.

'That's what it's like to hold things here, to touch you,' she near whispered. 'Like your body is being splintered into tiny pieces. Breaking the shackles you wore – that caused pain I cannot even begin to describe.'

I stepped in hurriedly, and tried to comfort her, though she brushed me away.

'The door was bolt-locked,' she whispered, breathlessly.

'Are you all right—'

'Not with a key,' she cut in. 'Someone locked it from the inside.'

I looked from her to the space around us, as dreadful excitement surged through me. Someone was in the house.

Nothing stirred but the rain against the windows. We stood in a small hallway, with stairs rising to the upper landing. There was a dining room to our left, and Dorothy edged into it, though her steps seemed laboured. I followed her, looking towards the stairs as I went, mindful that Jack might be resting in the rooms above. An empty vase stood on a table with chairs neatly tucked around it. No artwork adorned the walls, no family photographs could be seen. A clock was ticking, though the time was wrong. The place was clean but barely lived in.

Towards the back of the dining room was a set of cherry wood double doors. I recalled that they led to a lounge or study of sorts. The doors were shut, and I listened for any sound from the other side. I heard nothing but Dorothy's shallow breaths and the ticking of the clock. For some perverse reason I pictured Lavernock in the next room, waiting for us (for me!) with a gang of officers and sergeants. Mindful of leaving fingerprints, I took a corner of my shirt in hand and pushed down gently on a door handle. I tried to compose myself, for what good it would do, then eased the door open as quietly as I could. Dorothy stepped into the next room before me, though stopped abruptly. I had to move around her to see what she saw. Indeed, Jack was in the room, though not in the manner I had expected.

There was blood everywhere. A thick streak lined the far wall with trickles dripping down to the skirting board. The colour was vibrant, fresh. Jack lay in the centre of the room, his body sprawled on the floor in the most undignified manner, his head turned towards us, his open eyes staring at the door we had just walked through. His expression was heart-breaking, for it was clear his death had been slow, and he had grown dreadfully scared and confused. Blood pooled around him and soaked through the rug he lay on. Papers and documents were strewn around the floor. The room smelled of smoke and urine.

I rushed to Jack's side, meaning to roll him on his back, then stopped myself. He was dead, there was nothing to be done about that. Yet I had to be cautious, to think clearly. I couldn't leave any evidence that could falsely prove I was behind Jack's murder. Awkwardly, and with less dignity than Jack deserved, I used my elbows and wrists to roll him over onto his back. Dorothy moved around him awkwardly, staring at his corpse.

Jack's miserable end was made clear to me when I saw the deep and bloody gash across his throat. He had been left to bleed out. I quivered and nearly broke down, but Dorothy wouldn't let me. She knelt beside me, looked me in the eyes and spoke to me sternly.

'I know this is hard, but you have to separate yourself from this. We have to hurry.'

Her resolve gave me strength. I nodded feebly, took a breath to compose myself then cleared my throat.

'It appears someone wanted Jack to suffer.'

'The Wraith, the real villain?'

I shrugged. 'Perhaps. But why would they come for him?'

'Maybe Lavernock was an accomplice who needed silencing.'

I nodded, thinking of what Henley had said in the interview. *He didn't believe you could have any involvement in all this.*

Grabbing a portion of my shirt, I carefully felt inside Jack's jacket, rummaged through his pockets. There was nothing; it seemed even his cigarettes had been taken. On the far side of the room, a chair lay on its side next to a small cluttered desk. The drawers were all open and had clearly been riffled through.

'Can you see a weapon?' I muttered looking about. Dorothy pointed beneath the desk. There I spotted a pistol, no doubt Jack's. I envisaged a struggle, and the gun being kicked out of Jack's reach as he lay dying.

Dorothy stepped over to a fireplace and knelt at the grate. 'Someone burnt something in here, letters or papers of some kind.'

I stood beside her, staring at the ashen grey leaves in the fire. A few scraps of pages were visible, though there was nothing discernible on them.

'They tried destroying all Jack's notes, I'll wager. Seems they were in a hurry.' I stepped back to the body. Jack's eyes were still open, staring at me, following me as lifeless eyes often do. I knelt, took a corner of my shirt to hand and carefully closed the eyelids. 'Jack could still be guilty of some crime, an accomplice silenced as you suggest.' I looked at the streak of blood along the wall. 'This depravity however, the manner in which he was killed … I'd wager more that Jack was onto something, maybe even confided in someone.'

'There's still evidence against him though,' Dorothy said, stepping towards the desk.

'Circumstantial, as we said. The real guilty man is the one who killed Jack.' I looked up and down Jack's body, at the tackiness of the blood around his neck. 'He was killed less than twelve hours ago, which means the killer knew of my escape.'

'They wanted to frame you further?'

'They wanted the opportunity to tie up loose ends. Regardless of there being any evidence that I was here, or at the scene of this other disappearance, it won't matter. The Yard will simply place the blame on me. We have to find the real killer before they flee – there's nothing else for it.'

Dorothy wasn't really listening; she had spotted something discarded on the floor, close to Jack's hand. 'Look at that.'

Amidst the pieces of paper strewn close to Jack's body, I saw a flimsy map, one that had been folded regularly and was badly creased. It was spattered in blood, obscuring the street names and locations. Still, it was clear that the map was of London.

'What do you notice about it?' Dorothy muttered. I didn't understand her; the blood was dashed in no noticeable pattern or fashion, far from it. Lines of ruby red streaked across the page, cutting across streets from west to east. She knelt down and pointed at a single area, where it appeared a circle had been made.

'There's another here,' she said pointing, 'and another.' Indeed, it seemed now there was some purpose to the markings, for the small circles were surely not made by chance. A few were over the west of the city, one or two in the north. More were made around the East End, and when I spotted the location of one such marking, I seized the map up quite suddenly, with no concern for fingerprints.

'Flower and Dean Street,' I said nervously. 'This was where one of the victim's was taken, uh, Chenko, I believe her name was. I saw Jack there the morning before I travelled to Scotland.'

Looking at the other small circles it dawned on me. 'These must be the locations of the other victims. The wealthy in the west, the poor in the east.'

'Chelsea,' Dorothy muttered. 'He's circled the streets around my home. What does it mean?'

'I don't know, it was done quickly, made in blood—' I looked back at Jack's corpse. 'Jack was trying to tell us something; he was marking the map with his own blood.'

The lines, the streaks cutting across the city, took on a relevance now, a sudden importance. Yet as I stared at them, I couldn't discern what they meant.

'He tried to write something.' Dorothy pointed to the top corner of the map. A single bloody letter was marked feebly, what was surely an E, though it had been smudged badly.

'His killer was in a hurry. No doubt they tried destroying his notes in the fire before fleeing. Jack must have still been alive; they just left him to *die*.' I spoke the last word with venom. 'He held on long enough to try and tell us something.'

'These lines have to be relevant,' Dorothy nodded fervently. 'They have to tell us something about who did thi—'

There came a thudding from the front door. It made us both jump in fright. Someone spoke, their words muffled. They knocked again; this time harder. I quickly closed the doors from the study to the dining room.

'Who could it be?' Dorothy whispered, panicked.

I thought I knew. 'The police. Come to find Jack.' I stuffed the map roughly in my pocket. 'We have to hurry. There's a back door, a garden, I think. The killer must have fled that way.' I stood and led her out of the room via another door. After a moment's hesitation I returned, scrambled beneath the desk and took possession of Jack's gun. I checked it was loaded and thrust it in my pocket.

'What are you doing?' Dorothy mouthed.

'I may need it,' was all I replied before dashing from the room. The knocking was louder, and I could discern a man's voice.

'Jack. Open the door. We need you.'

An officer from the CID, surely. We hurried through the kitchen and a rear door that led to a garden. Here, with great difficulty owing to my weary body, I was able to hitch myself over a low wall into a back lane that led around the row of terraced homes. When I turned back to look for Dorothy, she was gone.

Slowly I glanced out onto the street and up the road towards Lavernock's front door. There was a plainclothes officer, kneeling at the door, looking through the letterbox. A constable in black uniform and cape stood behind him. As I watched, the officer gestured to the constable and the pair began forcefully shouldering the door.

'What are you doing?' Dorothy whispered then from my side, making me lurch with fright. 'We have to go.'

I watched a moment longer as both men began thudding their heavy boots at the door. It crashed open suddenly and they stepped inside. Exchanging a brief glance, Dorothy and I scarpered.

'Where are you going?' she asked me as I moved briskly along the streets.

'The East End, Flower and Dean Street.' I took out the map, saw the circle around Lucinda Chenko's home. 'I need to know what Jack was telling us.'

Through the Eyes of a Child
September 13th, 1905

Exhaustion struck me down like a steam engine, suddenly and with no warning. I'd gone south of the river, walking indirectly from Lavernock's home back to the East End. I was skulking through All Hallows when my legs buckled and the last of my strength gave way. I fell to the floor and Dorothy looked at me gravely.

'It's nothing, we need to go on.' As I took another step I nearly fell to the floor once more. 'I need somewhere to sit, just for a moment.'

I struggled a little way further, came in sight of a workhouse and moved up a thin road lined on either side by dishevelled and dreary-looking tenements. Halfway up the road, a thin passage cut between the houses on the left, and stepping through, I came to a courtyard that smelt frightful. It was filled with all manner of waste, rot and filth, no doubt thrown from the windows of the rooms above. The place was deserted.

I slid down a wall and settled in something wet and unpleasant. It hardly mattered, for the rain still beat down upon me. I rested my head back against the wall, heard Dorothy talk to me, though I paid her no attention. My entirety was throbbing with pain – I needed to eat, to drink and to sleep. I took out the map from my pocket, gazed at the bloody marks and the incoherent lines.

The lines began to blur as my eyes grew heavy, and a moment later all went dark.

I felt Dorothy's unnatural touch, and roused myself enough to tell her to leave me. 'I need a few minutes, that's all.'

'It's been hours,' she growled into my ear.

When I prised open my eyes, I saw the change of daylight, and felt the biting chill of evening. The map was still in my hand. My body felt no better though.

'We have to go,' Dorothy insisted. 'People have seen you.'

I gazed up fearfully towards the dark windows of the surrounding tenements, hearing voices from inside. I hauled myself to my feet, keeping my head low as I stumbled from the courtyard and back into the street. Here, too many men and women looked upon me, for many sat or stood in the doors of the houses and buildings, taking the cool air or smoking. I hurried from the place as fast as I could, though this was no great speed. I had wasted too much time, time in which the Wraith's latest kidnap victim – the innocent snatched away the previous night as the papers had reported – could have been murdered, their body disposed of. Time in which the Wraith may have slipped back into the shadows or even fled the city. Time in which the police may have closed their net tighter around me.

I crossed Southwark Bridge, moved along the river and past the Tower to the docks. I'd spotted constables along the way, and I moved as casually as any other man down the street, though in truth, every sighting had twisted my stomach in knots. There were more as I came to the East End, some patrolling in pairs. The grubbiness of my appearance was all that disguised me, and I pulled the cap I wore down low across my brow. The coming of eve and the dreary elements aided me, and as gas lamps around the city began to light, I came to Commercial Street, where the drunkards, the revellers, the broken and forgotten, moved along in cackling droves. Flower and Dean Street was all but empty by comparison.

'Her home is down here?' Dorothy asked, and I nodded, pointing to the end of the road. A rolling boom – the sound of the nearby docks or thunder – bellowed out as we came to the ramshackle door of the house I knew Lucinda Chenko shared. No one could afford to live alone in places like Flower and Dean Street; four, maybe five families would share each of the squalid dwellings. I recalled Lavernock telling me of a family of five, living in the adjacent room to Chenko, how they had noticed a terrible smell, and discovered Chenko's dead child.

Now standing before the door, I struggled to think what best to do. I pulled out Lavernock's map, gazed at it in the gloom and thought hard on what the intersecting, bloody lines could mean.

'What are we to do?' Dorothy seemed agitated, nervous. I shook my head.

'Now we are here, I don't know. These lines connect the crime scenes together but not in any way that's coherent.' I glanced up either end of the street, stepped back and examined the front of the building. 'Jack must have thought of something. There has to be a reason he did this.'

I folded the map carefully and tucked it in my pocket. 'Are you going to go in?' Dorothy muttered.

I shook my head. In truth, I was fearful of entering the place. 'I don't know what we may find.' I rubbed my brow, frustrated, agitated. I stepped back to the door and impulsively reached for the handle. The door opened before I pushed against it; a man stepped out into the street, something heavy and metallic in his hand. He pushed me back with his broad chest, nearly knocking me to the floor.

'Wot you wan' eh?' He stepped towards me and I was so start-led I couldn't think what to say. 'Gawd blimey, if you're another man from papers you'll 'ave this.' He shook the metal object – an iron poker – at me. I raised my hands. 'Come on 'en. Speak up!' He was near yelling and I could see curtains being drawn back from the adjoining homes.

'I'm investigating the disappearance of Lucinda Chenko,' I stammered. 'I'm not a reporter.'

The man lowered the poker a little. 'Copper are ye?' He looked me up and down, at the filth still covering my clothes and skin.

I nodded. 'Of a sort. I'm following up on some lines of enquiry.' I gestured at the dirt on my sleeves and shirt. 'I'm afraid it's been quite a difficult day. You may have spoken to my colleague, DI Jack Lavernock, previously.'

The man seemed to relax then, no doubt recognising the name. 'Oh. Come 'ere at this late hour?'

I apologised. 'This case is very important – we're working around the clock.'

The man shrugged. 'Wot you want then? You comin' inside?'

He stepped back inside the building and I glanced at Dorothy nervously. She stepped in before me, though I admit even then, I hesitated to follow her.

Inside I saw an open door on my right, spotted a cluttered room that smelled of wet laundry and thick smoke. A woman was cradling a small baby, one who began crying as soon as I set eyes upon it. A young boy, dirty and wearing little more than rags, sat close to a dwindling fire. A girl of maybe four or five stood at the open door and looked up at me with wide, curious eyes.

She met my gaze for only a moment, turning to look down the narrow corridor where Dorothy was following the man, no doubt her father. Her stare changed then, her eyes flooding with fear. I looked down at her, as she in turn seemed to stare after Dorothy. It was impossible, for I knew the girl couldn't see her. Yet still, her eyes widened unnaturally, and the colour of her complexion changed dramatically...

'You comin'?' The man was standing at the end of the corridor, in front of a door that was tucked almost entirely below a flight of rickety stairs. I nodded, glancing at the girl who still stood watching Dorothy. The man opened the door with a heavy shove from his shoulder. A putrid, stale smell seeped into the corridor, heavy and overpowering. Whether the man was perturbed by the smell, or had simply grown accustomed to it, I cannot say, but he didn't flinch or even wrinkle his nose.

'Was far worse before we foun' the little un.'

I nodded and stepped into the room. It was totally dark. I had no matches to strike and the man still standing in the dim light of the corridor seemed unwilling to offer me a candle or lamp. I let my eyes adjust for a moment, then began fumbling around carelessly, though any possessions the poor woman had were long gone. The small space was barren, and not even a window could be opened to let in any air. After a few minutes I realised the futility of my task and wondered whether I had made a mistake in coming here. I stepped back into the corridor, shot Dorothy a quick glance and shook my head feebly as the man pulled shut the door with a thud.

'The night Miss Chenko was taken, you didn't see or hear anything?'

'No. I was 'sleep. So was the wife.'

'And in the days that followed, you didn't notice Miss Chenko was absent from the building?'

The man shook his head.

'She kept to 'erself. Spoke to the missus when they crossed paths. She made her keep fixin' clothes so she didn' go out much.'

'And was it yourself or your wife who discovered the baby's body after Miss Chenko had been kidnapped?'

'Was me, though everyun''ere noticed the smell. Baby use' to cry a lot. When we didn't 'ear it for a while, it made us think summin was wrong.' The man frowned, his face twisting. 'I tol' all this to the coppers when they come. Why you askin' me the same things?'

I shrugged. 'Just following up on something, a piece of information that likely isn't relevant.' The man was clearly growing suspicious of me; I noticed the poker move as he clenched his hand tighter around it.

'Did you notice anyone suspicious – unusual – around the area, outside on the street, in the days before the kidnapping is believed to have happened?' The man gave no reply. I nodded feebly. 'Thank you for your time.'

I moved down the corridor, Dorothy walking before me. The young girl was still watching us, and as Dorothy drew near, she recoiled and stepped back into the small room. I saw the abject terror on her face then, the pained effort it took the child to stifle a scream. The man was close to my back, though when I stood beside the girl I stopped and smiled at her, though it was clearly little comfort.

I glanced at her father. 'May I ask the girl a question?'

The man seemed confused. 'Wot for?'

'Children can, uh, often hold valuable evidence, even when they don't realise. She may have heard something, seen something.'

'She didn't!' The man was growing angry. Still I knelt to the girl's level, gestured to Dorothy standing to my right by the open front door.

'You ... you see something?'

The girl stepped away from me. She glanced towards Dorothy and pulled on the ends of her filthy blonde hair. She nodded without saying a word. I tried to maintain my composure, though the sick excitement welling in my chest was overpowering. I took a deep breath, glanced from the girl to Dorothy.

'You're sure? You see … *her* … now?'

'Wot is this!' the girl's father yelled.

The girl paid him no attention. She stared at Dorothy and nodded again, before speaking very quietly. 'She's not really here. I can always tell when *they* are not really here.'

I didn't have time to think of any more questions. The girl's father grabbed me under the arm and hauled me upwards. 'I dunno who ye are but get out!' He pushed me towards the open door and slung me onto the street. I turned back, slammed my body against the door to stop him closing it. I saw the rage in his face but looked beyond him to his daughter.

'The girl knows something,' I spluttered, trying hard to keep the door open. 'She knows something, please.'

The man's strength was overpowering. He pushed me back into the street and slammed the door shut. I heard him yell at the girl, his words vicious and cruel. I rushed back to the door, hammered my fist against it repeatedly but to no end. I turned to Dorothy, who seemed truly mortified.

'The girl saw me?' She held a hand to her mouth.

'She knows something,' I groaned. 'I feel it – I know it!' I pulled out the map and shook it in my hand. 'The fact she sees you and was so close to this terrible crime has to be connected. She may know something that helps us with this.'

'That poor child,' was all Dorothy could reply. 'She must be so frightened. She must not understand.'

I felt great pity for the girl too, for surely if she saw Dorothy, she saw other spirits as well. Maybe spirits of a far more malignant appearance. I couldn't let myself dwell on the notion.

I looked towards the shut door in frustration. 'We have to go to the nearest crime scene circled on this map. We'll find something, we will.' I was trying to convince myself more than Dorothy.

I walked a short way up the road, but Dorothy didn't follow. She stood, staring morbidly at the house with the little girl inside. I returned to her side, tried to speak some words of comfort to her.

'That girl is safe; no harm will come to her.'

'How can you be sure of that?' Dorothy murmured. 'She is just a child, yet she sees the dead. Look what that has done to you.'

'There's no time for this,' I exclaimed, ignoring any sympathies I felt. I turned away and once more headed towards Commercial Street. A door creaked open and a soft voice called out to me. When I turned back, I spotted the young girl, rushing towards me. Dorothy was nowhere to be seen.

The girl was breathless when she stood at my side. Her father was behind her, yelling into the night.

'I see her,' the girl said quietly.

I knelt and nodded. 'My friend. Yes, I know you see her.'

'No,' the girl shook her head as her father drew near, 'the woman. The one next door.'

Her father grabbed her savagely by the arm then. 'You get back inside before ye get an 'iding.'

The girl didn't yell or scream as she was dragged back towards the house. I stood and called out to the man to wait.

'If ye don' clear off I'll have the coppers 'ere—'

'She knows something,' I exclaimed. 'Your daughter knows something.'

'Like hell she does. She's makin' up stories for fun!'

'You have to listen to her—'

'Clear off or I'll break your neck!'

To my dismay, the argument was drawing attention. Men in particular were coming out of the squat, shared houses and standing in doorways, looking at all the commotion. In the midst of it all, the father grabbed at my shirt and shoved me roughly to the cobbles. The girl got free of his hand and cried out with surprising volume.

'She goes over there!'

It stopped both me and her father short. She pointed towards the Brick Lane end and began running from us both. Her father stood where he was and barked at her to come back. I scrambled to my feet and rushed after her.

She ran south on Brick Lane a short distance, then turned left onto Finch Street. By then, I was struggling to keep any sort of pace with her and could hear the girl's father following at my back. Finch Street was black, for not a single light shone down it. For a moment, I panicked when I lost sight of the girl. She waved to me from the edge of a thin alley; by then her father was close at my side. He roughly pushed me and spoke to his daughter.

'Mary! Get back inside before this gets worse for ye!'

She disappeared down the alley. When we both caught up to her, she was but a shapeless form in the shadows. She stood then, waiting for us. Her father tried to grab her, but she dodged him quickly. In the dim light, I saw her point towards the ground.

'She walks here. She goes down here.'

I was baffled. 'What do you mean?'

'Lyin' girl. You're 'avin it now!'

She pointed to the ground once more as her father took hold of her. 'There. She goes down there. I see her, I hear her.'

She was pulled away, this time unable to struggle. The man was furious, and for a minute I thought he would surely give me a clout as a parting gift for causing such trouble. But he didn't. His concern and anger was directed solely at his daughter.

I crouched down, felt the wet and dirty alley floor, ran my

fingers in a growing arc. I stepped forwards, feeling the cool metal of a sewerage manhole cover, slick from the rain. It was surely what the girl had been talking about. I grabbed at the map – a futile errand for it was so dark I could see nothing scrawled upon the page. But I pictured the red, bloody lines, the last efforts of a dying Jack Lavernock.

The sewers – Jack had been trying to draw London's sewers, cutting across the streets beneath the city, running from west to east. I called out to the girl and her father, running after them.

The father grabbed my collar when I came close enough to him.

'The sewers,' I said to the child excitedly. 'You see her go down the sewers?'

She nodded. 'I hear her sometimes too.'

Her father looked from me to her. 'Stupid girl! You're lyin'.' He looked back at me then. 'You come near me or my family again, I'll 'ave ye in a box.'

'I'm police,' I growled. 'The girl has information. Important information.'

The man nodded. 'O' yea. If you're police, you could do with some 'elp then. Oi!'

He called out down the road. I turned, and to my dismay, spotted a dark figure, with a lamp strapped to his belt, and a truncheon brandished in his hand. The man was tall, his helmet taller. The Metropolitan Police badge shimmered in the dingy light.

I began to tremor. 'No, no, you've got this wrong.' The girl's father gripped my collar tight.

'What's goin' on,' the constable called out, stepping over to us quicker.

'This bloke reckons 'e's a copper,' the girl's father replied.

'Let go of me,' I said in a frenzy. 'The girl knows something. It's important.'

'Causin' trouble are we, mate.' The constable was at my back. 'Had one too many 'ave we?'

'Came knocking at my door. Said 'e was a copper. Been askin' funny questions.'

'Has he now?' The constable placed a hand on my shoulder. 'We got enough goin' on to have some drunkard makin' a fuss.'

He spun me around, and how his expression changed when he held his bullseye lamp to my face. His mock incredulity vanished, replaced by curiosity, confusion. Then fear.

'It's you. My God it's you.'

He was panicked at the sight of me, enough so that I could pull myself away from the girl's father, and clumsily grab Lavernock's pistol from my pocket. As the constable pounced at me, I shoved the barrel of the gun in his chest.

'Get back. I don't want to use this!'

The terrified constable dropped his truncheon and raised his hands. The father held the little girl tighter and tried to hurry away from me. There seemed no sense in stopping him. I struggled to think what to say.

'You-you're under arrest, Bexley,' the constable muttered in some vain attempt at bravery.

'Quiet!' I rubbed my jaw, trying to make sense of what the girl had told me. 'I'm not the Wraith of London. I had no part in any of the kidnappings.'

The constable said nothing.

'The other victim, the one taken last night, have they been found?'

'Put down the gun—'

'Answer me!'

'No.' The constable winced as I thrust the gun closer to him. 'No, we haven't found them.'

I nodded, encouraged. 'There may still be time. Come with me – move.'

I gestured with the gun, made the constable walk the short distance to Finch Street and the pitch-black alley. There I demanded his bullseye lamp from him, and ordered he pull up the sewer grate.

'You-you're not taking me down there?' he stammered as I stood over him, the terror in his face now clear in the warm glow of his lamp.

'No, far from it.' When the grate was lifted away, I looked down into the dark abyss of the sewer. 'I need you to bring other men.'

He was confused then, his face twitching. 'Mo-more police?'

'Yes. You remember where we are.'

'Off Finch Street.'

'Good. Now listen to me. I think Detective Inspector Jack Lavernock realised the Wraith may have been moving bodies through the sewers. The little girl claims to have, um, *seen* something, though she was too scared to tell police before.' One more lie seemed to matter little then. 'Get every officer you can into the sewers; tell Flynn and his men this is where I went down.' I pulled out the map, tried to think which direction to head in. 'I-I don't know where I'm going. Just get men down here.'

The constable merely shook where he crouched upon the floor. He held my gaze, reached for the shackles upon his belt.

'Y-y-you're under arrest…'

I pulled back the hammer of the revolver and fired into the air. He leapt away then, yelping as he did.

'Get more men here now!' I yelled, and he ran from the alley without so much as a glance at me.

I tucked the gun in the waistband of my trousers, took the bullseye lantern in hand and lowered my legs over the open manhole. Warm air rose up to me. It was laced with foul smells, though I paid these no heed. I was more concerned for Dorothy, for she had vanished and in truth I wished to have her with me. But there was no time to wait. Stoking some courage from within, I held tight to the lantern and gingerly set my foot down onto an iron ladder.

Slowly, I began my descent into the city's underworld.

What Hides Beneath the City
September 13th, 1905

My feet splashed in water and unspeakable filth. I reeled and gagged, covered my nose but to no avail. I tried to breathe through my mouth as best I could.

The tunnel was narrow and low, six feet high at most, just enough for me to stand up straight. I shone the bullseye lantern in both directions, trying to decide which way to travel. I realised the foolhardiness of my endeavour then, for I knew that there were miles of such tunnels beneath the city and had no real way of knowing where the Wraith may be hiding, if indeed he was even in the sewers at all. The notion that a kidnapper, a killer, could move about such loathsome, rancid places – with his victims in tow! – was quite absurd. And yet, as I shone the lamp onto Lavernock's map, staring at the haphazard red lines he had drawn, I felt certain that his killer lurked somewhere in the shadows with me.

I moved with the flow of the water. The air was thick, warmer than the night above. I cast my eyes over the brickwork of the curved walls and scrambled straight for perhaps two hundred yards, by which time my trousers were all but soaking and rank. It was then I stopped and held my breath, for far off, I heard the high-pitched screech of police whistles. They were gathering on the streets above; the young constable had raised the alarm quicker than I had anticipated. They would be on my trail soon, down in the dark and festering labyrinth with me.

I felt a surge of panic, for it was more than likely they would capture me before I found any signs of the *real* guilty party. I had to move fast.

The first tunnel connected to another, this one moving perpendicular so that I had to choose to head either left or right. This second shaft was slightly larger and as I stepped into it, my feet sank deeper into the muck and brown water. I cursed aloud, wading along to the left, where the water moved downwards gently. Strange shapes, peculiar reflections caused by my lamp light, danced around the curved ceiling.

The water began to rush faster as the decline of the ground grew steeper. The shaft was growing tighter, and I was forced to arch my back. A dark tunnel appeared on my right, sloping upwards, the sewage gushing from it. I stopped for a moment, trying to decide which way to travel. I knew, in some corner of my memory, that the water of London's sewers flowed from west to east, with the current of the Thames. But I couldn't help but hesitate and grew agitated as I stood at the watery crossroads. To my horror, above the lapping and flow of water, I heard the sounds of wading boots and officers calling out to each other.

I shook my head, for in truth I had no idea what I was doing. In a moment of blind compulsion, I stepped downwards, following the flow of the water, moving, almost certainly further east. I nearly slipped, and with some fortune stayed standing.

Within a few yards I spotted a foul thing slithering beside my leg. Black and slick, the dreadful creature touched upon my ankles as it encircled me. It was as long as an eel, though far larger, its back ridged and cracked. Startled, I stumbled away from it and fell backwards, dropping the bullseye lamp as I went. The light inside remained, though barely; I lunged for it as though my life depended on it.

Sewage flowed about my hands and midriff. I struggled to stand and heard a terrible snapping and clicking from the darkness before me. Too breathless even to scream, I held the lantern outright, searched in the water for the strange, unholy thing that had so shocked me. In the dim light, I saw it, rising from the water. Contorted, misshapen, broken, it changed and grew, slowly resembling something that was almost human. Indeed, a face formed from twisting black dust: eyes thin and ferocious; a mouth filled with yellow teeth. The spectre was a woman, a horrid thing with nails over an inch long, ribs that broke through her skin and hair matted and twisted beyond recognition. Leeches covered her entire body like a gown; she rippled like the water, shifted and moved even as she stood still. And she held a tiny shape in her hand, a bundle covered in black and moulded rags.

I knew then that the spectre was the ghost of Lucinda Chenko, cradling her child.

The smell of her was abominable. I stammered as I tried instinctively to shield myself from her gaze and splashed in the water as I moved backwards from her. She made no motion towards me, though her body cracked and broke, her shoulders and neck twitching and convulsing.

I groaned aloud, for whilst the appearance of the woman was most dreadful, the manner with which she clung to her dead child was worse still. I wished Dorothy was beside me then, to bolster my nerve and courage. The thought of her alone seemed enough to focus my mind, to take a breath and calm my heart. Awkwardly I managed to stand, and with the lantern still held out before me, I spoke to the ghost as I would any other woman.

'I am searching for a villain, for the man who took the lives of you and your child.'

Leeches fell into the water; it was growing warmer around my legs, bubbling from the base of the dreadful figure. Spiders crept down from hanging webs and wrapped themselves around her hands. I mustered my resolve and spoke on.

'I do not fear you.'

The wicked thing hissed then. I held my ground.

'You are surely here for the same purpose.' I spoke without any real knowledge of what I was saying. 'You want to find answers,' I stammered quite feebly. 'I do as well. I want to find those responsible for your death.'

The ghost said nothing. She brought the child closer to her face, which cracked into a dreadful smile as it looked upon the babe in rags. I nodded assuredly, for at that moment I believed myself to be right.

'Tell me, were you awake when he brought you down here?' The water was growing hotter, as though her presence was boiling it somehow. Quite suddenly she lurched closer to me and I nearly fell backwards as I recoiled. The child in rags was gone from her arms. She held her hands at her sides, her fingers twisted and broken.

'Do you know the man I seek?' The woman stayed still. 'Would you show me the way to him?'

She hissed once more; perhaps the closest she could come to speaking.

I held my nerve. 'Answer me. I am here to find a killer, to find a man who will not stop killing.'

She tilted her head and held my gaze with dreadful, reptilian eyes.

'You will not tell me? You cannot? Do you fear him still?' The thing remained unmoved. 'Does he go in that direction?' I pointed behind the spectre, in the direction of the water flow. Her hands held steady. 'Or this way?' I pointed to the tunnel sloping upwards on my right, where the water flowed from. The ghost stayed still.

I turned for just a glance at the way I had come. As I did, I heard a rush of air, a gale battered into a ship's sail. When I looked back, I saw the spectre was gone. No trace of her remained. Spiders climbed quickly up hair-like strands of web that rose to the ceiling. The water grew cold once more.

I gasped and held a hand to my chest. How my heart then did heave. I rested against the brick wall for a moment, shaking my head for the madness I had just experienced. My lamp grew brighter, though only a little, its flame feeble in the darkness of the maze I moved in. I gathered myself as best I could, heard the not too distant sounds of men calling back and forth to one another, and realised the troop of police hunting for me was dreadfully close. I stared down the tunnel where the water sped away, deciding in an instant that the spirit of Lucinda Chenko had appeared to stop me going any further. I turned and began ascending the narrow passage from which the water flowed.

My head brushed against the grimy masonry. I shuffled with cautious steps, struggling against the flow of spilling sewage. When the way levelled off somewhat and the passage widened, the water came up to my shins. The tunnel continued straight for as far as I could see. Smaller tributaries, archways into greater depths of darkness, fed into that which I walked.

The sound of the constables was distant now, hard to hear unless I stopped and held my breath. Whilst I needed to search for the villain in this dreadful place, I couldn't afford to lose them entirely. I was in no position to arrest anyone, let alone the Wraith of London. I had to keep the officers close to hand, had to ensure they didn't lose track of me.

A spindly branch of dead wood stuck up in the water, like a hand reaching out to me. I removed the cap I still wore and hung it on the branch. It was plain to see and not easily missed, provided any officers came down this tunnel, they were sure to spot it.

I was petrified. Such unseemly places as sewers, hidden from sight, cannot be imagined unless one has descended into their depths. The darkness alone was enough to bleed me of my courage. How my heart wished me to search for the officers, to turn back and find them, to hand myself to them, so I could be returned to the fair air and lamp-lit glow of the streets above. My resolve was wavering, even when I closed my eyes, trying to dispel all feelings of terror and misery to think only of Dorothy. I called out to her meekly, for I wished she would come to my side. It seemed in that dreadful place my pleas went unheard; I didn't know how long I had been wandering alone.

I came to a juncture in the tunnel, where the throughway I moved along continued straight ahead, and where another narrower shaft connected on my left. It was partly collapsed, water and filth trickling over a pile of bricks and crumbling mortar. I held my lamp out in both directions, tried with pained effort to consider which direction to travel. With the strangest sense of relief (for it both eased my mind and panicked me greatly), I heard a voice echo from far off, back in the direction I had come. Turning around, I squinted into the gloom and knew then the officers were still following me. When I turned back, the wretched figure of Lucinda Chenko stood before me once more.

Her hand was stretched out to me.

I reeled and fell into the filth. I splashed and scrambled away from her, though it felt as if something held me down in the grimy water.

She knelt, crept with crooked arms towards me, leaned over and above me, her face riddled with moving parasites.

I panted and gasped and struggled to breathe. Her reptilian eyes – lifeless, hopeless – focused upon mine. She seemed to study me.

'P-please,' I begged like a child, afraid of what she would do to me.

With a suddenness she stood, thrust her arm out towards the adjoining tunnel and stepped back from the faint hue of my lamplight, evaporating into the shadows. I struggled to my feet, lurched in the direction she had pointed and began down the collapsing tunnel, gasping and groaning as I went.

After a short distance, I realised how little water was flowing about my feet. I was heading upwards, an ascent so gradual it was barely noticeable. Soon, having passed a few small drains built into the stone on my left and right and from where the trickling sewage flowed, the brickwork below my feet revealed itself, and my way was dry and clearly visible. I noted the strangeness of this, for though I had no great engineering knowledge of the sewers, I knew all of it was in near constant use.

It was then that the last light of my lamp ebbed away. All around me turned to black. I fumbled to the wall, my breathing ragged and fast, feeling along with my hand. Unseemly things slipped beneath my fingers, things that bore no thinking about.

I moaned, shook the lamp, cursing the damned thing. I heard scurrying then, drawing nearer, nearer still. Rats – how I hoped such scurrying was caused by vermin and nothing worse. The terror brought on by real darkness extinguished any courage or strength that had brought me down to this place. I needed to flee. I needed to escape.

The glass of the bull lamp smashed as it hit the floor. The rats, for then I pictured hundreds, screeched in unison. I lashed out as best I could, and blind to all around, moved as fast as I dared. My hands lay upon cold brick. I stumbled but held myself upright. I continued in vain for a time, but wailed in agony as I felt a sharp pain around my left Achilles, a pain that made me twist down and strike out madly. Sharp teeth had bitten me.

I limped maybe another ten yards, then fell hard, jarring my back as I did. To my surprise, I felt steps carved into the stone, leading upwards. They were uneven and damp; I laboured up them on my hands and knees. They were covered in rats that moved about my ears and face, scratching at me with dirty claws.

I hoped the steps would lead to my escape, but they climbed only a short distance to another tunnel. I crawled as quickly as I could, looking instinctively behind me, kicking blindly as I went, thrusting myself away from the vermin as they crept across my legs. Their claws dug into my skin despite my efforts to shake them off. When I was a short way from the top of the steps, I began distinguishing each terrible pair of black and red eyes. When I looked ahead, I saw light at the farthest end of the passage I now crawled in.

With what pace I could muster, I headed towards the light. The rats dwindled in number as if repulsed by the mere sight of themselves. I snarled and stamped at the last of them, and when I was certain of my safety, I stopped to regain my breath and examined my ankle; dark blood was seeping from a deep, burning wound. There was nothing to be done for it, and I continued to move to the light as slowly and quietly as I could.

The walls were distinctly different from the curved brickwork of the sewers. The passage was tall and straight, broken up by archways of stone that stretched some ten feet high. Dust puffed up with each of my laboured steps. The source of the light soon became apparent; a dirty oil lamp left hanging from a rusted nail. As I stood beside it, I held my breath and listened, hoping to catch sound of something from deeper inside the strange chamber. I heard a muffled noise, too distant to truly distinguish. I thought to take hold the lamp and carry it with me, but decided against it, noticing another dim beacon further ahead. I scuttled towards it and came to the end of the passage, where the space around me opened up considerably. It seemed I had entered some vaults or catacombs beneath the city that I had never known existed; antechambers and gated corridors; a stairwell curving downwards; a rickety scaffolding of timbers set upon a platform.

I took Lavernock's revolver in hand. I moved to the curved stairs; faint light shone up from below. Kneeling, I heard the sound of rushing water, the steady drum of it churning. Not merely a stream but a torrent, for it grew louder with every precarious step I took down, down, down. I couldn't dwell on the policemen hunting me, or ghosts or spirits or drink or misery; all I could do was force myself down each narrow step and ensure my shaking hand held the gun firm.

Distorted by the sounds of the water, I heard murmuring. Voices – the deep timbre of a man and the terrified pleading of a woman.

The latest victim – in my heart I knew it was her.

I moved down the stairs hurriedly, excited and terrified in equal measure. Only when she cried out and was silenced abruptly did I stop, fear pulsing through me.

The Wraith was below me. The terror of London was finally close to hand.

The Wraith of London

September 13th, 1905

I had to hurry, for the sake of the unknown woman. I crept down the last steps quickly and with bated breath, certain the wicked villain would lunge towards me, brandishing some unspeakable weapon. The light remained dim, though as I came to the base of the stairwell, I spied the edges of a vast chasm carved from the rock. It's true scale was difficult to judge.

The water raged, flowing along a channel that stretched the length of the chamber, cascading down into a chasm close to the stairs. Above the torrent, I heard the woman once more, begging for her life, weeping as she spoke. She offered money, as all in such a miserable position do. The kidnapper, whomever he was, said nothing in reply. I heard the tapping of metal. I inched myself forwards and looked into the space.

The figures were closer than I realised, silhouettes against the relative brightness of a few lamps. My eyes struggled to adjust, though when they had, I saw neither figure was facing my direction. The woman was staring at the man. To my surprise, I saw her raise her hands to him, to even stand clumsily from a seat, though it was clear this took a great effort. Listening closer, I realised she was slurring her words. The manner in which she collapsed back into her chair, her head rolling lazily to one side as if too heavy to sit on her neck, was perhaps the clearest sign that she had been drugged.

The man, the Wraith, had his back to me. He was standing at a table, laden with things that I couldn't see. A case of some sort was open beside him, and in the glint of the light, I spied he wore high riding boots, perfect for traipsing in the filth of the sewers.

The fellow made some remark too quiet to be heard against the gushing of the water. I saw the woman's reaction though, how her hands began to quiver, how the volume of her voice rose considerably. She stood fully then and made to dash deeper into the chamber. But her legs wouldn't carry her and she fell badly on her knees, crawling a few pitiful yards. The man seemed unconcerned. When he did move, I noted the manner of his gait, the awkwardness with which he walked. It startled me, for he leaned heavily on the table and struggled to stand on his own two feet. He grabbed the woman furiously and dragged her back towards the chair, rasping at her to sit. When she didn't and lay collapsed on the floor, he snarled at her, and slowly returned to the table side. How I strained to see his face, to make out the contours of his features. But the light was against me; the man was but a shadow.

I looked at the gun I carried and concealed myself for a moment. I could not steady my hand. Whoever the devil in the chamber was, I needed him alive, to prove my innocence to Henley and the Yard. Having framed me, he would surely know that; he had an even greater advantage against me beyond his captured hostage and knowledge of the catacombs. As I pulled back the hammer of the pistol, I heard the woman cry aloud. I had so little time to think on what to do; all I knew was that I needed to get her away to safety.

I readied myself, craned my neck around the wall. The

kidnapper lifted his head and spoke to the woman. The churning water concealed his words. She looked up, unmoved, from where she lay sprawled beside the chair. I took a step to move into the chamber, just as the kidnapper brandished a gun. I cursed beneath my breath and moved back into hiding, resting my head against the wall as a swathe of nausea and panic overcame me. How was I to best this dreadful fellow? He seemed to hold all the cards.

When I looked back, the woman was struggling to stand. She moved towards the lamps, where now I spotted another table or wooden bench. She staggered like a drunkard, as her kidnapper gave another order. The woman stood beside the low table, looking down towards it. He gave her a moment, before aiming the gun at her and barking his command once more. To my astonishment, she began to strip off her clothes and it was this vile act of indignity that spurred me to move. I stepped out from the cover of the stairwell, the gun raised, my nerve as steady as it would ever be.

I made it some ten yards into the room, just under half the distance to where the kidnapper stood. He was looking squarely at the woman, his attentions so fixed on her, he didn't notice as I readied my stance and aimed the revolver at his back. I could have shot him outright; how easily I could have killed him in that moment. But I needed him alive.

The woman whimpered as the kidnapper yelled at her. I in turn jolted where I stood and called out with waning volume, startling both man and woman alike.

'Police,' I said somewhat feebly. 'There's more men on their way.'

At that, the woman gasped and began staggering towards me. I kept my gaze and gun fixed on the kidnapper, his head now turned towards me but still little more than a silhouette in the dim light. Slowly, he brought the gun to his side.

With gasps of relief, the woman came beside me, and there I saw for the first time the features of her face. She was surely mid-thirties, her complexion pale, her hair well kept. Her eyes were wide, pupils dilated. She strained to speak, struggled to form coherent sentences.

'Oh God, please … He took … Oh God … he's mad!' She wept, and for a moment, my gaze was fixed solely on her. I intended to lead her to the stairs, to tell her to run. She muttered something terrible then, something that stopped me entirely.

'There's another one.'

'What?'

A huge crack of thunder rang out. The poor, sorrowful woman whimpered and collapsed against me. Her arms wrapped around me and held me tighter than a vice, terrified to let go, even as the blood seeped from the wound in her back. She moaned a little, almost as if surprised. I dropped my gun as she sank downwards. As I crouched by her side and tried to comfort her, telling her of the approaching police, of men that would surely save her, my words felt cruel. What fear she must have felt in that strange place, with no one but a liar, and her killer, at her side. Tears streaked down my cheeks as she took her last painful breath, and in that moment, I lost all hope of leaving the chamber alive.

I made sure to close her eyes. The murderer stepped over to us, his gun still trained on me.

I stared at mine on the floor, thought to reach for it.

'The police know you're down here,' I said with some foolish defiance. 'They're close behind me, searching the tunnels. It's all ove—'

'Stand up, Thomas. Please.' The kidnapper spoke with a gravelled voice I recognised. 'And pick up your gun.'

I looked up at him slowly. He wore a strange mask that obscured his entire face, similar to that worn by a fencer, though any metallic mesh had been replaced with black material or gauze. Dark spectacles had been fitted into the material, though it was impossible to see into the villain's eyes. He pulled the mask off slowly, and finally I saw him for who he really was, though even then I struggled to believe it. I found myself doing as he had asked, taking the gun in hand and standing as straight as I could.

'It's you. How the hell could this be you?'

The Man Who Hated the Dead

September 13th, 1905

'You are sure she is dead?'

He gestured to the lifeless woman almost casually. I nodded, too stunned to say anything.

'Pity, great pity.' He mumbled the words beneath his breath. To my horror, he knelt and pulled a small medical vial from his coat pocket and gathered some of the victim's blood. I tried raising the gun in my hand, and it were as though he read my very thoughts.

'You're not going to shoot me, Thomas, I'm sure of that.' He glanced up at me and told me to sit down. I found myself obeying mechanically, stepping to the chair the woman had occupied only moments before. I finally saw that the array of items on the table were in fact surgeons' tools.

My ankle was throbbing mercilessly, my entirety weak. I pinched the bridge of my nose as I sat down and tried to compose myself, impossible as that was. 'Do you have a cigarette?'

'No. Quit some years ago. They are poor for one's lungs.' He stood slowly and moved towards the table, his back to me.

I nodded, thought how to begin, where best to start. But I was too tired, too battered and bruised. In truth I was miserable then, for looking upon the man responsible for such fear and grief gave me no sense of achievement or satisfaction. How I wished, in many ways, to be looking upon someone else.

'Is what you said – that police are following you – true?'

I nodded. 'If they are as close as I hope, they will not be long.'

'I'm sure you have questions for me ...'

'I'm going to bring you in.'

He shook his head. 'We both know that's simply not true.'

'Because you're going to kill me?'

He slowly took hold of his gun but didn't answer. My eyes focused on his fingers, how they bent and wrapped around the handle of the pistol. I saw the indentation, the slightly paler skin tone, where his ring had been worn for years. It shouldn't have been there – nothing of the fingers should have been. I'd seen the bloodied knuckles, the mutilation wrought upon both hands, in the miserable cellar of the manor. His body had been there – he'd died there. I'd been so certain of it.

And yet Hawthorn stood before me now, his hands undamaged, his body whole.

How wrong I had been. How badly I had been deceived.

'The hands have made a miraculous recovery,' I said.

Hawthorn gazed down at them, flexing the fingers and twisting the wrists. 'If only modern medicine was so good. Perhaps, one day.'

'The corpse in Scotland, in the basement of the manor, whose was that?'

'No one important,' he said coolly. 'Didn't bare the strongest resemblance to me but given adequate damage to the facial features, we lose most of what gives us our unique appearance.' He frowned. 'You believed the evidence put straight before you – I worried the ring might be too much.'

I felt tremendous shame then, for not seeing through the deceit sooner and for the burning desire to ask my next question above all others. 'Why me, Elijah? Why go to such lengths to frame me?'

'My reasons are my own. And not *all* of this was about you.'

I struggled to speak. 'You've gone to such lengths to frame me for your crimes – to send me to the hangman. How can you say it isn't about me?'

'You were a suitable means to an end. I knew I could use our friendship against you, knew even how I could connect a seemingly random group of victims to you—'

'Did you kill Timberwell after you got what you needed from his photography shop?' I muttered. 'Was he another one of your victims?'

Hawthorn paused for a moment but didn't answer.

'Framing you was not the end in all of this, though I admit I took great pleasure in it. My reasons were far more important than that.'

'Enlighten me,' I snapped.

Hawthorn turned to me slowly, the gun still held in his hand. He met my gaze for a moment, before his eyes shifted to the space behind me. His shoulders slacked; his mouth opened ajar as his jaw loosened. The arm holding the gun fell to his side.

'My God,' he muttered, 'so soon.'

For a moment, I thought with some blessed relief that the police had arrived, sneaking into the chamber without either of us knowing. But when Hawthorn pulled down his twisted mask to cover his face once more, I was baffled.

I turned and looked behind me.

The woman, the woman he had shot, the woman whose body still lay upon the floor.

Her phantom stood just behind the chair, her appearance not deathly, or twisted, or monstrous. She appeared as she had in life, identical in fact, though I couldn't see if her back was bloodied by the gunshot wound.

She looked at me in bemusement, tears streaming down her face.

'Y-you said they were coming. You said I would live!' She stepped towards me and I admit I reeled from the chair to Hawthorn's side. She was so real, as though the dead body had merely stood and walked over to us. Indeed, I had to glance repeatedly at her lifeless corpse to be certain it remained there.

She turned her focus to Hawthorn. 'Why? Why, you bastard, tell me!'

She stumbled to him, as black began to ooze from her lips. She coughed even, looked in horror at the strange substance, began to quiver tremendously as it seeped down her chin. I felt such pity for her as the misery of her death played out once more. She doubled over, cried aloud, screamed even, to such an unnatural volume I was pained by the very noise. Hawthorn seemed unmoved. He held tight the little vial of blood, his arm outstretched. When the phantom stepped towards him, I saw its appearance changing. Its skin smouldered; the features of its face contorted. In a single blink, the eyes turned a sickly yellow and the last of the woman was lost entirely to a raging monster.

When the spirit screamed out once more, Hawthorn bellowed. 'Silence!' He thrashed an arm out, dashing specks of blood from the vial he'd collected across the ghost. Like a scorched timber burnt in fire, the spectre crumbled and disappeared in an instant. I gasped at his bravado, his fearlessness.

He stepped back beside me and tossed his mask onto the table. He began gathering his things carelessly. He picked up the gun after a moment, as if keeping it to hand had slipped his mind.

'You see them too,' I said in astonishment.

He didn't answer.

'The dead. You see them as I see them.' I noticed a thin trickle of blood seep from his nose. He rubbed at it with irritation.

I grabbed him by the arm and he lashed out at me.

'How do you see them as well? How did you just banish—'

'I've seen far fouler things than you could dream of, Thomas!' His voice boomed in the cavern.

He moved towards his case. Only then did I notice the camera in it, a model I didn't recognise. He weakly kicked against it, almost losing his balance as he did.

'First it was merely in photographs. I saw things on every murder enquiry: yours, Jack's, anyone's. If photographs were taken, things appeared to me.' He glowered at me with real contempt. 'Is that how it began for you as well? Is it? Did you spy a measly mark that didn't belong in frame, a shadow on a lens cast by no object that existed in reality? Faces lurking in plain sight, faces that no one but you could spot.'

'Elijah—'

'You doubt your own sanity, don't you? For so long I did. Soon you accept you are mad.' He stepped back to me and grabbed at my shirt. 'If I am mad then so are you, boy. For many years I ignored it as best I could, for what else was there to be done? How could I admit to anyone that I saw strange things in photographs, things that were pertinent to our enquiries; secrets that revealed killers or their motives?' He stepped away, pointed to the spot where the woman's ghost had screamed in agony. 'Then they began appearing to me everywhere. Night. Day. No matter where I went, they found me.'

He grabbed a few instruments from the table, threw them carelessly towards the open case, casting many to the floor as he did. At last he snatched a notebook, which he tucked inside the jacket he wore. It hung loosely on him, for he was gaunt and dreadfully thin.

'You saw these things while you worked in the Forensic Crime Directorate?' I murmured.

'It started some time then.'

'Why did you never think to tell me?'

'Would you have believed me,' he growled, 'or called for the white coats to drag me to an asylum?'

'I don't know,' I admitted. 'We were friends, truly we were friends.'

He ignored that, attending to the case on the floor, snapping shut the latches quickly. When he stood back straight, he aimed the pistol he carried at my chest and began edging slowly to the water.

'The blood,' I said, looking from the body on the floor to the space the ghost had appeared. 'What did you do with her blood?'

'They hate it,' Hawthorn muttered. 'The dead fear blood from their mortal bodies – it is a means of warding them away. There was some truth in the lies I spun to you about cults and the importance of blood.' He nodded his head sombrely. 'The blood of the dead is important, though as yet I am uncertain why.'

'As yet?' I was lost, too overwhelmed by all I was hearing.

'Research. Since the day these wretched spirits first appeared to me, I have done all I can to understand them. I'm a man of science after all, always have been.'

He was perhaps ten yards from me now.

'I needed to know what these *things* were. I needed to know why they came to me and me alone. Believe me, I spent years observing them, recording them, indulging in all manner of pseudo-science, spiritualism and experimentation. That's how I learnt about the blood, how I learnt about a great many things.'

I tried to make sense of what I was hearing. 'Are you telling me you've done all this – all these kidnappings, these murders – for *research*?'

Hawthorn nodded. 'It began with men of loathsome standing, those who surely deserved their fate. If those I killed appeared before me, I could correlate the visions with their demise. It would give some reason as to why I saw them.' His brow furrowed. 'These things are not so simple, I'm afraid. There is little sense to what has befallen us.'

He reached inside his shirt and pulled a thin chain from around his neck. By now he was close to the water, and though I saw something looped upon the chain, I couldn't fathom what it was.

'What is that?' I asked plainly.

'None of your concern.' He stepped another few yards, before suddenly turning and throwing the chain towards the churning water. He looked back towards it repeatedly as he returned to the table.

'Did you start killing whilst we worked in the Forensic Crime Directorate?' It seemed such a petty question to ask, and yet for my own sake I felt I had to know.

'Towards the end,' Hawthorn replied plainly.

'How? How have you done all of this?'

'This isn't a trial, Thomas.'

'Then at least tell me why you framed me – you must hate me terribly to do such a thing.'

He slammed a hand down hard against the table. 'I do hate you, Thomas, but don't be so arrogant as to assume this was all about you.' He turned and pointed a finger in my face. 'My wrath spreads to Henley, to Critcher, to the seniors in the Metropolitan Police as well; with them I have greater grudges to bear so don't think yourself special, or unique. You were merely a part of something bigger. In you I saw an opportunity.'

His voice had grown manic, his eyes wild. I saw then how unhinged he had become.

'An opportunity to do what?'

'To get away with murder, Thomas. To get away with the most terrible spree of murders our fair London has ever witnessed. To walk away when I saw fit, so as to carry on my work in any other town or city I deemed appropriate.'

'How?' I asked plainly. 'Regardless of where you go, the police will surely learn of my innocence and come for y—'

I stopped as he shook his head. 'You're the Wraith of London, Thomas. I've spun an intricate web of lies with you trapped at the centre. That's all that matters. I'll find somewhere new, somewhere I can start again. When the time is right, I'll take all those I need under a different guise – the Strangler; the Butcher; whatever the press decide to call me. I'll frame another in the manner I framed you.' He sneered, his jaw flexing and moving. 'I admit I took great pleasure in showing up Henley for the fool he is, by making the Wraith of London a member of his own police force. The public will crucify him. They'll crucify *you* if they can.' He smiled manically. 'You deserve everything you get.'

I was dumbstruck. 'You did all this because they shut your Directorate down, didn't you? You framed me because you think I wronged you somehow all those years ago?'

He lunged at me, rammed the barrel of the gun in my face.

'You *did* wrong me, Thomas. Don't think otherwise. After all I did for you, all I helped you through, you betrayed me when I needed you most!' He shook me roughly. 'But this is about more than just righting wrongs done to me. My research is the most important thing – it must continue! I must have free rein to take the lives of whomever I deem necessary, whenever I choose. There are so many variables to explore, so much left to be understood.'

He shoved me backwards, though kept his gun trained on me.

'For years I knew my work would need to go beyond taking the lives of petty thieves and drunkard vagrants. I knew I'd need to extend my reach across every corner of London, every corner of the nation. It struck me, that if the police thought I was dead, were convinced of this fact unequivocally, they would never suspect me of any crime. Never would they seek me out or look for me upon the streets.'

He lowered the gun.

'I have no cause to tell you any of this.'

'You owe me—'

'Nothing,' he yelled. 'I owe you nothing.'

He gathered his case from the floor.

'The body in the manor. The body I so believed was yours. Who was it?' I stepped towards him when he didn't answer. 'Tell me who it was.'

'A man I stumbled upon some two years ago,' Hawthorn remarked dryly. 'A most boorish fellow whose life I spared if truth be told, on account of our rather amusing resemblance to one another. Even then I'd been thinking of how to get away with murder, and the thought of him acting as my "double" – if you take my meaning – was an intriguing one. Kept in contact with him until the time came.'

I took a moment to consider the notion. 'You murdered an innocent man just so the police would think his body was yours, just so they would think you were dead?'

'Yes. I kept in touch with him until the time was right, until everything was laid out as I needed it. Truth be told, your entry into the whole business was rather late, after I heard of your misfortune on that enquiry in South Wales.'

I felt blood rush to my cheeks. 'How did you hear about that?'

'I still have means of keeping abreast with what's going on inside the Yard. The stories about you were most intriguing.'

I saw another thin trickle of blood run from his nose.

'Seeing things in photographs that shouldn't have been there; claiming to be visited by the ghost of a dead girl. Ludicrous to many; all too familiar for me. I knew what was causing your absence from duty, knew what terrors you were trying to hide from. That's when my plan truly came to fruition. I knew how I could satisfy my need for bodies and get away with murder. And as an added incentive, I could show up Henley and his lackies for the fools they are, whilst knocking the great Thomas Bexley from his lofty perch.'

'I don't understand. I don't understand any—'

'I've known of the manor in Scotland for some time, have visited it in secret over the last few years.'

I saw the dead body in the bath, and the bloodstains upon the moth-ridden bed.

'You kill—'

'It seemed the perfect place for my research,' Hawthorn continued. 'Quiet, isolated. Far from prying eyes. But it wasn't enough. Even there I drew too much suspicion.'

'The two brothers,' I muttered.

'Were happy to take my money and turn a blind eye.' He was speaking quickly then, with a ferocity, his hands fidgeting and drumming upon the table. 'I told them my guests on the island were friends, colleagues, even staff doing work around the manor. As the months went by, I knew they suspected the truth, that something far more nefarious was taking place. But they were poor, and penniless and fearful of what I might be capable of. Those I killed were not missed by many. The act of killing is not difficult, Thomas, but finding suitable victims has its challenges.'

'Yet you returned to London,' I said. 'You came back just to frame me?'

'I came back in the interests of my research,' he snapped. 'I needed greater access to victims, more equipment to experiment. This city is festering with the damned, the wicked and pure of heart, all of whom I needed. It was always my intention to frame *someone*, but I learnt of your condition upon my return and it struck me how easily I could manipulate our friendship for my purposes. Soon after, I began putting things into motion. I met with Critcher in January, feigning interest in working for the Yard once again. I visited Timberwell's shop, hoping to find something I could use to connect you to a series of new kidnap victims.'

'You did kill him,' I groaned with fury.

He gestured to the cavern around us. 'Then I vanished, hid in miserable places like this. I started taking bodies as I deemed necessary, ensured the police knew each crime was connected with that ludicrous cult symbol. In mid-August I returned to Scotland briefly, whereupon I met with my boorish doppelganger and convinced him to join me on the island.'

He stopped abruptly, looked towards the stairs that had led into the cavern. The blood was still trickling from his nose.

'You butchered him so that anyone who found him would be convinced his body was yours.'

'You were always going to find that man, Thomas,' he said, his eyes still gazing about the cavern. 'I planted my own bloody thumbprint at the scene of James Mortimer's home and ensured the letter supposedly written in January was placed amidst your correspondence. That and the evidence concealed in your home—'

'How did you conceal such thing—'

'You're a wretch – a drunk, a waste. There was ample time to conceal such things on days you no doubt can't even remember, days in which you wandered the streets, fearful to return home. It could have been done with you asleep in your damn bed, you still wouldn't have noticed! You did the rest for me. You bought the narrative of the cult so easily, of a conspiracy against me—'

'I looked for you because we were friends,' I snarled, stepping to Hawthorn without thought, grabbing the scruff of his jacket. I heard the snap of a gun hammer, and felt the cold barrel pressed against my neck. I eyed the pistol, realised it was the same model Enfield I had carried since my days in the Forensic Crime Directorate.

'You're sick,' I said as I eased my grip. 'This insanity you have committed; the blood streaming from your nose.'

He rubbed a hand along the top of his lip. 'Say another word—'

'You're sick because I am as well. Whether it's caused by these visions we have, some symptom perhaps. A doctor looked me over when I was being questioned; he claimed I may have some neurological disorder—'

'What difference does it make?'

'It could have changed you,' I said, gripping a hand tight upon his shoulder. 'The fact we see all that we see may have made you ill, brought on this desire to kill,' I spoke pleadingly. 'You're not the man I knew; not my dear friend. I never betrayed you, never slighted you. Yet you have gone to such *extremes* to see me fall and even now, claim all you have done is not about revenge.'

He shook his head, shrugged me away.

'It makes no damn difference. None at all.'

A noise, a quiet thud from somewhere away in the darkness, cut him off. He looked, panic-stricken, towards the source of the sound. In the gloom, a light appeared, trickling down steps that were revealed one by one. Quick footfalls could be heard; the arm of a figure holding a lantern out was revealed.

'Go back!' Hawthorn yelled, and for a minute I thought he

was making some threat towards approaching police constables. But the manner in which the figure paused, hesitated even, dissuaded me of that notion. I saw what was surely a gun being pulled, though this only panicked Hawthorn more. 'Go back!' he yelled again, shaking his hand. I took a step forwards, tried to see more of the figure. But suddenly they turned, the little light around them vanishing as they fled quickly back up the steps.

'Who was that?' I said quite breathlessly, tempted even to chase after them.

'The devil who stole this woman from her bed,' Hawthorn said, pointing to the body on the floor. 'A devil who steals people away *without thinking*.'

I turned to the man slowly. He looked aggrieved, angry even.

'Your accomplice? The one who aided in your scheme.'

Hawthorn said nothing.

'You couldn't have done this all alone. It makes perfect sense—' I stopped myself. 'Henley believed there was a failed kidnap attempt; a figure dressed in black broke into a man's home south of the river but was chased away.'

Hawthorn's face twisted.

'Henley claimed it was me. The victim claimed the man who broke in couldn't have been in his sixties.'

'This is of no concern to you, Thomas.'

I glanced at the woman's body upon the floor. 'Why kidnap another victim so soon after I had been arrested? If you sought to frame me …'

I tried to meet Hawthorn's gaze, but he wouldn't look at me.

'You didn't take this woman,' I said slowly. 'Whoever that was – your accomplice – did they take her without your knowledge?'

I knew I was right by the way the man scowled.

'You've lost control of them, haven't you? Whatever influence you have over them is waning. They've developed a desire to kill that doesn't neatly fit into your plans.'

Hawthorn stayed silent.

'Did they butcher Jack Lavernock or was that your doing?'

'Lavernock had a theory about how we—' He caught himself and pursed his lips tight. 'He knew too much.'

'He'd figured out how you were moving the bodies. He knew who your accomplice was.' A terrible thought occurred to me. 'Someone in the Yard, someone who could plant evidence in my home, could feed you information.'

Hawthorn fired suddenly, and how he missed I cannot say, though I dived feebly backwards and raised my gun to him. The sound reverberated around us, and it felt an age until I could hear the panting of my own breath. With unnerving calm, Hawthorn pulled back the hammer of his smoking pistol and stood over me. He held the barrel towards my temple, even as I raised my gun to him.

'You won't shoot me, Thomas. It's over for you. I put one bullet in your head and make this look like a suicide.'

The gun was shaking dreadfully in my hand, a useless, heavy weight.

'You don't have to do this, Elijah. You don't have to do any of this.'

'It's too late for that. My work must continue, anywhere I see fit. My research is all that matters.'

To my disgust, I saw the desire in his eyes, the *lust*. The man was surely going to kill me, take my blood as he had the innocent woman's, and wait for my very spirit to return and look upon him. Nothing of my former friend remained in those hungry eyes, and I was certain, in that moment, that my life was about to end.

Something cold dashed across the nape of my neck, like

a hand grazing my skin. The lanterns in the cavern flickered. Hawthorn didn't seem to notice.

'T-t-tell me one thing,' I muttered, trying to quell my nervous excitement. 'Dorothy Clarke, the woman you took from Chelsea in her sleep. How did she die?'

Hawthorn seemed genuinely baffled. His hand wavered, and he frowned at me.

'She was given too much sedative. Died somewhere in the sewers before I had time to conduct any ... *tests* on her.' He pushed the barrel harder into my temple, failing to notice how the lanterns were starting to dim. 'Why are you asking about her?'

'You repel them with their own blood. Is that why they fear you? The mask disguises your identity and the blood wards them from your side.'

At last Hawthorn seemed to notice the sudden cold. He looked away from me.

'What is th—'

'You didn't take Dorothy Clarke's blood, did you?'

Hawthorn pulled the gun from my head, and in an instant, his expression turned to one of terror. Darkness enveloped us both, and he moved from my side, his breathing ragged and fast.

The darkness lasted an age, seconds that passed as slowly as hours. I heard Hawthorn moan, clatter against his case and rummage for things blindly, all the good it would do him. Finally, he stilled. His breathing even seemed to stop, the unbearable wait drawing the air from his lungs.

Suddenly the lanterns burst to life, flooding the cavern with white light. Dorothy stood at Hawthorn's back, her face filled with rage. She waited for him to turn and look at her before she clawed a hand around his shoulder.

He screamed; such a petrified, animal scream. His body wilted, he arched his back and tried to pull away from her, though her hold was too tight. The gun in his hand fired, his finger barely capable of pulling around the trigger. I yelped in terror, as Dorothy brought Hawthorn to his knees, leaned down to him, so close that her face nearly touched his. I felt her power from where I lay, for then it was inescapable, beyond anything I had ever experienced.

'You killed me,' Dorothy cried, tightening her grip on his shoulder. 'You stole me away and killed me whilst I slept. My husband still hopes I will return to him, that I will come walking through the door of our home, alive and well.'

Hawthorn was grimacing, struggling to speak.

Dorothy seemed to be growing before my eyes. Her shoulders sharpened, the soft edges of her face became hard and severe. The fingers that clasped Hawthorn grew to razor points that cut into his flesh. He wailed and tried to free himself from her.

The space began to darken once more. Dorothy seemed to breathe in the light of the lamps. They flickered out completely as her skin began to crack and blister; veins of white fire erupted and spread throughout her entirety. Her eyes widened and grew to consume much of her face. When she spoke, her teeth were jagged, splintered edges.

'You took all those people, those innocent mothers, fathers, children.' Her voice was not human, far from it. Her words rose from the depths of forgotten nightmares. They pierced through both Hawthorn and I, so that we each winced and tried to block out the sound.

'You killed those undeserving of your cruelty!'

She shoved Hawthorn to the ground. He gasped, struggled away from her, though she moved and loomed over him, her charred flesh burning.

'You did this to me. You did all this to me!'

She lunged down at him, grabbed him by the throat. The man tried to scream, but the air was choked from him in her fiery grasp. His complexion changed dramatically; he wrestled and pulled on her monstrous hands but to no avail.

'Dorothy,' I mumbled. 'Dorothy,' I said louder when my courage had returned. 'Don't, don't do this.'

She turned her black eyes towards me, stared at me with all the ill will and malice she had for Hawthorn. I crawled back away from her, raised my hand.

'Not this way,' I begged, though my words seemed hollow. 'He must face justice; he must face those he has wronged—'

'He's facing me!' she screeched. 'He's facing me. He did this to me!'

Hawthorn swung loosely at her, though he was clearly growing weak. His body slumped; his lips drained of the last of their colour. Dorothy turned back to him, watched with gruesome fascination as his bloodshot eyes bulged, as his tongue slathered pathetically from his open mouth. I stood and moved closer to her, felt the heat radiating from her terrible body.

'You can't do this, Dorothy. Please, it's, it's ... it's not you.'

She looked at me once more, though I held my ground, not backing away from her terrifying stare.

'You're better than him, so much better. You've sought justice all this time, sought to find the man who wronged you and so many others.'

She appeared unmoved, as I saw with horror Hawthorn's arms fall loosely at his sides.

'I'll make sure he is revealed to the world. All will know his name and revile it for years to cōme. He'll tell us of his accomplice – they're still on the loose.' On this latter point I was desperate for her to understand, for Hawthorn's co-conspirator would no doubt be the most wanted man or woman in the country. 'Dorothy, please. Don't stoop to his level. I'm begging you.'

She stared a moment longer. I thought with dread she wouldn't listen, resigned myself to this fact, for her dreadful face was lifeless, completely blank. The hand clutching Hawthorn's throat surged with light, pulsing like blood pumping through veins. She would surely snap his neck. She would surely crush him in her palm.

To my relief, I saw her grip loosen slightly. Hawthorn coughed, wheezed and hacked for air. Dorothy's malevolent eyes began to shrink as I stared at them; the fire across her skin dwindled.

'He can't be allowed to get away with it,' she said, her voice returning to its soft timbre. 'He can't ... he can't ...' She began to weep as her entirety quickly shrunk and returned to its normal form. She let go of Hawthorn, and the miserable wretch spluttered and rolled upon the floor, still in agony.

The light returned to the lanterns. I wanted to comfort her, but she gestured that I leave her, her hands visibly shuddering. She couldn't bring herself to look at Hawthorn.

'I want him to suffer, as he's made so many suffer,' she groaned. 'He's taken so much from me.'

She lunged and kicked at him suddenly, in a desperate, futile way. A human reaction, a deserved one. I grabbed her arm, felt the ice-cold of her skin, the dreadful sensation. I could only bear to touch her a moment, and she seemed to know it. She stormed away from me, her anger so raw, so visceral. I had such pity for her then, and such great admiration.

So many would have succumbed to their desire for vengeance. So many would have killed Hawthorn had they stood in her place. She was far better.

'He'll face a judge, a jury,' I said to Dorothy's back. 'He will stand trial for all the wrong he has done.'

She didn't reply, didn't move.

'Dorothy—'

I stopped. Beyond the gushing water, I heard voices, calling out to one another. I turned and looked towards the stairs I had descended. I saw faint light growing stronger.

'The police,' I said, and how relieved I felt. 'The officers are coming, they'll take him awa—'

Dorothy had gone. I couldn't help but feel disappointed. I thought to call out to her, but didn't. With shoulders slumped, I stepped over to Hawthorn, gasping still, his eyes wide, filled with abject terror. He reeled away from me, though I manhandled and pulled him to a sitting position.

'They're coming for you, Elijah. You'll face up to all you have done.'

He tremored in my grasp. 'None of them have tried to hurt me. Even without blood they fear me. How-how…'

I saw the deep lesions across his shoulder and shook my head. 'I don't know what you are talking about.' I gestured to his arm. 'These wounds were caused whilst you were resisting arrest.'

'She was going to kill me.' He barely seemed to acknowledge me then, his gaze vacant, his eyes darting back and forth to the chamber around us. 'She was going to kill me.'

I let him slump back to the floor. I turned as the sound of voices grew louder, as the light coming down the stairs only brightened. A moment later, a burly officer in uniform came storming into the space, followed closely by a plainclothes officer with a rifle. The gun was aimed straight at me.

'Drop the pistol, Bexley.'

I'd almost forgotten I was still carrying the gun. I dropped it lazily and raised my hands.

'The man beside me is Elijah Hawthorn. He's the one responsible for all this.'

'Keep quiet and get down on your knees.' Another troop of men suddenly appeared from the stairs. Mostly uniformed constables, though two more were plainclothes officers. They shone lights and aimed rifles, though all seemed wary to approach Hawthorn and me.

'This man is Elijah Hawthorn,' I repeated calmly. 'He has framed me for the Wraith kidnappings; I was charged with his murder.'

The men spread out around the chamber. Some were stony-faced, glaring at me intently. The plainclothes officers, however, men from Flynn's unit no doubt, soon carried expressions of shock and confusion. They were better informed about the case, likely knowing who Hawthorn was and what significance his discovery meant.

'His accomplice has fled up a passage over there.' My arms were still raised, though I gestured with my head. One of Flynn's men took a step closer, looked from me to Hawthorn upon the floor.

'Jesus,' he croaked, the rifle aimed at my chest wavering. Only then did he seem to notice the dead woman on the floor. He turned suddenly to a constable by the stairs. 'Raise the alarm. Find Flynn and the commissioner. We'll get 'em up top side.'

He shouldered his gun, stepped closer to me and told me to turn around. As I did, I saw him pull shackles from his belt; without a word I clasped my wrists together.

'You have questions to answer.'

I didn't reply. Hawthorn was staring at me from the floor. As he raised his hand to his neck, I saw how badly it was shaking.

'Someone get this fella,' the man at my back yelled, and I heard boots trudge across the dust and dirt. Hawthorn flinched at the very sound.

'You can plead insanity,' I muttered to him, not with spite or ill will but genuine regret. The man had fallen so far. 'You're mad, Elijah, and they'll see that.'

He nodded his head a little, looked up at the officer who began pulling me away.

His eyes fell to something on the floor.

'I'll see you soon, Thomas.'

It happened so suddenly I could do nothing to stop it. As Hawthorn scrambled for the pistol I had dropped, I tried lunging forwards to it, held back by the officer clasping my shackles. I yelled out, as Hawthorn pulled back the hammer and put the barrel to his temple. Then it was done; I don't recall even hearing the gun shot. His body crumpled to the floor like a ragdoll and all manner of misery, guilt and contempt surged through me.

I'd told Dorothy he would face justice.

I had failed her.

A Sombre End

October 20th, 1905

I woke with a start, thrashing my arms, expecting to fall and hit the cold stone of the cell floor as I had so many times over the previous month. Only when I prised my eyes open fully, when the warm light of morning made me squint and look towards the window, did I realise I was in my own bed, in my own home. Having been released from the Yard two days previously, I was still not accustomed to soft sheets and privacy.

My head hurt as it did most mornings; my body remained stiff as I stretched and sat up lazily. The deep bruises from the beating I had sustained in Walthamstow Station were all but gone, though the lasting damage was still felt. A discomfort, a dull pressure, burned on my right side when I breathed in too deeply, though I knew this would pass in time. I reached for a glass at my bedside, sunk the clear liquid in one swallow and felt all the better for it. No booze that morning, only water, though I was far from a sober man. My weeks imprisoned had gifted me an opportunity to clean myself up somewhat, though upon my release I had been quick to buy two bottles of rum. Now, at the very least, I refrained from drinking until after noon.

I pulled back the sheets and felt the chill of the air. I didn't know the time, though guessed it was late morning. I had stayed awake through much of the night, sitting downstairs with a few lit candles. Waiting. Waiting for her, for Dorothy.

I hadn't seen her (or anything of the dead) since the day Hawthorn had died. I feared I would never see her again.

I lit a cigarette, inhaled the rich smoke fully and wrapped a robe around myself. I headed downstairs and heard the pleasant sounds of life beyond my front door. For the first time in over a year, I was seeing my world as it had been before I was plunged into a realm of hauntings and the supernatural. I felt *safe* – safe in the knowledge of my innocence, though that was still to be proved to many.

I opened the front door; a shower of rain had broken out and a few men in fine suits began dashing quickly along the pavement. The sun still shone brightly though, for the clouds overhead were meagre and had not concealed it in any great manner. The effect was a rather pleasant one, for the light reflected off the pavements and cobbles spectacularly, giving all the appearance of being cast in purest gold. I leaned against the door frame, smoked my cigarette down to a stub and took in the morning. I could have stayed that way, in a comfortable, dreary state, for hours, had it not been for the loud crash that startled me from somewhere inside the house.

Where once panic would have overcome me, excitement arose. I burst into the lounge, looking all around before stepping into the adjoining dining room.

'Dorothy?' I exclaimed. I waited in eager anticipation, hoping she would appear before my eyes. A minute became two. Two minutes became three. Nothing stirred throughout the house, though still I waited. How I longed to see her.

A quick knock at the sitting-room door.

'Mr Bexley.'

I near leapt from my skin, turning to spy the constable taking a step back from me into the hallway. He was young, barely a man.

I gasped in air, my heart racing. 'What the hell are you doing?'

The constable apologised, clearly nervous. 'The front door was open.'

I rubbed a hand across my face, took a moment to regain my composure. 'Well, what do you want?' I snapped rather rudely.

The constable stepped further away from me.

'Orders from the commissioner. He's asked that I escort you down to the Yard.'

'What the hell for? More questioning?' I searched about the room, looking for any signs of Dorothy. Between her lack of appearance and the constable scaring me senseless, my good mood had suddenly evaporated.

'I don't know, I was just told to fetch you.'

'Am I under arrest?'

'No.' The young man shifted uncomfortably. Regardless of my release, he was clearly wary of me. Many more harboured deep suspicions about my character.

There seemed no sense in arguing with him. 'All right. I'll get dressed and head down presently.'

'Shall I wait outside?'

I sighed. 'There's no need for you to wait at all.' I left the lounge and led him back to the front door. 'If the commissioner has deemed it appropriate to release me, he should realise I pose no risk of running.'

'But, my orders—'

'Take my advice, constable. Policing is not always about following orders to the letter but often a case of reading the situation before you.'

He stepped outside and I tried offering him a smile. 'Tell Henley I'm getting dressed and I'll be along presently.'

The constable protested a little, before yielding. I could tell, from the look upon his face, that he was relieved not to have to share my company. He left in the direction of the Yard and I watched after him, before closing the front door and returning to the lounge.

Dorothy was still nowhere to be seen, much to my disappointment.

The rain had stopped by the time I left. My face was clean-shaven, my suit neatly pressed. At the sight of clear blue skies, my mood lifted substantially, and although it seemed Henley would surely berate me with more questions, or ask me to clarify some minute detail of the whole sordid affair, it seemed no great trial or inconvenience. I would enjoy my quiet walk, do what was needed of me, and be on my way.

Lower James Street was not busy by then, nor was Piccadilly Circus or Regent Street for that matter. The carts and carriages that passed by in the road moved serenely, their nags, drivers and passengers alike, all in no hurry. Those I passed seemed jovial and pleasant; shopkeepers smiled at customers, tradesmen joked and laughed amongst each other. Children scampered away from nannies and mothers, who laughed merrily at the sight. I watched a family, a father with daughters and wife, pass me by on the street. And how to my surprise the proud man did tip his hat and bid me 'Good day', and what pleasure it was to bid him 'Good day' as well, and revel in the normality of the brief encounter.

I wondered, as I turned and watched after the family, if I would find need to take any drink that day, if the pleasantries and good cheer of those around me would help stave off the need for liquor. I knew, with some regret, it was a naïve notion; although my mood was fine that morning, it could just as easily be dark and pensive by the coming eve. The flask of rum in my pocket was testament to that. Overcoming addiction is far from easy; to this day of writing I have not succeeded in the endeavour.

My gaze was distracted, looking about the road, peering into shopfronts and the like. A man thundered into me at the crossing for Charles Street; I begged his pardon before realising who he was.

'Mr Bexley, funny runnin' into you like that.'

It took a moment to recall the man's name. Edward Sanders, the hack reporter. As he smiled up at me, his crooked teeth looked darker than they had when we had last met. His whole appearance seemed ragged, in fact; his clothes were riddled with stains and dirt, his hair oily and unkempt.

I tried to pass the man, but he moved his body in front of me.

'Been tryin' to speak t'you last day or two, ever since Henley cut you loose.' His breath was repulsive, yet he held his face close to mine, taking some pleasure from my disgust. 'Thought I might run into you somewhere round these ways.'

'What do you want, Sanders?' I spoke confidently, with force. It did little to dissuade the rotten man. He smiled wryly and scratched at his brow.

'*Nothing*. Nothing really, Mr Bexley. I'm just curious why Henley and the CID thought to let you go, after all the allegations, the evidence stacked against you.'

I barged by him roughly then, and he laughed quite wickedly.

'How did you ever convince them of your innocence?' He walked just beside me. 'They said the real Wraith 'ad been apprehended but won't comment on who the guilty party was. There's a lot of anger in the streets, a lot of questions left to be answered. Not to mention the death of Jack Lavernock—'

I turned on him then and thrust a finger close to his eyes. 'You mention that man's name again—'

'And what?' He revelled in my outburst. 'What y'guna do about it?'

I shook my head, turned away from him and walked on.

'I have a theory about it all, a notion I may run by the editor at the *Mail*. He always likes printing a good conspiracy.'

'Really,' I said dryly, not stopping or turning back. 'What's that?'

'The Wraith couldn't have worked alone, no doubt needed someone to help 'im with all the bodies. I reckon you were his right-hand man, made some deal with Henley if you spilt the whole truth.'

He stopped me then, though the notion was wholly absurd.

'Admit it,' he smiled, goading me. 'You admit the whole thing to me, and I'll make sure to write it up friendly. I swear, you'll be like another victim, an innocent pawn—'

I lunged at him, grabbed him by the shirt and barged him to the floor. He scrambled away from me, got to his feet laughing, much to the shock of a few fine-dressed onlookers.

'Get out of here!' I snarled as Sanders brushed down his trousers and straightened his jacket.

'I'll be seeing you soon, Mr Bexley. Be sure of that.'

He walked away then, back down Charles Street. I watched after him until he was out of sight. Then, with no hesitation, and in full view of all those on Regent Street, I grabbed the flask from my pocket and took a long swig, my fine mood forgotten.

The waters of the Thames were busy, vessels moving sullenly along the murky surface. Big Ben struck twelve, though no one paid it any heed. A portly man stopped and gazed out across the river a little way from me. I watched as he smiled, pulled a paper from his coat and unfolded the great thing, spreading it on the wall that I leant upon. He looked over the front page carefully, the headline of which I could clearly read.

QUESTIONS FOR THE MET –
WHO WAS THE WRAITH OF LONDON?

I watched the man read through the story carefully. I took a cigarette, fumbled in my pockets to find a light.

'I may have one.'

I turned and saw Robert Henley standing behind me. He pulled out a box of matches from his waistcoat and struck one for me. He wore no jacket, and to my surprise, no tie. The sleeves of his crisp shirt were rolled to the elbows. I puffed on my cigarette and thanked him as he leant against the wall beside me. He sighed deeply.

'Fine day.'

I nodded. 'It was until about thirty minutes ago.'

'Something happen on your way here?'

I shook my head. 'It's of no concern.' I took another drag, wondering if Sanders was being serious, fearful even that he may run his story, paint me out to be the contemptible Wraith's accomplice. I pushed aside the thought. 'I assume you have some more questions for me, commissioner.'

'One or two, though really I thought you should be brought up to speed on developments. You were there when Hawthorn died, he brought you into all this. It seems right you know the truth.'

'You're convinced at last I played no part in this?' I said curiously. 'What finally persuaded you?'

'We questioned you for weeks, Bexley. You're either a bloody good liar or had no part in the disappearances. The fact Elijah

Hawthorn was found alive; the notebook we discovered on his person detailing where he disposed of the victims' bodies; the tools he had that we were able to link with several of the victims' wounds. If you and Hawthorn were working together, why would he have faked his own death and framed you for the murder?'

He stared out across the water, his expression subdued.

'That in itself was enough for me to release you. The new evidence we uncovered yesterday exonerates you fully.'

'What evidence would that be, sir?'

Henley took a deep breath. 'When we arrested you initially, Bexley, you were deranged. You spoke as if one of the victims was beside you, as if you'd been with her the whole time?' He turned on me, looked me straight in the eyes. 'Tell me about that, truthfully. After Hawthorn shot himself you said nothing of it, as though your derangement had gone completely.'

I felt my chest tighten – what was I to say to him? I couldn't tell him the truth of what I saw, of all I had seen in the past sixteen months. He'd never believe it, would have me institution-alised within the hour. My palms grew sweaty; the shirt and suit I wore suffocating and hot.

'I can't, sir.'

He frowned. 'What do you mean, you can't?'

'It's, um, it's not very clear to me.' I feigned sincerity as best I could, certain that Henley would see straight through me. 'I had been quite sleep-deprived prior to my arrest at the home of Lord Cavendish-Huntley. Furthermore, I have some suspicions that Hawthorn may have possibly drugged me whilst I was in Scotland.'

'Drugged you?'

'Yes, sir.' I was saying the words before my conscious mind had thought of them. 'I explained that I had seen a man fitting Hawthorn's description at the station in Adanburgh. We know he or his associate must have been in the area at the time, owing to the poisonings in Pike Ness and the assault on Lachlan Montgomery.'

'Indeed.'

'Well, sir, there's every possibility Hawthorn may have managed to drug some food or drink of mine around that time. Depending on what he used, it could account for the, um, delusions I saw.' I paused briefly, then added for good measure, 'Either that or the delusions themselves could be the consequence of the neurological disorder the physician prognosed. He's made several examinations of me over the last few weeks.'

'He has,' Henley concurred. 'From what I gather, his findings have been inconclusive.'

I nodded. 'The onset of my symptoms has been quite sudden. With all that has transpired over the last few months, a number of factors could have led to the seizures I experienced inside Walthamstow Station. Not least the beating I took.'

Henley was unmoved. 'Have you sought clarification on the matter? Has any treatment been recommended?'

'No, sir. The physician explained that a new scientific technique, using unseen rays of light to take photographs of the brain inside the skull could reveal the cause of my seizures. Even then, he was somewhat sceptical, owing to the suddenness of my symptoms.'

Henley was frowning at me. 'Photographs of the brain, *inside the skull*?'

I nodded. 'Science is changing the world at quite a pace, sir.'

'Hm,' he grunted. 'Well, your explanation for the delusions is reasonable. Very reasonable.' He turned and leant back against the wall, casting his gaze out across the water. 'But the manner with which you spoke, the assuredness that you had been with Dorothy Clarke since arriving in Scotland. That troubles me.'

'I'm afraid I can't give you more of an answer, sir. Either Hawthorn drugged me or this neurological disorder may have had some effect that really made me believe I had seen her.'

'Hawthorn saw things too.'

My heart stopped beating.

'Pardon, sir?'

'His notebook. He wrote of sightings – timed them, marked them with dates, descriptions of individuals.' Henley's voice remained completely level. 'Quite ghastly descriptions, in fact, the stuff of nightmares really.'

I nodded, though couldn't find my voice. Henley continued.

'We had the complete autopsy report back on him. Due to the sensitive nature of the case – names being withheld and so forth – it took considerably longer to collaborate our findings, to compile them fully. Do you know what we found?'

'As cause of death,' I murmured nervously. 'Gunshot wound to the head, no doubt, considerable damage to the cranium, the soft tissue—'

'A tumour.' Henley turned his head to look at me, his eyes narrow in the midday sun. 'In his brain. Almost the size of a golf ball, would you believe.'

I could. Hawthorn's nose had bled twice in the brief time I had been with him. I'd speculated then that he – we – may have some illness, some physical symptoms caused by the terrible things we'd witnessed, the dead walking about us day after day. It seemed Henley may have confirmed the theory for me. I tried to stifle a shudder, tried to maintain my calm disposition. Henley was staring at me like a hawk, watching my reaction.

'We've asked several specialists to examine the tumour, to provide some insight. None so far have ever seen or heard of anything like it before. All concur that it was no doubt growing inside Hawthorn's head for years, maybe even as far back as his time running the Forensic Crime Directorate. They speculate it may have resulted in a drastic change of personality over many years, could even be attributed to his compulsion to kill.'

I thought of my own recent symptoms and wondered, with sudden panic, if I were walking the same path as Elijah Hawthorn. Each of us had first seen ghosts in photographs; each of us seemed blighted by the dead for some unknown reason. Perhaps Hawthorn's symptoms had once been like mine; nose bleeds, seizures. Perhaps, unbeknownst to me, something akin to what grew and festered inside Hawthorn's brain for many years was now growing inside my skull. Perhaps such a thing was *caused* by my seeing the dead. Perhaps such a thing would only worsen, would drive me mad as it had done to Hawthorn...

Henley let the silence hang heavily between us. I nodded slowly, hoping I was giving the impression of deep thought rather than sheer panic.

'Peculiar though,' he eventually said in his calm tone. 'We find evidence that Hawthorn was *seeing* visages of the dead, of victims, individuals, that he could identify by name. The discovery of this tumour shows clearly that he suffered from some untreated condition for years.' He brushed a finger against his moustache. 'You *saw* Dorothy Clarke, even if you now acknowledge you were hallucinating. A physician has diagnosed you with some neurological condition, as yet unidentified.'

'What are you suggesting, sir?' I spoke rather abruptly. Henley shook his head.

'Merely pointing out a parallel, one that you yourself must acknowledge.'

'I do, sir. But I don't see what pertinence it has to the whole affair.' I was lying of course, struggling now to maintain my composure.

'Maybe none.' He shrugged. 'Perhaps it is merely a coincidence.'

He cleared his throat. 'In truth, I'm not sure I want to know.' The way he looked at me then was startling, his unfaltering eyes saying far more than a thousand words ever could.

He knew. Maybe not the entirety of my dark secret, maybe none of it, in fact. Only that a secret existed, a secret both I and Hawthorn had shared, one that had dramatically changed the course of our lives.

'I'm a man of the law, Bexley. I don't deal with the unknowns of this world, only the facts. All I can suggest to you is that you seek to uncover the truth of your *condition*, before it sends you down a similar path to Elijah Hawthorn.'

I nodded, mechanically reaching for another cigarette before asking for another match. Henley provided me with one, and didn't speak until I flicked the stub into the water.

'That's not why I brought you here. I wanted to talk to you about the evidence we discovered yesterday. We think we've identified Hawthorn's assailant.'

'Really?' I said excitedly. 'How?'

'In the account you gave of your confrontation beneath the city with Hawthorn, you claimed he took an item from around his neck and discarded it in the water.'

'Yes, it was a small item, on a chain.'

'A key.'

I looked in total disbelief as Henley pulled a small brass key from his waistcoat pocket. He dropped it in my open palm, and I stared closely at the unremarkable thing.

'Clearly, when Hawthorn threw it, it didn't make the water. After your statement, I ordered men to look for it, on the off chance they may find something. Seems we got very lucky.'

'How long have you had it?'

'Over three weeks,' Henley replied. 'There's no identifiable marks on it as you can see. Hawthorn clearly feared it falling into our possession, so I ensured every available resource was used to identify what the key is for. Care to hazard a guess?'

I turned it over in my hands; there wasn't a single scratch upon it.

'I don't know – it could be for anything. Whatever it unlocked surely held valuable information.'

'We started with that assumption and worked from there. Hawthorn didn't have a safe in his home, but we made the presumption this was some form of safe key. There's a safe in the manor on that island in Scotland but its lock doesn't match this key type.'

'There must be thousands of safes throughout the country – it could belong to any one of them.'

'True,' Henley nodded. 'But Hawthorn committed the majority of his murders in London. Furthermore, if the key belonged to a safe outside the city, our search would have been nigh on impossible. Hawthorn likely wouldn't have seen the need to discard it.' Henley took back the key. 'For him to have disposed of it on the chance he may have been captured, the information it unlocked must have been very important, and somewhere we could access it.'

'You searched all of London then?' I couldn't conceal my disbelief.

'Started with banks and safety deposit boxes – believe me, it took considerable manpower. Day before yesterday we had a breakthrough. A jeweller's, with all of twenty deposit boxes in a back room. The owner identified Hawthorn when shown his photograph, though didn't recognise the name.'

A couple walked slowly by us and Henley said nothing until they were far from earshot. 'How much do you really think you knew Elijah Hawthorn? Before all this, I mean?'

'He was my mentor,' I said plainly. 'A father figure when I needed one.'

'Yet you didn't know he had a ward, an adopted son?'

I was baffled. 'An adopted son?'

Henley nodded. 'No one of senior rank had a clue either. Seems Hawthorn kept secrets from everyone and kept them well.'

I struggled to say anything, as much as I tried. A hundred questions flitted through my mind in an instant, leaving me speechless. Henley spoke on.

'About five months after the Forensic Crime Directorate was formed, March or April of eighteen ninety-two, Hawthorn took guardianship of an eight-year-old boy named Albert Fayweather. The boy's parents – friends of his – were killed in an accident whilst travelling to visit their country estate on an island just off Aberdeenshire–'

'The manor off the coast of Pike Ness,' I exclaimed.

'The very one. Hawthorn took ownership of the property when he began caring for the boy. I have no idea why he would keep the matter secret. Perhaps he feared his guardianship of the child would jeopardise his role in the Directorate.'

I tried to think of the numerous times Hawthorn and I had spoken in depth about our private lives; our wants, our ambitions. Never once had the man mentioned anything about children; as far as I was concerned, he was an unmarried man who had dedicated his life to his work.

'We learnt of this from what we found in Hawthorn's deposit box. Along with further information regarding the victims – and his plans to frame you – there were numerous papers regarding Hawthorn's guardianship of the Fayweather boy, and the state of his upbringing. He was educated privately at Hawthorn's home; spent much of his time with a nanny who cared for him.'

'Hawthorn couldn't have been with the boy much, not with the volume of work we had in the Directorate.'

Henley concurred. 'We know that a year before the Directorate was disbanded, Hawthorn relieved the child's nanny of her duties. Seems the boy would have been left alone in Hawthorn's home for much of his young life.' He shook his head. 'No friends to speak of. No one to love him in the way a parent should. We found a number of diaries in the deposit box, containing rather disturbing information.'

My heart sank. 'Hawthorn abused the child in some fashion?'

Henley shook his head once more. 'No. Not in any way most would understand at least. He speaks fondly of the boy throughout his entries, cared for him quite sincerely. But the man was clearly mad, writing evermore about his *visions*. Seems he wanted the child to see them as well.'

'Well, what happened?' I asked. 'The boy would be in his early twenties by now. Where is he?'

Henley glanced cautiously around us. He leant closer towards me, seemed to pull back a moment in hesitation. I sensed he didn't want to tell me.

'We believe he's Hawthorn's accomplice, the one who aided him in all of this. The lad changed his name; there are men looking for him as we speak,' was all he muttered.

'You have hope of finding him then?'

'Hope is all I have. From the evidence you gave, we know it was the young man who kidnapped the final victim, even though Hawthorn put the fatal bullet in her back. We believe the young man was also responsible for the failed kidnap attempt of Daniel Pinkney in mid-August. From what we gather, Hawthorn was losing control over him. He's dangerous, a threat to anyone he comes across.'

'Let's hope you capture him soon,' I muttered. 'At the very

least,' I said flippantly, 'his arrest will get Edward Sanders off my back.'

Henley, who had been looking out across the water, turned on me suddenly. He grabbed me roughly by the shoulder and I admit he took me quite by surprise.

'Sanders. Edward Sanders?'

'Y-yes,' I said nervously. 'The journalist – the hack. The one Jack seemed to despise so much.'

Henley's eyes widened as he looked at me; his fingers dug deeper into my arm.

'It's him,' I said then, bile bubbling in the pit of my stomach. 'He's the boy.'

'Where did you see him?'

'I don't understan—'

'Where did you see him?' Henley growled.

'Regent Street, on the corner of Charles Street. Just before I came here. He headed north—'

Henley let go of my arm, walked briskly across the road and spoke with a group of constables standing outside the Yard's main entrance. Two of the men scampered off quickly in the direction of Regent Street; another ran inside the building. Henley came back to me quickly.

'We thought he would have fled the city after Hawthorn's death.'

I barely heard the man, thinking instead how Sanders' involvement made perfect sense.

'He was always at the crime scenes. Always the first reporter there. He may have had sources inside the force feeding him information.' It dawned on me then. 'Jack. When I found him dead, there seemed no signs of forced entry into his home. Whether he liked Sanders or not, he knew the man. Maybe he convinced Jack to let him in, claimed to have some information that may be relevant.'

'You can't speak about this to anyone.' Henley's face was dark, his tone darker still.

'The map Jack left. He started to write on it – he'd written E for Edward Sanders.'

'Are you listening to me?' Henley said louder, grabbing my attention. 'You speak of this to no one, understand? Not a soul. Until Edward Sanders is found, he is a danger to every man and woman in this city.'

'He'll slip up, sir,' I said, trying to reassure myself more than Henley. 'He'll make a mistake and be caught out.'

Henley nodded. 'Let's hope so, Bexley.'

He turned to walk away from me. As he stepped off the pavement, I called after him.

'I could help. The man has some fascination with me – why else would he seek me out as he did?'

Henley stepped a little way back to me, glanced over his shoulder towards the red brickwork of the Yard.

'You know as well as I, you have no future here.' His regret seemed genuine. 'The constables who know about the case question your innocence. And the rest have heard enough rumours to fear you. With what I know, I can't risk—'

He stopped himself, but I implored he speak on.

'I can't risk you taking decisions and making enquiries in the name of the Metropolitan Police. Were anything to happen, were you to … *snap*, as Hawthorn did …' He shook his head. 'I won't let it happen, not now or ever.'

I wanted to protest, but there seemed no point. He was right about it all. Too much damage had been done. Too much of my reputation had been lost within the force. Few would have any confidence in me and in time I doubted any constabularies outside of the city would even want to seek my assistance.

It seemed my career was over, not with any great flourish, but merely a few words shared on a gorgeous day down by the river.

'You're a smart man, Bexley. You'll move on, I'm sure of it.' Henley held out his hand to me then. 'If there's anything I can ever help you with.' He said the words slowly, his eyebrows raised somewhat. I nodded, took his hand and shook it firmly.

With that he stepped into the road, back towards the Yard's main doors where more constables and sergeants had gathered, waiting to be dispatched. They all stood straight as Henley spoke to them, before he stepped inside without so much as a glance over his shoulder. The men began moving away quickly, but not before a few eyed me with clear suspicion.

As I looked upon them and the building I had once been so proud to enter, I doubted I would ever walk through its corridors again.

An Uncertain Future
October 20th, 1905

I didn't know what time it was when I returned home, but it was dark and miserable outside. I had been wandering for hours, thinking of my future, my career, now seemingly in tatters. I closed the front door quietly and lit an oil lamp, feeling the small but pleasant warmth from the burning flame against my skin.

In the light I spotted a letter lying on the floor. A nondescript thing, stamped and marked appropriately, my address scrawled in messy black ink across the envelope. I picked it up and stared at it, felt its edges and examined the handwriting with great scrutiny. It was not Hawthorn's. I shook my head at the thought of this. The man was dead, yet still I waited for his letters.

I'll see you soon, Thomas.

I stepped into the living room, still looking down at the letter, and placed the lamp upon the mantel. I intended to stoke a fire before I set about making some food.

'Hello, Thomas.'

I leapt in fright, reeled away from the fire and looked towards the dining room. Dorothy was sat at the table, her hands clasped loosely. She smiled a little as I grabbed at my chest and inhaled deeply. In the dim light I noticed the faintest hue around her skin and wondered if it had always shone in such a way.

'You scared me!' I wasn't angry, far from it in fact. I was more than merely relieved, but jubilant to see her.

I snatched the lamp and came into the dining room. She said nothing as I pulled out the chair beside her and sat down clumsily, the lamp clattering onto the table. In its light, I saw the melancholy etched into her face, the sadness laced in her thin smile.

'I feared you were gone,' I spluttered. 'Feared you may have ... *moved on*.' I didn't know how else to say it. 'I thought I would never see you again.'

Her eyes were wet, shimmering in the orange light. 'I have. I mean, I've *moved on* from here.' She looked about the room.

'I'm so sorry,' I said quietly.

'What for?'

'Hawthorn, of course.' I felt embarrassed then, ashamed. 'He died because of me. I swore to you he would face justice and he didn't. I failed you so badly—'

She hushed me. 'That doesn't matter. You found out the truth. You uncovered it all.'

'For what good?' I asked bitterly. 'It changes nothing – it won't bring you back.'

'It will save so many more.'

'Will it,' I scoffed, sitting back in the chair. 'Until the next madman starts snatching people in the night. Until more bodies appear, until more lives are taken needlessly.' I rubbed my brow. 'I spoke to Henley today. The Yard learnt who Hawthorn's accomplice was, a man named Edward Sanders.'

Dorothy nodded. 'Will you go after him?'

'No,' I sighed. 'I don't know. He's surely the country's most wanted man. I doubt he will make it out of the city.'

'And if he does?'

The idea didn't bear thinking about. 'It won't come to that.'

We grew silent then, each of us staring down towards the table, glancing up at the flickering light of the lamp or fidgeting where we sat. Dorothy wiped tears from the corners of her eyes, and how I wanted to reach out a hand and touch her.

'You want to ask me where I've moved on to,' she said bluntly. 'You want to know if there's an afterlife.'

I felt my body tremble. 'There is; surely there is? How else could this be happening if there was not a place beyond this one?'

Dorothy smiled. 'In truth I don't know – I haven't found it yet.' She laughed a little as the tears streamed down her cheeks. 'Since last we met, I've been searching for it; that's the only way I can describe it really. It's as though I've been travelling through a world built on dreams. I don't know what I'm looking for, but I think I'm getting close.' She hesitated. 'It's not easy coming back here. In fact, I think this may be the last time I can. I just, I just…'

I couldn't bear it any longer. I reached my hand out to hers and clutched her fingers tight. The pain – the shocking, cold pain – was more terrible than I could have expected. She saw my discomfort, surely felt it and tried to wrench her hand away. But I wouldn't let her. After a moment, she wove her fingers around mine. She squeezed them gently, before letting go her grip. I let go as well, for then I could take no more.

'You don't owe me anything, Thomas.'

'You saved my life,' I murmured. 'Had you not freed me from police custody, I would surely have thought myself mad all the way to the gallows.'

'It could never have been you, Thomas. Never.'

'Aren't you afraid?' I said.

She nodded. 'Always. Since the day this began, since the day he took my life.' She smiled again and reached towards me, setting her hand down close to mine. 'Things were easier with you though. There were times when you made me feel safe.'

Together we sat quietly, neither of us needing to speak. Her presence was a great comfort to me. I wished she would never go.

'You're cold,' she said sometime later. As if on cue I began to shiver. I moved to the fire, set about lighting it clumsily and knelt beside it, holding my hands close as the flames grew tall.

'Did you and Henley speak of much else today?' Dorothy asked quietly.

'Yes.'

She waited for me to elaborate.

'My service with the Metropolitan Police is over.' I couldn't conceal the regret in my voice. 'I don't know what I expected really, but too many bridges have been burnt, too much damage done.'

I said nothing of Hawthorn's tumour, or my theory that it was caused by the presence of the dead and the ability to see them. I rubbed my temple slowly.

'What will you do?'

I stood from the fire, feigned light-heartedness as best I could. 'I'm not sure. No doubt I can make some good of my skills in other ways.' I didn't believe my own words and could see the disbelief on Dorothy's face. 'Such things seem so trivial compared to you—' I stopped myself from saying any more. 'Sorry.'

'They won't stop,' Dorothy said. 'The dead. They will keep coming to you whether you like it or not.'

I grimaced. 'Why? Such terrible things will destroy me. You are the only one ...' I stopped, took a breath. 'You are the only one I have not feared.'

She looked at me with such sympathy. 'Whether you fear them or not, you are bound to them now. They need you; all those like me who were wronged so terribly. They need you, and you must continue to help them, regardless of whether you work for the police or not.'

I ran a hand through my hair. 'I'm afraid it's not as simple as that.'

'Why not?'

'Well…' I paused. 'I can't – I can't just interfere with murder enquiries as and when I like. I'll be locked up inside a month or two.'

I sat back down at the table. Dorothy was staring at me, and I struggled to hold her gaze.

'You have to find a way to help people,' she said sternly.

'Henley will take no pity on me. There can't be a single constable in the whole Metropolitan Police who trusts me anymore.'

'Then look beyond the city, as you always have.'

I laughed, exasperated, shaking my head. Dorothy pointed across the table.

'What's that?'

I looked down at the letter, at the scrawled handwriting, at the faded, almost unreadable postal marks.

'I have no idea.'

'Aren't you going to open it? You told me you received letters from those asking for your help. You told me of that girl – that girl already murdered – who wrote to you—'

'Dorothy—'

'Listen to me.' She reached out across the table, resting her fingers close to mine. 'Whether you call it a gift or a curse, you possess something that few others surely do. *And you must use it.* You can't waste your days, drinking yourself half to death and reminiscing on simpler times.' She tilted her head, so that our eyes met. 'You have to help others as you helped me. You have to do good, and not let any of this destroy you as it did Elijah Hawthorn.'

Slowly, I reached for the letter and ripped open the envelope. In the light of the lamp I read it silently. Dorothy could barely contain herself.

'What does it say?'

I rubbed a hand across my jaw, reading the first lines of the letter again.

'It's from a police sergeant, based down in Devonshire.'

'And?'

My heart was fluttering, trepidation and excitement cutting straight through me. 'He fears a man's suicide may not be what it seems. His superiors have already closed the case based on substantive evidence. But this sergeant is certain someone has staged the man's death.'

'To conceal a murder?'

'Indeed.' I quickly read through the last paragraph. 'The sergeant has been trying to contact me via the Yard for the past six weeks. Clearly he has no idea what's been happening.'

'Will you go to help him?'

I shook my head. 'I have no business interfering with such matters anymore.'

'Thomas—'

'I can't,' I said bitterly. 'This man, this sergeant, who I have no knowledge of, may be mistaken or have some vendetta against his superiors. If, as he claims, the evidence points to a suicide, then that is surely what it was.'

'Thomas—'

'Dorothy,' I said, interrupting her. 'I can't simply barge my way into police stations and demand to have enquiries re-opened. That is not my place anymore; if Henley found out he would have me arrested.'

'But you need to help those like me who have been wronged, whose killers roam free.'

'Who's to say this is such an instance of that? What evidence is there but the word of this sergeant?'

I realised then that Dorothy was not looking at me. Slowly she raised her hand and pointed into the lounge at my back. I turned, the flutter of my heart erupting quite suddenly.

In the corner of the room, concealed partially by the thick, open curtains, a man stood motionless. His face was beaten and bruised; his clothes dirty and torn. Around his neck hung a noose, thick and heavy.

Blood trickled slowly down every knot of the rope.

'Is he evidence enough?' Dorothy said plainly. 'Will you help him as you helped me?'

I struggled to find words, to find the strength to speak.

'C-can you not stay? Can you not stay with me?'

I turned back to Dorothy, stretched out a hand to hold her, no matter the pain it caused.

To my horror, she was gone.

I leapt from the chair, knocking it backwards. It clattered to the floor as I turned to the lounge. The morbid figure with his hanging noose was gone as well. I searched for Dorothy, calling out her name futilely.

I stood alone, with the letter in my hand. After a few moments, I caught my breath and lit a cigarette. I stayed awake for much of that night, reading and re-reading the letter, thinking about my conversation with Henley, hoping Dorothy might appear to me once more.

She did not, nor did I see her in the weeks or months that followed. I grieved at first, though in time I grew happy – happy in the knowledge that she was at peace, happy that somewhere in a world indescribable to mortal souls, she flourished.

Some part of her remained with me and still does to this day – her conviction, her courage, her resolve. In those daunting weeks that followed, when I had to pick up the pieces of my life, when I had to build something anew and walk a path most lonely, it was as though she were at my side, even in times of great peril, when all hope seemed lost to me.

I did what she wanted, of course. I went into the world; I investigated. What else was there to be done? I was – *am* – an investigator, bound to the dead in a way few would ever dare dream of.

Acknowledgements

Thanks to Alice, who's listened to me prattle on about ghosts for hours and helped make sense of this book when I've been totally lost. Cheers Al – you've been brilliant (even when you've been a complete pain in the arse).

Credits

Sam Hurcom and Orion Fiction would like to thank everyone at Orion who worked on the publication of *Letters From The Dead* in the UK.

Editorial
Lucy Frederick

Copy editor
Clare Wallis

Proof reader
Linda Joyce

Audio
Paul Stark
Amber Bates

Contracts
Anne Goddard
Paul Bulos
Jake Alderson

Design
Debbie Holmes
Tomas Almeida
Joanna Ridley
Nick May

Production
Ruth Sharvell

Finance
Jasdip Nandra
Afeera Ahmed
Elizabeth Beaumont
Sue Baker

Editorial Management
Charlie Panayiotou
Jane Hughes
Alice Davis

Marketing
Lucy Cameron

Publicity
Alex Layt

Sales
Jennifer Wilson
Esther Waters
Victoria Laws
Rachael Hum
Ellie Kyrke-Smith
Frances Doyle
Georgina Cutler

Rights
Susan Howe
Krystyna Kujawinska
Jessica Purdue
Richard King
Louise Henderson

Operations
Jo Jacobs
Sharon Willis
Lisa Pryde
Lucy Brem

'Gothic, claustrophobic and wonderfully dark' *GUARDIAN*

A SHADOW ON THE LENS

1904. Thomas Bexley, one of the first forensic photographers, is called to the sleepy Welsh village of Dinas Powys. A young girl named Betsan Tilny has been found murdered in the woodland.

One night, he develops the crime scene photographs in the cellar of his lodgings. There, he finds a face dimly visible in the photographs – the shadowed spectre of Betsan Tilny.

In the days that follow, Thomas senses a growing presence watching him as he tries to uncover what the villagers of Dinas Powys are so intent on keeping secret...

'Top notch historical crime fiction, with a dash of the supernatural. A gorgeous book and a riveting tale'
DAVID YOUNG

'An intriguing debut' *THE TIMES*

Available in Hardback, Paperback and eBook now